HYPATIA'S DIARY

DAVE BARTELL

ISBN 978-1-7328626-3-0

To my editor, Annie Tucker, who makes my stories better.

PROLOGUE

Libyan Desert on the edge of the Great Sand Sea
391 CE

Hypatia stood in the largest chamber of Alexander the Great's tomb and surveyed the arrangement one last time. Seven years of meticulous planning and dozens of journeys across the western desert had led to this moment. She was not given to tears, but felt a constriction in the back of her throat as she realized this was a burial. *I'll never see you again, nor will I be alive when you return to life.*

The chamber was lined floor to ceiling with the surviving scrolls from the original Library of Alexandria. The rising powers in the Coptic Church were intolerant of pagan beliefs, which included many of the ancient Greek works. Calls were being made to destroy texts that did not align with the new and growing faith. Hypatia grieved for the ancient knowledge they buried here, but hoped that a future generation, more accepting of broad ideas, would find it.

She sighed and walked down the sloping passage cut just large enough for a human. The oil lamp cast a tight circle of light, reaching only a few body lengths ahead. Some distance later, a wall emerged as the corridor pivoted hard right, and she grabbed the side for support against the steeper downward slope. Grit trickled down her collar from her hair brushing the ceiling, and she wiped her neck. The space seemed to close in on her, and she paused to take some steadying breaths. *It's just this part. Keep going.*

A short distance later, the corridor widened and doubled back on itself. It continued downward through a series of steep switchbacks, before coming to a long, straight passage that flattened out. She felt her trembling leg muscles ease after walking a couple minutes on the near-level surface.

Hypatia stopped for a brief rest before the most challenging section, rough-hewn steps that descended at a severe angle. She braced one palm against the rock wall for balance in the chimney-like space and leaned backward as the lamp's flame threatened to ignite her tunic. At last, her feet reached bottom, and she saw a distant light.

"Come, Hypatia. It is almost sunrise," said Synesius, his voice warm and melodious. She smiled at her most trusted pupil. *He could charm a viper,* she thought, and knew he had with all the bribes they had paid people to look the other way as they moved the scrolls.

"Is it ready?" she asked.

"Yes. Hurry," he said.

She squat-walked about thirty feet, her leg muscles burning again, and then stood up in a round-walled chamber. Natural light poured in from above, and Hypatia looked at the gray dawn sky. She blew out the lamp and rubbed her lower back.

"Up. Up," said Synesius, grasping her elbow and directing her to the ladder.

She climbed, and a small group of men helped her over a wall and onto the ground. As Synesius joined her, several of the men, digging tools in hand, descended the dry well.

"How long will it take?" asked Hypatia, looking down at them, already some twenty feet below.

"Before the sun is high," said an old man leaning on a staff.

"Good. Do you trust them?"

"Ammon has told them their families will be blessed as long as the secret is safe. You have nothing to fear," said the old man.

Hypatia stepped closer to him and took his hand. She gazed at him for a moment, trying to fathom his thoughts, then said, "Masnsen, I thank you with all my soul. As you have guarded the oracle, I trust you to guard the mystery of Alexander's tomb. Someday, when the outside world is less troubled, the right person will come to open it. As the oracle foretold, it will reveal to your descendants who is worthy," said Hypatia.

Masnsen closed his eyes and nodded. A yell from below signaled that water flooded the hole, and the ladder creaked as the men climbed out.

"Go now," said Masnsen. "By tonight, this will be just another well in the oasis."

Hypatia and Synesius went to the edge of the lake and paddled a raft across. After a meal of dates, olives, and flatbread, they walked to the main settlement of Ammoneion, where they joined a caravan readying to leave for Alexandria. Hypatia was glad for the relative cool of springtime, as it meant they could journey during daylight.

A few hours later, the camel's slow, rocking steps colluded with the sun's warmth to lull her into a lucid dream, in which people dragged her out of her home. A man snatched her diary and yelled, "We have it!"

She shuddered awake, heart pounding and breathing hard. *I can't let that happen. I can't keep it.* She slowed her camel and removed the diary from a satchel beneath her robe. Clutching the small volume, she marveled at the simple invention that transformed the written word. Instead of a long roll of papyrus that could be crushed or disintegrated with the smallest amount of moisture, the codex, as it was called, had been made from fine lambskin that was cut into small rectangles, then neatly stacked and bound on one side. The compact form also allowed her to write on each side of the skins. A leather-wrapping protected the codex that could be easily held with one hand. *It's so much smaller and less fragile than the scrolls. If only we had time to copy them.* She sighed and maneuvered alongside Synesius.

"I need you to take this. You said you had a safe place, a new library. Hide it there," she said, handing him her diary.

"I will go there next month," said Synesius. "I have business with—"

"Do not tell me where it is! You know how valuable this secret is."

"Understood. I will hide it where it will be forgotten until the proper time," said Synesius.

Hypatia guided her camel back into line as a strong breeze erupted from the east. She looked behind her at the sand billowing off the top of a nearby dune and burying the camels' tracks. *A good omen.* She smiled.

1

Rome, Italy
Present Day

"Here it is," said Joseph to his aunt Tessa Santarossa. They were deep in a cave beneath their family's restaurant and wine shop, legendary for its old vintages. Joseph had taken an interest in his grandfather's shop at an early age, and now twenty-three had been cataloging the rare wines to sell them online. This idea for the family business was long overdue.

They stood in a cramped space, with decaying wooden crates stacked haphazardly against the walls. The air was close and damp molds competed with a cloying sweetness that emerged from a sticky dark purple puddle. Tessa held a tissue to her nose.

"I cleaned it up as best I could," said Joseph, looking at Tessa's raised eyebrows. Several wooden crates had come apart, loosing their bottles onto the floor. About half a dozen had broken, spilling liters of wine. Much of the substantial leakage had flowed under the crates.

Tessa picked up one bottle that Joseph had stacked along with still intact crates. A 1925 Biondi-Santi Brunello di Montalcino Riserva, a spellbinding Tuscan red. She gasped at seeing a pile of glass.

"What happened?" she asked in a gentle tone. The broken bottles were not from his carelessness.

"This crate in the middle fell apart, and the box on top tipped over. I couldn't catch them all. I'm sorry," he said. A rotted wooden box lay on the floor.

"No. No. It's okay. How did you find this place?" asked Tessa.

"A few weeks ago, I found a key hidden in the sorting room, but didn't know what it was for," he said, referring to a small office-like area they had passed through. "Yesterday, I moved a few rows of boxes stacked against the back wall and discovered this door. I remembered the key, and it worked."

"My god. It's true," she said.

"What?"

"Your grandfather once told me about a secret space where they hid wine from Mussolini's fascists..." she trailed off and shined a light around the other crates. Most of them were in similar distress. Decades of neglect had put these old vintages at risk. "You found it."

"Yeah, but..." he looked at the mess on the floor.

"It's not your fault, Joseph. This box would have collapsed under its own weight. When I was a teenager, your great-grandfather Vito went apoplectic with rage one night at dinner. He blamed his brother for a collapsed shelf. His brother blamed him. It was the best supper in years.

"Anyway, I'm surprised the lot hasn't fallen down," she said, holding up one of the Tuscans. "Looks like you've cleaned up well enough. You ever tasted this?"

"No," he said.

"Well, it's time to deepen your education. You need to know what you're selling."

She walked back and collected a couple glasses from the sorting room, skewered the cork, and coaxed it out. She poured the rich liquid, and they swirled the wine. She breathed in and was transported to the hills in Tuscany. Fruit, punctuated by musky earth and raw stems. Hot sun blazed on her bare shoulders as her grandfather showed her how to trim the vines, leaving just enough leaves to shade the delicate grapes. Her hand curled with the memory of vineyard soil rolling through her fingers.

She looked at Joseph. He swirled the glass, held it to his nose and then, eyes closed, inhaled. He sighed and grinned like the Cheshire Cat. He tipped the glass, and she watched his mouth swish the liquid across his palate.

"Holy Mother Mary," he said, wild-eyed. "It's..." He swirled the glass and took in a larger mouthful.

"A miracle," she said.

Halfway through their second glass, Joseph turned and stared down the rows of crates lining the walls. "How far does it go?" he said.

"I don't know," she said. "Grandfather Marco wouldn't tell me about this place. Said it wasn't safe and to stop asking about it."

"Well, it's mine now," said Joseph, standing and tugging down his skinny-leg jeans. "C'mon."

Tessa followed. *No wonder Grandpa Marco left him the wine business.* She read the labels and vintages as they walked. *My God, even if half this wine is corked, there's still a fortune in here.*

The cases of wine stopped after a hundred meters, and the cave became danker. Slimy water trickled down one wall and streamed along the floor, making it difficult to walk even without the wine affecting her balance.

"Joseph, wait. Let's do this another day. It's dangerous."

"Aw, Tess. Where's the girl who taught me how to climb trees?

She grew a brain, thought Tessa, remembering a fearless six-year-old Joseph edging farther out an oak tree branch. She had been seventeen at the time and heading to university that fall.

"Joseph?" she called. He had disappeared around a corner. "Wait up."

She rounded the bend and saw him running his finger over something on the wall.

"What is it?"

"I don't know. A symbol. It's old. Looks more in your line of work," he said.

"Let me see," she said, squeezing in next to him.

"I can use this as the logo for my wine business!" he said and snapped a photo of a bird-like symbol chiseled into the rock. Seven points were connected with scored lines in a shape where the bottom resembled a child's kite and the top two points extending to form a head and beak.

Tessa covered her mouth to hide her surprise.

"What is it?" asked Joseph.

"It's an Aquila," she replied and continued explaining after seeing Joseph's face screw up in perplexion. "It's a constellation in the northern sky. The Aquila, or eagle, was the most powerful icon of the Roman military."

"Cool. The ancient Roman army was here, but so what?"

"It's the same symbol a guy discovered last summer in that lava tube between Iceland and Scotland. What's it doing here?" her voice drifted off in wonder.

An archaeologist by profession, Tessa had followed the discovery closely. The initial news had caused a sensation because of a massive diamond cache found halfway between the two countries. It had also led to a revolution in geology as researchers scrambled to find similar structures.

She was further intrigued when the lead archaeologist, Darwin Lacroix, revealed an ancient Roman connection with the lava tube and suggested that lava tubes occurred in multiple places across Europe. She had highlighted a quote in one of his interviews: "What if the ancients knew about these lava tubes and used them to store or hide scrolls? We've lost so much ancient knowledge. Imagine if we could find a long-lost library."

A few years earlier, while cataloging an archaeological dig in Rome, she had come across a note in the inventory:

```
Papyrus fragment - reference to Serapeum
scrolls and Synesius, unclear meaning
```

The fragment was found among artifacts brought from Alexandria and dated to the time when Christian rulers gained control of

Alexandria around 400 CE. Synesius was a common name in that time period, but there was a Synesius who was a student of Hypatia, the famous teacher and philosopher. She was rumored to be one of the guardians of the Serapeum library, which some scholars thought was the last known place that contained scrolls saved from the original Library of Alexandria.

Tessa asked colleagues if the remains of the Library of Alexandria could have been consolidated in the Serapeum, but no one took her seriously. The evidence was lean, she knew, but many great discoveries began with a hunch. The fragment contained the words "hidden..." and "Rome church..." Against all reason, she convinced herself that Synesius wrote this scrap of papyrus as a clue pointing to more.

She figured there was only one church in Rome where important scrolls from the ancient world would go and began submitting research requests to the Vatican's archive. But, so far, they declined her requests.

Tessa's mind swirled in a hive of activity and an idea formed. She searched her mobile for a blog post published by Darwin Lacroix the previous summer. She found it and skimmed the text until she reached a photo about halfway down the page. Darwin was pictured sitting in a lavish Vatican reading room with a Cardinal and a Priest. The caption read, "Darwin, Cardinal Santos, and Father Ndembele discussing access to lava tubes beneath holy territories."

That's it! This Darwin guy can get me access to the Vatican Library.

2

Reykjavík, Iceland

Darwin Lacroix watched a late February storm race over a distant glacier, sweeping up snow and whipping it into a spray of stinging ice crystals. He shivered reflexively behind the glass in the warmth of his condo in Reykjavík, Iceland, and breathed in the smoky caramel aroma of the cappuccino he made a few minutes ago. The mug's heat stung his hands. He sipped the frothy beverage and set it down, rubbing his hands over his forearms to sooth the burn. He then returned to the task that had consumed him the last couple months.

Maps of Rome, ancient and modern, lay atop most of the flat surfaces in the condominium he had purchased last fall shortly after becoming engaged to his fiancée, Eyrún. Darwin, French by birth and educated in London, was on extended leave from the University of California Berkeley to continue his research on the lava tube network he had found in Iceland the year before.

Darwin's family, the Lacroixes, hailed from Corsica and had descended from Genoese traders who had built a shipping empire across the Mediterranean Sea. A couple hundred years earlier, one of his forebears had discovered a box of Roman scrolls beneath the ruins of the centuries-old eruption of Mt. Vesuvius. Those scrolls described how first century Romans had used lava tubes beneath Europa for military and mining purposes, but no entry points could be found to back up the claims.

His grandfather, Emelio, had thrown away a promising career chasing evidence of the lava tubes existence, and Darwin's father had been aghast when Darwin himself had taken up the Lacroix quest. A few years later, a lucky break at an archaeological dig on the west coast of Iceland unearthed a lava tube, which traversed the North Sea and connected with Scotland. An almost bigger surprise was finding a diamond chamber two-thirds of the way through.

The discovery brought him temporary fame and significant wealth as well as an introduction to Eyrún Stephansdottir, the lead volcanologist. They had begun the journey as reluctant rivals and found themselves falling in love. But Darwin had not yet found what he wanted, the proof the Romans used lava tubes for both covert military travel and hiding wealth.

As the son and grandson of archaeology professors, Darwin's world was full of travel and cultural immersion. He loved archaeological digs, and one graduate student had nicknamed Darwin "The Great Finder" for his uncanny knack at locating prime objects. Whereas many kids thought of being famous rock stars or athletes, Darwin was drawn to the ancient world and dreamed of making a great discovery. He imagined himself unearthing a tomb of wonders, like Howard Carter's discovery of Tutankhamun's golden death mask.

Darwin's fascinations matured with age and took a more intellectual turn when he read an article in high school that listed missing works by Greek masters. He had asked one of his teachers what happened to the missing works and was told, "They were lost."

"Lost? What do you mean? asked Darwin.

"Just that. Lost. No one knows. They probably decayed over time," said his teacher.

"But what if they still exist? You know, like the Dead Sea Scrolls, stashed away in a cave," said Darwin. His teachers, and later, professors would shrug their shoulders as he pressed them for answers. The recovery of lost knowledge transfixed Darwin, and he vowed never to become a lazy scholar. *What if I found a lost Greek tragedy or a previously unknown Persian mathematical formula or an ancient Hindu cure for cancer?*

He considered the destruction of the Library of Alexandria a tragedy and read all he could on the theories of what happened to the scrolls. *How could something so large just disappear? If I could find evidence of the library or even just a few scrolls, I'd be as famous as Howard Carter.*

As he completed undergraduate and advanced degrees, his daydreams had remained fantasies until the first time his grandfather showed him the box of Roman scrolls. Right away, Darwin sensed the lava tubes could be a hiding place like the caves near the Dead Sea, and he soon built on Emelio's work to patch together a series of discoveries at sites in central France and London, which led to the Iceland lava tube. There was a strong correlation between the locations. For instance, the lava tube sections in London and France had identical geology, but to advance his theory about the Romans and publish in respected journals of archaeology, he needed multiple proof points.

He laid a tracing of Rome circa 100 CE atop a modern street map. Great structures like the Colosseum drew the tourist hordes, but most of the ancient city lay buried under the modern metropolis. He had lined up the famous seven hills as best he could and read the main scroll again:

> *...stand with your back to the ridge and align the morning sun above the middle of the three hills. Enter the crevice behind you and follow the cave to the right. Look for the symbols.*

Agrippa Cicero, an engineer and miner from Rome, had authored this scroll as well as a series of letters to Emperor Nero, his financial and political backer. Darwin had used these scrolls to make his discoveries, but Agrippa also mentioned a cache of gold concealed by Nero in a lava tube under Rome.

This could turn up previously unknown evidence about Nero's last days, he thought, looking at the map he considered the best candidate from the many strewn about the condo.

Darwin had started with the obvious, trying to figure out which of the famous seven hills of Rome were the three described in Agrippa's scroll, but soon figured out it could be any point in the city. Agrippa had mentioned an area close to Nero's palace. Unfortunately, a later emperor, Flavian, tore it down to build the Colosseum.

Agrippa also described an above-ground route from the crevice with the cave to Nero's palace, but all the main streets in Rome led to the city center. He was stuck. Despite several short visits to Rome to scout potential locations, the centuries of build-up and the height of modern city buildings made it impossible to see the hills. *It's like the blue-sky section of a puzzle where you have to try every piece.*

The front lock clicked open, and Eyrún pushed her way in. Darwin hurried over to take her bags.

"Cold out there?" he asked.

"It's Iceland," she said, hooking her coat and beanie on the rack and ruffling her hair.

They kissed, and Darwin carried a bag of groceries to the kitchen, while Eyrún kicked off her boots and put her backpack in her office.

"How did it go today?" he said.

"The usual. The contractors and the government lackeys are fighting over who's in control."

"I thought you were in control," he said. She was now head volcanologist for exploration of the North Atlantic Tube or NAT, that was now entering a phase of commercial development. Eyrún's company, Stjörnu Energy had the rights to build a pipeline through the NAT to deliver flue gas to the UK.

Iceland had abundant geothermal energy, but its far-north location across an ocean made energy exporting uncompetitive. The NAT meant Icelandic energy could be transported to the United Kingdom profitably. But because the project crossed multiple international boundaries, she also had to navigate a tangle of environmental laws.

"Some days, I feel like I work in a daycare getting the toddlers to play nice and share their toys," she said, padding barefoot across the heated wood floors and throwing her arms around Darwin's neck.

He gazed into her glacier blue eyes and ran his fingers through her dark brown hair. They kissed again. A few moments later, she slipped her hands into his jeans' back pockets and whispered, "Dinner's not for a couple hours."

3

Later that night, they sat at a cozy two-seater of Occam's Reindeer, a farm-to-table restaurant in Reykjavík with a reputation for food and wine as eclectic as it was fresh. The chef-owner was an Israeli who had lived all over the world. Her last restaurant in Istanbul reached The World's 50 Best Restaurants list and she was eager to achieve the same in Iceland.

Darwin ordered a Tanzanian coffee-wood roasted Roe deer, and Eyrún chose an Arctic Black Cod done Tagine style with fenugreek. The server slid a Macadamia Nut pâté between them.

They had decided to celebrate early as Eyrún would be underground next week on Darwin's actual birthday. Her trips into the lava tube were so far beneath the earth it was almost an off-planet affair that made real-time communications impossible.

"It's like a six-hundred-mile-deep mine, except sideways," their friend Zac had once described in a blog post.

"Happy birthday," said Eyrún. Their glasses chimed as they toasted and looked into each other's eyes.

"Thanks," said Darwin.

"Oh, God, that's good!" said Eyrún after sipping the wine. "How much was this?"

"A lot," said Darwin, taking a mouthful. While his family was not poor, he now had more wealth than he could imagine running out of. His discovery of diamonds in the NAT had earned him close to a billion dollars.

"Good choice. An excellent year," she said, clinking his glass again.

"So was 1984," said Darwin, referring to his birthday.

Eyrún was also part of the original group that discovered the tube. Between her share of the Roman diamonds and stock ownership in Stjörnu Energy, the company building the pipeline, she, too, had more money than she could spend.

After a dessert of Greek yogurt topped with toasted Pan del Indio and Rainberry's from Tierra del Fuego and drizzled with Ghanaian honey, the chef walked over and greeted them.

"How was the meal?"

"Lovely as always, Hilani," said Eyrún.

"I would come here every night if I wouldn't grow large," said Darwin, patting his belly.

"Darwin, I don't think you could get fat if you tried," laughed Hilani.

"Where did you find that wine?" asked Darwin.

"Did you like it?" asked Hilani. "It came out-of-the-blue from a twenty-something Italian dealer who only sells by personal referral. He has a special cave in Rome and sent me a case to try out on some of my special clients."

"Spellbinding," said Darwin tipping the glass back to get the last few drops.

"Can you introduce us to him?" asked Eyrún.

"Sure. Calls himself Aquila Cellars," said Hilani.

Darwin gasped and locked eyes with Eyrún.

Here's his website," said Hilani, holding out her mobile. A chiseled bird-like logo appeared that looked identical to the symbol he had found in the lava tubes beneath France and Iceland. It was an eagle drawn from the shape of the Aquila constellation that Roman legions carried as their talisman.

"You recognized this?" asked Hilani.

"Yeah," said Darwin, staring at the photo. "Rome you said?"

Hilani nodded.

Darwin grabbed his mobile and Googled it.

"This has got to be the tube in Rome," he said to Eyrún.

4

Back at their condo, they sat by the fire for a short while before Eyrún went to bed as she had an early start in the morning. Darwin said he would stay up "a little while longer" and used his iPad to zoom into Google Maps of Rome. *Sometimes you get lucky*, he thought. The address for Aquila Cellars aligned with the possible locations for the ancient cave, but was closer to Nero's old palace than he had thought it would be. He zoomed to street level to explore the neighborhood.

The building containing the wine shop was wedge-shaped and came to a point at the convergence of Via Quattro November and the narrower Via di S. Eufemia. A restaurant, it's main entrance on the triangular corner, occupied the downstairs of both sides. The streets sloped upward from the corner. He clicked up Via di S. Eufemia past a hotel.

There was nothing to show a famous wine shop, not even a number, but he guessed it was number seven as it was the only door between the hotel at five and a neighboring business at nine. Its bow window displayed an elegant scene of vineyards and places for bottles to rest during open hours. A tiny sign in the lower corner listed hours of operation.

Darwin switched to the website for Aquila Cellars. Aside from more common wines, a section for the "discerning palate" described wines of great pedigree and vintage. These were available by invitation only, but had no link to get an invitation. He flipped over Hilani's business card to see the proprietor's name—Imperator—Darwin chuckled and typed the address into an email app. Imperator, or commander, was a title given to victorious generals in the Roman Republic and later used by emperors.

He introduced himself in the email, mentioning that he got the address from Hilani, and wrote a few lines about the rare Masseto from Tenuta dell'Ornellaia they had drunk with dinner. He concluded by asking for a personal tour, if possible. Darwin then moved to the condo's floor-to-ceiling windows and smiled at swirling snow that had turned Reykjavík into a giant snow globe.

5

Rome

A little less than two months later, Darwin waited at a traffic light in Rome, scooters swarming around his taxi. Aquila Cellar's had taken weeks to reply to his email, and then he had to work around a long-planned trip to California to clear out his apartment in Berkeley. The traffic light switched green, and the two-wheeled plague buzzed away, filling the street with a noxious blue cloud.

He tried picturing Rome in Leonardo da Vinci's day. Different sounds and smells. *And a different sense of speed.* The fastest transportation then was a single rider on a horse. *Does it matter how fast we get there? In the end, we all end up in the same place.* His brain, always busy, played through a series of random thoughts. Until it got to last night's fight with Eyrún, and his stomach plunged.

"I wanted us to go to Rome together," she had said, referring to Darwin's promise to take her on his next trip. But he had already been forced to postpone it several times because of Eyrún being pulled in to solve issues with the NAT.

The increasing frequency of her trips into the NAT caused

tension in their relationship. Darwin argued that there had to be someone else who could to this, and she countered that the project was a critical phase.

It's always at a critical phase, he thought. From his perspective, she was obsessed with the NAT.

"It's not like you need the money anymore," he said last night and instantly regretted it. She had been the main source of income for her family after her father had died years ago, but her sister was now grown, and her mother had met a new partner.

"Yeah, and it's not like Rome's going anywhere, either. I've seen you moping about. You're missing the attention."

"But this could be the tube that connects to Nero's gold," he said.

"So now, you want to run off and see if you can recapture the limelight? It's not always all about you, Darwin," she said.

The words still stung twelve hours later. They had gone to bed not speaking, and Darwin had stared at the ceiling for what felt like half the night. This morning, Eyrún got up before sunrise, and after working out, left for the office. She had kissed him goodbye and wished him a good trip, but her words felt flat.

Am I looking for attention? He did not consider himself drawn to celebrity, and the media had stopped calling him months ago. He had gone through a period of boredom before extending his leave of absence at the University of California Berkeley and settling in to write a book about the Lacroix curse — his family's generations-long hunt for the Roman lava tubes. *It's not about attention. I need data to finish publishing. There's more to find. I know it.*

His face, one side deep in shadow, reflected in the car's side window. A green eye squinted back from the sunlit side of the face beneath brown hair hanging low across his brow, a reminder he was to visit the barber yesterday. *I'll find one in Rome.* A three-day beard stressed a prominent cheek bone that, together with a creased forehead and clenched jaw, painted a grim expression, like a man who didn't get his way.

Merde! Lighten up. Darwin lifted his eyebrows and forced a smile. *Better.* He rolled his shoulders and took a deep breath while stretching his arms outward. He smiled and the face in the window transformed, like a politician entering a room full of voters.

"Almost there, *signore,*" said the driver.

"Oh, thanks. I'm just tired from the early flight," said Darwin.

A few minutes later, the car stopped, and Darwin recognized the wine shop. The sun radiated off the neighboring building, and the warm humid air reminded him he loved the Mediterranean. His pleasant moment burst as a scooter nearly took off the car door in its hurry to be somewhere.

6

"*Buongiorno,*" said a young woman arranging wine bottles on one side of the shop.

"*Buongiorno. Come stai?*" asked Darwin.

"*Bene grazie e te,*" she said. "You are English. No?"

"Corsican actually, but I live in Reykjavík at the moment."

"Well then, welcome to Rome. How may I help you?

Darwin's gaze swept the room. Like most wine shops, the cases served as the platforms for the displays, the top boxes peeled open. This shop seemed also to go upwards forever. Shelving reached the ceiling of the two-story interior, with bottles arranged against the cool stone walls. A narrow industrial-metal catwalk jutted out midway up the wall to provide access to the bottles in the top half of the room.

"Darwin?" asked a young man standing on the catwalk with an armful of bottles.

"*Si.* Joseph?"

"I'll be right down. The restaurant just called and asked for a special wine," said Joseph, setting the bottles in a dumbwaiter. He tapped a button, and the wine descended in its small elevator as Joseph mounted a ladder beside it.

"Cool, huh?" he said, retrieving the bottles. "My cousin's a mechanical engineer. She designed it as a graduate project."

"It is," said Darwin.

"Give me a moment. I'll be right with you," said Joseph, moving the bottles to the front counter where several customers had queued to make their purchases. A woman tapped her mobile against the tablet on the counter, and a bright tone signaled the completed transaction.

Old and new, thought Darwin, imagining the exchanges of goods in this location over the centuries. *Value for value, only the currency changes.* He turned towards the rear of the shop, where a thick glass door created a modern partition to an older-looking cellar. The lighting was muted, but he could see bottles lying on their sides in brick alcoves. *These must be the more prized vintages.* A round table with four chairs occupied the room's center. The far wall contained an old door, with arm's-length hinges set between stout stone blocks. *And that must lead to the cave!*

"Shall we go in?" said Joseph, stepping past him and pushing through the glass door. Silence greeted them as the door swung closed, and Darwin felt the hairs on the back of his neck stand up as the much cooler air swirled about.

"Welcome to Aquila Cellars," said Joseph, spreading his arms like a ringmaster. "Let me give you the proper introduction. Please sit." He pulled out a chair for Darwin, filled two glasses from a decanter that had been waiting on the table, and sat opposite.

"Salute," said Joseph.

"Salute," said Darwin, swirling the ruby liquid and taking a mouthful. "This is excellent. What is it?"

"A Nebbiolo from a tiny producer in the Piedmont region near the city of Alessandria. Her land produces epic grapes, but it's so small she manages only a few hundred cases a year."

"Wonderful," said Darwin, swishing another mouthful.

"This one is young. Give it another dozen years. She has no capacity to age it that long, but my cellar here is enormous," said Joseph.

"You said you would tell me the story about the cellar when we met..."

"True. The website is purposefully vague as we only own the property on this block, and the cellar goes on for some distance beyond. My family has run this wine business for centuries, and I started working part-time in the wine shop at thirteen and discovered I liked it. A few years ago, I found some ledgers dating back to the seventeen-eighties," said Joseph.

"The business thrived until last century's wars and depression when demand for good wine fell as people could not afford it. The fascists became the main customer, but they tended to take and not pay, so we hid the best wines. There was a revival after the second World War, but the business fell into neglect in the nineteen-seventies when my granduncle's family focused on the tourist money with the hotel and restaurant.

"The shop was mostly wholesale by then as restaurants bought from distributors. I modernized our operations, and my grand-uncle let me run the place. I used the Internet to reach a wealthier clientele, and our profits went up. When my grand-uncle passed away a few years ago, he left the business to me," said Joseph.

"It's impressive," said Darwin.

"Thanks."

"When did you find the Aquila symbol?" asked Darwin.

"About a six months ago."

"Where?" asked Darwin.

"Deeper underground," said Joseph.

Darwin swirled his glass again, looking past Joseph at the oak door. *I need to get in there.*

"Let me show you something," said Darwin, tapping to some photos on his mobile. "I think it connects some of my discoveries to your cave. If it's true, then it will bring considerably more fame to Aquila Cellars.

And it may even lead to something even more valuable, he thought, swiping to a photo of an ancient text.

"I found Aquila symbols identical to yours in France, UK, and

Iceland. And then there's this bit about Rome," he said, handing the mobile to Joseph.

> *... the gold remains under the rubble of Nero's trap. I filled my pack, but at least a tonne remains...*

"You think it's here?" said Joseph, leaning in on the table.

"The Romans used the Aquila symbols to mark entrances to lava tubes. I think it's a real possibility there's a lava tube below your cave." He nodded toward the door.

7

Darwin returned the next evening as the wine shop closed and, after the employees had gone, Joseph opened the oak door and led the way into the cellar. The air was heavy with aging wine, and Darwin shivered at the drop in temperature beyond the door. *Here we go, Agrippa. Show me where you are.*

The main cellar was about ten meters deep and ran at least forty meters to the right. Here, the stone was the same cut blocks as the building's exterior, but as they approached the far wall with an arched opening, the blocks changed to a darker color.

"It's the foundation from an older building," said Joseph. "This arch crosses under the street on the uphill side of the building, but none of the city permits shows the cellar beyond this point."

"Which era?" asked Darwin, running his hand on the different blocks that had an older patina.

"Not my area of expertise, but we are in an ancient part of Rome," said Joseph.

Inside, the arch the cellar narrowed to a few meters wide and took on a disused look. Old wood shelves, mostly bare, lined the walls, and naked lightbulbs followed a single wire across the ceiling.

"This was the office for the old cellar before the new building went up in the early nineteen-hundreds," Joseph continued, referring to new construction that mingled with the old. An upturned barrel with a couple chairs served as a tasting area.

"Here we are," he said about thirty meters in and pulled back a drape to reveal an ancient door, its hand-hewn planks held by rivets hammered through two thick iron bands. A keyhole perforated an iron plate and also supported a saucer-sized pull ring.

"I found this last year when I moved stacks of old wine crates. I think my granduncle knew about it, but maybe not. I put the drape up to keep my staff from asking questions," he said, inserting a thick metal key in the slot and, turning it with both hands, shouldered the door inward.

A low groan reverberated in the space beyond, like an ancient guardian warning against entry. Darwin's nose wrinkled at the dank mustiness swirling out of the gloom. Joseph stepped inside and switched on a lantern.

"Best if we put on our safety kit here," said Darwin, buckling a caving helmet and connecting its light to a battery pack on his belt. He helped Joseph do the same, then followed him into the cave.

"This is where you found those amazing vintages?" said Darwin as they passed stacks of crates.

"*Si,*" said Joseph, who had moved some meters ahead. Darwin caught up as the slope dipped downward.

"How far have you gone?"

"Only to the junction up here. I got busy with the business and haven't had time to come back," he said and turned a corner.

Darwin reached the corner and saw it was an intersection. The left narrowed into a crack barely human-width, and the right turn angled downward. Joseph stood with his finger on the wall.

"Here it is."

Darwin stepped beside him and looked at an Aquila symbol cut in the rock about eye level. He snapped photos of it with his mobile.

"Is it the same?"

"Yes," said Darwin, feeling his heart thump and an urge to hurry forward. "If this is the place I think it is, we should find a pile of rocks in less than a hundred meters." He started down the slope and slipped on a rock. "Ow," he said, landing on his ass. He stood and rubbed the sore spot.

"Is this safe?" asked Joseph. "That's why I didn't come down here."

"Mostly," said Darwin, who had continued onward. About thirty meters farther, and they edged through a door-sized crack into a large space.

"Cool!" said Joseph.

The cave enlarged, and its walls rounded like a large storm drain or a single car tunnel. Parallel ridges eroded the sides, like a riverbed, and the floor was mottled and chunky but was all solid rock. Darwin touched the ceiling a moment before walking toward the right. The floor was smooth but undulated.

"What is this place?" asked Joseph.

"It's a lava tube," said Darwin.

"A what?"

"A lava tube. Sometimes, faster flowing lava cuts a channel that erodes deeper. The lava on the sides and top cools, leaving a lava river underground. When the eruption ends, the lava drains out, leaving a tube."

"Are they all this big?"

"Sometimes. We found one in Iceland. There are other large tubes in Hawaii and Australia."

A few minutes later, they came upon a rock pile that blocked the tube. Darwin surveyed the scene, picking up and comparing rocks in the pile. *Something's not right here*, he thought.

"What are you doing?"

"There's a difference in the rocks. Can you go back about twenty meters and bring back any loose rocks?

"Sure," said Joseph, heading back in the direction they came.

Darwin moved his light over the pile. Most rocks were fist-size and lighter than the lava tube wall. He recalled Agrippa wrote that *he triggered a mechanism that sealed the gold in a side chamber.* He stepped back and swept the light over the floor to ceiling rock pile.

The rocks... that's it! The rocks that buried the gold are not from this lava tube. They're too uniform, like someone quarried them elsewhere and carried them here.

"How about these?" said Joseph. He held a mixed bunch of rocks. One was the size of a soccer ball, and Joseph's arm quivered from its weight.

"Perfect," said Darwin, taking the larger rock and setting it next to those he had separated from the pile. He then picked up one of Joseph's found rocks and one of similar size from the rock pile and held them in his palms like a scale. The difference in mass was striking.

"Which one's heavier?" he asked, handing the rocks to Joseph to confirm.

"This one," said Joseph, holding up one rock he had retrieved.

"I'm not a geologist, but someone carried these rocks in here," said Darwin, pointing to the pile. "They are nearly the same size and less than half the weight of the rock you found up there," he said, nodding.

"The lava in the tube walls is dense, full of iron. These are scoria, heavier than pumice, but still much lighter than denser lava like this tube. I think someone moved this down here," he said.

"Why would they do that?"

"To bury Nero's gold," said Darwin "I think the answer lies on the other side."

There was a gap in the top left, and he climbed. The pile moved underfoot, and some rocks slid down around his ankle. He hastily retreated, bumping into Joseph.

"Sorry," he said. "It looks like it goes through, but I need to get up there to confirm it."

"Do you think it's still there?"

"Dunno, but I think we've gone as far as we can tonight," said Darwin. "And you have to open the shop tomorrow."

8

Darwin scratched the back of his scalp under the hard-hat as the midday heat produced beads of sweat under the unbreathing plastic. Joseph was busy all day in the wine shop, so Darwin explored the probable end-point of the tube they traversed last night — Emperor Nero's ill-fated palace, the Domus Aurea. Meaning gold house, the former palace was now just another Roman ruin on the must-see list.

He had joined a tour and listened as the guide said something about the palace grounds occupying a couple hundred acres before being reclaimed and buried after Nero's death until a cave-in during the 1500s led to its rediscovery. *Modern dictators have nothing on this waste of the public treasury*, Darwin mused while taking in the towering arches and remaining mosaics.

Standing in the Domus Aurea's underground rotunda, he also scanned the frescos, recalling their rediscovery and beauty provided creative inspiration for Raphael and other Renaissance painters. *Old becomes the new,* he thought, refocusing on the task at hand. *Agrippa wrote that Nero used a lava tube to move in and out of the palace in stealth. It must be under here.*

He waited for the tour group to move on to the next lecture spot, then wandered over to a map of the complex. Pulling out his mobile, he opened the scans of Agrippa's scrolls and found the one he needed.

... face the shrine of Apollo. Approach the alcove and enter the opening on the left. Go down the hole in the floor. Follow the left passage and go down again. Find the Aquila...

He studied the map. Nothing referred to Apollo, and they had stripped the alcoves bare centuries ago. *Probably before they buried this place. But if I built a shrine to Apollo, it would be bigger than the others,* he thought. He turned, and sure enough, one was larger. It had a deeper back wall and a wrought iron barrier across its front. He approached, using his mobile to mimic taking a panoramic photo and checking that no one was looking, moved over the waist-high barrier.

The left wall had a narrow opening, invisible from the front. He tapped the flashlight app on his mobile and pushed through. Dust from the ancient concrete swirled, and he sneezed, banging an elbow on the wall.

Merde. Small lights danced about as he rubbed out the sting is his arm. After the mental fireflies retreated, he stood up in what looked like a storage closet, a meter wide, and maybe two deep. The floor was first-century concrete, crudely poured. He stepped forward to take photos of a section that must have been filled in after they poured the original floor.

"*Signore, cosa stai facendo? Non si può essere qui*, what are you doing? You can't be in here," came a voice from behind.

Darwin turned to face a blinding light and shrugged, *I don't understand* even though he was conversant in Italian. The security guard motioned him to squeeze past.

"I'm sorry," said Darwin in English.

Back on the other side of the railing, the guard shooed him back to the tour group. Darwin rejoined, but only until the guard wandered off again.

Nero, you clever bastard. Hiding the unused gold just out of sight, he thought while hiking back to street level. After his eyes adjusted to the sun, he looked toward Joseph's wine cellar. *But if your gold's still there? How're we going to dig it out undetected?*

9

Darwin arrived at Trattoria Santarossa a few minutes after nine PM, where Joseph had invited him to join a monthly family dinner. The host, a young man in a smartly tailored black suit, and with fashionable white-soled sneakers, led him to a back room. A rectangular table set for at least a couple dozen ran the length of the room perpendicular to stout beams that crossed the ceiling. Large black and white framed photos of the kitchen staff in full action added movement to the space where five or six knots of people were engaged in loud conversation. Darwin leaned back toward the door. He liked people but was awkward in large groups.

"Darwin," yelled Joseph, stepping away from one of the nearer groups. "Welcome to Trattoria Santarossa. Let's get you some wine."

Joseph led the way to a sideboard where he poured Darwin a glass. "Try this. That customer the other day reminded me I had a few bottles of this beauty from Mount Etna. You can taste the ash. Come, let's meet the family."

Darwin struggled to keep the names and faces sorted as he shook hands around the room. The last group he had been eyeing for some time as there was a woman who had caught his attention. He noticed her laugh at first, and then how she drew the conversation to herself.

She was at least his height, standing in substantial heels. Her dark brown hair cascaded in waves past her shoulders and swished about when she laughed, which was often. Her arms and upper back were sculpted like someone who spent time in the gym and cared to be noticed.

When they reached her group, a rotund man named Marco slapped him on the shoulder. "Genoese. I knew it. You're one of us," he exclaimed after Darwin had mentioned being from Corsica.

They coerced him into giving a brief family history of the Lacroixes and their Genoese roots. Ajaccio Corsica had become their base of operations for the Mediterranean shipping empire begun in the late Middle Ages, and Darwin's grandfather still lived in the family mansion near Ajaccio harbor.

"And this is—" Joseph began.

"Tessa Santarossa," said the woman, taking Darwin's hand, not waiting for Joseph. "Pleased to meet you."

"Likewise," said Darwin. "Santarossa?"

"Yes. Her father owns the restaurant. She's my first cousin," said Joseph.

"You must be completely confused meeting so many people at once," said Tessa.

"Ah..." Servers arriving with large plates of antipasti saved him from answering more questions.

"Let's sit. I'm famished," said Tessa, guiding him around the table.

Darwin sat between Joseph and Tessa, and as he speared slices of cured meats and pickled vegetables onto his plate, Tessa said, "Try this. It's a papecchia, a little hot, and stuffed with tuna, anchovies, and capers."

She spooned a fire-truck red pepper with a light tan filling on his plate. He popped it in his mouth, and the pungent fish mixed in the peppery heat erupted. The roof of his mouth burned, and he felt his sinuses clear as a nasal drip threatened to roll down his upper lip. A dollop of burrata cheese put out the fire, and a mouthful of wine brought his palate back to earth.

"It's good," he said, blinking back moist eyes and reaching for a slice of prosciutto to absorb the grenade going off in his belly. A light bowtie pasta course with eggplant and basil sauce further put down the flames as he settled into the marathon meal.

"Watch out for my cousin. She's a troublemaker," said Joseph. Darwin noticed he avoided the stuffed peppers.

As the veal and wild mushrooms second course arrived, he asked Tessa about her archaeology work. "Joseph said you do a lot of work in Egypt. Do you teach?"

"Ha," she laughed. "I had to as part of my graduate work. I hated it."

"Field research? Writer?" he probed.

"Research on privately funded digs. My dissertation focused on the transition of beliefs in Alexandria during the fourth century—the switch from the Greek ascetic paganism to the Coptic and other competing Christian beliefs," she said, taking in a mouthful.

"Marco, this is fabulous," shouted Joseph to the rotund man whom Darwin had learned was the restaurant owner and Tessa's father. Marco raised his glass from across the table.

"What kind of private research?" asked Darwin, using his knife to sweep the brown gravy onto a forkful of veal and mushrooms.

"Various. Sometimes, its museums like the American Getty, or sometimes wealthy collectors."

"Like treasure hunting?" he asked.

"We could call it that. A lot of researchers sift through the small things, looking for how people lived, what they ate, how many people it took to build the great pyramids. I look for lost artworks," she said.

Darwin furrowed his eyebrows. *More like stealing cultural heritage. These pieces belong to the countries they're found in. Saying that wealthy collectors or museums fund your work is just a higher class of looting.*

"It's all legal," she continued as if responding to his thought. "We register our digs with the local governments and the antiquities authorities. Many times, our work funds projects that would otherwise be neglected, like building sites. For example, a construction site might wait years for an official antiquities exploration. We can do this within weeks or months."

"Archaeology for hire," he said.

"Not unlike what you and Joseph are doing in the lava tube under the wine shop," she replied coolly.

Touché. Darwin grinned through a mouthful of food and sipped some wine. The irony in archaeology, he knew, was that wealthy collectors were sometimes the best preservers of the past because they collected for artistic value, not just plunder and sell-off the gold by weight.

"What about the Aquila in the cellar?" she asked, smiling again.

Darwin talked her through the findings, including the rock pile that looked human made and how it might be connected to a scroll he had. "Perhaps it is connected to the lava tubes in—" he stopped. *Merde. What am I thinking? I don't know her from anybody.*

"Not to worry," she began. "I've followed your articles. I think I know why you are chasing these lava tubes.

"You do?"

"Yes. If what you said for Archaeology Magazine was true, that bit about using lava tubes as the ancient equivalent of storage lockers, then the Romans might have forgotten what they left underground when their empire collapsed."

"Exactly," said Darwin. "Gold is one thing, but so what? We spend it and it's gone. But suppose they stored other objects of less tangible value?"

"Like the Nag Hammadi scrolls," she said.

"Precisely!"

She stared at him a long moment as if measuring her next words.

"Come with me. I want to show you something," she said.

"Now?"

"Yes. It's only next door."

"In the cellar?" asked Darwin, scrunching his eyebrows. He was enjoying the dinner, and Marco had promised an amazing dessert.

"We'll be back for dessert," said Tessa, as if reading his mind.

"Okay, sure," said Darwin.

Tessa got up and walked around the table to Joseph. She bent and whispered into his ear. Joseph shrugged and handed her a key from his pocket. She stood and nodded toward the front door, motioning Darwin to follow.

10

The restaurant door closed behind them, and the humid night felt like a sauna.

"Where are we going?" yelled Darwin, his voice still adapted to competing with the loud diners.

"Next door," said Tessa. Music pumped from the hotel bar and smartly dressed people circled outside for smokes. She hooked an arm in his as they moved toward the wine shop. She activated the roll-up door and keyed in the alarm code and waved Darwin into the shop. She pulled the door closed, muting the buzz of a scooter flying up the street. Once out of the light that streamed in the front windows, the path between the wine crates became difficult to navigate, and she urged Darwin to stay close.

A few moments later, she reached the cellar door, unlocked it, and pushed through. The cool air rushed under her thin dress, and she felt her nipples gather against the chill, adding to the excitement for what she had planned.

Lights came on activated by motion sensors, and she led him past wooden crates and the small office tasting room to the old door to the cave. A short distance later, she stopped and motioned for him to sit on a crate.

"What are we doing here?" asked Darwin.

"Shh." She turned and reached for a bottle and two glasses she had placed earlier on a stack of crates. The hem of her dress followed her upward motion. She grabbed the glasses and, placing them on a crate next to Darwin, uncorked the wine and poured. He turned the bottle to read the label: a 1945 Chateau Margaux Bordeaux. Tessa heard him inhale sharply.

I knew you'd like that; she thought while removing a small leather folder from her purse and laying it on the crate between the glasses. "I have something to show you, but it needs a proper introduction," she said, lifting her glass in a toast and nodding for him to join.

He clinked her glass and smiled.

"A little something from your homeland kept safe in our Roman lava tube," she said, swirling the glass. She watched Darwin do the same, then close his eyes to sample the nectar. His lips stretched into a grin as his shoulders relaxed. He took in a mouthful. She did the same. Cool liquid flooded her mouth, and she pumped it around her taste buds. One by one, the wine's flavors distinguished themselves like the musical instruments in an intricately layered adagio.

"Wow!" said Darwin, and he started to say something else.

Tessa put a finger to her lips and refilled their glasses. She reached down and moved a lantern onto the crate next to the folder. *Now, for the coup de grâce.*

"Imagine that moment you told me about at dinner, when you found that Roman mark in the lava tube in Iceland," she said, turning the lantern on its lowest setting. A yellow pool spread on the table focused on the folder.

"Like it was yesterday."

"How did you feel?"

"Like everything connected in that moment. All time stopped. I just... I put my hand on Agrippa's handprint and was there! I knew it. Everything I looked for my whole life. I've felt nothing like it before."

Yes, you know the feeling.

"Would you like to feel it again?" she asked.

"More than anything," he said, tossing back the wine and refilling their glasses.

Perfect. A warmth gathered in her abdomen, and she smiled. She moved their glasses to another crate, shifted the folder directly in between them, and turned up the lantern.

"What if I told you I knew how to find the Library of Alexandria?" she said.

"I'd say you are in a long line of wishful people who have been saying that for two-thousand years."

"Basically, the same thing people said to you about lava tubes."

"Erm..." said Darwin.

"Exactly."

Tessa reverently opened the folder. A piece of papyrus lay under acid-free paper. She pinched the top paper with bright red fingernails and turned it back. Darwin leaned in close and tipped the lantern to brighten the text. The papyrus was torn and broken, and the ink faded, almost invisible in places. Missing sections interrupted the flow of letters, all Greek. Tessa watched him decipher and waited.

Let's see how good you really are, Dr. Lacroix.

"This is Greek. Old, but not ancient, and with a Roman influence," he said, looking up at her.

Very good, she nodded.

"It says 'Serapeum scrolls hidden...' it's broken up here," he hovered a finger over the text, "but continues 'her diary names location...' there's another chunk missing, then picks up again... 'diary hidden...Rome church... lib—' it cuts off. Could be a book or maybe library. Dunno. The last bit 'Synesius Alexa...'

"Wait! Her diary? Synesius? He's the most prominent pupil of Hypatia, the renowned philosopher and mathematician in Alexandria. He must be writing about her. And, some say she's one of the last guardians of the famed Library of Alexandria," said Darwin, looking up.

She remained impassive.

"There's also speculation that many scrolls were moved to the Serapeum library before they destroyed the Alexandria library. But then, the Serapeum itself was destroyed around four-hundred CE," he continued.

Tessa picked up her glass and drank. *Keep going*, she grinned. *You're almost there*. She crossed her legs, excitedly kicking one shoe-less-foot.

He glanced at her red-painted toes and continued, "this scroll is suggesting that Hypatia wrote a diary, and it's hidden. 'Lib' must mean library. And 'Rome church,' it's got to mean the Holy See. No other church could protect an important document that long. And the Holy See is..." He paused as if waiting for divine confirmation.

"Oh, my God...this papyrus is telling us Hypatia documented the location of the Library of Alexandria, and her diary is in the Vatican library!"

"Excellent, Darwin," she said, raising her glass. "You ARE as smart as the BBC said you are. Now, how would you like to find the Library of Alexandria?" she asked, grasping his hand hovering over the papyrus.

"More than anything!" said Darwin.

"Then I suggest we use your influence to get us into the Vatican Apostolic Archive," she said, draining her glass. She flounced her hair across bare shoulders and smiled like a cat who caught a mouse.

11

The next morning, after a couple cappuccinos, Darwin's hurting head could finally plow through the application form to research the Vatican Apostolic Archive. He also felt bad from the lingering emotional hangover from his fight with Eyrún and composed a text about finding a lead on the Library of Alexandria. He reread it before sending it.

It's not always all about you, echoed in his head, so he deleted what he had composed and wrote a simple: I love you!

She won't get it for days, anyway, he realized and turned back to the online form. Researchers applied to the Prefect of the archives with a proposed study and length of time. The website did not list how long it took for approval, but given they allowed only sixty researchers access each day, he knew it might take months. And submitting a proposal to find a sixteen-hundred-year-old diary would probably be dismissed as a folly. Now he knew why Tessa needed him to jump the queue. Darwin had a friend on the inside and sent him a message from his iPhone.

Darwin: I'm in Rome

That friend, Richard Ndembele, was personal secretary to Bishop, now Cardinal Santos, and had moved to Rome the previous fall. Darwin had met Richard in Clermont-Ferrand France last year while following a lead on his quest to find lava tubes Agrippa and the Romans used. Richard had caught Darwin after a breaking into the vault under the cathedral.

Darwin had discovered a lava tube but swore to not reveal its location in exchange for not being prosecuted. But Richard had been a miner and geologist in South Africa before being caught up in anti-apartheid riots. He had offered to help Darwin get the proper permissions for exploration and brought justice against Darwin's nemesis for racial crimes committed in South Africa.

I should have called Richard before I came to Rome, thought Darwin, feeling a twinge of guilt.

> Richard: Thanks for the warning. Fortunately, my trip to Brazil was canceled. What's up?
>
> Darwin: Got an urgent need to research in the Archives
>
> Richard: Naturally, you thought of me, your guardian angel
>
> Darwin: Of course. You always get me out of trouble. Can you talk?
>
> Richard: Not now. I'm in a budget meeting. Very important, but very boring. Email me. I'll see what I can do.

Darwin emailed that he was looking for a particular document without adding too many details, and that it would take only a few hours or a day to determine if the document even existed. He also added that a colleague needed access, if it wasn't too much trouble.

After emailing, he went in search of a barber and found one a couple blocks from his hotel. As the barber combed and clipped,

Darwin's mobile beeped, and he carefully lifted the device out of his jacket. He held the thing up to keep his head level and read:

Approved. You get two days starting tomorrow.

"Yes!" Darwin pumped a fist that caused an errant cut, and the barber threw up his hands in frustration. "*Mi dispiace. Mi dispiace.* I'm sorry. I'm sorry," said Darwin, and he sat very still as the barber tried to repair the damage.

12

Vatican City

The next day, Darwin sat in the Vatican library reading room among a couple dozen other researchers dispersed across large tables. The soft-tapping on keyboards and warmth of the mid-morning sun pulled on his eyelids. He stood to shake himself awake and smiled at Tessa, who sat across from him.

A sign on the table proclaimed, *Nelle sale di studio si prega vivamente di osservare il silenzio,* observe silence in the study halls, but most people were already alone in their universe of exploration. Like libraries the world over, books lined walls save for the high spaces between arched windows, where portraits of cardinals stared down like proctors in a university exam. Beauty was intricately woven into a tapestry of function as the religious art blended with the architecture.

Darwin hung his jacket on an empty chair-back and did a series of light stretches. Rolling his head to release a tight spot, his gaze swept across frescos of saints and cherubs on the vaulted ceiling. He did not consider himself deeply spiritual, but the sheer depth of history shrouded in the mysticism of the Holy See evoked a feeling of awe. His focus settled on the fresco in the arch directly above. *Not dissimilar to paintings of the Greek gods*, he thought, *except we think of the Greek gods as fiction*. He rotated his shoulders a few cycles and sat back down to work.

Research rarely produced quick results, and they had found nothing in their first three hours. They exhausted various searches using keywords and phrases from Tessa's scrap. The Vatican project to digitize the library had been underway almost five years now, but he knew would probably take another decade. *What we want is probably not in the stacks. We need another approach.* He turned to Tessa.

"Where did you find it? The papyrus, I mean," asked Darwin in a whisper, thinking it may lead to a clue.

"I didn't," said Tessa.

"I'm not following. You have it. That means you found it someplace."

"Let's say it's borrowed, and don't ask any more questions," she said, turning back to the search screen.

"You stole it," said Darwin too loudly as people in the surrounding rows turned to towards them.

Tessa stood and motioned him to follow her. She hurried through the double-glass doors into the atrium and turned on him.

"Keep it quiet," she began through furrowed eyebrows. "It's complicated."

"I exposed a lava tube network. I can handle complicated."

She crossed her arms and looked around the gallery. Darwin slipped his hands into his pockets and waited.

"You know, collecting antiquities has many faces and we all look for answers to fundamental human questions to make sense of life. But who owns the gold buried in tombs? The Egyptians? What claim do we have over someone's grave? What if you came across bones buried on your land? Are they yours to keep along with the valuables?"

"It depends. Some countries have laws, but finders also get to keep a share," he said.

"And then there are the costs to explore and universities are stingy. Sometimes, you need private investors, like the one you had in Iceland," she asked.

"How do you know that?" said Darwin, feeling his face flush.

"It doesn't matter. We both know how to fund projects creatively," she said.

"Where's this going?" he asked.

"I sometimes help a collector on private digs and in return I get to browse what her people bring in. This piece was lying in a folder, uncatalogued, and probably never would be," she said.

"In other words, no one would miss it, so you took it," said Darwin.

Tessa shrugged and looked at the marble floor where the tiles made up a southward pointing arrow of a compass. He followed her gaze down to her intertwined fingers. *She's not as innocent as she sounds*, he thought, and immediately felt a pang of guilt, remembering the times he broke into the London Underground and a cathedral in Clermont-Ferrand France. *But I didn't do it for the purpose of selling relics to private investors. There's more to this collector and looting, but I need to find out if diary really points to the library of Alexandria.*

"It's okay," he said, deciding a forgiving tone would garner more trust. "I've done a few things that were questionable. You want an espresso? I could use a bump before we get back to the research," he said.

"Sure," she said, slipping her arm in his as they walked to the cafe.

Darwin thought of the Roman scrolls his family had found and the coin that he had taken from the University of Iceland archaeology lab and felt his eyebrows furrow. *I'm more like her than I thought.* He laughed out loud.

"What is it?" she asked.

"Nothing. Just remembered something funny my buddy Zac did," he lied.

13

Back in the reading room, they searched for another two hours before Darwin was stymied again and led her to a small cubicle where they could talk without disturbing other researchers.

"We're going about this in the wrong way," he said, leaning against the built-in desk. Tessa sat in the only chair.

"I agree," she said. "I've been looking a long time, but you're still new to it. What do you think?"

Darwin steepled his fingers against his lips and closed his eyes in thought. *I'm missing something. Hypatia gives her diary to Synesius, but who wrote that scrap of papyrus? Synesius?* "Let's go back to the beginning," he said. "Do you know anything about when and where this scrap was found?"

"When is early four hundred CE in Alexandria, but I can't ask *where* without exposing myself. People will want to know why I want to know, and I don't want to share this opportunity," she said.

Darwin raised his eyebrows.

"With anyone else, but you," she answered.

"Okay..." he said, wondering how much more she was withholding. "Then let's summarize what we know. First, Hypatia moved scrolls from the Serapeum in the three-nineties to a yet unknown location. And, many of those scrolls in the Serapeum had previously come from the original library of Alexandria. Next, she describes all this in a diary she gives to her most trusted pupil Synesius for safekeeping, and then she's killed in four-fifteen without telling anyone else. Right so far?" he asked.

"Yes."

"At some point, Synesius hides Hypatia's diary in a church in Rome. And, we are guessing this church is the Vatican," he said.

"Correct," she said.

Darwin pinched his lips between thumb and forefinger in a pose resembling The Thinker statue and closed his eyes to run through what he knew of the Christian history of Rome. *Something's not right*, he thought. Then, after a few more moments, he said aloud, "Wait, there was no Vatican as we know it today in the later three-hundreds. So, where did this diary go originally? Which church in Rome?"

"There were many churches, but the most logical would be the Old Saint Peter's Basilica," she said.

"The *Old* Saint Peter's? Tell me about that."

"It's called the *old* to distinguish it from the Saint Peter's that Michelangelo designed. When Emperor Constantine converted to Christianity in the early three-hundreds, he commissioned a basilica to be built on the site of the Christian martyrs' graves, including Saint Peter's. It was a large wood structure that stood until the middle-ages when the new domed Saint Peter's replaced it," she said.

"Okay, I've seen photos of the crypt, but the diary's a book. Would they have kept a library somewhere in the basilica? We know they kept important documents like the Gospels because they needed proof of Jesus' life and teachings," asked Darwin.

"Possibly. We know relics, objects, and bones of saints were translated from other tombs around Rome to St. Peter's," she said.

"Translated?" he asked.

"It's the early Christian term for moving relics. They wanted all the most holy remains to be in the most holy place," she said.

"Makes sense, but you can't store documents in a crypt. Too dank and damp," he said and tapped his iPad to search "old Vatican library." Tessa leaned in as they read the results. She pointed to a link, and Darwin clicked on it.

"Here's our answer," she said, reading the screen. "It says the popes carried important documents with them until they inhabited the Lateran Palace. That's right. Now I remember my early church history. Like all things in Italy, the history is convoluted. The Vatican is an ancient holy area going back to Etruscan times, that's why the martyrdoms occurred there, and the basilica was built. The popes lived in the Lateran palace on the other side of Rome. They didn't move to the Vatican until after the papacy returned from France in the middle ages," she finished.

"That means Hypatia's diary would have been kept in the Lateran Palace, not St. Peter's, and later moved to the Vatican, meaning the papyrus referred not to a literal church, but to the institution," Darwin speculated. *And I thought the lava tubes were full of mystery. This is crazy to think a random non-Christian document was saved.*

"Why would there be no record of it?" she asked, beating Darwin to the question.

"Given how much change was going on in Rome back then, I'd be surprised if it survived. You have to admit the evidence suggesting it ended up in the Vatican library is thin at best," he said.

They were silent for a long minute. Darwin gazed out a narrow vertical window in the door at the other researchers in the reading room.

"There's another possibility," she said, and Darwin looked at her. "What if there's something in the diary that no one wants us to see?"

"Like what?" asked Darwin.

"I don't know, but what if the Vatican has a place for documents that it does not want to make public for security or political reasons? You know they declassify some documents, like the ones we can find here, but they keep others classified. Like the CIA or MI6," she said.

"MI6? That seems like a stretch," said Darwin.

"Does it? There's no organization on earth more cabalistic than the Vatican. They'll tell you they answer to no one, but God," she said.

"I'll give you that," said Darwin.

"Ask Richard if there is another, deeper archive. You admitted yourself we're going about this the wrong way. There's nothing to lose," she said.

Darwin studied her face, debating about asking Richard what appeared to be a foolhardy question. *Nothing to lose? Except his respect. He'll start to think I'm nuts. Chasing phantoms.* He deliberated a while longer, then decided, *What the hell. He already knows I'm impulsive.*

He began writing a text and stopped a couple lines into it. *I need to ask this in person.* He tapped the call button instead. Richard answered after a couple rings.

Tessa listened while Darwin recounted their lack of progress on research and posed the question about a more special archive. Darwin pulled his mobile away from his ear as Richard's gregarious laugh boomed through the device. "What makes you think..." came Richard's voice as Darwin moved the mobile back to his ear.

"Well, the Vatican's been keeping secrets long before modern countries existed," said Darwin.

The conversation continued a couple more minutes until Darwin wrapped up with, "Okay, I'll meet you for coffee tomorrow."

"What time are we meeting?" asked Tessa.

"It's only with me. He also has a private matter to discuss," said Darwin as Tessa protested. "Sorry, I'll fill you in right afterwards."

14

Rome

Darwin arrived first at the coffee shop the next morning and ordered his usual.

"*Una cappuccino triple si prega*," he said to the barista who raised her eyebrows in response. Two extra shots of espresso in a cappuccino was Darwin's standard drink. Baristas in his local hangouts were used to his eccentricity and had named the beverages. Thor's Hammer still topped the chalkboard of a coffee bar in Reykjavík where Darwin was a hero for discovering the lava tube that connected Iceland with Scotland.

He took the drink and a couple biscotti to a vacant table on the sidewalk. The mid-morning sun radiated off the metal cafe table, an early warning of the day's heat. He placed his jacket on the chair-back as a large man stepped out of a car and called his name.

"Darwin," said the man walking over, his cassock billowing like a storm. He set down a bag in the opposite chair and crushed Darwin in a hug.

"Richard," said Darwin with the last of his breath.

"It's good to see you. You got thinner," said Richard, holding

Darwin by his shoulders. "You are a settled man. Engaged. You should eat."

"Eyrún doesn't cook."

"She's a modern woman. You should cook for yourself. Let me get an espresso. Watch this for me," he said, pointing at his laptop bag.

He watched Richard retreat into the cafe and thought about their first meeting in France. Richard had pushed Darwin to disclose why he was looking for lava tubes, and he remembered Richard's words as if it were yesterday, "Think about how you will tell the world about your discovery. And think about what you don't want to happen."

After the discovery of the Iceland lava tube, Darwin had followed Richard's advice and people had been angry at his slow responses to questions and cautious publishing of research. Fortunately, Eyrún and her company dealt with most of the politics between Iceland and Scotland. But even so, Darwin was careful about naming possible locations of the other lava tubes, both to keep looters from tearing up historical sites and to keep the discoveries for himself. There was still a lot of fundamental archaeological research needed to support how the Roman military used lava tubes.

Richard returned and sat down. He grasped the demitasse and tossed back the espresso one swift motion.

"I see you've adapted to Rome," said Darwin. Richard was South African by birth and since had lived in Brazil and France.

"When in Rome..." said Richard. "I have some news, but before I tell you, how is Eyrún? It was lovely to meet her in Clermont-Ferrand and I'm still sorry we could not show her the crypt."

"She's great and sends her love. We had a wonderful time in Clermont-Ferrand. How did you know about that romantic bed-and-breakfast?" asked Darwin.

"Part of my job is hearing about people's marriage troubles and a good counselor has a wealth of tools available. Sometimes, couples need time together. Alone. Speaking of couples, when will you marry?"

Darwin laughed nervously at the question and steered the

conversation to Richard's move to Rome. "So, what's the news?" asked Darwin.

"The church has approved your request to investigate Clermont-Ferrand," said Richard, handing Darwin an envelope from his bag.

"Merde..." said Darwin, looking at the Papal Seal at the bottom of the document. "I almost forgot about this."

"I told you I'd get it done. Now, what was it you wanted to ask me?" said Richard.

"It's about our research. We can't find any record of what we're looking for in the archive. Sorry if this sounds a little crazy, but is there a restricted archive? You know, like classified documents?" asked Darwin.

"Restricted archive? I have heard of no such thing, and why would we let *you* see if there was?"

Darwin showed Richard the picture of the scroll fragment that mentioned a diary hidden in the "Rome church."

"It could be any church. Rome has hundreds," said Richard.

"Yes, but there is only one that matters in the long scope of history and this is about the Library of Alexandria," pleaded Darwin.

"Is this from the woman?"

"Yes. Why?"

"The head of Vatican security called me about her. They profile everyone. She's associated with a sophisticated antiquities theft gang that operates out of Cairo. Let's just say security is nervous having her in here and now you ask about a secret archive?" said Richard.

"But the fragment seems genuine. I saw it. These things are hard to fake. I'm sure you have facilities to validate it," said Darwin.

"I'm just saying be careful Darwin. She may be using you to get to the archives," said Richard.

Darwin paused as Eyrún's voice played in his head. *You need to be less trusting of people and think more about their motives.* He took a breath and started again.

"Understood," he said with more humility. "I was thinking it's more than a coincidence that she happened to approach me. But, whatever her rationale, I've been looking for the Library of Alexandria as well. There can't be harm in asking about it, can there? If there's no such thing, then we've lost nothing."

Richard stared at him a long moment before saying, "You are amazing, Darwin. Just when I think I know what you are up to, you come up with another crazy idea."

Darwin raised his shoulders and turned his palms up in a please-just-this-onetime gesture.

"Okay. Okay. I'll ask, but don't get your hopes up," Richard scolded. "And, don't look so down. I saved a surprise."

"What?"

"His Holiness is a fan of your lava tube discovery. In fact, he would like to meet you," said Richard.

15

"How did it go?" asked Tessa when Darwin arrived at the Lavazza coffee bar a few blocks away.

"He said there's no secret archive," said Darwin.

"What? I don't believe it."

"That's what he said," said Darwin.

"But you said he was a friend," she said, eyebrows tightening like a bow ready to loose its fury.

"Well—"

"Jesus, Darwin—" she said sharply but stopped herself and turned to look out the front window at a group of tourists following a lady with a small blue flag. Her chest rose and fell with several deep breaths, and Darwin waited for her to reengage. The people outside cleared the window, and she turned back to him.

"Sorry… I-I get excited because it seems we are so close, and you had blogged about working closely with the Vatican. It just feels like we're close to finding the diary," she said.

"Are we?" asked Darwin.

"Yes. Besides, I have resources lined up to help us. The library's got to be in Egypt. Hypatia couldn't have moved it far."

What's she up to? Resources lined up? Richard's right. I don't know her or these people. We can't risk the library falling into their hands. We'll never see it again, he thought, and said to her aloud, "Let me talk to Richard again. We're having coffee again tomorrow."

"Okay, my resources can wait. For a little while," she said.

16

Vatican City

Driving rain greeted Darwin the next morning, and he secured an indoor table at the coffee shop where Richard arrived about a quarter of an hour later.

"Not my favorite weather," he said, wringing out a corner of his cassock. The storm had turned Rome into a wet mess and rain thrashed the window next to their table as a thunderclap rumbled the old building. "You'd think it never rained here," he said, bemoaning the traffic made worse by the weather.

Darwin half-listened to the comments, his mind racing on his audience with the Pope this afternoon. He sipped another triple cappuccino, the first gone within a few minutes of arriving. *Slow down. You'll get there*, he told himself.

Yesterday, while wandering the streets after coffee with Tessa, he had decided he could not go to the meeting in jeans. He found a shop and, as he was trying on an exquisite Brioni suit, asked if they could complete alterations by evening.

The salesman said their tailor was fully booked until reading Darwin's note about a Papal audience. "Alonzo!" yelled the salesman.

"Get in here!" They had measured the suit, and both of them later delivered it to Darwin's hotel where they insisted on taking a selfie.

"Let's get to this afternoon's meeting," said Richard.

Finally. Darwin threw back the last of the cappuccino.

"His Holiness has a general audience today from 10:30 that lasts about an hour and a half. Hopefully, the rain lets up for the poor souls standing in St. Peter's square. He will have a brief lunch, then move to his private office where you will meet him at 12:30," said Richard.

"How do I get in?" asked Darwin, sliding forward in his chair.

"I will accompany you during all phases of the visit, which means picking you up at your hotel at ten o'clock. We'll clear Vatican security, expect more questions. They've done a background check, but they're like the Israelis and believe in personal questioning."

Darwin's eyes went wide.

"Don't worry. No one's getting out latex gloves," laughed Richard. "After security, we will have lunch in the Vatican cafeteria. Cardinal Santos may join us. Then we see His Holiness. Now, are you ready? Any questions?"

"No," said Darwin.

17

That afternoon, while waiting in the Pope's antechamber, Darwin licked his index finger and reached down to rub out a scuff mark on his shoe. His stomach rumbled. *Something from lunch?* He massaged his belly, thinking through the lunch with Richard and Cardinal Santos. He chose a delicious Insalada Nizzarda, the Italian equivalent of Salade Niçoise.

"His Holiness will see you now," said the Pope's secretary, rising from his desk and opening the door to the receiving office.

Richard motioned for Darwin to go first.

The Pope's office where he met heads of state and other dignitaries felt even more spacious due to the spartan furniture. Warm light flowed in from large windows onto a carpeted sitting area, atop a black-and-white marble tile floor set on the diagonal. A cross with Jesus featured prominently above a large credenza on the inner wall.

The Pope stood and squared his shoulders before striding around a large desk at the far wall. His hair had remained as black as the photos the press ran from time to time, highlighting his days as a rugby fullback for Italy.

"Darwin Lacroix. *Je suis ravi de te rencontrer* I'm pleased to meet you," said the Pope in Darwin's native French and reaching to shake his hand.

"*Saint Père, le plaisir est à moi,*" said Darwin, taking the Pope's hand and bowing his head in respect. Richard had coached him that this Pope relaxed the traditions and did not expect people to kiss the Papal ring.

"I'm afraid I've exhausted most of my French," said the Pope, motioning them to chairs atop the carpet. He picked up a small red case and a book from a small table beside his chair. "My gifts to you, Darwin. A medal commemorating our visit and my book on the care for our common home—the Earth. I hope you will read it."

"Thank you and I have a gift for you," he said, extending his palm with what looked like a piece of dirty glass encrusted with rock. "It's a diamond from the chamber in the Iceland lava tube."

The Pope took it between thumb and forefinger and held it up to the light streaming in the windows. "Magnificent. Is this what they look like before being cut?"

"Yes. Not much to look at," said Darwin.

"And yet they can cause so much suffering to extract," said the Pope. He sat, and they followed.

"Thank you for seeing me," said Darwin.

"I have followed the news of your lava tube discovery and the energy project. But I wanted to ask you about the other lava tubes, especially the one under the cathedral in Clermont-Ferrand. It must be wondrous to stand in such a place," he said, smiling with a youthful vigor that belied his age.

"It is."

"Tell me how you discovered these tubes."

Darwin rolled into the story of how a relative found a mysterious box of scrolls buried in Herculaneum under the ruin of Mt. Vesuvius that documented lava tubes crisscrossing Europe. He recounted the Lacroix family quest over the centuries and the accidental discovery in Iceland that led to solving the puzzle.

Out of the corner of his eye, he saw Richard tap his watch,

reminding him of their limited audience, and he wrapped up the story.

"I'm fascinated, but I'm afraid our time is almost up. They keep me to the clock around here. Is there anything I can do for you?"

Richard wagged his head no.

"There is," said Darwin. "When I first searched for the lava tubes, I was hoping to find clues to ancient knowledge. One of my scrolls hints at Romans using the lava tubes for storage of supplies and valuables in times of threat from enemies. They're dry and a perfect place. Anyway, I found a clue about the library of Alexandria, and it points to a document hidden in your library. I think in a restricted vault. May I have your permission, Holy Father, to look?"

Richard winced.

"We've made the library available to all. Why do you think there is a restricted vault?" asked the Pope.

"It's a guess, but I'm thinking there are controversial documents and the one I seek is probably written in code."

"And if there is such a vault and coded document, why should we let you see it?"

"Because I know how to decode it," said Darwin.

A side door opened, and a young priest stepped through, indicating the meeting was over and motioned Darwin to follow.

"Darwin, I'm so glad to have met you and I'll consider your request. God bless you," said the Pope, making the sign of the cross.

"Pleased to meet you, too, Holy Father," said Darwin, bowing after the blessing.

They turned to the door.

"Richard, a moment, please," said the Pope as Darwin left and the door closed.

A few minutes later Richard emerged from the office and Darwin returned his mobile to a back pocket after messaging his grandfather Emelio about meeting the Pope.

"What was that about?" he asked.

"Walk with me," said Richard.

They walked in silence until they reached the Vatican gardens. Brilliant sunshine sparkled on the vegetation, and the morning's rain steamed off the pavement, recycling back into the heavens.

"That was a ballsy request back there. What were you thinking?" asked Richard as they strolled toward the far wall of the garden and the physical border of the smallest nation-state in the world.

"Sorry, it was the only way I could think of."

"Humph," said Richard. "You could have warned me."

"Would you have agreed?"

"No. But, somehow, His Holiness agreed to let you in the special archive—."

"Yes!" said Darwin, looking skyward.

"With conditions," Richard added. "His Holiness is concerned about your motives. I gave him my word that you are a man of honor and less concerned for personal gain. He agreed to let you explore because he sees an opportunity for the Church if you find the Library of Alexandria. It would be the Vatican helping you, and the Pope hopes it could be the olive branch he seeks to improve relations with the followers of Islam.

"He gave me three firm conditions: Only you are allowed. I am to be with you at all times. And His Holiness's office reviews anything you publish about the Church," Richard finished.

"Agreed. When do we start?"

"Midnight."

"What?"

Richard slapped him on the back and laughed. "I thought you enjoyed breaking and entering. Just like Clermont-Ferrand. No?"

"No," said Darwin sheepishly.

"C'mon. Let's go now. The Pope just gave us unlimited access to His library, but we probably have to make arrangements."

18

Rome

"When did you take these pictures?" Tessa asked the caller after Darwin's meeting with the Pope.

"This morning," said the man who had called after emailing photos.

"What did they talk about?"

"A visit to the Pope. I followed them later from Darwin's hotel to the entrance to Vatican City. I had to stop at that point."

"Shit!" Tessa spat, sweeping a pile off her counter, papers flying like startled pigeons.

"What do you want me to do now?"

"You bugged his hotel room?"

"Yes."

"Can you get access to his email? Find out what he talked to the Pope about. And whatever else he's doing," she said.

"We have some people who can work on the email. When do you want reports?" he said.

"When you find something!" she ended the call and muttered, "You idiot."

God dammit, Darwin. I found Hypatia's diary. It's mine. You will not take it from me. She typed a message on her mobile.

Tessa: change of plans, need your help

Nahla: tell me

Dammit! How did I allow Darwin to manipulate me? Tessa hated relying on Nahla as the true price always came later. She looked at the mess on the floor and moved to collect the papers. *Get yourself together.*

Calm down. Look at this objectively. You've lost control of nothing important, said a voice. Tessa first started hearing a voice she took to be Hypatia's shortly after she had stolen the papyrus scrap.

"But I wanted to find the diary," said Tessa to the empty apartment.

No, you want to find our library. The diary is just a clue, a starting point. Look what you've accomplished, said Hypatia.

Tessa smiled. Her apartment occupied half the top floor of an envious Rome neighborhood, bought with money she had earned.

At thirteen, they had given her a hostess job in her family's restaurant. She had argued with her father to work in the kitchen or wine shop so she could use her hands and brain, but he had replied, "You're pretty, and the customers want to see a girl up front." Worse, the men in the restaurant harassed her, slapping her butt and making crude remarks. She protested to her mother who answered, "That's just the way men are dear."

She turned to her grandmother, who had been a resistance fighter in the war against Mussolini. Tessa had spent summers with her grandparents at their vineyard in Tuscany. They understood her need to learn and showed her how to tend grapes and make wine. Her grandmother taught her how to defend herself against men's unwanted advances and about women who led a strong intellectual life despite the confines of traditional society.

At sixteen, Tessa got her wish to work in the wine shop after breaking a junior chef's arm. She levered him around by his groping hand, after his unwanted advances in the walk-in refrigerator, slammed his forehead into the wall, and closed the heavy door on his other arm. Her father moved her to the wine shop to become *my brother's problem*.

Later that year, she left home to attend university in Sicily. With her grandparents now gone, she wanted to be as far from her parents as possible. She was drawn to archaeology and anthropology since her days as a little girl digging in the dirt, pretending she was an explorer. The past fascinated her, and life changed one day during a lecture on the rise and influence of Alexandria Egypt that also introduced Hypatia, a philosopher and mathematician of unrivaled intellect.

The professor told how people had traveled across the ancient world to hear Hypatia's lectures, and the fact she was beautiful added to her allure and power. Men subjugated themselves looking for love, but romantic love was a distraction and a folly of lesser minds, and Hypatia would have none of it. Tessa identified with Hypatia's intellect and strength of character. She resolved to be more like her and move away from menial work.

She traveled to archaeology digs across the Mediterranean when she could and showed a knack for finding antique objects that drew notice from Nahla Al Mahwi a purveyor to wealthy collectors. Nahla suggested "setting aside some valuable pieces" a temptation that Tessa resisted until suffering a shortfall in rent money one month. Without thinking, she pocketed a flat gold object, a winged scarab pendant.

"Exquisite," said Nahla when they met at a coffee shop. "Where did you find it?"

"In an ancient latrine. Someone must have dropped it," said Tessa.

"Good work," said Nahla, passing Tessa a fat envelope. "Think about my offer. There's more where this came from."

The cash more than paid the rent and, for days, Tessa felt as if the professor's eyes followed her every move. And something else, a turn-on, a feeling of desire tempered by guilt, like sneaking upstairs for sex during a family party a few years ago.

A week later, her appetite for thrill prevailed as she slipped more gold in her pocket. Tingles ran down her scalp. A sense of hyper-awareness led to an arrogance that changed her attitude. Her professors loved digging in the dirt, marveling at the flotsam and jetsam that pieced together ancient life, but they were poor. Discovery did not pay the bills, at least not well.

Soon, Tessa found other pieces and learning from Nahla, which objects were most valuable, set aside her own collection. Their lucrative partnership grew, and Tessa accrued places for herself on the more promising digs. But, despite transacting small treasures on her own, Tessa had become dependent on Nahla's connections for the big money exchanges.

Let me find your library Hypatia, and I won't need anyone's help again, she asked while switching on the espresso machine in her luxurious apartment.

19

Vatican City

Darwin followed Richard through the doors of the Archivum Secretum Vaticanum. He knew that 'secretum' translated to both private and secret, and the Pope's private library memorialized the vast dealings of the church. The library included famous documents like Galileo's heresy trial for suggesting the Earth orbited the Sun and vanity records of prominent families like the Borgias.

Most volumes were stored on shelving that would stretch the width of the Italian peninsula if put end-to-end, with special documents, like Galileo's, stored in acid-free cases in climate-controlled rooms. The archive had been open to all researchers of any faith since the 1880s and most of the collection was being digitized for global access via the Internet. But, secrecy pervaded the Vatican like the incense in its chapels. Despite the current pope changing its name to the Vatican Apostolic Archive, conspiracy theorists still maintained that the Vatican withheld knowledge.

Darwin entered the same reading room as he and Tessa had occupied a few days ago and walked to the front of the queue at the document request desk. A couple people scrunched their eyebrows at this pushing to the front and one man looked about to protest when a librarian approached from a side door.

"Mr. Lacroix? Pleased to meet you. I'm Franz Ehrle, the head librarian. I understand His Holiness has granted you special access," said Franz, tall and slim with black hair that matched his cassock.

On hearing this exchange, the other researchers' expressions changed to wide-eyed stares.

"I think it best if we discuss this in private," said Richard, nodding toward the people in the queue.

"Of course, let's sit in my office," said Franz, motioning to the door where he had entered. He led Darwin and Richard into a small office lined with bookshelves that mostly contained photographs of dignitaries and celebrities who had visited the library.

"Espresso?" asked Franz.

"Please," said Darwin. Richard nodded.

Franz made three cups of espresso using a portable machine in his office. He sat behind the desk with Richard and Darwin taking the chairs opposite. Franz tossed back his espresso.

"What brings you to Vatican City, Mr. Lacroix?" asked Franz.

"Please, call me Darwin."

"Of course. Darwin's a most unique name. Any relation to the great biologist?

Darwin laughed. "No. My parents are both professors and, I guess, they thought it clever to name their children after famous scientists. My sister is Marie after Madame Curie."

"Well, it's a name to remember," said Franz.

"Don't encourage him," said Richard.

"How can I help you today?" asked Franz.

Richard held up a hand when Darwin started to speak. "Darwin has evidence that points to a document in a special section of the library. He seems to think there is a part of the archive known only to a few. His Holiness gave permission for Darwin to see *any* document, but I think we need to make this official."

"Ah, yes," said Franz and reached into a drawer. He withdrew a document and slide it across the desk to Darwin. "This is a non-disclosure agreement and you must sign it before we may talk further."

Darwin scanned the paper. It was the standard legal language binding him to silence about anything in the library that was not publicly available. The non-disclosure included not telling family, even spouses. He frowned, but took the offered pen and signed.

"I'll email you a copy," said Franz, putting it to the side. "Now, tell me what you seek."

"Does the NDA go both ways?" asked Darwin. He knew the answer from reading the document but wanted to let Franz know that his search was not for sharing either.

Franz looked at Richard who said, "Fair play."

"Yes," said Franz.

"I have a scrap of papyrus dated in late fourth century AD," said Darwin, using the Vatican's favored anno Domini versus the non-religious CE or Common Era. "It's written by someone named Synesius and claims that he sent a diary to 'the Church' in Rome. This Synesius calls it *her* diary and says the diary contains the location of the Library of Alexandria."

"Leaving aside the incredulity of the diary's claim for the moment. Why do you think it's here? There was no Vatican library until much later," said Franz.

"It's a guess. If this diary went to the Church, then it must have been important and eventually found its way into the Lateran, the early Church library."

"Yes, but if this diary, as you say, reveals the location of the Library of Alexandria. People would have found it. If it ever truly existed," said Franz with a slight dismissive tone.

"I get it. I'm skeptical, too. There are too many false connections that we may make, but let's speculate further. Synesius in the latter three-hundreds was the most famous pupil of Hypatia of Alexandria. She was a mathematician-philosopher of indisputable renown.

"The Serapeum library was built partly to replace the library of Alexandria and to continue the city's reputation for learning. Historians posit that the Alexander library scrolls moved to the Serapeum.

Following Hypatia's death, it disappeared into ruin. What happened to those scrolls? Did they fall into decay, or were they moved to another location?" said Darwin.

"If you hadn't come in here with the Holy Father's permission, I think I might toss you out about now," said Franz.

"And I might have helped," said Richard.

"I know. I know. I've heard all this before," said Darwin, "but suppose the Serapeum contained the scrolls from the Alexandria library and Hypatia moved the scrolls from the Serapeum."

"Why would she move them? And where?" asked Richard.

"Good questions," said Darwin. "If we extrapolate history backwards, maybe the decline of Roman power and the rise of the young Christian religion threatened the library. We know the advance of Christianity destroyed a great deal of Pagan culture. No judgment here. It's happened countless times in history when a new truth replaces the old," he concluded.

"Like science?" asked Franz.

"Yes. If people think of science as a religion instead of a method of disciplined observation," said Darwin.

"Okay. So, the Library of Alexandria moves to the Serapeum library. Hypatia sees a threat and moves the scrolls to some location that she writes in her diary. Her pupil Synesius takes her diary to Rome, and it ends up in our archive," said Franz.

"Correct," said Darwin.

"Why didn't someone read her diary and go find the Library of Alexandria? That kind of thing could not have escaped historians," said Franz.

"I think she wrote it in code," said Darwin.

"What?" asked Franz and Richard together.

"She's a mathematician. She has a huge secret. How else to hide it?"

"Why haven't we cracked it?" asked Franz.

"No doubt we can today, but back then simple ciphers like the Caesar Cipher were impossible to crack without the key," said Darwin.

"Refresh my memory on the Caesar Cipher," said Richard.

"A simple letter shift. You use a number to shift the actual letter to the coded letter. For example, your name Richard with a shift of three letters becomes..." Darwin paused, wrote on a scrap of paper and held it out.

uldkdug

"Without knowing the number shift, you can't decipher it. Well you can, but it takes a long time by hand. A modern computer can crack it in minutes. I'm guessing there are documents reserved from view because of potential controversy. For example, a document in an unbroken code," said Darwin.

"True, but we could have decoded it in recent years as you suggested is possible," said Franz, turning back toward them.

"My guess is you have a lot to do, and it's on someone's to-do list, but very low in priority," said Darwin, imagining the bureaucratic minutia of Vatican City.

Richard smothered a laugh.

"You have me there," said Franz, pausing before he continued. "What we're about to discuss stays with you. I know you've signed the NDA, but that's just a piece of paper. There are many enemies of the Church who would relish our demise. And, yes, there are many dark periods for which we are ashamed."

"Understood. I am here for scholarship. If there is such a diary, we can find ways to bring it to light," said Darwin.

"Sure, but let's focus on today. There is a section in the bunker that is *Papal-only* restricted access. Any entry immediately flags Vatican security. I can enter with you, but I must first see the order from His Holiness. When I get it, I will contact you," said Franz.

"How long will it take?" asked Darwin.

"If he granted you access, his office should have it to me within a day or two," said Franz, standing to conclude their meeting.

20

The next day, Darwin and Richard were following Franz to the elevator leading to the basement.

"We built this in the 1980s," said Franz in the practiced voice of a tour guide. "Pope Paul the Sixth commissioned it to preserve the valuable documents from the environment and protect against fire. It's nicknamed the bunker."

Darwin thought it was an apt moniker—the vast concrete space was a warren of steel shelving and metal cabinets, possessing none of the elegance of the upstairs library. Rough wood grain imprints of planking that held the concrete ran in long lines that converged on the far walls. It looked like any other research library where function guided form and physical retrieval relied on accurate location.

Franz led them to a hallway where the ceiling lines created an infinity point at a red door some fifty meters distant. *Cool,* thought Darwin, as the perspective illusion caused the door to grow as they approached. Recalling his caving techniques, he figured they were about twenty meters below ground and under the garden towards St Peter's Basilica.

They reached the red door where Franz tapped his badge on a small white square next to its frame. Lights blinked yellow and a small panel containing a retinal scanner opened. He leaned in to scan his left eye, and a few seconds later, multiple latch points in the door *clicked*, and Franz pulled it open.

"Wow," said Darwin.

"It's a two-person failsafe. When I tap my badge here, the head of Vatican security verifies it's me through a camera. The retinal scan ensures it is not someone disguised as me," said Franz.

LED lights switched on as the door swung open, revealing dozens of drawers like the ones in the rest of the climate-controlled areas.

"May I?" asked Darwin, stepping to one.

Franz nodded.

Darwin pulled out the drawer. It moved silently. A parchment about half a meter square began in large block text proclaiming its purpose and importance. Gold seals indicating various approvals were bound to bits of braided silk attached to the document bottom.

"Best if you don't read it," said Richard. "Knowing something and not being able to tell can be quite a burden."

"Yeah, good idea," said Darwin, who had a facility with languages and read Latin, Greek, and Aramaic. He closed the drawer and asked, "Where do we start?"

"I think what you're looking for would be in this section," said Franz, leading Darwin to the far wall. "These drawers contain documents that are not readable."

Franz pulled open a drawer that contained multiple documents, mostly fragments. Each had a card describing any detail known such as date and location found.

"These look too small for a diary," said Darwin, pushing the drawer closed and opening a taller drawer with larger documents. He picked up one of the paper-bound bundles and read its card.

```
Codex returned with the Papacy from Avignon.
Language: Old French. Found in a chest with
other documents marked Templar.
```

He held it like a kid in an amusement park store where his

parents said he could only have one item. *Oh, my God, the Knight's Templar,* he thought, then sighed and placed it back in the drawer.

"Are these filed by age?" he asked, replacing the French bundle and closed the drawer.

"Yes. The oldest are in the bottom drawer near the wall," said Franz.

Darwin knelt and opened the drawer. He scanned the description cards. Only one fit.

```
380 AD +/- 50, carbon dated in 1983.
Language: Greek. Coded. Undeciphered.
```

He lifted it from the drawer. *Could it be this easy?* He carried it to an examination table and unwrapped the acid-free paper binding. A plain blank leather cover protected a stack of vellum pages a couple centimeters thick. It was in a modern book form as opposed to papyrus. He guessed maybe thirty pages. *Someone wrote this at great cost, that's thirty sheep to produce the vellum.*

The leather protested with a crackle when he lifted a corner. He let it down and carefully opened the volume at a middle point. The vellum creaked like wax paper but separated without breaking. He stopped at about forty-five degrees and moved the book so the light shone directly onto the open pages. Tightly written script filled the front and back of the open pages. There were no line breaks, but tiny circles seemed to show where new sections began.

"It's Greek lettering," he said to Richard and Franz looking over each shoulder.

"Can you read it?" asked Richard.

"Not in any way that makes sense. The letters form words, but it appears written with a cipher."

"What do we do?"

Darwin closed the book and re-wrapped it in the acid-free paper wrapper.

"Does the Vatican have any code breaking ability?" asked Darwin.

"Not that I know of," said Franz.

"No," said a voice from the ceiling.

They jumped at the sound and looked to the spot with a perforated circular cover and a tiny camera.

"We monitor real-time when anyone is in this room," said Miguel Suarez, the head of Vatican security.

"What about the Italian military cybernetic command? I read something about them," said Richard.

"Too many outside eyes," said Miguel.

"I have a resource. I could personally take the volume there," said Darwin.

"Who is this resource?" asked Franz.

"Barry Hodgson. He's Chair of the Archaeology Department at the University of Newcastle. I'd trust him with my life."

"I doubt His Holiness would approve," said Miguel.

They argued about permission to do this for a few minutes when Richard reminded them that the Pope wanted this work done.

"How about this?" Darwin continued. "You have scanners in the restoration labs. We can scan a handful of pages and learn if the algorithm can crack it."

"No electronic transmissions," said Miguel. "But a hand-carried copy might work. Franz?"

"We have to clear this with His Holiness's office. It may take some days. What are you doing?" Franz asked Darwin who had reopened the package.

"Writing some notes. I'm copying a few lines to ask my resource how much text we might need to decipher," said Darwin.

Another argument ended in a tenuous agreement that Darwin would read his copied text over the phone to his resource. It wasn't perfect, but nothing was.

21

Rome

Tessa stopped pacing and looked out the floor to ceiling window of her apartment at the late morning sun glinting off the television satellite dishes that forested the rooftops. *They're like a modern fungus ruining ancient cities.*

She focused on her reflection. A long white robe in the fashion of Greek philosophers flowed over her figure and spread on the floor. Gold piping accented one shoulder, and a matching band pressed her wavy hair tightly to her head and gathered it into a ponytail. She had taken to dressing privately in the fashion of Hypatia, seeing herself as a modern version of the ancient philosopher.

Calm down, said the Hypatia voice. *You know where he is, and he can't take it out of the Vatican.* She walked to another window, gathering a handful of the robe and lifting it from under her feet.

She stood a few moments longer before retrieving her mobile from the desk and messaged the same man who had taken photos of Darwin a few days ago:

Tessa: Where is he now?

Man: Back in the library. Arrived at opening

Tessa: Can't you get in

Man: Not in the Bunker

Tessa: Let me know the instant he comes out

Damn! She tossed the device onto a soft chair and walked to the shower, untying a braid at the neckline. The robe slid to the floor as she turned the water on scalding. The burn satisfied her need for pain, to feel intensely present. She flipped the handle to cold and gasped at the shock.

Her brain focused like a laser. *Get our diary.*

That evening the doorman at the St. Regis Hotel rushed to open the car as Tessa stepped out. She felt his eyes on her legs as he hurried past her to open the hotel door. *Weakling, so easy to manipulate*, she thought and made her way to Le Grand Bar.

"Hi, Tessa," said Darwin, sliding onto a stool next to her a short time later.

"Did you find it? What did it look like? How heavy was it? Could you read it?" she asked in rapid-fire.

Darwin described the diary as smaller than expected in terms of pages, but also larger because of the vellum's thickness as compared to a modern palm-sized paper diary. *I should have been there. Not this amateur,* she thought while crumpling a paper napkin and grinding it in her palm.

Patience, he'll deliver it, said the Hypatia voice.

"Did you at least take a photo?" she asked as a mounting disappointment edged into her voice.

"No. It wasn't allowed, but I copied some of it." He held up his notebook.

She snatched it from him.

"Whoa," he said.

"I can't read it," she said.

"It's encoded like we thought," he said.

"So, how do we decode it?"

She moved her mobile to snap a photo of the text. Darwin pulled back the notebook.

"No digital records. That's the stipulation."

"Whose?"

"The Pope. Well, the librarian's, too, and Vatican security," he said.

"Ugh," she said, rolling her head in disgust and gulping some wine. "What happens next?"

He explained that they would scan, print, and deliver a few pages to a resource that could decipher and code. If successful, they would decode the rest.

"Who is doing this work?"

"A Vatican source," he lied. "I'll share everything when we're done. I promise. This is your find. Like I told you yesterday, this meeting with the Pope came out of nowhere and it seemed like our best chance. If he hadn't said yes, we'd still be poking around the library."

Be grateful. You need him to do this part, said the Hypatia voice.

"This is amazing. It really exists," she said, smiling. "After all these years and with so many ways an old document could be lost or destroyed."

"I know. I'm starved. You still want dinner?"

"Yes. I'm sorry for how I started off. I guess I'm still mad at not being invited to meet the Pope," she said with a playful pout.

22

Darwin awoke to bright sunshine and went out for a brisk run before the day's heat. An email from Eyrún greeted him when he checked his mobile shortly after waking up. She wrote a short update on her work in the NAT and, more importantly for him, an apology for "getting mad" about his going to Rome. She confessed that work had consumed more of her time than she had wanted, and he should not have to sit around and wait for her.

He rounded the corner to his hotel and smiled about her last remark, "Just don't find anything amazing without me." The warm feeling stayed with him as he showered, got dressed, and returned to the bunker as soon as it opened.

Darwin's iPhone rang just after he cleared the library security scanners. The previous night after dinner with Tessa, he had dictated a few lines of the diary to Barry Hodgson, who said he would get an answer back the next day.

"Good morning, Barry. That was fast," said Darwin.

"I told you Lupita was a genius. She said the sample I gave her is not large enough to decrypt," said Barry.

"That shouldn't be a problem as we're scanning the entire volume today. I can't send it electronically but will courier some pages overnight. I'll let you know," said Darwin.

"Where are you?" asked Barry.

"Er, nice try. I said this is sensitive. If I told you where I was, you'd know why it's so important. Don't worry. If this is what I think it is, you'll figure it out for yourself," said Darwin.

"Only the best mysteries with you, eh Darwin?"

"I try Barry."

The scanning had already started when they caught up with Franz, and Darwin marveled at the technology as they walked through the conservation section of the library. The restorers cleaned documents that suffered damage from earlier restorations that proved insufficient or worse, caused more damage. They devoted one section to examining documents where the original writing had been scraped away and written over. These texts underwent special scans that revealed the ancient writing.

Darwin paused to watch a woman use an ultrahigh-resolution camera to capture images simultaneously in multiple wavelengths of light. She explained that this minimized the destructive exposure of the fragile texts.

"Once we scan these, why do we need to save all the paper?" asked Richard.

"For the same reasons we still want to see the painting on the ceiling of the Sistine Chapel," said Franz. "There is a human connection to seeing the masterwork of another that we cannot experience looking at a reproduction. We look up where Michelangelo dabbed paint on the ceiling and see, feel, and smell the whole place."

"Like collective worship?" asked Richard.

"Yes. Viewing it together binds us in the experience."

"We're also learning that digital reproduction can be faked," said Franz. "Forgeries exist, for sure, but we can date this paper and ink. You cannot yet fake carbon dating. And, libraries also preserve provenance. Like an evidence locker, this fragment will always be here, and we know its history."

As they moved on to the workstation where Hypatia's diary was under a scanner Richard asked, "How much of the library is being scanned?"

"All of it," said Franz.

"So, in theory, all recorded human history could be made available," said Richard.

"Yes. Most of the world's libraries are digitizing their ancient texts. Scholarship is no longer limited to a privileged few. Anyone can search anything," said Darwin, picking up one of the scanned pages. "Hopefully, that will soon include the library of Alexandria."

Richard raised his eyebrows.

They watched the scanning process for about an hour and went to lunch in the cafeteria. The completed scans would be ready in mid-afternoon, and Franz moved them away so the library workers could do their jobs undisturbed. Darwin booked a flight for early evening to the UK and messaged Barry that he would meet him the next morning.

23

Newcastle, UK

The next morning Darwin awoke to rain pelting the window of his hotel room. *Late spring in the northeast of England,* he mused, watching umbrellas in the street below flap in the wind as if trying to take flight. He showered and dressed for the day.

Slinging his bag over his shoulder, he thought of the rain and rummaged the plastic laundry bag from the closet. He removed the bound diary scans and wrapped it tightly in the plastic and returned it to his bag.

A ride share car pulled up at the hotel, and Darwin sat in quiet after the driver's attempt at conversation faded. The rain had abated when he arrived at the University of Newcastle where he exited the car into air fragrant with lush foliage and walked across the car park to avoid the trees shedding rain in post storm gusts. He stopped on the steps between the columns of the elaborate entry to the Armstrong Building and exhaled, flushing the tension from his body. Its elaborate portico reminded him of The Treasury at Petra in Jordan, except for the frequent rain.

"Darwin!" a familiar voice shouted across the car park. He turned to see Barry Hodgson converging with his path.

"Hey, Barry," said Darwin.

"Bloody awful weather," said Barry, shaking the rain off his collar.

"You should have picked Tel Aviv University, if you wanted decent weather."

"Now there's a thought," said Barry, holding open the front door. "So, which far off Roman outpost is it this summer?" he asked Barry as they climbed the stairs to his office.

"The Vatican."

Barry stopped and stared at him.

"Keep going. You'll want to see this," said Darwin, patting his bag.

Barry took the remaining steps two at a time. After a detour to the break room for coffee, they arrived at Barry's office. Darwin locked the door behind them and threw his coat on a chair back, shivering as his body adjusted to the warm office.

"Sorry for the formality, but I need you to sign this before we continue," said Darwin, sliding a legal document towards Barry.

"Jesus," said Barry, reading The Vatican letterhead.

"Not quite," said Darwin, "but I think what I have may be close."

Barry sped-read the pages and scribbled his signature on the last page. Darwin took the document and laid a brown paper wrapped bundle on the desk.

"What's this?" asked Barry.

"We think it's a diary written by Hypatia of Alexandria describing the location of the lost library of Alexandria," said Darwin.

Barry's lower jaw dropped, but he quickly regained composure and paged through the document. Darwin moved to the office window where blue sky now peeked out from the last of the rain clouds and gusts shoved the trees around like a playground bully. Shafts of sunlight hinted at a pleasant afternoon.

"This is the text you read to me, right?" said Barry, flipping over the last page.

"Yes."

"We'll need help."

"I figured, so I brought extra copies of the NDA," said Darwin as Barry messaged someone.

A few minutes later, there was a knock, and a tall woman entered after Barry unlocked the door.

"Darwin, meet Lupita," said Barry.

"Pleased to meet you. I'm Darwin Lacroix."

"Lupita Kimani," she said. "You have warm hands."

Darwin blushed.

"No, no. It's okay. It's so cold here in England, it is nice to feel warmth." She beamed.

"Let's sit," said Barry, clearing off a small conference table.

After signing the NDA, Darwin explained the document to Lupita and what they hoped to learn. Lupita studied the text on the top page.

"We've made great strides reading the old scrolls from Herculaneum," said Barry. "Many of them are copies of known works, but about a third of them are new. We're on the verge of announcing a couple discoveries. Lupita, here is the genius behind it."

"You are too kind, Doctor Hodgson," said Lupita.

"Not at all. Tell Darwin how you did it."

"Our biggest challenge has always been differentiating between the carbon of the papyrus and the carbon in the ink. Because of the intense heat of the Vesuvius eruption, both were converted into charcoal. The older machines could not see a difference. This new scanner uses carbon nanotube technology from semiconductor manufacturing and can *see* down to one nanometer," said Lupita.

Darwin's eyebrows furrowed.

"A human hair is about 80,000 nanometers wide," she explained.

"We're the first in the world to use a new scanner," said Barry, smiling.

"How does it work?" asked Darwin.

"The plant material shrank when the volcanic heat scorched the papyri. Like burning paper that curls when the carbon converts to gas and energy. The ink added extra carbon to the papyrus, leaving behind thicker marks."

"And the scanner can detect the differences," said Darwin.

"Precisely," said Lupita. "But the scan data was tightly compressed because of the scrolling. This is where the software takes over."

She rolled a piece of paper and held it in her fist. She held it so Darwin could see the coiled end.

"You and I read left to right and top to bottom. So did the Romans. The letters begin at the top and spiral down the page one line at a time. The scan showed the discrete separations between each coil. The software program reads the letters in each coil and lays them out in a long line," she said, circling her finger around the paper.

"When she says the program, she means her program," said Barry. "No one else could visualize the data the way Lupita did."

"That's amazing," said Darwin. "How can it help with the diary?"

"They wrote some scrolls with a cipher and we had the double problem to unravel the text and decode. We have a large data set to help us decipher Greek, Latin, Etruscan, and even hieroglyphics," said Barry.

"Awesome. How do we start?" asked Darwin.

"We scan these pages which won't be hard as they're readable. We must do some hand typing in a few spots like this page," she said, flipping a couple pages. "And these notes in the margins may not render. But we can do it. No problem. If I may..." she asked, reaching for the pages.

Darwin nodded his assent and handed over the document.

24

When Darwin and Barry returned from lunch, Lupita was waiting in the office.

"Done so soon?" said Barry.

"It was a simple shift. Only five letters Alpha to Epsilon," said Lupita.

"Did you read any of it?" asked Darwin. "It's okay if you did. I'm just wondering."

"A few pages to validate the decoding. Here," she said, handing him a copy.

Barry excused himself to deliver afternoon lectures, and Lupita returned to her lab, leaving Darwin her mobile number if he had questions.

He plopped down in a soft chair and felt the sun warm his neck and shoulders. Wriggling into a comfortable position, he swung one leg over the chair arm and began reading.

We arrived in Ammoneion two days ago. After eleven days in the desert from Marsá Matrûh, we were desperately thirsty and hungry. We had to take shelter as we could from a surprise sand-storm that fortunately lasted only two days. This oasis is a true miracle. It has the most delicious dates I have ever tasted, and there is a type of olive that does not reach Alexandria.

"Ammoneion?" he asked aloud to an empty office and pulled out his mobile.

Using the biometric facial scanner on his iPhone, he logged into a Virtual Private Network to secure the Internet connection and then opened a Tor browser to disguise his identity. It was not foolproof, but these two steps combined to conceal his digital trail. Zac showed him last year how easy it was for sophisticated hackers to impersonate someone and steal money, or worse, valuable data. Darwin remembered his jaw-drop feeling when Zac also showed the daily inbound cyber-attacks from North Korea alone.

"D-a-r-w-i-n-4-5-6 is your password? You bone head. My mother could hack you," chided Zac when showing Darwin how to use the more sophisticated tools. "And be careful of Google search too. They save everything you've ever done. Let them build great AI, but not on top of your intellectual property."

A search for Ammoneion turned up a raft of links many for chemical processes and many in German. A couple clicks and quick reads pointed him toward the Siwa Oasis. He entered Siwa Oasis on the maps site and watched a green splotch appear in the vast western desert of Egypt. Zooming out, he saw Marsá Matrûh to the north on the coast of the Mediterranean Sea. Alexandria lay a few hundred kilometers to the right, and a vast emptiness occupied the space between Cairo and the Siwa Oasis. *What's in Ammoneion?* It sounded familiar, but he could not conjure the snippets of history lectures swirling in his brain into a coherent memory. He returned to the diary, skimming until:

Today, I visited the oracle a most curious experience. Its walls and structure are in a state of decay. The locals tell me it was more impressive at its height when Alexander was here six hundred years ago. Were it not for his visit, I fear this place would have been forgotten long ago.

That's it. The oracle of Ammon! Grabbing his iPhone, he tapped through various links until he had the basic history. The Siwa Oasis was famous throughout the ancient world for its oracle of Ammon, a manifestation of Amun-Ra, the chief deity of the Egyptian Empire. Ammoneion more or less meant the oasis of Amun-Ra. Oracles required consultation in person, which was why Alexander the Great had traveled to Siwa in 323 BCE. He emerged from his visit proclaiming that the oracle named him the "son of Ammon" meaning a direct descendent of Amun-Ra which gave Alexander a god-like legitimacy to rule Egypt. He picked up reading again:

I carried a candle to the innermost chamber where I endeavored to lay aside expectations and experience. I prostrated myself before the oracle and felt my emotions carry me to feel something ancient and then, to my disappointment, nothing more. I had traveled this great distance for nothing.

But, when I emerged an old man, who was not there when I entered, was waiting for me with a message. He told me that a woman would come "in possession of great knowledge from the Son of Ammon. That a coming storm threatened to destroy Alexander's creation, and she must safeguard this knowledge for future generations."

When I asked him what this meant, he replied, "I do not know. The oracle only told me to deliver this message to the woman teacher." I told my guide about this man, and he said no one has ever seen this old man.

What's this coming storm stuff? thought Darwin.

I must write this while it is fresh. Last night during my sleep, men kidnapped me. At first, I feared for my life thinking Berber invaders had taken the oases, but my guide said the men were taking us to the Son of Ammon's tomb. I was blindfolded and rode two hours on a donkey. Then a rope was bound about my waist and we were guided up a steep slope and taken inside a cave. I only knew this because the sounds became closer, and the smell of dirt and dust was overpowering.

At last, the blindfolds removed. I stood in a large space a room carved in rock. Its walls were painted with wondrous frescoes of Alexander identical to his tomb in Alexandria.

Alexander's tombs! She's not talking about one, but two. One in Alexandria and another in Siwa. Darwin's heart punched at his rib cage. He sat straight and read straight through the remaining pages, then flipped back to a page he had dog-eared.

I placed a special scroll in Alexander's unused sarcophagus. Written in His hand, it lists locations of stored treasures from his conquests. I have carried it on my person since finding it years ago embedded in an anonymous scroll. No one else knows I have done this.

Alexander's treasures? My God. He conquered half the world. It would be an inconceivable fortune. He looked at the window and imagined caves lined with gold and silver.

25

Darwin had been making notes when Barry and Lupita joined him a couple hours later. There were also spots in the decoding that needed clarifying.

"I thought Julius Caesar destroyed the Library of Alexandria," said Lupita.

"We don't know," said Darwin. "There is so much legend behind the library that some people question if it ever existed. True, no one has found it, but we can say the same for many things."

"Like much of history, Lupita, it's complicated," said Barry.

"Which is why I'll stick with data science," she said. "But supposing this is true, what do you think happened?"

Darwin paused a moment before answering.

"Alexander the Great founded Alexandria in three twenty-three BCE when he conquered Egypt. Founded is a misnomer as there was a town, but small according to the records. He didn't stay long, and the library was begun by his successors, Ptolemy one and two. All great ancient cities competed to be centers of learning, and a library showed a core of knowledge that would draw scholars to the libraries.

"The Julius Caesar story happened during a civil war a few hundred years later in forty-eight BCE. We don't know how much of the library was destroyed, and they rebuilt another center of learning, the Mouseion, around it just before Christ's time. After that, the history is vague as Alexandria suffered ongoing strife and centers of learning shifted to other cities.

"We think they moved Alexandria's main library to the Serapeum, an offshoot library, but even it was demolished in three ninety-one CE. The truth is, we don't really know if there was a great library at Alexandria," said Darwin.

"But maybe this diary changes all that. It's exciting stuff," said Barry.

They worked on Darwin's questions for some time, and Lupita excused herself when they had finished. Barry walked to a spot on the wall containing multiple maps and brought a map of Egypt to the front. Darwin joined him.

"Alexandria is here," said Darwin, pointing and traced his finger westward along the Egyptian Mediterranean coastline. "Marsá Matrûh is here. That's about three hundred kilometers." He measured the scale with a finger and laid it along the route.

"That route would have been well travelled even in ancient times," said Barry.

"The Siwa Oasis is another three hundred kilometers south, but in open desert," said Darwin. "Not much margin for error, and only one other oasis in-between. No wonder Hypatia freaked out about the sandstorm."

"Come look at this," said Barry, who had gone back to his desk and zoomed into a map of the Siwa Oasis.

"I was looking at this earlier. Where does the water for farming come from?"

"It's ancient ground water. This whole section of Egypt is below sea level," said Barry, running his finger in an arc from Siwa across to Cairo. "Deep aquifers poke through here and there to form the oases. The nomadic peoples know the locations and how to move about."

"Zoom out," said Darwin.

The top half of Egypt filled the screen with the curved edge of the Mediterranean Sea with Cairo to the east. Libya bordered Egypt's western edge, and Siwa was less than fifty kilometers from a border that Darwin knew had been fluid in ancient times. South of the oasis spread the Great Sand Sea, an unimaginable expanse of sand. Before modern air travel, setting off to the south of Siwa was akin to sailing west from Europe before Columbus.

"Listen to this, the paved road from Marsá Matrûh to Siwa was only completed in nineteen eighty-five. Before that it was the same sand route that camels traveled," said Barry.

Darwin scrolled through Wikipedia as they both developed a mental picture of a place that, to them, had been just another spot in the sand a few minutes ago.

"Find the oracle of Ammon," said Darwin.

Barry zoomed into Siwa.

"Here." He pointed.

"Closer."

Barry clicked in as close as the resolution allowed and a mound of ruined structures filled the screen.

"Not much to look at, but more than we've worked with at many sites," said Barry. "Let's look at people's photos. I swear these maps have saved me thousands of dollars in travel."

"Stop. Can you enlarge that?" asked Darwin, pointing to a sign in front of a ruined structure.

Barry clicked, and they read:

> Known as Amun revelation temple, this archaeological ruin dates back to the Pharaonic era (26th dynasty: 663-535 B.C.). The visit by Alexander the Great in 331 B.C. gave it historical significance.

They looked at photos posted by visitors and saw there was not much to the remains. Some hieroglyphs remained on the walls, but it was, overall, poorly preserved because of centuries of exposure and high tourist traffic. Barry zoomed out, and they continued a virtual tour of Siwa hitting its high points such as Cleopatra Spring, a ten-meter brick ringed pool. Overall, Siwa was a mixture of ancient with modernity coming in waves, and Darwin thought the tsunami of modern civilization would soon cover everything.

"What about Alexander's tomb? What does the diary say?" asked Barry.

"It's buried in a mountain, but she doesn't give its name," said Darwin. "Listen to this,

> *To find the mountain, stand outside the outermost gate of the Oracle in the second hour after sunset in March. Find the Aldebaran star in the Taurus constellation. The tomb is in the lone mountain across the lake."*

"It's April. We missed it," said Barry.

Darwin walked to the window. *We have to wait an entire year? Merde!* The sun's angle cast long shadows, and people in the car park had scarves pulled tight against the strong wind. His gaze fixed on nothing in particular as he considered options. Just then, his iPhone blasted the song by Björk that he had set up as ringtone for Eyrún and he grabbed for the device almost knocking it off the small table next to the chair.

"Eyrún?"

"Hi, Love. Of course, it's me. Did you forget I'm out of the NAT today?" she said.

"No. Well, yes, you won't believe what I found. I'm in Newcastle with Barry."

"Wait. What? Slow down. I thought you went to Rome," she said.

"I did," he said and spent the next few minutes catching her up on finding the lava tube location of Nero's gold, meeting Tessa and learning of Hypatia's diary, getting Richard's help and meeting the Pope.

"You met the Pope!" she squealed, and Darwin heard her yell away from the phone, "I can't believe it. Darwin met the Pope," and then back to him, "OMG, what's he like?"

Darwin talked her through the visit and assured her he had gotten a suit when she said she hoped he hadn't worn jeans. He started to describe finding the diary but paused and a brief silence separated them.

"I miss you," he said. "I'm sorry for being so self-centered."

"I miss you, too. I'm sorry for the way I left in Reykjavík. It's bothered me the whole time I was in the NAT."

"It's okay."

"No, it's not. You were right. This whole project is getting out of control," she said and launched into a litany of complaints about the over-the-top egos and infighting over ownership. Darwin listened and reminded himself to pay attention as her problems were their problems if they were going to make a life together.

"Sounds like Sveinn is the same old asshole," he said when she finished.

"Ugh. Screw him. When are you coming home?"

"I have to take this document back to the Vatican. They want it hand carried. Maybe day after tomorrow I'll fly back," he said.

"What if I come to Rome?"

Darwin felt a surge of warmth, like someone had switched on a heat lamp.

"Really! I mean, yes! I'm at the Hotel de Russie close to the Vatican. When could you arrive?" he said.

"I'll get there when you do. Saturday," she said. "I love you."

"Love you, too," he said. "Can't wait."

26

Late that same night, Darwin swayed while fishing his room key from his wallet and swiping at the keypad. *Maybe not the best of ideas.* He thought of the scotch and cigar Barry had insisted upon after dinner to cap off their celebration. A champagne cocktail and heavy Bordeaux had already laid the foundation of tomorrow morning's hangover.

He filled a glass from the tap and gulped a few times. Opening the room window, he sucked in deep breaths, hoping the extra oxygen would clear his head. He was tired, but the alcohol also spurred a desire to talk with someone about Hypatia's diary. He tapped his iPhone to call Eyrún and froze his finger over the button. *Don't, she's asleep. Always goes to bed early when she gets out of the NAT.*

He thought next of his grandfather in Corsica. *No, it's way too late. He goes to bed at nine these days.* He looked at his watch, 2:03 AM. *Who's awake?*

Zac! It's daytime for him and tapped the number for his buddy in California.

"Hey, Darwin. What's up, man?" said Zac, who picked up after a few rings.

"Dude, you won't believe what I found," said Darwin.

"Dude? You must be drunk, you French-wanna-be-Californian. It's what... two in the morning over there. Where are you?"

Zac had founded a startup in Palo Alto California with the money from their discovery in Reykjavík Iceland and was pouring his considerable energy into developing an earthquake early warning system. His former employer, the United States Geological Survey provided access to data and Silicon Valley was ripe with data scientists and software coders.

"Newcastle... in the UK."

"I know where it is. Gotta be something with Barry. Tell me," said Zac.

"I think we found the library of Alexandria," said Darwin, looking out his room window at a dog sniffing around a lamppost. Its owner texting on his mobile.

"Where?"

Darwin filled Zac in on the initial discovery with Tessa, including the work in the Vatican Library.

"But I hear some hesitancy. It sounds like you don't trust this chick. Am I wrong?"

"Dunno," said Darwin. "She seems nice, but then she gets in these moods."

"That's the hot Italian blood," said Zac.

"No. It's different. Like someone is behind her actions. I dunno, maybe it's the wine," said Darwin, watching the man lean on the post as the dog wandered off.

"When are you going to Egypt?" asked Zac.

"Dunno. The diary mentions a location based on a constellation's position in March. Shit, that's a year away."

"Bad luck, dude. Uh, wait a sec..." said Zac, and Darwin heard a muffled conversation before Zac came back. "Look, Darwin, I got to go. Some VC is here, and I've got a pitch starting. Call me tomorrow... if you remember," said Zac, laughing.

"Yeah, sure. Sorry didn't mean to interrupt," said Darwin.

"Always make time for you, bro. Catch you later," said Zac, ending the call.

Darwin dropped his iPhone onto the bed and continued to stare out the hotel window at the now empty pool of light across the street. *What is it about Tessa? Why don't I trust her? She was the one who invited me into this.*

No answer came as tiredness compounded the alcohol, and he side-stepped to balance himself. He tossed his clothes on the floor, chugged more water and crawled under the covers.

Just before sleep pulled him under, he thought of Zac's comments about pitching the VC to fund the launch of a new ground-penetrating radar. Some combination of private ròcket companies and a micro-satellite startup. Silicon Valley sounded like a science fair of hairball ideas funded with blank checks.

A few minutes later in Rome, Tessa's phone vibrated from an incoming message. She fished it out of her purse and read a message from the man she had hired to follow Darwin. She did not trust him and suspected the Vatican would influence what was shared with her.

> Man: They deciphered the scrolls. Darwin keeps the copy with him at all times. Can't break in
>
> Tessa: Who else knows about it?
>
> Man: A research assistant who broke the code
>
> Tessa: Bribe him & get me a meeting ASAP
>
> Man: On it, and it's a her.

Bastard! I knew it! Tessa tossed the device and reached for the wineglass on the counter.

It's what you would do, said the Hypatia voice.

"Shut up!" she said aloud, knowing the voice was right. Antiquities procurement was a competitive business and lying to protect sources was considered a best practice.

27

The next morning, Darwin stared at the vertical pattern covering the wall and willed the pain behind his eyes to stop. It did not obey. The sun streaming in the window cast his shadow on the back wall. His horizontal form looked like a mountain range, and the sound of rushing water had him imagining a waterfall splashing off his shoulder.

After a minute, the noise resolved into plumbing inside the wall. He sat up and drank the remaining water in the near-empty glass, remembering he had filled it twice last night. *God, what's that taste?* His tongue felt around for the source of the wet socks and burnt coffee. *The cigar, you idiot.* He recalled the memory of Barry insisting on smoking cigars he had bought in Cuba.

"Ugh," he mouthed and looked toward the window and drapes he forgot to close. Through narrowed lids, he could make out bright sunshine. He turned to the bathroom and squeezed a blob of toothpaste on a finger and rubbed it around his mouth while rooting in his bag for the toothbrush.

He spit and rinsed and cranked on the shower. Saliva filled his mouth. *Great. Mint flavored socks.* He stepped under the warm water. After a couple minutes, the knot inside his head loosened, and the pain eased. *Not bad. This will pass. Get some food, and I'll be fine this afternoon. Barry's got to be worse.* He smiled and soaped up.

A knock on the door a short while later delivered breakfast, and he directed the cart to a pool of sun streaming in the window. He tipped the server, pulled a chair into the sun, and poured a cup of coffee while looking at a message waiting on his mobile.

Tessa: did it work?

He started to message back and paused. *What to say?* He needed to buy some time.

Darwin: We got some of it, but there were errors. Had to run it again overnight.

He stirred cream in his cup as the iPhone chimed again.

Tessa: How long will it take today? When are you back in Rome? I need to get resources lined up.

Darwin: Rome late tonight or tomorrow morning. What resources? We don't know where to go yet.

Tessa: We will. Hurry.

Thought I was impulsive. He toggled the switch that silenced the device and put it face down on the table. It vibrated almost immediately. *Dammit!* He flipped it over.

Eyrún: Good morning, Love. Land Saturday at 1. Hope you and Barry behaved last night

Darwin: Yay! And no Barry got out cigars again

Eyrún: Stupid boy ;-)

She knows us too well, he thought and went to the bath to get some ibuprofen from his kit. He swallowed the tablets and returned to the table where he opened the diary to the map of the tomb and brought up a map of the Siwa Oasis on his giant iPad. Hypatia had drawn a crude approximation of the tomb with a single line representing what Darwin took to be a path through the tomb from entrance to exit. She had written it was beneath a mountain, but there was no reference to geography only to the constellation Taurus from the oracle.

Siwa was surrounded by mountains or more precisely, plateaus, as the entire area, the Qattar Depression, was an ancient ocean. He imagined Paleolithic times when Libya and Egypt were forested. No doubt humans had lived nearby and had learned to travel as water and food became scarce, eventually isolating them into tribes as the oases shrank.

Hypatia's legend on the map put the entire underground tomb at "three-hundred passus". He recalled a Roman mile was one thousand passus, the length of one Legionnaire's full stride, that is the distance between the two left feet during a march. In modern terms, a stride was about a meter and a half. *Five-hundred meters!* He read on.

Two chambers, offset from each other, branched off each side of the main tunnel. A larger chamber measured twenty-seven by nineteen passus or, he scribbled on a notepad, about forty-one by twenty-nine meters. The smaller chamber was twenty by thirty-one meters. He looked around his hotel room, remembering the reservation app listed it at thirty-three square meters. *This tomb's more like the grand ballroom*, he whistled. *I guess Alexander did everything super-sized.*

On the edges of the drawing, Hypatia wrote about four traps showed by dots along the underground path. *But what does underground mean? Is it underneath a mountain like the Valley of the Kings? And she wrote about an exit. Does it loop around? No, she drew a straight line. And what types of traps?*

He zoomed in on the satellite maps, but the resolution was too low, so he wrote questions for later research and studied the drawing again. The entrance and exit, he could not tell which was which from the drawing or if even it mattered, were more obscure. One side she labelled "sealed," which he took for an entrance. Hypatia listed "down" and "steps" and "well." It appeared to Darwin that once they had put everything in the tomb, they would seal the entrance.

The other opening, or exit, would be a back door that few people knew about, like priests who chose not to be buried alive with their dead ruler. Unfortunately, it was also the way in for thieves. He put that thought aside and gathered his notes to head back to the university where Lupita would have a final translation ready.

As he walked out of the hotel room, a Wookiee tone alerted him to a message from Zac. Darwin smiled at a boy in the corridor who had a surprised look from also hearing the tone. He fumbled the mobile from his pocket and looked at the message.

Zac: At dinner with a VC. Can't talk but remembered that one of my developers is a PhD astronomer. Might help us with your star problem. Stay tuned.

28

Roissy, France

Three hours? Darwin fumed that evening when an Air France agent in Charles de Gaulle Airport informed him of the next available flight. A delay in Newcastle caused a late departure, and he missed the connecting flight to Rome. He wheeled his case aimlessly around the shops when he remembered the champagne bar in terminal 2E. Maneuvering against the crowd, he struggled onto the airport inter-terminal shuttle train and, twenty minutes later, slid onto a bistro chair at the bar.

Its art deco interior and lower sound level eased the mind-numbing chaos in the terminal and restored some luxury feeling to air travel. He slid onto a bar stool and felt the chill of the black granite on his forearms as he scanned the menu.

"*Bonjour*," said Darwin as the waiter approached from behind the bar.

"What do you choose?" she asked in French.

"Which champagne do you recommend?"

"I don't know what you like." she said with a shrug.

It was an honest response and so French. He had grown used to

California, where the staff cheerily introduced themselves and offered suggestions at the slightest hint. He ordered a half-bottle of Blanquette de Limoux and a dozen oysters. A smile spread on his face in anticipation, not expecting to find a gem from Pyrenees foothills in an airport bar. Legend had it that the monks in Limoux invented the technique, but the more famous Champagne region had stolen the idea and relegated all other producers to mere sparkling wine.

He read feeds from archaeologists he followed on Twitter and Instagram as the waiter returned, popped the cork, and poured. He sipped and bubbles tickled his upper lip and nose as the gas ballooned in his mouth.

"*Délicieux,*" he said, raising the glass. The waiter put down the bottle and moved on to an American couple. The Blanquette reminded him of a trip with Eyrún to Limoux and Carcassonne during a holiday to explore the geography and get to know each other. It was their first extended time together after falling in love during their lava tube adventure in Iceland.

His iPhone made the Wookiee noise again, and he grabbed it as the waiter looked up.

Zac: Got a solution. Check email

Darwin tapped the mail app and read:

```
Hey Darwin, no need to wait a year. My guy
pointed me to https://www.timeanddate.com/
astronomy/night/egypt/siwa-oasis
Use it to view the night sky any time of
year. Straight forward UX, even an archaeol-
ogist like you could figure it out. ;-)
Zac
```

The link sent him to a page titled *Planets Visible in the Night Sky in Siwa Oasis, Egypt*. He scrolled down to a window that showed a black silhouette of hills beneath a deep blue sky. The navigation-bar at the bottom showed the current date and time set between controls for compass direction, calendar, and height above the horizon. A Play/Pause button activated the twenty-four-hour sky position and a red dot showed progress, just like a YouTube video.

Cool, he thought, fiddling with a red dot and making the day darker or lighter. He watched the time display mirror his movements. Tapping the Calendar icon, he entered March 15 on the pop-up calendar, then scrolled the red dot until the time was 9:00 PM, two hours after sunset. He studied the window.

Draco, Ursa Minor, Cepheus, he noted the constellations in view. *No Taurus. Where's...* He touched the star field and saw that it moved up, down, left, and right just like looking at the sky and noticed two light grey triangles on the nav-bar: N and NE. *Duh! Stupid!*

He dragged a finger slowly to the left. *Cassiopeia... Perseus... Aries... this is so cool. Taurus! Not exactly a bull, but I guess nights were slow for the ancients.* A bright orange star showed Aldebaran, the main star in the constellation. He looked at the navigation bar. *West!*

He opened a map app and zoomed into the oracle mount in the Siwa Oasis as far as possible. The structures on the mount were blurry, but the layout looked fairly wide open, meaning the view westward would be clear. He zoomed out to see the whole oasis and used a napkin-edge to mark an east, west line from the oracle.

The main oasis dwellings ended at Siwa Lake, and he followed the napkin line westward to a large peninsula that jutted into the lake. Zooming in, he saw the spit of land contained a single large mountain. *C'est top! That's it.*

He wanted to jump up and yell at the top of his lungs, *I just found Alexander's tomb*, but did the next best thing—he raised his champagne and said aloud, "To the Library of Alexandria." He smiled and drained the glass.

The waiter circled by and refilled his glass as Darwin's iPhone buzzed.

Tessa: where are you?

He ignored it. For all she knew, he was on a flight and could not receive texts. The alcohol spread a gentle warmth spread in his belly, and he relaxed as the oysters arrived. Darwin picked the first, used the cocktail fork to ensure it was properly shucked and tipped the shell into his mouth. A small ocean wave broke onto his palate, conjuring up an estuary, sea grass swaying in the onshore breeze. Biting down a few times, he released the oyster's flavors and let it slide down his throat. A follow-on sip of the blanquette foamed in his mouth like a retreating breaker.

Halfway through the plate, he paused. The wine had calmed his busy brain and precipitated an idea, or rather a problem that needed an idea. Since his conversation with Zac the previous night about trusting Tessa, he realized Hypatia's diary had all the directions to find Alexander's tomb, including the hand-drawn map. Once he handed it over, she would not need him.

He ate another oyster, this time with a squeeze of lemon and a dash of sauce, its heat spiking his sinuses.

Damn. Would she really go after this without me?

Another oyster with a larger dash of spice rendered water from the corners of his eyes.

Wait! But no one knows what's in the diary until I share it.

He watched a trail of bubbles rise in the wine and settle on its surface as another idea formed. He sipped and opened the diary text on his iPad. Scanning it, he smiled. *Only I have the full deciphered text. Well, Barry, too, but he won't let it out. No one else will know about changes, but it needs to be convincing.*

Opening a notes app, he wrote a couple places where he could alter the diary. He knew working too quickly after a couple glasses of wine could lead to mistakes. *Best to do this early tomorrow morning before meeting Franz at the Vatican.* He reread the notes and drained the wineglass. *Wait!* He set down the glass and paused, realizing there was a problem. *Tessa will only have the copy I give her, but the Vatican has the original. Once they figure out the cipher shift, they'll know my deception.*

He gazed out the tall windows as a new Airbus A350 rolled

towards the runway. He worked through different scenarios and people's motivations, recalling both Eyrún and Zac cautioning him to be less trusting. *Why does everything have to be so complicated?*

"*L'addition s'il vous pla"t*," he said to the waiter, taking some Euros from his wallet.

29

Vatican City

"There it is," said Darwin the next morning back at the Vatican library and laid a copy of the diary on Franz's desk. He was in a foul mood, as Eyrún had called him a little after six AM. Another emergency required her to go back in the NAT, but his initial anger defused quickly when she said a close colleague had been hurt in an accident. She had sounded almost in tears at missing her trip to Rome and vowed that she was "done with the project."

He had done his best to console her and asked if she knew how long she might have to be in the NAT this time. He knew the colleague and hoped she was okay, but he spent the morning in a funk even after running to burn out the frustration. Being made to wait thirty minutes by Franz's arrogant assistant did nothing to change his disposition.

Franz opened the folder and read the first page. He closed the cover and asked, "Does it tell us where the library of Alexandria is?"

"Yeah. More or less," said Darwin.

"Be more specific," said Franz.

"It's somewhere in the Siwa Oasis in Egypt. Hypatia describes moving the library from Alexandria to a tomb that Alexander built, but never used."

"Can we find it?" asked Richard.

"Dunno," said Darwin. "Her directions are based on lining up some landmarks, but that was seventeen hundred years ago."

"But you can find it right?" asked Franz, looking at the document again.

Richard looked at Darwin, flipped his palms up, and mouthed, "What's up with you?"

Darwin shook his head, closed his eyes and sighed. *Get over it. She's not coming, but it's not their fault.*

"Yes. Sorry, I didn't mean to sound rude. I slept poorly last night," he said. "We can find it, but a big part of the problem will be the Egyptian antiquities authority. We'll need permits."

"That's never stopped you before." Richard grinned. "What about the Vatican's antiquities group, Ufficio Scavi?"

"Maybe..." said Darwin knowing Ufficio Scavi partnered with archaeologists throughout the world. He knew the current pope sought to reconcile the historical feuding between Christians and Muslims, but he doubted the Egyptians would ever cooperate with the Vatican. *I need to be careful here. Too much government help, and we get tied up for years trying to get political permissions and permits from the antiquities authorities.*

"But it might take too long to get them up to speed. How about we see what Tessa's resources can do. She also has ways to get things done without the authorities," said Darwin.

"Absolutely not! I forbid it! The scrolls might have content that could damage our faith, especially if introduced in the wrong way," said Franz, slapping his palms on the desk.

Darwin rocked back in his chair as if avoiding a blow. *Who is this guy? His kind of small-mindedness has controlled history for too long. No, the Library belongs to humankind.*

"I think the Catholic church has damaged itself enough with its current scandal," said Darwin.

Richard opened his mouth to protest, and Darwin held up a hand.

"This news could be the kind that changes focus. Think about it —a new discovery, ancient knowledge shared, a peaceful collaboration between two great religions. You can't fix the past, but you can create a different hopeful future. Islam is struggling with extremist acts. This could be a change of times for them, too," said Darwin.

"I don't think—"

"AND," Darwin cut Franz off. "The library will need a skilled librarian. Aren't *you* a strategic advisor on the board at the Bibliotheca Alexandrina?" he finished referring to the reconstructed library in Alexandria that opened last decade.

Richard smiled and said, "You are still full of surprises, Darwin."

"I'll agree on one condition," said Franz. "You can use Tessa's resources, but you must email Richard every two days with a progress report."

"Agreed," said Darwin, knowing it was a strange bargain for once he reached Egypt, Franz would have no hold on him.

But, best to play the long game, he thought while walking the marble corridor outside Franz's office. He envisioned the controlled archive and its many drawers. *What of those other documents? What's in that Templar package? Maybe once I'm done with Tessa...*

He reached for his mobile and checked for missed messages as he had expected to hear from her this morning. *Odd. Where the hell is she?* He re-pocketed the device and pulled on a pair of sunglasses as he stepped out the main entrance into bright sunshine.

30

Newcastle

Tessa slid into a seat across the small table from Lupita at a coffee shop in Newcastle after arriving the night before.

"Lupita, it's so nice to meet you," she said.

"And you," said Lupita.

They had agreed to meet after the man Tessa had used to follow Darwin approached Lupita with a request to scan some ancient scrolls from a private collection. The client would pay handsomely, but the work had to be discreet.

Lupita had been reluctant at first, but the man had given her an envelope with a sample of the scrolls and a stack of pound notes. His research had shown that Lupita regularly sent part of her scholarship to her family in Kenya. The extra cash would be welcome.

"Ugh," said Tessa, untangling her scarf. "The weather's horrid. How do you stand it?"

"It's okay. I don't go outside much."

Tessa picked up her coffee with both hands to warm them against the wet chill. While she was in a hurry to ask about Hypatia translations, she knew trust like savings was built on regular deposits and slow withdrawals.

"You're from Kenya, right?" asked Tessa.

"Yes."

"Where? I studied at the Turkana Basin Institute for a year."

"When was that?" asked Lupita.

"Twenty-twelve to thirteen. Early spring to end of winter. Absolutely spellbinding to be in the cradle of humankind."

"I grew up in the Great Rift Valley. My family is Maasai," said Lupita."

"How did you come to be here?" asked Tessa, sipping again mostly to keep her mouth occupied and allow space for an answer.

"I was always good with maths and puzzles. My family got me good schooling, rare for girls. A great teacher recognized my talent and helped further my education. After my undergraduate degree at the University of Nairobi, I got a scholarship from Total, the oil company."

"Aren't they French?" asked Tessa.

"Yes, but my French is too poor for me to have studied in Paris. Besides, Newcastle has a focus on satellite imaging. The same technologies allow us to peer underground and into objects like burnt scrolls."

"Burnt scrolls? Fascinating. Tell me more," said Tessa.

Lupita talked a few minutes about her research merging images from satellites and ground penetrating vibration tests for oil company sponsors, and they had experimented applying the technology to the burned scrolls found in Herculaneum under the Mt Vesuvius volcano. She described developing the algorithms to resolve the text in the scans was a welcome challenge, a chance for more meaningful discoveries than more oil.

"What is your request?" asked Lupita. "I have a lecture in half an hour."

Tessa smiled inwardly. Cash was a good spark, but curiosity and a sense of purpose fueled the hottest fires.

"I'm an independent archaeologist, I choose my own projects. My backers are sometimes well known like the Getty organization in America, but many times they are collectors," Tessa paused, seeing a frown on Lupita's face.

"You're like a grave robber?" asked Lupita.

"No." Tessa laughed, imagining herself as Angelina Jolie in Tomb Raider. "It's much less exciting. We perform investigations at private sites or, like in this case, validate the authenticity and provenance of artifacts. The money we earn funds more private research such as seeking ancient settlements," said Tessa.

"Like what?" asked Lupita.

"We think there are many more caches of ancient knowledge. But it's slow and costly finding them," said Tessa, stopping to drink her coffee. *C'mon, Lupita, take the bait.*

"Why the ancient scrolls?" asked Lupita.

"The truth," said Tessa, letting her words sink in.

"The truth?"

"Yes. Think about it. There's the work we do to pay our obligations, like your oil company research, and then there's the work we do that matters. What's the most valuable thing we can discover?" asked Tessa.

"I don't know. Diamonds. Gold, maybe," said Lupita.

"Knowledge," said Tessa.

Lupita cocked her head slightly as if to say prove it.

"Your ancestors told stories that preserved the past. Your elders had an oral culture that communicated how to live, which plants were safe to eat, and how to treat illnesses. Other cultures eventually wrote the stories and life hacks on clay and plant skins, then paper and, finally, in digital space.

"What happens in a clash of cultures?" asked Tessa, knowing this question would hit home.

"The dominant culture displaces what it doesn't like," said Lupita.

"Exactly! It purges the ancient knowledge. You've heard of the Nag Hammadi scrolls? A find as important as the Dead Sea scrolls. Men, in a political power grab, ordered destruction of all versions of Christ's life that they couldn't control. Seventeen hundred years ago, someone risked their life to take a few of those scrolls and bury them in a jar. These are writings that offer a wider perspective—the truth.

"This is the truth I want to find. We don't have endless money, but we're passionate. We take on corporate work to pay the bills," said Tessa.

Several people sitting near them had looked over as Tessa's voice rose in volume. Tessa stared down one couple who returned to their coffees. She looked back at Lupita and grinned in apology.

"Let me get to the point," said Tessa. "You're deciphering a document written by a great fourth century philosopher—Hypatia of Alexandria."

"How do you know that?" exclaimed Lupita. "They told me it is a secret and had to sign an NDA."

"That's what the *men* in the Vatican want us to believe. Remember the buried Nag Hammadi scrolls? Hypatia was doing the same thing, saving the truth from destruction. The *men* in the early Christian church, the roots of the Vatican, were on a power grab. Did you know they murdered Hypatia?"

"No," said Lupita, putting a hand to her mouth.

"You see it today. How hard it is for women to break into male-dominated fields. This is why we need your help. Maybe there's nothing left of the library of Alexandria, but imagine the wonders it might contain," said Tessa.

"But isn't this Darwin's find?" asked Lupita.

"Is that what he said?" asked Tessa in the tone of a schoolmaster scolding an innocent who had been led astray.

"Now that you mention it, I don't think he said anything."

"Precisely," said Tessa. "I found the original papyrus that led to Hypatia's diary in the Vatican. But the Vatican only allows men into the restricted vault. More *men* suppressing the truth. Why do you think they buried it in their bunker?"

"But Darwin seems genuine."

"Maybe, I like him too, but do you think he can go up against the Vatican?" said Tessa. The couple next to them looked over again.

"What do you want from me?" asked Lupita.

"I want you to help me ensure that the Vatican doesn't hide the truth. Let me see a copy of the decrypted diary."

"I could lose my scholarship and be sent home. Disgraced," said Lupita.

"We're in this together. If we betray you, we also get cut out of discovery. Think about it. The world deserves to know the truth," said Tessa, sliding a fat envelope across the table. "I trust you to do the right thing."

"What if I decided not to do it?" asked Lupita glancing about as she slid the envelope into her bag.

"We'd be disappointed but, either way, keep the money and use it for a good cause," said Tessa.

"Let me think about it," said Lupita. "I have to get to my lecture. I'll text you my answer this afternoon."

They said goodbyes and parted ways in front of the shop.

31

Rome

Sunday turned out to be a casual day for Darwin, and he had begun by sleeping in or at least lying in bed an extra hour, splayed diagonally across the king-sized mattress. Expecting to be with Eyrún, he had booked the Picasso Suite that overlooked the hotel's Secret Garden, where birds now reveled in a late spring frenzy.

At least they're getting some, he mused. A knock at the front door reminded him that he had ordered breakfast the evening before, and slipping on one of the plush cotton robes hanging in the bath, he directed the breakfast service through the French doors onto the terrace.

The service set the table and poured coffee before asking, "May I get you anything else Signore Lacroix?"

"No. *Grazie*," he replied and carried the cup to the railing and watched the birds zip through the trees as he considered what do to with himself in Rome.

I've already seen the Pope. He laughed aloud and then grew quiet and absorbed the easy warmth of the morning. An older couple moved in the garden below, the man taking pictures of the woman by various plants. Then they moved together for a selfie in front of a fountain. Her fingers lightly stroked his back as they reviewed the photos. They kissed oblivious to Darwin, watching them and, after a moment, he turned away feeling uncomfortable as a voyeur in their love scene.

His stomach growled, and he went to the table and started breakfast. The aromas of the frittata swirled around him as he bit into a firm, but light layering of eggs, peppers, ham and parmesan cheese. His appetite grew, and he plowed through the dish with single purpose. He tore off a piece of cornetto and dabbed on a generous slather of butter. The light flaky pastry, an Italian cousin to the croissant, melted in his mouth, and he chased it with a sip of coffee. *This is nice. I haven't eaten breakfast like this... I dunno... since Eyrún and I were in Provençe.*

32

Rome

Monday morning brought the workday rhythm back to Rome as Darwin noticed an uptick in the hum of the vehicle traffic filtering onto the terrace during his breakfast. He had slept well again after a lazy day in the Italian capital. At one point he found himself at Nero's old palace and had walked the distance to Joseph's wine shop on the chance he might explore the lava tube, but the shop was closed.

The Santarossa's restaurant on the corner was jammed with families gathering for a Sunday communion, and he asked if anyone had seen Tessa. A cousin, working as a chef, laughed and said, "Tessa's like the weather, unpredictable."

Another family member who overheard their conversation said, " I heard she went to London for the weekend."

That perplexed Darwin for several hours. After Franz and Richard had agreed on Friday to let him pursue working with Tessa, he could not find her. *What would she be doing in London?* But he had eventually let it go and spent the later afternoon researching for his publication before delving into a fantasy fiction novel he had been meaning to pick up again.

This morning his iPad, zoomed into a first century map of Londinium, lay on the terrace table in front to him as he talked on the phone with a research librarian at the British Museum, when both devices chimed with an incoming message.

Tessa: Lunch today? I heard you have the diary

Darwin: Sure. Where have you been?

Tessa: London. Something personal came up

They agreed on one-thirty at a restaurant near the Vatican. *Something personal? I don't buy it.*

Darwin reached the restaurant about one-forty and found Tessa pacing the pavement, engrossed in a phone conversation. She smiled when she saw him and held up two fingers meaning a couple minutes. He was seated at a sidewalk table under a red and white striped awning that shaded them from the brilliant sunshine and provided a fabulous view of St. Peter's domed basilica.

"Hi, Darwin," she said, sliding into the opposite seat and the woven café chair creaked as she scooted it in place.

"Hey, Tessa. It's beautiful today," he said while dying to ask what was so important in London.

"Rome is heating up. In another month, there'll be so many tourists, we'd never get a seat here."

They ordered a bottle of Rosaro Negroamaro from the Puglia region. Darwin asked for an Insalada Nizzarda, remembering the seashore-meets-vegetable-garden freshness from his lunch at the Vatican. Tessa requested the same, but with the dressing on the side.

"What did you do yesterday?" she asked.

"Enjoyed a casual Roman Sunday, played tourist a while and caught up on some reading. And you? Is everything okay," he probed.

"*Si.* A former lover texted that he had a free weekend in London without his wife. It was...well, I'll leave it at that," she said with a dreamy smile.

The server delivered their salads, carefully arranging the large plate on the small table and refilling their wineglasses.

"What's in the diary?" she asked after swallowing a mouthful.

Former lover, my ass? She's like a bloodhound chasing the diary and jets-off for a romp in the sheets just as we decipher the text? If the guy was in Rome, maybe, but London, no.

He studied her face a few moments longer and was about to ask where they stayed in London to draw her out in a lie, but decided there was nothing for it. Instead, he summarized the diary in between bites of salad, concluding with the tomb in Siwa Oasis.

"The Siwa Oasis? It makes sense. Alexander went there to meet the oracle of Ammon and that gave him legitimacy to rule Egypt. I wonder..." she paused. "Most scholars believe Alexander's tomb is somewhere in Alexandria, but there's an archaeologist in the late eighties who claims to have found his tomb in Siwa," she said and tapped on her mobile, searching for something.

"That's the problem," said Darwin. "They carted Alexander's body around for two years after he died in Babylon. The claims for his tomb are all over the middle east."

"Here it is. I saved the article. It's a Hellenistic royal tomb with carved lions at the entrance and Greek-style decorations and inscriptions. The archaeologist, a Greek woman, also claims there are inscriptions written by a Ptolemy, one of Alexander's descendants," she said.

She held out her mobile for Darwin to look at a photo of the decaying lion sculptures found in the tomb.

"Which Ptolemy? There was more than a dozen, with Cleopatra the last," said Darwin.

"It doesn't say. But, problem is, there're no references to any names."

"So, it could be any Ptolemaic royal figure. Where's the site?" asked Darwin.

"Not listed. The article writes that the Egyptian government blocked further access to the site for political reasons. But you said the diary says the tomb is in a mountain and this looks like a flat area," she said, holding the device out again.

They continued the conversation through bites of salad and, after paying the bill, walked to the Vatican library reading room where Darwin handed Tessa a copy of the diary. She read it while he fetched coffees from the cafeteria. A few minutes later, he returned to find her tapping on her mobile.

"There's a flight tomorrow morning for Alexandria. I bought us tickets and booked rooms for us at a hotel near the new library of Alexandria," she said.

"Isn't this a bit fast?" he asked.

"Is there something you need to do in Rome? The library's in Egypt. There's nothing more to find here," she said.

That afternoon Darwin visited a couple of outdoor adventure type stores to buy clothes for Alexandria and its desert beyond. He tried on a dark brown fedora that the salesperson had offered. "You look like Indiana Jones," she said. He admitted the hat gave the khaki trousers and off-white shirt a retro adventure look, but decided wearing a felt hat in blazing heat would not be comfortable.

Back in the hotel, he had arranged for the hotel to ship his new suit and warmer clothing back to Reykjavík and was packing for Alexandria when his iPhone rang.

"Hey, Barry. Long time no hear," said Darwin.

"Darwin, are you still in Rome?" asked Barry, sounding urgent.

"Yeah. Why?"

"Lupita's here in my office. Let me switch this to speaker mode," said Barry, and Darwin heard rustling papers and then Barry's voice came back with a hollower sound. "Darwin?"

"Still here."

"Okay good. Lupita came in my office this morning pretty upset," said Barry. "Here, you tell him."

"Hi, Darwin," said Lupita.

"Hi, Lupita. Are you okay?"

"Yes, I'm fine. Tessa was here yesterday—"

"What? Why?" Darwin burst out and threw a shirt he was folding.

"She tried to bribe me to get a copy of the diary—

"I knew that sneaky bitch was lying. She told me she went to London to meet an old lover. Sorry Lupita. I cut you off. Go on," said Darwin.

She continued and described how Tessa posed as someone who wanted to scan damaged scrolls similar to work they had done with the charred Herculaneum scrolls. But the legitimate sounding request then turned into a bribe to get a copy of the deciphered diary. "She made it sound like you and the Vatican had some conspiracy to control the knowledge," said Lupita.

"Did you give it to her?" asked Darwin.

"No way! I tried to sound sympathetic, but then she gave me an envelope with two-thousand pounds and said I could keep it whether I sent the diary or not. I didn't know what to do, so I talked to Barry," said Lupita.

Darwin's mind raced, trying to figure out what Tessa was up to. He heard Lupita sniff as if she had been moved to tears as Barry offered her some soothing words.

We could ignore her. No, we can't risk it. She'll just find some other means to get the original diary. Darwin ran a few more scenarios in his head and decided on the simplest.

"Okay, here's what I think we should do," he continued. "I edited the decryption in exactly two places: one, I redacted the part about Alexander's scroll hidden in the sarcophagus and two, I changed the location of the mountain by substituting the Taurus constellation in the west with Polaris in the north. There's a mountain that fits the description."

"Sounds like it will work," said Barry. "What should we do?"

"I just emailed you both a copy of my changed diary. Lupita, wait for Tessa to contact you. Make it sound like you are thinking about it. Call me when she makes contact, then send her the changed diary you got from me," said Darwin.

"What about the money?" asked Lupita, sounding very worried.

"Put it in the safe in Barry's office. Document the conversation you had with Tessa and what we've agreed to do. You'll be fine, Lupita. I promise," said Darwin.

33

Alexandria, Egypt

The next morning Darwin watched the Italian coastline disappear under the wing of the Airbus 320. Clouds blurred past the window as the jet banked over the Mediterranean Sea towards Alexandria. Rattles in the airframe and various system dings at once gave a pit in-the-stomach feeling and a reminder that all was normal. After a few more minutes, the pilot throttled back to ease the angle of attack on the way to cruising altitude while an announcement told everyone to stay in their seats.

Darwin looked out the window at the white ridges streaking the water a few thousand meters below as a cruise ship labored towards one of the ports on its endless circumnavigation of the Mediterranean playground. Tessa tapped his arm. The flight attendant was taking drink orders.

"Water. No ice," said Darwin and returned his gaze to the window.

This is all happening too fast. She's a liar and bribing Lupita... He had thought about abandoning the project, but after talking again with Barry, they decided Darwin needed to go with Tessa to Alexandria.

They did not have enough to go to the authorities and, with Lupita taking the cash, they did not want to risk having her accused and deported.

What the hell else is she lying about? I give her the diary, and she decides we need to go to Alexandria today. She's barely had time to read it, let alone investigate its contents.

Three days ago, he was in Newcastle and today en route to Alexandria. Normally the one in control, or at least the one whose spontaneous actions gave the sense of being in control, Darwin felt himself struggling to keep up. *What the hell's driving her sense of urgency?*

He had figured the redacted diary would keep Tessa from abandoning him in the search and give him time to work out a better plan. The changed reference points to the mountain containing the tomb and removal of the part about Alexander's scroll should have slowed things down. *Instead, she's speeding up. Shit! I need a new plan.*

She passed him the cup of water, head rocking to music pumping from her ear buds. He smiled, sipped the water, and put it on the open tray table between them. So far, he knew they were meeting Tessa's contacts in Alexandria and to see if they could find the location of Alexander's tomb Hypatia had described.

They expected nothing given the centuries of development, but they planned to work around the ruins of the Serapeum which would give them ground-level access to ancient Alexandria and perhaps useful clues. Finding the lost scrolls in Siwa would be sensational, but proving that Hypatia moved them there would validate the provenance that the scrolls were from the lost library of Alexandria.

Nothing came to him. *Merde! Merde! Merde!* He emptied the glass and stared out the window as if willing an idea from the clouds veiling the blue-green ocean. His body sagged in the seat as the pilots throttled back to begin the descent. On the horizon, a sand arc marked the edge of the African continent, followed by the farmland of the Nile delta. Verdant fields striped the landscape as if an artist had painted various shades of green on a canvas, searching for the perfect color. Splotches of human civilization clustered tightly to maximize arable land, as this was the breadbasket that fed a nation and kept fruit on the tables of Northern Europe.

The window turned skyward as the plane banked into the landing pattern and, returning to level flight, the lush farmland gave way to desolation that ran over the horizon, reminding Darwin that Egypt was over ninety-five percent unlivable. Somewhere out there lay a series of oases that sustained human life. Siwa was but an outpost in a desert that could swallow all of Europe with room to spare.

An hour later, they had cleared Egyptian customs and hired a taxi. Chaos reigned on the streets as their driver pulled away from Borg El Arab Airport. Horns flared from every direction as six cars attempted to drive abreast in the space of three lanes, each gap contested with the ferocity of a nine-puppy litter.

Darwin's anxiety increased at finding himself in a sea of Arabic speakers. While having a facility with languages, he had not been in an Arab country in over five years. He knew basic phrases from working on several digs in Syria and the Sinai Peninsula, but only visited Egypt once, mainly the key sites along the Nile.

I can't completely depend on her.

From the moment they landed Tessa had taken control beginning with a clothing change. He had looked out the plane's window a few minutes while taxing to the gate and turned back to see her transformed into a modern Egyptian woman. She had expertly covered up with a turquoise hijab and slipped a few gold rings on her fingers. Once curbside, she had negotiated the taxi price like a flea market veteran.

Get it together. You're not a university newbie.

He pulled out his iPhone and checked the translation apps and searched his cloud storage account for a cheat-sheet he wrote some years back. He downloaded it and reviewed the basic phrases. Tessa was talking to someone on her mobile in rapid Arabic, and he caught a few words. He felt a glimmer of confidence return.

You've done this before. Focus. Don't be lazy, he thought and looked out the taxi window, practicing the phrases for greetings.

Pulling into the hotel drive, the driver braked hard to avoid a few women who walked obliviously into the car's path. Darwin heard the driver mutter something that he thought sounded derogatory toward the women, but was not sure as the translation pinged around in his brain.

Tessa sprang forward from her seat and unloosed a fusillade at the driver that continued for a half a minute after he pulled away. The man hunched down behind the seat back to avoid the verbal beating.

"Asshole," she said as the car disappeared into traffic.

"What was that?" asked Darwin.

"Education, not that it will help. Welcome to the world of men, Darwin. Get my bag," she said and stalked off toward the lobby.

34

Early the next morning, Darwin ran along the shore as the city came to life, preferring the quiet promise of the new day despite his French heritage of late-night dining and sleeping later. A light onshore breeze carried the fragrant Mediterranean Sea air and its skin softening vapor. Fat gulls stood at the water's edge as if reserving their energy for aggressive panhandling of the tourists later, while the smaller birds ran up and down the beach with each slapping wave.

Endorphins coursed through his limbs, making everything right in Darwin's world as his feet swept forward in easy effort, chasing his shadow projected by the eastern sunrise. The return would be hotter as the sun god Ra advanced across the heavens.

Alongside him, the traffic on El-Gaish Road flowed free of the incessant one-hand-on-the-horn habit that seemed to possess all the drivers once coming within five meters of each another. But for now, the only other inhabitants sharing the post-dawn calm were fellow seekers of physical and spiritual space. A group of men rolled up their prayer rugs and a few meters farther a mixed group followed a yoga instructor's lead through various positions. On a basketball court, some older people swept through tai-chi with the grace and coordination of a dance troop.

This was why he ran in the mornings, visible harmony. *It always was*, he thought. *But the full motion of midday blinds us and makes it easier to find conflict, missing what we love.* At that thought, Eyrún popped into his head. *She's due out of the NAT in six days, then our holiday in Greece.* He envisioned the photo she had texted in her new bikini. *Wow. I can't wait.* His pace picked up and, about half an hour later, he finished running and walked down to the water. He bent and braced his hands on his knees to recover from a short sprint as sweat dripped off his nose and pitted the sand.

His thoughts returned to the present. Tessa had been like a Terrier on a hunt since landing yesterday, gathering supplies and preparing for the journey into the dessert. But, so far, she had said nothing about the translation. Running was partly to steel himself for today's exploration of the few remaining traces of the Library in Alexandria and preparations for the journey to Siwa Oasis. *There's more going on*, he told himself. *Be on guard.*

A few minutes later, he crossed the now much busier road and stepped into a Starbucks where the cacophony of music, espresso machines and human voices drove away any sense of calm. The queue for ordering better resembled a scrum. This was natural selection in all its glory—only the fittest would get their coffee before the call to mid-morning prayer. Darwin shouldered in and a woman stepped on his foot. He smiled and held his ground.

While Darwin jostled with the locals for a cup of coffee, Tessa stood at the window in a penthouse overlooking the harbor. She drank tea from a fine porcelain cup and watched a cruise ship arc outward into the Mediterranean Sea. Servants cleared the breakfast dishes while Nahla took a call at the opposite site of the apartment. Floor to ceiling glass offered a 360-degree view of Alexandria, but except for the ocean, Tessa felt it was much like her view of Rome—rooftops and TV satellite antennas.

The ancient city of Alexandria existed under a modern mountain of concrete. Some twenty kilometers to the east, obscured by haze, lay farmland. To the south and west was desert survivable only to those who could navigate between the pin-prick-sized oases in the Martian landscape.

Wondrous finds lay beneath the city and in long-buried crypts, pocketing the desert. Unfortunately, no maps existed or had been lost to time. And as much as archaeologists plotted and searched, many discoveries were accidental, like the golden mummies in Bahariya Oasis. A local man's donkey tripped on the exposed edge of a tomb, tossing him to the dirt. His misfortunate tumble opened a hole, exposing a hundred gold gilded mummies in the structures below.

Sometimes, archaeology resembled gambling where luck combined with skill came up a winner. *But you can't win if you don't play, and I have to play this carefully*, thought Tessa. She knew Nahla was only interested in Alexander's tomb and its valuable objects. Scrolls were valuable for sure, but to a smaller group of collectors.

"I never tire of this view, but I'm thinking of moving. Too much of that floating plague," Nahla nodded toward the massive barge-hotel. She had finished her call and now stood next to Tessa. "What's your plan?" she continued as she turned her gaze toward the silver dome of the Bibliotheca Alexandrina, the twenty-first century incarnation of its ancient namesake.

"We begin at the Serapeum and retrace Hypatia's route to Siwa," said Tessa.

"Waste of time. Just go to Siwa. That's where you say the library is," said Nahla.

"True, but I don't trust Darwin. I need to find out what he knows."

"You think he's hiding something?"

"I know he's hiding something. Part of the translation doesn't read right. The Greek is too ancient, too perfect like someone who only studied it in textbooks wrote it," said Tessa.

"Why would he do that?" asked Nahla.

"I'm not sure what Darwin's playing at, but he says he wants to give it away to a museum when we find it," said Tessa.

They watched the ship shrink toward the horizon, and Tessa waited for Nahla's response. She wanted help, but knew better than to ask for it.

"No," said Nahla after a long minute. "Giving the library away is not good. You better take Fathi with you and besides, he's from Siwa."

Fathi Hamdy was as seductive as a snake charmer, but lethal when it served his purposes.

Tessa smiled while riding the lift down from Nahla's penthouse. *This is coming together nicely*, she thought. Fathi had worked with her on several digs that yielded priceless objects, and she had hoped to bring him into this project. Besides his many talents, being a Siwa native would also give them an advantage with local resources.

Fathi had been a bright student and fortunate to study in Cairo where he caught the eye of the chief of Egyptian antiquities while working on a project in Saqqara, the site of the step pyramids. They brought him into an elite team of archeologists where Tessa met him during her graduate work and remembered him as playful, always smiling yet passionate about the need for change.

He was nearing completion of his Ph D in 2011 when the Arab Spring swept him up in its revolutionary fervor. She had returned to Cairo that season, but left as the uprising escalated. A month later, she was shocked to see Fathi on a news report, gun in hand, leading a group of the Muslim Brotherhood against a military blockade.

A half-dozen years later, Tessa ran into him again, this time on one of Nahla's projects in Crete. Tourism, the lifeblood of the Egyptian economy, had dried up like the Nile in summers before the Aswan dam. Fathi told her nothing had changed in Egypt except the overlords.

"A new group of thugs displaced the other. Only now there is no work," he had said.

He still had a passion for archaeology, but she observed he was different, more mature, yes, but bitter and cynical. He had learned to play both sides: the official projects where he published in academic journals and Nahla's more personally lucrative schemes.

Everyone had an angle. Bribes were paid and heads looked the other way. When workers protested, Fathi silenced them. Capitalism, but ruled by jungle-law, and she figured Fathi would have no problem keeping Darwin in check.

35

Later that afternoon, Tessa and Darwin arrived at the Serapeum, a once massive Greek temple built by Ptolemy III, a ruler whose family rose to power in the wake of Alexander the Great's collapsed empire. Darwin knew many considered the Serapeum a daughter to the Library of Alexandria, but there was not much to look at as the site had been heavily plundered in the centuries following its sacking in 391 CE.

He held a hand over his eyes against the slanting sun and scanned the site. A few kilometers inland made the air feel drier, but the ever-present gulls reminded them of the nearby ocean. They rested in clusters, having exhausted the scraps left the previous day, but a few skittered toward the arriving food vendors hoping to secure an early snack.

They entered a gate set in a series of recently built columns between a row of one-story buildings that contained small collections and curated history of the Serapeum. The bright smooth color of the new structures created a modern divide between the city of the last couple hundred years and the crude tumble of the ruins.

Darwin guessed the entire complex would fit inside a modern football stadium and the exhibit was but a glimpse of ancient Alexandria. The rest he knew would remain buried under the current city until new construction precipitated the need to dig down into the past.

Gravel crunched underfoot as he stepped into the deteriorated streets and foundations. He had been on this kind of site many times and, to the untrained eye, it appeared to have been left in this condition. But he knew that anything of value had been scavenged long ago and the site buried over. Even exposed blocks were recycled into new foundations or breakwaters for the Alexandrian harbor.

On closer look, he could see signs that they had refurbished parts of the rough-hewn rock with stone quarried in different locations and probably recycled from various buildings. Broken sculptures, mostly Greek and Roman, lined one path. But all made in Egypt during one of those superpowers' occupations. *Strange that we go on holiday to look at a pile of rocks*, he thought and shut his eyes.

His mind formed a vision of columns and statues newly constructed. Cut stone blocks fitted together, undecayed by an age of exposure. The main building rose atop wide steps where hundreds could gather to listen or a single person experience awe.

Gleaming columns supported a red tile roof as was the Roman fashion, and the immense triangular gable of the building writhed with human action in an odd mixture of chariot riding warriors, scholars, and healers plying their craft. A woman descended the steps, her arms overflowing with scrolls as she lectured to a trailing flock of young men eagerly absorbing every word.

A scuff in the dirt alerted him to another's presence.

"It was magnificent in Hypatia's day," said Tessa, standing at his shoulder.

"No doubt," he said, opening his eyes to a small black bird that had landed on one rock.

"How many scrolls do you think they moved?"

"I was thinking about that," he said, returning to the vision of Hypatia's arm-full of scrolls. "Depending on the size, maybe a dozen. If they carried more than that regularly people might ask questions."

"The diary mentions six trips a year to Siwa for five years. The library of Alexandria had, what, four hundred thousand scrolls. If they moved half of those to the Serapeum, that would make over six thousand scrolls per trip," said Tessa.

Darwin used the calculator on his mobile to run the numbers, then looked around the city as if imagining the clandestine movements.

"She must have recruited dozens of people, if not more. I can't imagine she went to Siwa six times a year. That would raise questions."

"Agreed," said Tessa. "I think it was a carefully crafted conspiracy. Someone had to prioritize which scrolls were moved. Others had to change the records in the library. Five years is a long time, and someone would notice too many missing scrolls, even if replaced with fakes."

"Possibly. There was a great deal of tension between the scholars and the rising Coptic Christian leaders. Theophilus was Pope of Alexandria at the time, and his paranoia over the pagans would have pushed Hypatia into high-gear," said Darwin.

He recalled the news coverage of Islamic extremists who destroyed a centuries-old religious site in Afghanistan. They killed those who opposed them and crushed the monuments into rubble.

Would I have risked my life to save artifacts? He tried to imagine the massive cultural upheaval in this region: Egyptian, Persian, Greek, Roman, Christian and Muslim. Mostly people of differing beliefs coexisted, but there were periods of zealotry and wholesale destruction. *Is it any different now?* He shuddered.

"What?" asked Tessa.

"I was just imagining Theophilus leading the destruction of the Serapeum in three ninety-one."

"Bastard. Accomplished women are so few in history, they're less than rare," she said.

That night she and Darwin had met Fathi for dinner whom she introduced as a regular archaeologist she worked with, in addition to being a Siwa native who would provide local expertise. As Tessa suspected, Fathi and Darwin got on well and after dinner they returned to the hotel for tea and to plan the journey to Siwa.

At one point, Tessa slipped a sleeping drug in Darwin's tea when he left the table to use the toilet and, soon after drinking the tea, Darwin left for bed saying he was tired from the few days of non-stop travelling. That was a couple hours ago and had Fathi gone up to Darwin's room to copy the contents of his iPad.

He now strode from the lift toward her table in the lobby bar. Her metal bracelets jangled as she adjusted the bright red hijab that matched her slacks.

"Did you get it?" she asked when he sat down.

"Yes," said Fathi.

"Let's see it," she said, looking over his shoulder as he copied the files from the USB drive onto his laptop, found the document labelled 'diary' and opened it. He opened the diary file that Darwin had given Tessa and moved the windows side by side. Tessa pulled the laptop toward her and compared the two diary files.

"They look the same to me," said Fathi when she had scrolled to the end of the documents.

They read both again.

"Shit, shit, shit," growled Tessa, shoving the laptop away. *I just know you're hiding something Darwin. I know because it's what I'd do.* She picked up her mobile and wrote an email.

```
Hi Lupita, we're still eager to hear from
you. What have you decided? My backers said
they can offer another £3,000.
Regards,
Tessa
```

36

Darwin drove his own Land Rover, following Fathi and Tessa through the coastal resort city of Marsá Matrûh where the traffic was thick with Egyptians on holiday. Drivers jockeyed with each other, weaving around the occasional donkey cart, and Darwin braked hard to avoid a blind man crossing the road. The painted lines on the pavement mattered little as cars filled every space, sometimes three across. His stomach gurgled. *I can't be hungry again. Can I?*

They had left Alexandria at sunrise to beat the traffic and had stopped for breakfast at a resort across the highway from the ancient Ptolemaic temple of Taposiris Magna. Darwin had wolfed down a plate of eggs cooked in ghee and served with dried beef, then torn off a piece of pita bread to scoop up Ful Madamas, a mashed fava bean dish generously seasoned with cumin and topped with tomatoes, goat cheese and olive oil. The breakfast had only been missing bacon, but he knew that would not happen in this part of the world.

That had only been ninety minutes ago, as the traffic sprinted away like a Formula One race after it bunched up in the first corner. Fathi jumped ahead several cars with a deft move around a cart, and Darwin gunned the engine into the same gap. Horns flared as he narrowly avoided a parked car.

"Shit!" he yelled and swerved to the left, following Fathi, and catapulted around a traffic circle towards the Siwa road.

Over the next ten minutes the buildings thinned, and the desert pinched the road into a strip of blacktop just wide enough for two vehicles. No line divided the black surface that cut through the tan desert, and there would be nothing for the next two hundred kilometers but sand and the occasional curious camel. He tapped the cruise-control button on and exercised a foot cramp. Looking at his iPhone clipped to the dashboard, he could see a strong signal.

"Hey, Siri, call Barry," he said.

"I found several websites showing berries," came the mechanized reply.

"*Merde,*" he said.

"*Merde* is the French word for—"

He swiped a finger on the screen, cutting off the insipid voice and tapped B-A-R-R until Barry's contact info came up, and he tapped "call". Three rings later, Barry answered.

"Hey, Darwin," said Barry.

"Hey, Barry. You got a few minutes?"

"Sure. Where are you? Sounds like you're driving."

"Yeah. I'm in Egypt on the desert road to Siwa. How's Lupita?"

"She's doing okay, but Tessa emailed her and offered another three-thousand pounds," said Barry.

"Shit!" said Darwin

"Should we go with the plan?" asked Barry.

"Yes. Text after Lupita sends it. I've got nothing to do the next few hours, but watch for camels," said Darwin.

In the car in front of him, Tessa's mobile chimed with an incoming email.

"She sent it," said Tessa, pulling out her iPad and tapped open the diary. She opened the documents from Darwin and compared it side by side with the one that Lupita just sent.

"What do you see?" asked Fathi.

"Shh, and turn down the music," she said.

Fathi thumbed the volume switch on the steering wheel and glided the SUV into the far lane away from a curious camel standing on the side of the highway, but whose nose extended over the pavement.

Tessa reached the end of both documents. *This can't be*, she thought and started over again.

"They're identical," said Tessa after a quarter hour and looked in the side mirror at Darwin's Land Rover one car back. Some crazy driver in a car that was a throwback from Eastern Europe had moved between them and moved out of her sight as it rattled past.

"Dammit!" Tessa banged the dashboard and stared out the windscreen at the road's infinity point. *They must have talked. There has to be something different.*

You knew people would try to deceive us, said the Hypatia voice. *Focus on the task. Our library is in Siwa.*

Yes, I know, Tessa replied to the voice. *What about the Oracle?*

Visit the Oracle. It helped me find the right path, said the Hypatia voice.

After a couple minutes, she said to Fathi, "The copies are the same. She probably called Darwin. I should have anticipated it."

"You want me to have someone—"

"No!" said Tessa, cutting him off. "She's a no-op. Just drive."

"What's so important about these scrolls? You know the Egyptian antiquities authorities will take them away," said Fathi a few minutes later.

"There is another section of the papyrus I found. The piece I showed Darwin only mentions the diary and a church in Rome. The second piece, which I did not share, mentions a scroll written by Alexander himself," she said.

"So."

"The fragment describes Alexander's scroll as a list of where he buried looted treasures from his campaigns across Asia."

Fathi whistled.

"Exactly," said Tessa. "We need to get it before Darwin does."

Darwin turned up the music on a *desert groove* playlist he found while in Alexandria and tapped the beat on the steering wheel. Small plants clustered at the side of the road in their desperate bid for life, and large patches of rocks emerged every so often where the desert winds had scoured away the sand. His only sense of progress was closing the gap on a large petrol truck.

He thought of Eyrún back underground and calculated that she had been in the NAT more days in the last month than she was out of it. *That sucks. She's got to be hating it. I need to do something nice for her.* He ran through some ideas and caught up on a couple archaeology podcasts when about three and a half hours into the journey, signs of modern human activity began popping up.

Earth moving equipment scraped up sections of the surrounding soil for minerals, he guessed. The road snaked around tabletop hills rising twenty meters with sides heavily eroded by rain and an ancient retreating sea. It reminded him of the Monument Valley in the American southwest, but with a more moonscape appearance as vegetation was nonexistent.

Two of the hills channeled the road into a hard-right curve that sloped downward, and a kilometer later, the road offered the only decision in four monotonous hours of driving—go straight into the Siwa Oasis or turn left toward Al Bahariya Oasis, another five hours of mind-numbing desert.

Rounding a bend, he passed several buildings that looked like recent construction, one with a sign, Siwa Water Company, in both Arabic and English. He lowered the window and blinked rapidly as the oven blast dried his eyes and propelled bits of sand into the Rover. The thermometer on the dashboard read thirty-eight degrees, just over body temperature. Darwin closed the window as a truck pulled off the road into the water company, raising a storm of dust.

Passing through the cloud, the oasis unrolled before him in a breathtaking carpet of green. Palms by the tens of thousands filled most of the oasis and looked furry, like a shag carpet he remembered in his grandparent's house. Low flat-topped buildings sprouted in patches among the palms.

To his right, the mountains marched westward and wrapped around a lake whose surface looked like a mirage because of the haze. Several oddly shaped conical hills poked upwards through the otherwise flat oasis, and the only things taller than the palms were metal towers bristling with cellular antennas.

A man on a donkey cart stacked with long green vegetation was talking on a mobile phone as Darwin drove by. He saw five bars and LTE on his iPhone. The Internet had arrived in the Siwa Oasis. *The great leap forward*, he mused. He recalled reading that they completed these roads in the early 1980s. The camel track, used since before Pharaonic times, would have been a butt-busting journey, whatever the vehicle.

What a study in civilization, he thought, counting the technological advancements that had poured into the oasis in a few decades. The contrasts between the ancient and the current were striking.

The palms rose above him as the road dipped toward the oasis floor. The far horizon resolved into a wide tan stripe that separated the green of the oasis from the pale blue sky. Its height eclipsed one hill in town, and Darwin realized he was looking at the shore of Great Sand Sea looming like a tsunami. Nothing but sand for hundreds of kilometers. A sharp gust of wind rocked the vehicle, and the windows hissed from the sand. He shuddered at the memory of an ancient Persian army swallowed by sand: 50,000 men en route to Siwa that vanished without a trace.

37

Siwa Oasis, Egypt

The number of people and donkeys increased in number as the road reached the oasis floor some twenty meters below sea level. There were dozens of donkeys pulling carts and vehicles that were a rolling museum of transportation, including motorcycles and Tuk Tuks, but nothing newer than the previous decade.

Darwin turned a corner into a sea of humanity—market day in Siwa. Fathi parked, and he pulled alongside. The road spilled into a wide square surrounded by two storied dwellings and single floor homes that hoped to have an upper floor, their partially complete cement columns bristling rebar like an old man's stray hairs.

An official looking building occupied a central part of the square, its main entrance made more important by wide wrap around steps. Ornate tiles and stonework decorated the arched windows and doorway, and its roofline was punctuated with carved crown-like blocks.

Mounds of brightly colored vegetables and other produce filled each vendor's stall where buyers sniffed the quality and ripeness as they haggled over price. Children ran and played, and it took Darwin a few minutes to figure out what felt different about the market. No women. He scanned the crowd more closely. About a third of the people wore robes and some with headscarves, but he was right. He looked at Tessa.

"What?" she said.

"Where are the women?" asked Darwin.

"At home," said Fathi. "The Siwan culture is even more conservative than most of Egypt."

"Even for market day shopping?" asked Darwin.

"Men do the shopping," said Fathi.

"Let's walk around," said Tessa, coiling a sky-blue patterned hijab over her head. Paired with dark sunglasses and a long-sleeved blouse over jeans, she looked like an Alexandrian native on Safari.

After touring the market, they checked into The Palms Ecolodge nestled in a palm grove. Darwin had dozed as the combination of the heat and a gurgling fountain outside his room propelled him onto the bed. He awoke in the late afternoon and watched the fan blades chase each other around the ceiling, making soft woofing sounds as they beat the air. A few minutes later, he checked email and saw only Eyrún's message from yesterday updating him on her progress. He smiled at her usual signature that included hearts and a volcano emoji. This email also included a photo of her in the bikini she had bought for their upcoming holiday. His groin swelled.

When did I see her last? He counted backwards from Alexandria to Rome, back and forth to Newcastle and when he had left Reykjavík. *Ugh, seventeen days. But only ten more days to Mykonos.* He imagined her standing on the bow of the luxury sailboat they had chartered. Her dark brown hair fluttering in the Mediterranean breeze, the translucent wrap pressing against her body. A warmth spread through him at the thought of gathering her into his arms.

Not now, we gotta get to the tomb; he thought looking at the time and rubbing the back of his neck sticky from dried sweat. He cooled off with a shower and spent a few minutes under the water when he remembered a promise to email Zac. He toweled off his shaggy hair and combed it backward with his fingers. He threw the towel across the chair and sat with his mobile on the edge of the bed to cool down under the fan.

> Hey Zac, arrived in Siwa. Tonight, we're going to the oracle to see how my misdirection works. Read Hypatia's diary here. If you don't hear from me by day after tomorrow, then something went wrong. I don't expect it to, but you said don't work alone, so here's the email I promised.
> Darwin

He tapped send and got dressed. They were going to the remains of the oracle where he would help Tessa determine the location of the mountain that contained Alexander's tomb—that is the mountain he wanted her to find.

38

Darwin's shadow stretched toward the eastern horizon as he climbed into the Land Rover with Fathi driving, as he had grown up in Siwa. As a passenger, Darwin could watch the locals going about daily life: men sat in the backs of small trucks on their ways home from work and children played football in the street. A few of the kids wore jerseys from big league teams and several of those sported the name "SALAH" for the Egyptian sensation Mohamed Salah who played in England.

"What was it like when you were a kid Fathi?" asked Darwin.

"Some the same and some different," said Fathi.

"How so?"

"We played the same games you see, and daily life was much the same, but it was much smaller here. Before the road in nineteen eighty there were less than eight thousand people and a handful of tourists. Now the population is triple, and the highways brings tourists by the thousands."

"Isn't that good for the economy?" asked Darwin.

"Sure, but tourism is down because of the uprising and outside investors build most of the hotels. No money stays here. The locals see wealth, but it is always out of reach," said Fathi.

Darwin thought this complaint applied to many places, even Reykjavík, where he, an outsider, had bought a condo.

"Much of it is good," Fathi continued as if hearing Darwin's thoughts. "The road brought better food and access to markets for our small industries and TV, and the Internet relieves the boredom. Family is everything here, but there is only so much to talk about."

They continued through narrow streets lined with mud-brick walls and irrigation ditches flanked by tall grasses. A fine dust gave the vegetation a gray tone and settled on everything else, making even newly washed skin a gritty feel. Darwin waved at a family on a donkey cart, the mother and daughters in the back and son up front with the father. The kids waved vigorously, and the boy waggled a hand with thumb and little finger extended in the Hawaiian *hang loose* gesture. He laughed and returned the greeting. *Yep, the Internet has arrived.*

Fathi turned and parked at the base of a rock formation with what looked like a mud fortress on top. Its walls rose vertically from the layered rock base, punctuated only by small square windows about twenty meters up. Truck-sized boulders lay at odd angles around the car park, and Darwin figured these had broken off the rock foundation. The oasis had a half dozen of these hills. *Eyrún would know the geological names and how they were formed. I wish she were here*; he thought and smiled.

"What are you smiling about?" asked Tessa.

"What? Oh. My fiancée. She would know about these rocks," said Darwin.

"Inselbergs," said Fathi. "The harder rock stayed in place as the retreating oceans eroded away the softer soils. The ancients built on the hills as holy places or for defensive purposes."

"That's why the oracle's here," said Darwin in a half-question.

"Probably. It's far older than any of the big religions. The Greeks and Persians knew about it and humans have been in the oasis at least 20,000 years," said Fathi.

Tessa was just ahead of them on a wide path leading up to the oracle temple, and Darwin stopped to read a sign listing the brief history of the oracle and Alexander's visit in 323 BCE. It was the same sign that Barry had zoomed in on when they first read the diary in Newcastle.

"What do the locals make of it? The oracle, I mean," asked Darwin.

"They mostly ignore it. Think of it like your Eiffel Tower or the pyramids. It's part of your surroundings, but in the background."

"Makes sense. Never thought of it that way, but you're right," said Darwin.

"That tower," said Fathi, pointing to a tall mud-brick tower that narrowed toward its peak some twenty meters over the height of the walls, "was a minaret when more people lived in this part of the oasis."

The path continued upwards and passed through a gate in the outer walls. Most of the interior buildings had long washed away in the centuries of rain, scant as it was. Any wooden support beams had long decayed or scavenged for newer construction, leaving only walls of mud and stone outlines of rooms. The site looked to Darwin like any other abandoned dwelling. However, the next turn through another gate revealed a much different looking set of walls built with granite blocks that were quarried a long way from the oasis.

"The oracle temple," said Tessa, who stood by the first sculpted gate.

Three tall rectangular gates opened in a line, spaced just far enough apart that each gate framed the one behind it. Restoration work at various times past had preserved the form, but the original carvings had long worn smooth. Darwin walked under the first gate, and the close walls amplified the crunch of gravel underfoot.

The place was empty. The last tourists had been leaving the site when they arrived, and inside the second gate the air became stale as the walls mitigated the breeze. Steel framed the third opening and held a gate that protected the inner oracle chamber. A chain and padlock around the open gate hinted that someone must watch over this place.

"Not much to look at," said Fathi as they walked around the ten-meter square chamber, its roof open to the sky. "Two thousand years ago it would be dark in here except for candles brought each morning by the head priest. As darkness fell each night, the priest would extinguish the candles as Ra, the sun god, went to the underworld to return the next day."

"Why did it decline?" asked Tessa.

"New religions. First Christianity, then Islam. As the local people converted to Islam, they stopped coming to the oracle," said Fathi.

"How did it survive?" asked Darwin.

"Isolation. While we are Muslim, we consider these monuments part of our heritage. Egypt is to the east, but much of this culture, including its people, comes from ancient Libya," said Fathi.

"It must have been something special in its day," said Darwin, running his fingers over badly faded hieroglyphs also marred by graffiti. "Let's hope it's preserved for at least another two thousand years, *inshallah*, God willing."

Fathi nodded.

"Sunset in twenty minutes," said Tessa. "Let's get set up."

39

The sun had sunk to a few fingers' width above the horizon as Darwin shaded his eyes against the searing rays. Fathi set up a laptop in a forecourt to the oracle that overlooked the oasis, and Tessa withdrew a wooden box from her backpack.

Darwin scanned the eastern horizon. At this distance the mountains appeared as hills, but he knew their relative height was a hundred meters because of his location below sea level. A quick glance showed Tessa and Fathi still occupied, and he turned west.

The constellation Taurus with it main star Aldebaran would not appear in the sky this time of the year, but he knew from a stargazing website that it was straight west from the oracle. He opened the compass app on his iPhone and waved it about to activate the accelerometer. Holding it flat on his palm, he followed the compass west over a sea of palms that shone a deep green.

The mountains cut a tan gray line on the horizon and separated into individual peaks until one last mountain stood out. There was nothing to the south. He stared at the last peaks, recalling that Siwa Lake lay out there, which meant those mountains went straight to the oasis floor. The last mountain was a plateau as rectangular as a Lego block.

That's got to be over five kilometers away, he thought, quickly glancing at the north mountains then back. *Those vertical edges mean it's bedrock like this inselberg. And huge... at least a hundred meters. If I were Alexander and going to cut a large tomb out of rock—*

"Darwin, we're ready," said Tessa. "What are you looking at?"

"Nothing," he said, lowering his iPhone and slipping it into his back pocket. "Just imagining life here when the oasis was active."

The sun dipped under the horizon.

Fathi had laid a walking stick on the ground next to a conventional compass, its sharp end pointing towards the horizon. Darwin saw the other end of the walking stick pointed at the oracle gates.

"We know Polaris is always north," said Fathi. "But when it's dark, we won't be able to see the mountains. Fortunately, I have an astronomy website that tells us precisely where Polaris will appear."

"But just in case, we're also using the technology from Hypatia's day," said Tessa, holding up an astrolabe, a bronze instrument about half a meter round.

"It's beautiful," said Darwin. "I've only seen one in a museum. Where did you get it?"

"One of our collectors let me borrow it. Judging from the inscriptions, we think they made this one around eleven hundred."

She showed him how it worked by attaching the proper disk for this latitude and adjusting the sighting mechanism. She explained that when Polaris was visible later, the Astrolabe would also show them the point on the horizon where Hypatia wrote they would find Alexander's tomb.

"But," said Fathi looking through binoculars, "it's a formality, because it's in that mountain, Qārat al Mujahhiz. It can only be."

They each took turns looking at it while Fathi boiled water on a portable stove to make tea while they waited for darkness to overtake the heavens.

"What do you think, Darwin?" asked Tessa, handing him the binoculars.

A distant plateau, mostly black in the failing light, stood out almost as prominently as the plateau to the west. He breathed a sigh of relief as he had hoped his guess at a fake peak when he changed the diary would hold up. *Looks good enough to be an alternate choice for Alexander*, he thought, and lowered the field glasses.

"If I were Alexander, I would choose it. Nothing in the oasis is large enough given the description of the tomb. It's prominent and near the road to Matruh. Yeah, that's it," he said. *Careful. Don't oversell it.*

"I agree," said Tessa. "Let's confirm it with the astrolabe though."

An hour later, Polaris had brightened in the tail of Ursa Minor. It was one of his favorites, and his buddy Zac always made a point of finding the Little Dipper as they knew it in America.

Tessa lined up the astrolabe to Polaris and confirmed that the walking stick was spot on. "Confirmed. It's Qārat al Mujahhiz. We found you Alexander," she said, placing the astrolabe in its velvet lined case and locking the lid.

"This calls for a celebration," said Fathi, withdrawing a glass bottle from his pack. He filled their empty cups with the cloudy liquid from the bottle.

"Palm wine. Locally made," he said, handing out the glasses.

"I thought Muslims didn't drink," said Darwin.

"We don't," said Fathi, smiling.

They clinked glasses and tossed back the contents. Fathi refilled them, and they sipped more slowly the second time.

Not exactly vintage. Might make a better salad dressing, thought Darwin, trying to keep a straight face to not insult the local beverage. It was similar to a dessert wine, but also leaned toward a sweet balsamic vinegar. His belly warmed and, a couple minutes later, his head felt the lightness brought on by the alcohol. He stood, wobbled, and sat back down hard.

"This stuff is strong," he said. *Way too strong. I only had one glass.*

He tried to stand again, and the last thing he remembered was falling into Fathi's arms, who laid him carefully on the ground.

"That was fast," said Tessa. "How long will he be out?"

"Long enough," said Fathi.

40

The next morning Tessa tapped send on an email as Fathi walked onto the patio for breakfast.

"You look like shit. How did it go?" she asked, commenting on the bags under his eyes.

"Fine," said Fathi, pouring himself a cup of coffee and putting on dark glasses against the brightening day. "Darwin won't be troubling anyone." He forked a plate of eggs into his mouth and mopped up the remains with pita bread.

Tessa could tell he was in no mood for conversation and finished replying to emails inquiring about her objects for sale on a black-market antiquities website. She signed the last email *Hypatia* and logged out of the encrypted email service based in Zurich. Then she closed the TOR browser, cut the VPN connection and powered off the iPhone used solely for this purpose. Without power no one could track its location.

She had no illusions that this was a dangerous business. The technology hid her from clients, but also worked the other way. Seti2 could be a wealthy Russian or an agent of the US State Department, not that she had any intention of ever setting foot on American soil.

They left the ecolodge twenty minutes later and turned north toward Qārat al Mujahhiz, just off the Marsa Matrûh-Siwa Road.

"What are we looking for?" asked Fathi as the mountain loomed closer.

"Slow down," said Tessa.

A couple Land Cruisers rode his bumper, so he pulled into the parking lot of the bottled water company they had passed on the way into the oasis. He stopped their Range Rover facing the hill. Tessa leaned forward to look through a clear spot in the filthy windscreen. The wipers had cleared most of the dirt but left it badly smeared.

Where in hell did he go last night? She wondered.

We don't care. Darwin became an obstacle. Another man in our way. Focus on the treasure, said the Hypatia voice.

"Can we get closer?" asked Tessa.

"There's a small resort that's parallel to the hill," he said, starting the engine and driving back onto the road.

A half kilometer farther, he turned onto a dirt path of a modest hotel. They exited the vehicle and walked into the property where the manager greeted them. They asked for tea by the swimming pool, and he led them through a remodeled lobby, fragrant with plaster and curing grout.

They sat at a table beneath long dead grey palm fronds that shaded the dining area beside the pool. Like many of the hotels in the oasis, this one existed simultaneously in a state of construction and decay. Turning their chairs, they looked at the peak a couple hundred meters away.

"How far would you say this is from the oracle if you rode a donkey?" asked Tessa when the server had left.

"A couple hours. Why?" said Fathi.

"Hypatia wrote that she rode two hours by donkey to get to the tomb. Listen," she said, reading from her mobile.

> *Last night, during my sleep, men kidnapped me. At first, I feared for my life thinking Berber invaders had taken the oases, but they brought my guide. He said the men were taking us to the Son of*

Ammon's tomb. I was blindfolded and rode two hours on a donkey. We were guided by rope up a steep slope and taken inside a cave.

"Did she write anything about how high? Any markers?" asked Fathi.

"There's a later section where she wrote about transporting the scrolls from Alexandria..." she said, swiping across the small screen.

The tomb entrance faces east to catch the first rays of Ra on his journey. Halfway up the mountain, a dark band of hard rock forms a shelf. The opening lies beneath a vertical scar only visible from the shelf. Use these clues. Masnsen, the old man of the oracle, said he would rebury the entrance.

"That would be the dark band," said Fathi, moving his hand side to side across a prominent ridge.

The hill rose from a wide base and narrowed to less than a quarter of the width at its top where the peak plateaued. The ancient ocean had eaten away the softer tan rock, leaving rings like a giant caramel layer cake.

"It fits," said Tessa. "Let's get up there before it's too hot."

"*Min fadlik al-hasib*, the bill please," said Fathi to the server. He paid while Tessa used the toilet and met him at the vehicle.

A half hour later while hiking up the mountain, Tessa paused and dabbed her brow with the end of her scarf. *How do people live here?* She drank from one of her water bottles, rearranged the scarf covering her neck, and reset the wide-brimmed hat. A hot gust of wind ruffled her loose white blouse, but at least it provided some cooling effect on her sweaty face.

After driving as far up the slope as it felt safe, they had climbed up the north side to the dark band and followed it around toward the east face. As the hotel came into view below them, Fathi checked his compass.

"Just up here." He nodded forward and continued another thirty meters where he stopped.

Tessa looked down at the hotel pool. *God that looks good*, she thought and continued her gaze to the eastern side of the Siwa Oasis with its saltwater pools that looked like pale turquoise gems scattered on the desert. She had heard the water was so buoyant that it felt like you were lying on it rather than in it.

Beyond the pools was a dark scarred land that ran over the horizon and, eventually, the Nile River. She shuddered. Anyone without a camel or a vehicle would die within days.

They turned to face the mountain. Nothing indicated a tomb entrance, and no signs that anyone had ever been here: no human footprints, but a few small animal burrows looked active. *What do they live on,* thought Tessa?

A few meters above them a section of vertical rock rose to the height of two people, and the soil beneath it had eroded leaving a gap. Fathi scrambled up the steep slope to have a look. The loose soil and rocks caused him to slide back a couple times before he figured out where to gain purchase.

Tessa watched him disappear halfway into the opening, his legs paddling against the loose rocks to keep from sliding out.

"See anything?" she yelled.

"What?" he asked, swiveling his head out of the hole. Suddenly he jerked backward, then slipped and tumbled down the slope. Tessa jumped sideways to avoid being hit, and they ended up in a heap on the ledge.

"Did you find anything?" she asked.

"A viper's nest. It was just the eggs, but I wasn't going to wait for the mother to return," he said, brushing himself off and unfolding two portable shovels. "Let's get to work."

41

They arrived at sunrise the next morning to watch the light come down the face of Qārat al Mujahiiz, hoping that it might illuminate the *vertical scar* in the diary. Nothing stood out, but Tessa knew that time acted like an eraser. Each passing century rubbed out more evidence until none remained. However, she had a few modern tricks up her sleeve and, while a couple local men that Fathi had recruited did the heavy digging, she assembled a high-tech approach.

"Will this work vertically?" asked Fathi.

"There's only one way to find out," she said.

She fitted two aluminum poles together and attached a couple other pieces on one end. It looked like a large letter T. She clamped sensors to the ends of the upper part of the T and ran wires from each sensor to instruments in a large belt around her waist. The device measured the intensity of the earth's magnetic field. Anything of archaeological value like charcoal or concentrations of bacteria would leave magnetic traces. Tessa also hoped that any human carving in the rock would show the hard edges of an opening.

"I need you to place the probes in the wall in a grid pattern. Start there," she said, pointing to the left, "and place them every two meters until you run out of probes. We'll scan these, then move them until we've scanned the whole wall."

"How deep will it scan?" asked Fathi.

"Not sure in rock. I've been successful at a couple meters in soil. Remember that jeweled scimitar I found last year? Found it with this baby," she said, patting the aluminum.

"Yeah, I heard you and Nahla offloaded it for close to three million to some German collector."

She did not answer. The less he knew, the fewer details he could reveal and the lesser the bribes she had to pay. She trusted Fathi, but money was money.

Fathi opened the laptop and started the scanning app that would receive the data. Adjusting the shoulder harness to hold the sensors toward the wall, she awkwardly stepped back and forth until it balanced.

"Ready when you are," he said.

"Starting," she said and stepped slowly across the face of the mountain. She shouted for the men digging to take a break, and they moved to a shaded spot and lit cigarettes.

The scanning took the better part of an hour, and she put away the contraption while Fathi crunched the data into something more visually useful. The men went back to scraping away the vertical wall, shoveling the excess soil and rock over the ledge.

"What do we have?" asked Tessa settling in next to Fathi.

He turned up the screen's brightness, but it was still faint. Tessa unraveled her scarf and draped it over the laptop and their heads, creating a makeshift hood. One digger looked at the other and shrugged.

Under the cover, the screen was much more visible. Vertical graphic swaths marched across the screen as Fathi scrolled from left to right. "I see nothing. It's just random all the way across like undisturbed ground or, in this case, rock," said Fathi.

"What's that? Go back," she said.

He scrolled back, and the screen refreshed. He pulled the laptop closer.

"Zoom in," she said.

A short vertical line resolved.

"Which part of the wall is that?" she asked.

While Fathi zoomed out to measure, she noticed the stale air under the scarf. *One of us needs a bath,* she thought and realizing it was partly her threw off the scarf.

"*Hafr huna*, dig here," Fathi said to the men.

A few minutes later, they saw a vertical crack, but it was not manmade. Tessa re-scanned the wall and also worked farther along the ridge south and north of their location, but they found nothing.

During the men's afternoon prayer break, Fathi suggested they call it a day.

"We can't. It's here. I know it," she said while pacing back and forth.

"Tessa. We've been here since five," he said.

"We must have missed something," she said, stopping before the original spot.

"Let's widen the search again tomorrow. We have time."

"Time! We don't have time," she fumed, but the men had returned and Fathi instructed them to pack up for the day.

She wiped sweat out of one eye and thought again of the carved stone tub in her hotel room. *Yes, we need the break. Things will look different tomorrow. We have time. We'll find it*, said the Hypatia voice.

"Fine, let's go," she said and started walking back to their vehicle, leaving the men to pack the supplies.

A short while later, on the way back to town, she stared out the passenger window, arms crossed and furiously tapping her right fingers on her opposite elbow.

"*Cazzo!*" she said, slapping the dashboard. "Where is it?"

"Sometimes—"

"*Sta 'zitto e guida*, shut up and drive!" she yelled and turned back to the window.

Temper. You need his help, said the Hypatia voice.

I don't need anyone's help.

Yes, you do. Fathi speaks Siwi. You're a foreigner here and a woman. Use him, said the Hypatia voice.

"Ugh!" she said and hugged her knees to her chest, head tucked down. The conditioned air from the vent blasted her forehead. After a couple minutes, she straightened and sighed.

"I'm sorry, Fathi. I get angry. I shouldn't have—"

"Don't worry about it. I know you don't mean it," he said, and after a long moment added, "I had an idea."

"What?" she asked, turning toward him.

"My grandfather had a friend who helped the Italians during the war. Maybe he's still around," he said.

"Can you find him?"

"Yeah, if he's still alive."

Later that evening they drove to a group of houses in Shali, the old city. Most people had moved away as the dwellings decayed, but Fathi had said the old people held to their traditions.

"Let me go first, then you come in when I call," said Fathi.

Fifteen minutes passed and Tessa looked at her mobile again. She was about to knock on the door when he came out and led her inside a room lit only by candles set in niches in the mud-brick walls. A century of soot trailed up the wall above each candle. Several threadbare, but colorful carpets crisscrossed the floor and pillows lined the walls for guests to support themselves.

"Sheikh Omar this is the famous archaeologist from Italy, Tessa Santarossa," said Fathi. "Tessa, this is Omar Adballah, sheikh of the Awlad Musa tribe in Siwa."

"*Ahlan wa sahlan*, welcome to my home," said Omar shaking Tessa's hand.

"*Ahlan bīk*," said Tessa in the formal reply common in Egypt.

Omar poured tea into an ornately scrolled glass and offered it to Tessa. She breathed through slightly parted lips as her nose adjusted to the strong odors of spiced foods and human bodies. She thanked him and commented on its wonderful taste although she hated the stuff, almost syrupy with sugar. Like an accomplished actor, she built success by flowing with the customs like a native.

After several minutes of polite conversation about Tessa's family and her work in Egypt, Fathi steered the conversation to their question.

"*Sheikh*, we are exploring the route of Alexander the Great and his visit to the oracle. Our research pointed us to Qārat al Mujahhiz. What do you know of it?" asked Fathi.

"The Italians used it as a lookout during the war because of its closeness to the road. They hired me to show them around. I was just eleven years old," said Omar.

"Did they explore the mountain?" asked Fathi.

"Yes, they dug all over the mountain looking for gold and even blasted parts of it with dynamite, but they found nothing. It's just a rock," said Omar.

They asked him about other archaeological digs that he knew about over the years and learned there had been many, but mostly in the Mountain of the Dead and around the oracle.

"There is nothing new to find. People have dug in Siwa for centuries, and all they find is water," he said laughing.

After saying good night and thanking Omar for his hospitality, they returned to the Land Rover. Tessa did not get in right away, but walked to a clearing and looked westward.

"Damn. He fooled us," she said.

"The Sheikh?" said Fathi.

"No. Darwin. I saw him staring to the west from the oracle like he was looking for something."

"Like what?"

"Like the real mountain with the tomb. Go back and get him," she said.

"Now?" said Fathi.

"Yes, now," she spat. "And he better still be alive!"

42

The Great Sand Sea, Sahara Desert, Egypt

Darwin could not look backwards. As much he wanted to turn to see what was chasing him, his head wouldn't turn. Sand bogged down every step as he ran up the side of a dune. Heat burned his back from whatever was chasing him. *Water. Get to the water.*

He crested the dune and running became easier. He saw a lake. *Get to the lake. What? No!* The lake water receded as fast as he ran to it. A maelstrom in its middle sucked down the shoreline. *No!* The lake drained into the desert. He tripped and rolled head over heels, hot sand whipping around him. It got in his mouth. He spat and spat again until he wretched up a torrent of sand and something large pressed against his back—

Darwin's eyes snapped open to blinding white light. He snapped them shut again. Putting a hand to his forehead, he squinted while he adjusted to the light. The pain in his head felt like an ax blade had cleaved his skull, and the pressure on his back came again. Instinctively he pressed up on hands and knees and the coughing returned. Violent. Deep. He gagged.

Head on his hands, he sucked in deep breaths until the nausea receded and, when it passed, he wiped his mouth. *Sand? What the hell?* Woven carpets covered the floor of... *what?* He sat up and touched white nylon back-lit by blazing sunshine. *A tent?*

He scrambled to a black zipper and swept open its arched doorway. Sand. Hectares of it. *Water!* screamed his brain, and he drank deeply from one of several liter-sized bottles that lay on the floor of the tent. Nausea. *Too much.* He waited a few minutes, then drank again.

Where am I? He stepped barefoot out of the tent and felt the burn of the early morning sun. Shading his eyes, he looked around. *My Land Rover?* It was parked behind the tent. He trod through the sand and opened the driver's side door. Its key was in the ignition and the interior felt cool after a — *Night in the desert. How did I get here? How long?*

7:33 AM showed on his watch May seventh. *Think. Think. I arrived in Siwa on the sixth from the coast. We explored the town and went to the oracle at sunset. Tessa and Fathi found Polaris and the northern mountain.*

He stared out the windscreen trying to make sense of the situation and emptied the liter bottle. He drank from a second and leaned back on the headrest as his body rehydrated. Scenes resolved: walking around the oracle; Tessa with the astrolabe; Fathi naming the mountain and pouring a celebration drink. *They drugged me? Merde!* He pounded the steering wheel. Its vibration rattled his sore head.

The key fob was still in the cup holder and he pressed the Start button. The engine turned over, but did not engage. He paused, then tried again. Nothing. He looked at the fuel gauge.

EMPTY

Fuck! He lowered his forehead against the wheel.

A half hour and another half-liter of water later, Darwin had climbed a large dune a short walk south of his encampment. The yellow-orange glow from sunrise had faded, and the air grew warmer with each passing minute. Sand was all he could see in every direction.

I must be south of Siwa, he thought, remembering the mountainous and rocky terrain north of the oasis on the drive from the coast. He visualized the Google map he had studied. *Yeah, must be south. Or east towards Libya. I never really looked there. But either direction puts me in the Great Sand Sea. Merde. I'm screwed.*

What had once been an actual ocean in the earth's cycling climate was now an ocean of sand as large as the nation of Ireland.

Why would they want me here? If they wanted to kill me... He shuddered at the thought. He swiveled around and looked toward the Land Rover and the small tent a hundred meters distant. Two white specks on a khaki canvas. *No. They wanted me out of the way.* He traced the Land Rover tracks over the horizon and judging from the sun; he confirmed he was south. A second set of tire tracks angled northeastwards.

He watched a small cloud of sand whipped into a spiral up the side of a distant dune. *By the time they find me the wind will cover all the tracks. Bastards! They drove me here and to make it look like I ran out of petrol.*

His head continued to clear, although he had no memory of anything after Fathi handed him the glass of palm wine, and the growing heat caused his nausea to return. *What the hell did they give me?*

He returned to the vehicle and inventoried what they had left him starting with the bottles. *Two, four, six, eight, including the one I drank and this one, that's ten.* There was also a box of food: energy bars, dates and Siwan flat bread. *But I'll run out of water before I starve.* He recalled from his Iceland lava tube expedition that humans needed one liter per day at the bare minimum survival level. Surveying the makeshift camp, he saw two vehicles on the distant horizon and jumped, waving his arms.

"Hey!" he yelled, instantly regretting the pain in his head.

They disappeared down the opposite side of a dune, and he reckoned they were kilometers away at a minimum. *I need a way to call — Merde! The sat-phone!*

His memory had cleared enough to recall the satellite phone he had concealed deep in the wheel well.

"Zac! It's Darwin," said Darwin.

"Darwin? What's this number? I thought it was a robocall and almost didn't answer," said Zac.

"It's a sat-phone. I got it in Alexandria for an emergency—"

"What happened? I got your email yesterday," said Zac.

"They drugged me and dropped me in the desert."

"Jeee-sus. You okay?"

"For now. I've got a killer headache from whatever drug they used, but I have water for three or four days and some food. I guess they wanted it to look like an accident," said Darwin and filled in the events of the last few days that led up to the email.

"Where are you—exactly?" asked Zac.

"Hang on," said Darwin, switching the device to speaker mode. "I've got the GPS coordinates. Can you write them down?"

"Yeah, lemme get a pencil... okay, go ahead."

"28.084866 and 26.410418," said Darwin.

Zac confirmed the numbers and asked him to hold on while he mapped them. Darwin moved into the shade on the opposite side of the Land Rover.

"Got it. You are in the middle of bumfuck nowhere, let's see... about a hundred forty-eight kilometers southeast of the Siwa Oasis."

"Fuck! Am I near anything?"

"The closest road is... like seventy-five kilometers north of you. It's the Siwa-Bahariya Road," said Zac.

Darwin thought of the tire tracks going north from his location and figured they drove at an angle from Siwa, then went straight to the road for a faster return trip.

"Zac, I need to get out of here," said Darwin, his voice breaking.

"We'll get you out. You'll be okay. Do you have shelter?"

"Yes. A tent and the Land Rover."

"Okay, with that and the water, we've got plenty of time to get you."

"How?"

"Let me think," said Zac.

Darwin's felt his heart thrum and closed his eyes and breathed. *He knows what to do. Be patient.* Zac had been a Ranger in the US Army special forces in Afghanistan and had firsthand experience surviving life-threatening situations.

"Wait! I'm an idiot. Stevie's in Cairo," said Zac.

"What?"

"Yeah, she went there last week to investigate a fungus growing on the paintings in some underground tomb structure. She can get you."

"How?"

"We've got your coordinates. She can drive from... let's see... yeah, here it is, a road from Cairo to the Bahariya Oasis that connects to the road north of you. She can go off-road and get to you no problem," said Zac, making it sound like a day trip to the seashore.

"How long will it take?" Darwin asked.

"Maps is showing a little under five hours from Cairo to Bahariya and about half that distance to a spot on the road to turn off. Then it's seventy-five clicks over sand to your location. I'd say between ten and twelve hours, give or take," said Zac.

"So, maybe tonight?"

"I wouldn't recommend night travel out there, but definitely by tomorrow if I can reach her today."

"What!"

"No, no Darwin. Sorry, man. I'll get her. It's just that she might be in some tomb and I can't get her right away. Listen, sit tight. Let me work this a while and call you back in, say an hour. Okay?"

"Okay," said Darwin, and they disconnected.

He got a couple energy bars from the cooler in the Land Rover and moved one rug onto the shady spot. A tear welled in one eye as he wondered what Eyrún was doing today.

43

Vik, Iceland

Eyrún found herself back above ground three days sooner than planned and put on sunglasses as her eyes adjusted to the bright sun. Her work as the chief scientist for the North Atlantic Tube that ran between Iceland and Scotland was fulfilling and challenging, but the project had dragged on.

Darwin's right. I don't need the money; she thought unconsciously rubbing her finger. It turned out this latest emergency, a close colleague who had broken her leg, did not require Eyrún's personal involvement. Her team lead had even pulled her aside to suggest she give them more space to do their jobs.

Maybe it's time to let go... focus on other priorities. She took off the safety helmet and bent over to shake her hair free of its pressed down shape. *Ugh. I need a shower.* Almost a week underground with limited toilet facilities had made common place activities like a daily shower seem like a luxury. The early afternoon weather felt great despite the cool Icelandic air, so she peeled off her jacket and stood facing to the sun to absorb its light and warmth.

After a couple of minutes acclimatizing to above ground life, she looked across the plain at the ocean and thought of Darwin in Rome. She grabbed her mobile and checked messages that stored on the mobile carrier's server until she was back in service range. Normally, they messaged each other a dozen times a day, but he cut back to just give highlights when she was underground .

1 May, 1:53pm
Missing you in Rome, but hope your colleague is okay

4 May, 2:17pm
In Alexandria. Moving fast since I gave Tessa the diary.

6 May 5:31pm
In Siwa Oasis. Feels like a place out of time. Cute eco-lodge, you'd like it. Going to oracle later. Don't worry. I'll be fine.

Siwa Oasis? Ugh, where the hell is that? She Googled Siwa Oasis and as the page loaded, recalled her first meeting with Darwin. She loved his unbridled enthusiasm and genius for finding things, but he also tended to get into trouble because of his naïvety in the workings of people and politics. "A charming risk taker," one of the government leaders called him as they tried to seize control of his lava tube discovery in Iceland.

Eyrún was the consummate planner and had almost followed their advice to cut him out of the project, and, in an uncharacteristic move, advocated for Darwin to stay on the project. She was glad she did so, although at the time she could not articulate why.

Because he IS charming... came the answer she now knew. *And impulsive... Full of surprises and sometimes a bit maddening... Everything I'm not.* A warm feeling coursed through her picturing his smile and unruly hair always in need of a trim. She reread his last message that ended:

Don't worry. I'll be fine.

Which is why I should worry. He's also a genius at finding trouble and not recognizing it until it's too late.

A quarter hour later, Eyrún sat in the backseat of a coworker's car on the return drive to Reykjavík. She had called Darwin, but it went to voice mail. *Strange*, she thought while opening the email app and checking her personal account. She found an email that had arrived yesterday and began reading:

```
Hi Love,
I'm in Siwa Oasis in far western Egypt
chasing a solid lead on the tomb containing
remains of the Library of Alexandria.
After I met the Pope, I found a diary in the
Vatican Apostolic Archive that Hypatia of
Alexandria wrote. Can't wait to tell you the
whole story, but best to read the diary
document I saved here
Call when you're out of the NAT. 10 days,
then Greece.
xoxo
Darwin
```

He'd better come back here first. I'm not flying to Greece alone. God, he gets blinded when he starts something.

She clicked the link that opened the diary document and began reading, oblivious to the conversations going on in the car. About a half hour later, she finished and looked out the window at the lunar landscape rushing by. They were passing an area of southern Iceland that had experienced a lava flow in the recent past. Mosses and grasses had regained purchase, but everything else was a tumble of basalt rock.

Is this for real? Alexander's tomb? The lost library of Alexandria? She remembered the day they had discovered the lava tube that crossed the north Atlantic. She thought him somewhat wimpy for tearing up after finding a handprint left by a Roman. His ideas were romantic, too far-fetched, and because of that she insisted on partnering with more experienced men. But it was Darwin who kept them going and led them out safely when the partners turned out to be killers.

He seemed driven like something was calling him and his sense of wonder was infectious. And the way he pulled us together. The way he cared for us... for me.

She shivered and felt gooseflesh on her arms, remembering his smile when they found the diamond chamber. "We did it Eyrún," he had said.

Not I, but we. And now he's going to open Alexander's tomb and find the long-lost library. I want to be there!

She Googled flights from Reykjavík to Cairo on her mobile. Her company owed her a lot of holiday time.

44

The Great Sand Sea

Darwin spent a nervy day waiting for Zac's calls and trying to stay cool in the oppressive heat. It was too hot in the tent, so he rigged it as a lean-to against the Land Rover and lined up the water bottles by day. *What if it takes longer than three days for Stevie to get here? No, she's coming. But...* he tried to push away the negative thoughts.

Zac called him back in the late afternoon when he had finally got Stevie on a call. She planned to set out around midnight and figured on reaching him by early morning. A couple guys on her project would go with her as they intended to drive through most of the night.

When the sun slanted low on the western horizon, he re-rigged the tent for the night. He scanned the horizon again as he moved about, but saw nothing but wisps of sand blowing off the tops of dunes. The only sounds were the synthetic tent fabric flapping in the hot wind and the soft scrunch of the sand pressed by his boots. The desert yawned about him, its silence like a vacuum. He crawled in the tent and lay back, staring at the darkening fabric. Sleep soon overtook him.

Ting!

He jerked awake at a metallic sound. He focused on the fine mesh of the inner screen of the tent, but everything beyond was black. The sound came again. He looked left toward the source, heart racing. *What do I have*? He mentally inventoried anything in the tent to defend himself. *Satellite phone, water bottles, boots...*

A white shape sprung up just outside the tent. *Fuck!*

Ting!

The zipper pull on the outer tent door struck one of the aluminum support poles, and he blew out a breath, almost a laugh. The breeze cast the fabric about like a loose sail. He sat up and drank some water as his breathing and heartbeat returned to normal. The Land Rover glowed in the light cast by the waning moon, and the surrounding sand was a study in gray similar to photos he had seen of the moon missions.

A glance at his watch showed just before midnight, and he lay back and studied the thick swath of stars overhead. Without the light pollution of a modern city, the Milky Way appeared true to its name. *I shouldn't have dropped that astronomy class*, he thought, trying to identify constellations. He settled for counting satellites, a game his grandfather had taught him at the Lacroix family mountain house in Corsica. *One... two...*

Three... four...

Another gust rattled the tent fabric, startling him awake again. The wind was picking up. *Not good. What time is it?* He looked at his watch: 4:33 AM. A strong hot blast bowed the south facing tent panel, its fabric hissing from the sand. Darwin got to his knees and closed the outer doors. He sneezed from the dust and powered up the satphone. He and Zac agreed to conserve its battery as they knew Darwin's precise location and Stevie was on her way.

"Darwin, what's up?" asked Zac, answering the call.

"The wind is picking up. Anything in the weather forecast?" asked Darwin.

"Lemme check. What time is it there?"

"About half past four. Still dark."

"Nothing in the forecast about wind, but a heat wave is due over the next few days," said Zac.

Darwin opened a small top panel to look outside. The desert now had a misty quality, like a morning fog.

"How far is Stevie?" he asked.

"They stopped for sleep a few hours ago. She left her phone on so I could track them. Let's see..." said Zac.

Darwin heard the clacking of a keyboard.

"Within seventy clicks of you. They must have pulled off the road to not be noticed," said Zac.

"I don't like this Zac. One of the locals said something about being careful going in the desert. The winds... er... khamaseen, that's it, comes up suddenly in springtime," he said.

"How bad is it?"

"Not too bad right now. It feels a lot hotter, though. That's one of the signs the guy said."

"Okay, I'm calling Stevie. They've got to be in the same weather. Sunrise should be in ninety minutes, but they'll have enough light to see you earlier. Unless the storm gets—"

"Zac!" Darwin almost shouted. "Just call her."

"Oh, right. Sorry," said Zac.

Darwin tried to sleep again, but the tent moaned as the wind bore down. He remembered a similar sound a couple decades ago during a winter storm in Paris as his younger sister Marie squeezed the life out of him. Thinking of his family brought more pleasant memories, and he dozed.

45

A couple hours later, the sun had cleared the horizon, but was reduced to an orange disk because of the amount of sand in the air. He had moved to the Land Rover as soon as it was light and watched the storm through the windscreen as a mini dune built up against the glass. He plugged the sat-phone into the vehicle and nervously chewed a snack bar as he scanned the northern horizon.

Zac had spoken to Stevie two hours ago, and she and Darwin had talked a couple times in between. *They should be here!* He squinted, hoping it would help resolve any object on the horizon. The sat-phone chirped.

Zac: They show almost on top of you

Darwin: Don't see them

Darwin called her and, when she answered, said, "Stevie, he says you're almost on top of me."

"I know. We're going slow. There's so much sand blowing," she said.

"*Où*, where?" he answered reflexively while climbing to the driver's side and pressing his face against the window.

"*Je te vois! Je te vois!* I see you," she yelled.

"*Te voilà*, there you are," he said, looking at a shape resolving on the horizon.

Two minutes later, Stevie pulled along Darwin's lee side, and he ran to their vehicle. Its rear door opened, and Darwin jumped in colliding with the man who was pushing the door that now slammed behind them from the force of the wind.

"*Désolé*, sorry," said Darwin to the man.

"Darwin!" said Stevie, leaning over the front seat and kissing his cheeks.

"This is Pierre and Jacques," she introduced the driver and the guy Darwin had bowled into.

"*Nous devons partir*, we must go," said Pierre, who gunned the engine and backtracked toward the road. He explained the dangerous unpredictability of the khamaseen as he leaned forward on the steering wheel and squinted into the murk. Stevie explained that Pierre had been living much of the last decade in Egypt and knew the desert. Jacques was a colleague from Lyon who joined them to investigate the fungus in the tomb.

"Nice to meet you guys and thanks for coming out to get me," said Darwin.

"No problem," said Pierre, "What about your car?"

"Fuck it. Her problem, she rented it," he said and tossed his pack in the rear compartment and kicked a small pile of food wrappers under the driver's seat. The car reeked of sweaty humans, but the conditioned air felt like a godsend.

Stevie peppered Darwin with questions about what he was doing and how he got in his current predicament. He recounted what happened, and after a couple minutes of being bucked around by the rocking vehicle while facing backwards, she asked Jacques to swap places. They awkwardly squeezed past each other.

A few minutes later, although they were still deep in the desert, Darwin noticed he was breathing more easily, thanks to the company of a close friend and conversing in his native French. That comfort grew into confidence when, an hour and a half later, they intersected the Siwa-Bahariya Road and turned right towards Cairo. But, progress was slow as the khamaseen drove the sand across the road at an awkward angle and Pierre reduced their speed to thirty kilometers per hour. At one point, he stopped on the road to swap driving duty with Jacques and, a short while later, they stopped again when Stevie said she had to pee.

No one wanted to open the doors due to the blowing sand, and they risked getting stuck if they went off the roadway, so Darwin watched for approaching cars while the other guys looked away. The sound of pee in the cup was too much for his own bladder, and they ended up passing the cup around.

"Get the lid on tight," said Pierre. "I put my personal card as a deposit on the car."

Over the next hour, the khamaseen abated and by late morning they reached the Bahariya Oasis where they stopped for breakfast.

"What?" said Darwin through a mouthful of eggs.

"It's good to see you again Darwin. And I'm happy to see your appetite is normal," said Stevie, joking about the vigor he always brought to a plate of food.

After the meal, Darwin offered to drive and the others soon fell asleep. They had told him over breakfast that yesterday's traffic leaving Cairo had been so bad that they had gotten only a couple hours sleep.

46

Cairo International Airport

That afternoon, Eyrún disembarked at Cairo International Airport walked to baggage claim as the excitement of being in Cairo replaced the lingering fatigue of inconsistent sleep while in the NAT. It did not help that she was up half the night packing. After the long drive along the Ring Road on Iceland's south coast, she visited a mountaineering shop in Reykjavík that stocked gear for all climates. Fortunately, she had slept a few hours on the plane and tried to look cheerful in the customs and immigration queue.

"Iceland?" asked the officer when it was her turn.

"It's cold. I want see the pyramids and get warm," said Eyrún.

He stamped her passport and slid it back under the plexiglass partition. "Welcome to Egypt. Enjoy your stay."

She had caught an early flight through Paris to Cairo, where it was now early afternoon. Darwin did not expect her to be out of the NAT until tomorrow, and she wanted to surprise him in Siwa, but it was too late to trek across Egypt today, so she would spend the tonight in the Four Seasons Hotel. The concierge had arranged a helicopter journey for late morning. He said the two-hour journey was much faster and safer for a single woman of means. He sealed the deal by booking her a spa appointment that afternoon.

After a lovely massage and a mani/pedi, she stood at the window in her room waiting for room service. The distant pyramids danced in the colored light show that had become a tourist staple, and the traffic in the streets below moved at the frenetic pace that was modern Cairo.

All of Reykjavík would fit between here and the pyramids. And there's more than four-thousand kilometers of Africa beyond... Darwin's out there.

She looked him up in the Find Friends app, but it showed: "Location not available." Her eyebrows furrowed, and she had a sinking feeling. *Stop it,* she reprimanded herself. *The stupid app doesn't work half the time outside Reykjavík and Siwa's in the middle of the desert.* She texted him anyway, knowing he would get it when back in range.

Eyrún: Got out of NAT early. Can't wait to see you.

There. Gets him excited without giving away my surprise. A knock at the door heralded dinner, and she ate by the floor to ceiling window. An hour later, she climbed onto the cool bedsheets and stretched her arms and legs outward like making a snow-angel. *I'll see camels and swim in warm water springs.* She imagined the bright blue water in photos on the Web, glad she packed both new bikinis. She thought of Darwin. *We need a break together.*

47

Cairo

The sun dipped low behind them as Darwin approached Cairo and Pierre took over driving as the vast city grew denser. Darwin's forehead leaned on the passenger side window as he watched the sea of people and vehicles flow past. *I'm done with this. Screw Tessa and her scrolls*, he thought. A couple hours ago, Stevie had woken up before the guys and they had talked through everything that had happened.

"She's a sociopath Darwin," said Stevie after hearing of Tessa's mood shifts.

"*Putain*! She tried to effing kill me," he spat. "Sociopath makes her sound semi-rational. No, that bitch is a psychopath, but whatever, I'm done with her."

"I'm sorry Darwin. I didn't mean to—"

"It's okay. I'm sorry and I'm beyond grateful for you coming out here to get me," said Darwin.

A couple minutes later, she had added, "I've been thinking, why don't you go back to Iceland. Let Tessa move on and we go after the tomb in the winter when it's cooler. We can get Zac to help using his new satellites," she said, referring to the small geographic satellites that Zac's start-up company was using to map the earth's plate tectonics.

"Will they work on archaeology stuff?"

"It's software. They use the images and ground penetrating radar to triangulate perturbations in the soil. I don't know how it all works, but you know how Zac loves to geek out. Ask him," she said.

"Cool," said Darwin. "How are you and Zac getting on?"

Stevie had related a short version of their long-distance relationship since meeting in Iceland. She had gone to California for three months following the NAT discovery, but as Zac got deeper into his start-up company, Stevie went back to her passion exploring rare life-forms in underground environments.

"We hookup every couple of months," she said. "Now, tell me the answer to a more important question. When are you and Eyrún getting married?"

He had answered, "Dunno." Everyone kept asking him and Eyrún, but they wanted to get married on their own terms and in their own special way. *It will happen. Why does everyone keep bothering us about it?*

Pierre rolled into the Four Seasons entry to let off Darwin, who thanked them again and offered to buy dinner later after they had showered and rested. Once in the hotel room, he left his filthy clothes in a heap and stood in the shower a long time. Memories of the past week replayed as the dirt circled the drain. After a few minutes, he thought of vacation and Eyrún. *I should text her.*

He turned off the water and grabbed a towel. Just then, a knock at the door meant his clothes had arrived. He pulled on a robe and dried his hair as he approached the door. The hotel went out of its way for high-value clients and had engaged a shopping service on his behalf. Darwin had chosen Hugo Boss from the options offered as he knew the fit, and one store was only couple kilometers away. Fathi had left Darwin's wallet and passport with him in the Land Rover, but in the rushed transfer to Stevie's vehicle, Darwin had left his iPhone in the abandoned vehicle.

After tipping the delivery person, he finished drying off and pulled on a pair of lightweight jeans; its cotton felt soft on his clean skin and had that unique retail smell. He immediately felt lighter and the long mirror reflected his improved mood. The ordeal in the desert was retreating to the dark graveyard of bad memories. He glanced at the bedside clock. *Shit! I'm late!* He finished dressing and ran out of the room. The switched-off sat-phone stayed in his pack by the dirty clothes pile.

Twenty minutes later, he joined them mid-conversation at the restaurant that Pierre knew. Stevie turned to Darwin and said, "You won't believe the underground structures in Saqqara. It's so far underground it feels like a lava tube."

"We're lucky as few people get access to the deep levels," said Pierre. "And it has more evidence to support our theory that the ancient Egyptians didn't have the technology to carve the rock with such precision."

"How so?" asked Darwin, popping a large olive in his mouth.

"The tombs and sarcophagi are fashioned from granite and cut at precise angles and finished with a high polish. There are also thousands of vessels perfectly shaped like a machine turned them. The conundrum is the ancient Egyptians only had copper tools which are much softer than granite," said Pierre.

"Then who carved the tombs?" asked Darwin. He had heard of this speculation before.

"That's the big question. We're not saying the ancients didn't do it, it's just there is no evidence in the archaeological record showing how they did," said Jacques.

"And the antiquities authorities give us so little access that we can only make guesses in between our occasional visits," said Pierre.

"Maybe Darwin can use his influence to change their minds," said Stevie. "He saw the Pope. Perhaps he could see the president of Egypt."

Darwin said sure, but his mind was on getting a real night's sleep, in a bed, in an air-conditioned room, and getting the hell out of Egypt. That the restaurant served no alcohol was fine with him. *One glass and I'd be on the table.* At the end of the meal, Stevie coordinated getting an Uber with him to the airport as they were on the same flight to Paris.

Back in the hotel, Darwin fell into bed, but sleep eluded him as the drama of the past week played over and over. After an hour, he got up and went to the window, his naked body reflected like a hologram above the lights of Cairo. He missed working out but saw that his muscles still held the tone he had developed in the home gym he had built in Reykjavík.

Good, he thought, pinching the skin above one hip. The inconsistent eating over the last week had helped take back ground in the battle against his lazy middle. He settled into a series of stretches to relax and found his legs to be tight. *I've been sitting too much.* He thought of the hours driving in the last week. He grasped an ankle and pulled it back towards his butt to stretch his quads as his mind returned to the oasis.

Could she find the tomb? He thought of Tessa who was still in Siwa. *Perhaps—Alexander picked a logical place—but she would have to make a lot of guesses and would need to spend a lot of time in Siwa to figure it out. And how long before she gives up? She's impatient.*

He switched to stretch his other leg and breathed into the burn.

She's also like... I dunno... flashy and manipulative. He thought of her performance in the wine cellar and pushed it aside, but an idea formed.

Barry warned me not to share the diary with her. But what if she's not sharing all she has with me? He moved into a downward-dog stretch and felt his thoracic vertebrae *pop.* A warm tingle flowed over his scalp and in the same moment he thought, *What if there's something else in that tomb? Something she thinks is worth killing over.*

He tried thinking of what it could be, but the released muscular tension brought on the heaviness of sleep that drew him back to the bed. He kneaded the pillows into place and let his gaze drift out the window before his eyelids closed. *Let it go. Give it time. A few months, maybe more. She'll forget and move on. Then I'll come back.*

He thought of Eyrún as sleep gathered him under its wing. She smiled radiantly in his favorite image of her, a touch of color on her face from the brisk Icelandic air and her dark brown hair tinged red by the setting sun. But as always, her glacier blue eyes drew him into their depths. *Tomorrow...*

48

The Great Sand Sea

The rising sun forced Tessa to peer under the sun visor and squint through her darkest sunglasses. She had been at the wheel since three AM when they left Siwa. Fathi had cautioned against driving in the desert in the middle of the night so they had slept at the ecolodge and began the drive early, figuring it would be sunrise when they reached the point to leave the highway. Watching the eastern GPS coordinate approach the number that showed their turn off point, she shook Fathi's shoulder, who slept against the passenger window.

"Uh, sorry, I fell asleep," he said.

"We're at twenty-six point three-nine," she said. "Anything look familiar."

Fathi scanned the desert south of the Siwa-Bahariya Road. He grabbed a small binocular set from his pack and looked again.

"No. It was nighttime," he said.

Tessa continued at highway speed as Fathi watched the GPS numbers.

"Close enough. Turn off anywhere here," said Fathi as the eastward reading hit 26.41.

Tessa slowed and rolled off the highway when their speed dropped under fifteen kilometers per hour and stopped the Land Rover.

"You drive. I don't like sand," she said exiting the vehicle. She stretched a couple minutes while Fathi walked about confirming their GPS location.

"He's about seventy kilometers due south from here. There's rough ground around a couple mountains that will slow us down, but all sand after that. I made it in four hours the other night, but that was in the dark."

"So, we can make it in two hours in daylight. Let's go," said Tessa, swinging into her seat.

She watched the north-south coordinate count down while the east-west number stayed within a narrow range as Fathi navigated around the hills. The warm sun and the undulating motion over the sand brought a heaviness to her eyelids, and she leaned back on the headrest.

A couple hours later, Tessa opened her eyes when their vehicle stopped before a white Land Rover, mounds of sand surrounded its wheels and windscreen. A tent beside the Rover had a similar slope of sand on the side that faced them, its white fabric straining from the weight.

"Do you see him?" she asked.

"No, but look at the desert. There was a storm," said Fathi.

"So. Everything looks okay."

"The storm was yesterday. I looked at the weather. It was not severe, less than—"

"Yeah, yeah, where's Darwin?"

"There're no footprints. He should have come outside... unless he got caught in the storm and it blew away his prints," said Fathi.

"Shit! Get over there" said Tessa.

Fathi shifted back into gear and closed the hundred-meter gap. Tessa shoved open the door when they slowed and ran toward the sand drenched vehicle.

"Darwin! Darwin!" she yelled, peering the windows of the Land Rover. She used her sleeve to scrub the dust off the glass. She yanked open one of its doors, peered inside, and then ran to the tent.

"Darwin!" She knelt on the side opposite the sand and unzipped the door. Nothing. The sleeping bag looked used and empty water bottles lay strewn about the tent along with food wrappers. *No, no. You can't do this to us. We need you.*

"Where is he?" she growled at Fathi. "Where could he have gone?"

Fathi had explored the vehicle while Tessa was in the tent and said he found the same signs of human presence, but nothing to show where Darwin was.

"He better not be dead," she said and hiked up the large dune that Darwin had climbed two days ago.

From the dune they encountered the same scene that had confronted Darwin, endless dunes whose surface rippled like waves at the seashore. The only wheel tracks visible were from their Land Rover. A soft roar brought Tessa's gaze skyward where contrails of a jet moved north toward Europe.

"What did you do with him?" Tessa accused.

"I left him right here! He should have been fine. The storm was small," he said.

"You should have checked the weather."

"I did. These storms come up without warning. He should be safe. Unless—"

"Unless what?" she glared at him as the unthinkable answer resolved in her mind. *He wandered off and got lost in the storm. He could be out there. Alive!*

The desert has swallowed many before, said the Hypatia voice.

"No, no, no." She ran to the car and jumped behind the wheel.

Fathi followed and swung into the passenger seat as she pressed the accelerator.

"Be careful. Not so fast. Turn straighter" said Fathi as Tessa angled up a dune.

"Don't tell me how to drive," she said, but understood his meaning from the tilting of the Land Rover and turned into the slope as it crested the dune.

After circling Darwin's camp a couple times, Fathi called a halt to their exploration saying they had a limited supply of petrol. Tessa looked at the fuel gauge at one quarter full and drove back to the camp. They had a hundred liters in fuel cans on the roof rack, enough to get them back to Siwa with a safe margin, but not if they kept driving around in the desert.

They examined the tent and vehicle again, looking for any explanation of where Darwin had gone. They reviewed dropping him off and who else might know he was here. Finding no plausible explanation other than Darwin had wandered into the desert, they cleaned up any evidence that they had been there and headed back to Siwa.

Tessa threw herself into the passenger seat, put her feet against the dashboard and hugged her knees. *Where did he go?*

It doesn't matter where he went. Our problem is he changed my diary, said the Hypatia voice.

Tessa screamed and stamped her feet against the dash. The Land Rover rocked as Fathi jumped and twisted its steering wheel.

"What?" he asked.

"Drive!" said Tessa and began to mentally inventory the copies of the diary. *One of them has the correct location. The Vatican has the original Greek encrypted version and the decrypted version from Darwin. But did he deceive them too? Think.*

A small oasis, literally a pool of water surrounded by thick grasses passed by her window. She watched a flock of birds rise from the grass and swirl in kaleidoscoping shapes as she worked the logical flow.

Darwin took the Vatican copy to Newcastle. Lupita deciphered the code, but she's not a classical language expert. That means Darwin must have translated the Greek to English, and he changed it before I got my copy. But the copy Lupita gave me also had the wrong mountain...

Wait...she must have called Darwin after I visited. I would have. I'll bet he told her to send me the copy where he changed the mountain location. So, who's... Shit, what an idiot, Tessa. It's in the original diary! And Lupita still has the deciphered, but untranslated, Greek version.

She smiled and sat up straight. "Lupita has it," she said aloud.

"Who" said Fathi, sitting tall to see around rocks scattered on the desert floor.

"Lupita, the lady in the UK who decrypted the diary for Darwin. She has the deciphered original," she said.

"Oh, her. You could send Mahmoud again."

"Good idea, but I need to confirm it's the right transcription. I'll have Mahmoud meet me there. How long to Siwa?"

"Less than three hours," he said.

"Good. I could get..." she said, looking at her watch, "a flight tonight from Cairo to London and go to Newcastle by train in the morning."

"Do you want me to go?"

"No. You wait here in case Darwin shows up. We need at least to put in a show that we are worried and looking. Tell the police he's missing, then drive around asking questions," she said.

"When will you be back?" he asked.

"The depends entirely on how cooperative Lupita wants to be," she said.

49

Siwa Oasis

Later that same morning, Eyrún arrived at the ecolodge in Siwa where Darwin was staying. The helicopter had landed at a small airport north of the oasis where she hired a taxi and, after tipping the driver, she looked about the property. Palms leaned over the roofline to provide deep shade from the broiling sun. She felt the muscles in her shoulders relax in the warmth, a relief from frigid air inside the helicopter and taxi.

She entered the lobby where a fountain gurgled and ceiling fans vigorously beat the air over a sign in several languages that read "hit the bowl to call the manager". She picked up a wooden hammer and struck the side of a large brass Tibetan bowl. Its resonant sound filled the room, and moments later, a man appeared.

"*Yawm jayid*, good day," he said.

"Hello, good afternoon. Do you speak English?" asked Eyrún.

"Yes, I thought you are Egyptian," said the man running his finger around his head referring to Eyrún's hijab.

"Oh, no, I am from Iceland," said Eyrún, adjusting the scarf and removing her sunglasses.

"I've heard it's freezing there. I studied in Edinburgh. That was cold enough for me," laughed the man.

Eyrún introduced herself and said she was looking for her fiancé, Darwin Lacroix.

"I have not seen him for two days. He went to the desert, but I heard he should be back soon. I can let you into his room," said the man.

Eyrún took the key and wheeled her case across the courtyard and around a swimming pool. Bougainvillea climbed the walls in the surrounding the compound and birds flitted across the pale blue water between the bushes and palms growing on opposite sides of the pool. She kicked off her sandals, hiked up her jeans and sat at the pool's edge.

It's like a bath. She moved her feet, sending gentle waves across the surface as she leaned back on her hands and closed her eyes. *God, it's been an age.* She tried thinking of her last time on holiday in a warm climate. After a few minutes, the shadows cast by the palms shifted and the sun seared her left arm. The relaxing heat now felt like standing near an open oven, so she collected her shoes and case and continued to the room.

The air inside the thick-walled building felt cooler and carried an exotic fragrance. She was not an expert on perfumes and tried to distinguish the complex aroma. *A smoky, sweet wood layered with rose... but there's something else underneath... darker and more sensual... musk?* She could not recall the exact scent, but knew they used it in many Middle Eastern perfumes. *I like it. It would smell good on Darwin.*

She reached number five, keyed the lock and pushed in. Everything was meticulously arranged even his dirty clothes were piled neatly. *It looks like Darwin's room;* she thought finding his iPad under the clothes in his case, but the bed was made and pillows in place like no one had slept in it the night before.

She went to the bath to wash her hands and marveled at the carved stone tub. *That's so cute!* She looked at her watch. It was a little before one o'clock, and she had been traveling almost non-stop since departing the mid-section of the NAT three days ago. Turning on the water to fill the tub, she tossed her clothes on the bed and got a package of bath salts from her case.

Feels like heaven. She leaned back and the water wrapped around her neck, enveloping her in gentle bubbles. The hot water eased the tightness in her neck and, a couple minutes later, her shoulders spontaneously slumped in another wave of relaxation. *Mmm...* she sighed and splayed her fingers and toes to release more tension. *What will we do here?* The helicopter pilot had told her about Siwa during the trip out and recommended an overnight desert trip as it was beautiful at night. "And romantic," he added when she mentioned meeting her fiancé.

I hope he'll want to go out there again. I wonder what he's been exploring? Beads of sweat blossomed on her forehead, and she splashed water on her face. The tub felt nice, but her stomach was growling. She toweled herself dry and slipped on a summer dress. Checking the mirror one more time, she stepped into her sandals and walked to the lobby to ask about food.

Eyrún tapped the brass bowl again and while waiting she messaged Darwin that she was in Siwa to surprise him. A couple across the lobby were arguing, in Arabic she guessed, and the woman looked at her briefly before turning back to the man. When the hotel manager appeared, Eyrún asked about restaurants and transportation, and he produced a copied sheet with a list of restaurants. He was calling a taxi when her mobile rang.

50

Cairo International Airport

Darwin and Stevie sat in the Air France lounge waiting the call to board their flight to Paris. He had just helped himself to more bacon to make up for his drought over the last few days and together with proper croissants; he felt half-a-step in France. The iPhone he had bought at the airport Vodaphone kiosk finished its set-up sequence, and he logged into his accounts. He had originally planned to buy one in Iceland, but with almost three hours to kill before the flight, he bought the newest model they had. It took a few minutes for Apple's servers to connect him and, once ready, he started to message Eyrún when his new iPhone chimed with her backlogged texts beginning with yesterday:

Yesterday, 14:03
Eyrún: Got out of NAT early. Can't wait to see you.

Today, 13:07
Eyrún: Surprise! I'm at the ecolodge in Siwa. The guy here says you're in the desert. 🩶

"What!" he jumped to his feet and tapped her picture to start a call.

Siwa

"Hello?" said Eyrún, not recognizing the number, but it was an Egyptian country code, so she guessed it might be important. She held up a hand for the hotel manager to wait a moment.

"Hi, Love. It's me, Darwin."

"Darwin! Where—"

"Eyrún, you need to get out of there now!"

"What?! Why?" she said as the couple across the lobby stopped arguing and moved quickly towards her. The woman started speaking to her.

"Hang on, someone's talking to me," she said to Darwin.

The next thing she knew, the man had seized her and put a hand over her mouth. Eyrún screamed as the woman wrenched the iPhone out of her hands.

Cairo International Airport

Darwin heard a muffled scream and something like "you can't..."

"Eyrún? Eyrún?" he yelled in the phone. People in the lounge looked up and stared.

"What is it?" asked Stevie.

Then a voice he never wanted to hear again said, "Hello, Darwin."

"What the fuck do you want Tessa?" he yelled. "What're you doing to Eyrún?"

"We're doing nothing to Eyrún, for now," said Tessa. "Whether we do something later depends on you helping us find the tomb." The call ended.

Darwin stood, dumbfounded.

"Darwin, what is it?" asked Stevie.

"They've got Eyrún."

"Where?" Stevie's hand went to her mouth, her eyes wide.

"In Siwa. I need to get there," said Darwin, shoving a few things into his pack.

"What? Siwa? I'm going with you," said Stevie.

"No. I don't want to get you involved."

The people in the lounge stopped whatever they had been doing and watched. Darwin looked about. Even the servers were listening.

"Let's go in here," he said, leading them into a small room for private calls and closed the door.

"Eyrún got out of the NAT early and went to Siwa to surprise me. Oh, God." He looked at the ceiling, his voice cracking. Stevie grabbed his hands and squeezed. He looked at her, the tears flooding his eyes now rolled down his cheeks. "They're holding her captive to get me —" he swallowed hard, "to make me come back and find the tomb."

The ceiling light shone down on Stevie's curly auburn hair and her green eyes blazed with action. She was petite, a full head shorter than Darwin and possessed the ferocity of a mother bear when threatened.

"*We*, Darwin. We will get her. You don't know who else these people have on their side and you said this Fathi guy is a local. You don't even speak the language. I do," she said.

"But I don't want you to get hurt," he said.

"I don't want that either, but she's my friend too," she said and sucked in a breath before spitting out, "Those assholes!"

"We need help. What about Pierre and Jacques?"

"Useless. They're academics. Jacques is afraid of his own shadow. No, we need someone who has experience."

"Zac!" said Darwin, looking at his watch and calculating the time in California.

Stevie had already started a call and tapped the speaker mode.

"Hey Babe. How did you know I was thinking about you? I just woke up and you should see the tent pole holding up the sheets—"

"Zac!" said Stevie, cutting him off. "I'm with Darwin."

"Oops, good thing you didn't FaceTime me. Wait, you guys're flying out today," said Zac.

"Eyrún's been kidnapped," said Darwin.

"What the fuck!" said Zac.

They filled him in on the situation, given what little they knew about Eyrún's surprise visit.

"Who's this Fathi guy?" asked Zac.

"Fathi Hamdy, an archaeologist who's worked with Tessa, but I found nothing he's published and, when I asked about his projects, said his career got sidetracked after the 2011 uprising," said Darwin.

"Hamdy, you said?" asked Zac.

"Yeah," said Darwin and spelled out the name. He knew Zac still kept access to the US Department of Homeland Security "persons of interest" databases, but thought it best never to ask questions.

"I found him. He's in some YouTube videos," said Zac over the sounds of gunfire. The sound muted, and he continued, "This guy's a bad actor, Darwin. He was a student, like you said, before the Arab Spring, but it looks like they radicalized him when the protests turned violent."

"Oh, my God. We need to get Eyrún," said Stevie.

"You can't go in there alone, babe. Too dangerous," said Zac.

"I'm going!" Darwin insisted.

"Hang on a second. Let's think this out," said Zac, and they heard fingers clacking on a keyboard. "There's multiple flights today from San Francisco... looks like I can be in Cairo early tomorrow night."

"I can't wait until then," said Darwin and described a plan where he would go to Siwa Oasis right away. "I need to get there to keep Eyrún safe. You and Stevie can travel from Cairo tomorrow night. The tomb's in a mountain near Siwa Lake and there's a luxury ecolodge at the base of the mountain," he finished.

"I like it," said Stevie. "We can show up as tourists."

"Good," said Zac. "Darwin, get going. Stevie, I'll call you once I decide on the flight."

"Got it," said Darwin, shouldering his pack. "There's solid mobile coverage along the road. Let's talk again in a few hours."

51

Cairo

Just under three hours later, Darwin had reached the outskirts of Cairo where he stomped on the accelerator of a stark-white Mercedes-Benz G550 SUV. Its bi-turbo V8 roared as it chewed up the highway.

He had called the Four Seasons concierge from the airport and explained that he needed a helicopter to Siwa right away. Unfortunately, the lingering sandstorms had grounded all flights into the desert. When Darwin said it was an emergency, the concierge put him in touch with a relative who sold cars and could circumvent the paperwork to meet Darwin's urgent need to get on the road. The choice of vehicles had been a couple sedans and the off-the-showroom-floor Mercedes. Darwin said he would pay an extra five hundred Euros cash if he could be on the road in thirty minutes. The only instruction he waited for was pairing his mobile to the SUV's infotainment system.

Turning right out of a roundabout, the black ribbon of highway ran away into the desert toward the Bahariya Oasis. *Like I ever wanted to go there again*, he thought. He set the cruise-control at 160 kilometers per hour. The coastal route through Marsa Matrûh was thirty kilometers shorter, but he remembered the heinous traffic and opted to make up the difference with speed.

The concierge had said the helicopters would fly again in the morning, but Darwin thought about it only a moment. A good night's sleep was no excuse to leave Eyrún a moment longer than necessary with those maniacs. His new iPhone rang as he adjusted the visor against the sinking sun.

"Hey, Zac," said Darwin.

"Hang on, Darwin, let me patch in Stevie," said Zac. The call went silent, then picked up a few seconds later. "Stevie? Darwin?"

Both answered yes.

"What's the plan?" asked Darwin.

"Zac's on a Turkish Airlines flight to Cairo at six-ten tonight, connecting through Istanbul, that gets here tomorrow night about eight. I pick him up at Cairo International and we head out for Siwa the next morning," said Stevie.

"I sent Stevie a shopping list of supplies that should keep her busy tomorrow," said Zac.

"What supplies?" asked Darwin.

"We need to assume someone is listening to this call," said Zac. "So, let's just say I contacted a buddy in Cairo who will help her with shopping."

Darwin imagined some of Zac's former special-ops buddies and what kind of work they might do in Egypt. While not his thing, Darwin deeply appreciated Zac's resources.

"We have a reservation at Adrère Amellal ecolodge under the name Cicero," said Stevie.

Darwin laughed at the use of the surname of Agrippa Cicero, the ancient Roman whose scrolls documented the lava tube in Iceland.

"Thought you'd like that," said Stevie. "We booked the Royal suite, which should give us enough room and privacy. Assume all the locals will gossip, so say nothing about meeting us. We'll find you."

"Got it," said Darwin.

"Listen, Darwin. Charge the sat-phone on and leave it powered on. Stash it somewhere in the car. We'll track it. Carry only your personal iPhone," said Zac.

"Okay," said Darwin, his voice faltering.

"It will be okay Darwin. You're not alone, and Eyrún is tough," said Stevie.

"Stevie's right. Hang in there, buddy. Remember your training. This totally sucks, but we'll get her back," said Zac.

Darwin steered the G550 through a series of curves. The road and desert shimmered in a mirage, and a quick glance at the in-dash thermometer showed thirty-five degrees outside. It had cooled a couple degrees in the last half-hour.

Where did this go so wrong, he thought, and returned to his questions from the previous night. *Tessa can't be trying to kill us over a bunch of scrolls in an empty tomb... wait... What if it's not empty? Hypatia wrote that she put Alexander's treasure scroll in the unused sarcophagus. But Tessa can't know that. I took it out of her version. Unless she's also lying to me.* He stared out the windscreen at the setting sun. The heat lines from the desert air smeared the egg-yolk orange ball until it was just a blip on the horizon before winking out.

His thoughts drifted to the previous night when he wondered what Tessa might be hiding. *She only showed me one papyrus fragment. What if there was more? What if that's why they dumped me in the desert?*

Headlights grew out of the blackness ahead as he pondered his worsening situation. *Oh fuck, if she hurts Eyrún...* and the highway flew beneath him as he thought what he would do if Tessa and Fathi harmed her. He recalled the training Zac mentioned, a special ops bootcamp he had attended last fall near a NATO base in Germany.

"It's good for your body Darwin. You think too much," Zac had told him.

A week into the training, Darwin had almost quit. The physical conditioning was brutal. But he turned a corner when the training shifted to living off the land and hand-to-hand combat. The fighting was urgent, real time, no thinking, only acting—if you knew the right moves. He learned fast and found the experience produced a rush of confidence and a balance to his sometimes overly intellectual pursuits.

He pictured Eyrún's bright smile and blue eyes. *Yeah, I could do it. I'll hunt them to the ends of the earth if they harm her.*

The SUV rocked as it flew past an approaching truck. *Shit!* He cleared his ears from the compressive airwave and eased off the pedal, realizing he had pushed it over 200 kilometers per hour.

Darwin pulled back on the road after a stopping for petrol and food in the Bahariya Oasis. He shoveled in bites of lamb shawarma as the last light faded from the western sky and sipped a Red Bull. It was not his caffeine weapon of choice, but the small market in the oasis had no coffee brewed.

An hour later, he rolled to a stop and relieved himself on the blacktop as he was not about to step into the desert. The darkness had brought cooling and the only sound was the SUV's engine fan. Out of the corner of one eye, he thought something moved. He turned, almost peeing on his shoe. *There's nothing out there*, he reminded himself, but his boyhood fear of the dark was hard to shake. He zipped up and jumped back in the SUV, its tires screeching as he accelerated.

The drive wore on, busy in pockets, three or four vehicles coming from the opposite direction, then nothing for a quarter hour. At one point he flew by a petrol tank truck like it was standing still and about thirty minutes out from Siwa; he called Eyrún.

"Darwin," said Tessa.

"Where's Eyrún?" he asked.

"Testy. She's right here," she said.

"I'm not in the mood Tessa. Put her on."

"Hi, Darwin," said Eyrún.

"Are you okay? They haven't hurt you?" asked Darwin.

"No. I'm fine except for being kidnapped and held in my room. Who the hell are these peo—"

"That's enough," said Tessa grabbing the mobile, then saying to Darwin, "Where are you?"

"Half an hour away. Put Eyrún back on," he said.

"You'll see her when you get here. We're in your room at the ecolodge and don't bother with the police, Fathi told them you and Eyrún are wanted in Cairo for antiquities theft," said Tessa ending the call.

Darwin banged the steering wheel, causing the SUV to wobble. He eased off the accelerator and brought the car under control. *Best not to die out here*, he thought, but he could not get the library off his mind. He kept thinking of scenarios where he found the library, but kept it from Tessa. *I can't let her get it.*

A short while later, lights from the outer communities twinkled, and he focused on his immediate priority. *First I get Eyrún, then figure out what to do about the Library.* He slowed for a bend in the road and called Zac.

"What's up, Darwin? I'm in airport customs settling some export permits for a couple drones," said Zac.

"I'm on the outskirts of Siwa. They've got Eyrún at the place I stayed. Just calling to confirm you're on the way," he said.

"Should wrap up here in a few minutes, then to the passenger terminal. Flight's on time with no weather delays forecasted," said Zac.

"Good. I stashed the sat-phone in the spare wheel well. Its battery should last three days."

"We'll be there before then. Be safe man," said Zac. "Stall them on the tomb if you can, but don't jeopardize Eyrún's safety. We'll get to you."

"She's all I care about. They can have their fucking Library!"

"Keep that attitude. See you soon."

Darwin rolled through a midnight quiet oasis, its modern street-lamps one of the few hints of the twenty-first century. The soft crunch of gravel announced his arrival at the ecolodge.

52

Siwa Oasis

An hour after his arrival, Tessa and Fathi left Darwin's room in the ecolodge. Darwin locked the door behind them, but realized they took the key, so he put a chair back under the door handle. He paused, listening to a sound like the scraping of wooden chair legs on a tile floor, and figured Fathi got the job of protecting against their escape.

"Oh, Eyrún, I'm sorry" he said, turning and squeezing her in a hug.

He had gone ballistic at Tessa and Fathi when he first arrived. Eyrún had stood with a wide-eyed look of horror as Darwin screamed, "It's just a goddamned tomb! You left me to die in the desert!" When Tessa had asked him how he got out, Darwin looked at her a long moment and said, "figure it out yourself." After an awkward stalemate, Darwin told them to leave and Fathi took their passports, wallets, key fob for the SUV, and both their mobiles.

After a few moments, Eyrún stepped back from their hug and looked him over. "Are you okay? Is it true she left you in the desert?"

"Yes," he said.

"That bitch," she fumed, staring towards the door, and then asked, "How did you get out?"

Darwin brought a finger to his lips for silence. He felt they had no chance but to cooperate and went to the small desk and wrote on a piece of paper:

assume they are listening

Eyrún nodded as Darwin continued writing:

Stevie got me out. She was in Cairo. I had a satellite phone. Zac is coming with her tomorrow.

Eyrún smiled and grabbed the pencil from him:

What time?

Darwin took it back and scribbled:

Late at night. Maybe early morning next day.

Eyrún read it and put down the paper.

"I'm beat," Darwin said aloud. "That was a long drive and I need to pee."

A minute later, he stood at the sink, rubbing water on his face, and looked in the mirror at dark circles that had formed under his eyes. His hair was raked to the right where he had combed through it nervously while driving. He ruffled it back in place with both hands, water droplets splattering the mirror.

Eyrún stepped behind him and massaged his scalp. "Maybe you need a fade," she said, running her fingers above his ears and referring the long on top and near shaved temples hairstyle in fashion with young men. "It will make you look younger."

"I look old?" he asked her reflection.

"No, silly. The rest of you is stylish, but your hair..." She paused as a sudden worried expression took over her face. "Darwin, what's going to happen?"

He turned and took her hands in his. "We'll get out of this. We're not alone. Our friends are coming," he whispered. "Besides, I know where the tomb is."

"Are you sure? What if there's no tomb?"

"We still get out and the longer it takes to find it, the more options we have," said Darwin, enveloping her and gently rubbing her back.

They got ready for bed and slid under the sheets. Eyrún sighed and spooned in closer as Darwin hugged her. After a few moments she turned and kissed him, and they eased into tender love making as the ceiling fan cascaded a cooling breeze across their bodies.

Tessa walked through the darkened lobby and motioned for Fathi to follow her out the front entrance. She turned on him as soon as they got far enough away from the lodge, where raised voices would not draw attention.

"How did he get out of the desert? Who's helping him?" she shouted, arms flailing. "How do we know Eyrún isn't helping him? Her arrival is too convenient."

"I'm sure she didn't want to be kidnapped," said Fathi.

"It's a trap. I know it," she snapped and looked up at the stars.

The answers aren't up there. Only Darwin knows, and you must force it from him, said the Hypatia voice.

He wants your library as much as I do, Tessa retorted.

Does he? You don't know his motivations. And who did he contact while in Cairo? He has powerful allies. You only have Nahla who must operate in shadow, said the Hypatia voice.

Darwin's guessing at what's in the tomb and his allies are not here, she countered. *And they don't know Siwa like we do.*

Don't be so arrogant. Look what he accomplished in Iceland, said the Hypatia voice.

Tessa waved away the thought like an annoying insect and turned back to Fathi, whose face glowed red-orange from a cigarette.

"We need to isolate them," said Tessa. "If they can't communicate, then whoever else is working with them will be equally confused."

"Agreed," said Fathi, blowing smoke into the breeze away from Tessa.

"Can you get your Brotherhood friends in the oasis to keep her? And I mean *hands-off* keep her," asked Tessa. As much as she wanted Alexander's tomb, she abhorred men's tendency to abuse.

"Yes. We can keep her with my friend's wife and daughters. She'll be safe and on the other side of the oasis," said Fathi.

"Good. We'll use the threat of harming the other one as the means to keep each of them from escaping."

"I'll go tonight," he said.

"No. Sleep now and go see them early tomorrow morning. I need you fresh," she said, dismissing him.

Weakling, she thought, watching him walk back into the ecolodge. She had seen him sway from fatigue the last few hours. She looked across the oasis and its lake toward the mountain with the tomb.

Small from this distance, she thought. Moonlight reflected off the water and created just enough contrast to offset the mountain. *Why didn't I see it before? So obvious. Of course, Alexander would put his tomb in such a place. And he did nothing small. You were brilliant to use it.*

Of course, I was. Don't let your ambition blind you, said the Hypatia voice.

53

Shortly after daybreak the next morning, a knock on the door roused Darwin. *Shit!* He got up, pulled a towel around his waist, and walked to the door.

"What?" he whispered through the narrowly opened door.

"Time to go to the mountain. Be ready in five minutes," said Tessa.

"Fine," said Darwin closing the door and noticed there was a different man sitting in the chair beside the door. A large man. He paused by the bed to watch Eyrún sleep, her arms stretched overhead, and hair splayed across the pillow. The rage he felt from last night's long drive resurfaced and, just for a moment, he envisioned attacking the man by the door. He willed himself back into control. *He's too large. I lose, Eyrún gets hurt.* "Goddamnit, Tessa," he said through gritted teeth.

"What?" She stretched and yawned. "You're up."

"Gotta find the tomb. I'll be back later," he said, kneeling next to the bed and laying his head on her chest. Her fingers ran through his hair, cascading tingles across his scalp. He felt her tighten.

"I hate this. What if I try to get away?" she said.

"You can't. There's a guy sitting by the door."

"What do I do?" she said, going slack.

"Wait for me to come back. I'll make sure they bring food," he said, wrapping her in a hug and whispering, "I love you. I won't let anything happen to you."

She sighed and said, "I know."

A second knock came from the door, and he got up. "In a minute," he yelled, walking to the bathroom to wash up. He pulled on a shirt and wrinkled his nose. It smelled from being sweated through during yesterday's drive, and he reached under the fabric to roll on extra deodorant while he ran through the timeline.

Zac lands in Istanbul about one and gets to Cairo about five. He and Stevie will be the road this time tomorrow morning or earlier and should be here by noon. We won't get much done here today and, if my car stays out front, Zac will know I'm here. Tomorrow we'll act.

Another knock at the door. *Assholes.* He walked to the bed and kissed Eyrún goodbye.

"Breakfast!" she reminded him.

"Okay, okay, the chocolate croissants are coming," he said, and he left the room to find Fathi now waiting by the large man watching door. Darwin closed it and said to the large man in the chair, "If you harm her, I'll kill you."

He did not react, so Darwin added, "*Sa'aeud inshallah*, I'll be back, God willing."

This time the man nodded. *No English. Good to know*, thought Darwin and followed Fathi to breakfast, mentally tallying what Eyrún wanted to order.

Darwin spoke as little as possible during the meal and continued his silence while Fathi drove through quiet streets, passing small groups of men returning from morning prayer. The sun ringed the mountains of the oasis and crests of the tallest dunes in the sand sea. Once they had left the palm groves, the White Mountain, also known as Adrère Amellal in the local language, came into clear view, and he studied it as the road carried them around the south side of the lake. The water had filled the space surrounding the lower slope of the plateau, making a peninsula, and they were heading toward a land bridge on the western side.

Geologically, it was one of a series of table-top mountains left behind when the ancient ocean retreated in the mid-Miocene era about eleven million years ago. The sea levels had risen and fallen across the epochs, creating a varied fossil record. This was textbook stuff, and he slept through much of it at university. But he knew it was vital to understand what kind of rock they would delve into and had grabbed a paper off the Internet before leaving Rome.

He read that the plateaus were siliciclastic sediments, a sandstone-quartz combination solid enough to resist the floods. They were also interspersed with limestone, dolostone, marl and olive shale, all sedimentary rocks that tended toward the soft end of the hardness scale. Easy to carve for tombs, but fragile when unsupported.

No diamonds here, he thought, watching the sun strike the mountain full on. Crisp shadows highlighted the yellow-orange striated layers, ranging from khaki, to caramel, to dark brown that matched the mountains ringing the northern edge of Siwa. However, the White Mountain appeared taller because it stood kilometers apart from its nearest neighbor and, from this distance, resembled an old wrinkled Panama hat.

Its base skirted outward like a down-turned brim, and the vertical sides bent inward just below a flat-topped crown. A distinct thick brown layer circled the mountain mid-height, giving the appearance of a hat-band. *That's the dark band that Hypatia described. The tomb should be just above it.*

They crossed the land bridge onto an empty plain and reversed direction alongside the mountain. To the left, the plain ran towards a thick palm grove about one-hundred-fifty meters distant, and to the right the road hugged the base of the mountain as they headed back eastward. Darwin now had to look at the mountain through the opposite window and leaned forward a little to see up its slope. He knew from studying the maps it was a kilometer east to west and nearly half a kilometer at its widest point. *This thing's huge,* he thought, trying to fathom the scale of a tomb inside the mountain.

Two minutes later, they parked under a few palms at the eastern side of the mountain. He got out of the vehicle and looked at the hundred-meter cliff face. He stumbled backward to recover his balance from looking up so steeply and moved toward the shore of Lake Siwa to get a better perspective. From the water's edge could see the entire cliff face without straining his neck, but he frowned at the fetid odor of decay rising from the mud. The lake had expanded from run-off over the last hundred years as the inhabitants drilled more wells, centuries of evaporation had left the water brackish, making it a haven for wildlife and not so much for humans.

Darwin pulled his sunglasses from atop his head to shade his eyes from the increasing solar radiation coming off the eastern cliff. His face grew warm as the day's heat built like a campfire on a cool night. He had thought about this moment standing before the mountain divining where Alexander would have carved his tomb entrance. He knew it would not be obvious, or others would have discovered it, but the sheer size of the cliff and two millennia of exposure to the elements made the task feel impossible. *This is so much bigger in real life.*

He turned slowly clockwise to study the surroundings. The main dwellings in Siwa lay five kilometers across the lake, its shimmering surface obscuring the far horizon, and the Great Sand Sea loomed on the southern horizon to his right. He followed the dunes as he continued rotating in a westerly direction and tried not to think about his time out there.

The luxury ecolodge where Zac and Stevie had made a reservation came into view. Named Adrére Amellal for the mountain, its buildings, constructed using local methods of salt infused mud and palm trunks, were nestled in a palm grove, and he judged the distance to the lodge at half a kilometer. He looked at his wrist for the time and an untanned ring of skin reminded him that Fathi had taken all his electronic gear.

Shit. This is more isolated than I thought... but it can also work to our advantage. I've got to find a way to communicate with Zac and Stevie. He turned back to the cliff.

"Where's the tomb, Darwin?" asked Tessa.

"Up there," he said, nodding towards the mountain.

"How do we know?"

"It says so in the diary. Unless Hypatia lied."

"You'd better not be lying this time," she said.

Darwin stepped towards her. "You kidnapped my fiancée. I don't give a shit about the tomb now. Once we find it, let her go and we get the hell out of Egypt," he said, jaw trembling.

Fathi stepped between them and shoved Darwin back. Darwin sprang forward and punched, his fist glancing off Fathi's cheek who twisted to avoid the full blow. Fathi swung at Darwin, who spun, flinging him by the shoulders into the dirt. Fathi sprung back his feet.

"Stop it!" yelled Tessa.

Neither man listened as they circled each other. Darwin flashed on memories of his desert abandonment. Fury seized him, heart pounding. He squinted against the sun behind Fathi and charged, driving Fathi to the ground. Fathi swung wild punches onto Darwin's back. Darwin rolled off and was about to kick Fathi when Tessa threw a handful of dirt. He blocked it with a forearm and backpedaled knowing that Fathi would have the advantage.

"Stop. Both of you," Tessa yelled, holding Fathi's shirt. "One call, Darwin, and you'll never see Eyrún again." She waved her mobile at him.

Panting from the exertion, Darwin wiped off his face and sucked in a breath. "Fine," he spat. "Just keep him away from me."

"You started it," said Tessa.

"Whatever," said Darwin and turned to walk toward the lake.

Fathi started after him.

"Leave him," growled Tessa. "There's nowhere he can go."

Darwin stopped at the water's edge and thought, *I can take him.* While he had punched Fathi in anger, it was also a test. He needed to know if Fathi could fight. Darwin replayed the skirmish and Fathi's movements. They were reactive, flailing. *No, he's not a fighter. He might be good with guns, but not at hand-to-hand combat*, he thought, and silently thanked Zac for recommending the bootcamp and his own decision to practice mixed martial arts. Darwin's instructor in Reykjavík had taught him how to size up an opponent while not telegraphing his own capabilities.

Time comes and I'll take him out. Tessa won't be a problem after that. Unless... Shit, unless one of them has a gun.

54

After taking a couple minutes to refocus after the fight, Darwin picked up a rock and skipped it across the flat water before walking back toward Tessa. He watched her look between her iPad and the mountain.

"Is this right?" she asked.

"Yes. I only changed the directions. The geology's the same; all the mountains have this layer," he said, pointing.

Halfway up the mountain a dark band forms a shelf. The opening lies beneath a vertical scar.

They looked up at the clear dark line that Darwin had thought earlier looked like a hat-band. From where they stood near the lakeshore, a field of dirt and rubble sloped upward at a forty-five-degree angle to about a third of the mountain's height. As they studied the cliff face, a dust devil spun off the flat summit and plumed outward, cascading another millimeter or two of sand onto the lower slope. Directly before them, a large section of the cliff had peeled away, leaving a clear vertical fissure and a massive tumble of boulders atop the debris slope.

"Do either of you see a shelf?" said Darwin.

"No, but what about that," said Tessa, pointing at the fissure. "Could that be the 'vertical scar'?"

Each brought a hand up to shade their eyes and stared at a crease in the rock that started just above the brown layer. The surrounding cliff face appeared somewhat lighter.

"Perhaps the shelf was broken off?" said Tessa.

"Maybe," said Darwin.

"That rock pile has been here my entire lifetime," said Fathi.

Tessa surveyed their surroundings and asked, "Will anyone at that ecolodge care what we're doing?"

"I doubt it. It's just wealthy tourists who want a spa experience," said Fathi.

"It didn't look busy when we drove by," said Tessa.

"Not as many tourists come here since the revolution," said Fathi.

"Yeah, that went well for you. Destroyed your main industry," said Darwin.

Tessa grabbed Fathi's arm and squeezed.

"Enough, Darwin. If there was a tourist industry in seventeen eighty-nine, I'm sure France would have screwed itself, too. As is, your people stole some of Egypt's greatest treasures. Save your morality and let's keep on task," said Tessa.

Darwin looked at Fathi out of the corners of his eyes and saw that he was grinning. *Asshole!* He turned and started hiking up the slope. Tessa and Fathi followed him to the base of the cliff. The loose rock and sand had made the hike much harder as they had slid a half-step backward with each foot forward.

Darwin wiped sweat from his eyes. He knew in a couple hours the cliff would concentrate the heat like a reflector oven. He looked up but could no longer see the vertical cut as cliff overhung and stepped outward to get a better view, sliding a few meters downslope.

"We can't see anything from here," he said after struggling back up.

"Can we climb it?" asked Tessa.

"Too soft," said Fathi, ripping a chunk of rock from the wall. "A friend of mine tried it years ago and fell. Lucky for him he landed in a sandy spot."

"We need to get on top. See if there are any clues," said Darwin.

They got water and basic supplies from the Land Rover before setting out for the mountaintop. Fathi drove them back along the same road as Tessa and Darwin sized up the mountain. At the western side, Fathi pulled off the road opposite the land bridge and drove over the rough ground onto the plain. The low angle of the sun left this side deep in shadow.

"Stop here," said Darwin and heaved his door open against the fifteen-degree slope. The debris pile on what they called the backside sloped twice as far as the front side and was mostly hard-packed sand. The surface was pock-marked like an old battlefield.

"What would looters dig for out here?" asked Darwin. He had seen enough evidence of it in satellite photos. While grave robbing was a time-consuming, low-yield activity, people of little means harvested what they could from ancient burials. It was a constant struggle between archaeologists who wanted to identify and catalog human history and looters who just wanted money, but he knew the argument also had another side: the internment of loved ones for their journey beyond life was private and sacred, not something for a doctoral dissertation and display in a collection.

"It might not be looting," said Fathi. "Look at the pattern. It's too grid like."

Darwin studied the holes more closely and concurred with Fathi's observation. The pits radiated around him in crude rows. "An old palm grove?" he asked.

"Likely. Something must have happened to the water, or maybe a disease," said Fathi.

"What about the trunks?"

"Used for building materials," said Fathi.

"Let's go. There's nothing out here," said Tessa.

As they drove away, Darwin made a mental note to study the plain from above. *What if the back entrance to the tomb is not in the palm grove over there?*

They stopped on the north side after a spine-crunching drive around boulders. At one point, Darwin had grasped the hold above the door with both hands after banging his head on the side window. The cliff had crumbled on this side to expose a series of steep, tight chimneys that they could traverse to the top.

Climbing was difficult, but they pulled themselves through. Sweat poured off Darwin's brow as he reached the summit where there was no relief as they immediately dropped into a depression that blocked the breeze and made their walk to the eastern facing side feel like a sauté pan.

Darwin climbed out of the depression on the eastern or front edge and stopped on the smooth wind-swept surface that ended in a one-meter drop onto a lower sharper slope that disappeared onto the floor below. He eased toward the edge but could not see down the cliff face.

"Be careful," said Fathi, tugging Darwin's sleeve.

"I know what I'm doing," said Darwin, shaking off Fathi's grip, but in the process felt the surface give underfoot. He jumped back as a dinner-plate sized section broke and slid downslope, gathering more rocks as it sailed off the edge. The trailing dust swirled from the updraft.

Fathi shrugged as if to say, "I told you so."

"What if we used ropes to climb down from here?" asked Tessa.

They debated how it would help them, and she suggested it might reveal the tomb.

"Not likely," said Fathi. "The ropes would hold us too tight against the cliff. We wouldn't see much."

Darwin agreed, and they abandoned the idea. He walked along the southern edge toward the back or western face, tightening his hat lanyard against a hot wind coursing off the desert. At one point he stopped and looked across the Great Sand Sea and its endless dunes, a tuft of one tiny oasis visible, as was a gathering of vehicles giving thrill-rides to tourists.

Tessa and Fathi followed him at some distance. He was stalling for time, knowing that Zac and Stevie would arrive this afternoon and that he would feel better once they did. *At least one of them can keep an eye on Eyrún while the other helps me get away from these idiots.*

It took twenty minutes to traverse the mountain top to the western edge where he studied the mottled oasis floor. The gridded hole pattern was clear from this vantage point, as were buildings at the perimeter of the large palm grove. The buildings used modern construction materials as betrayed by their smooth walls and sharp edges that indicated use of prefab blocks. Tan paint matched the look of surrounding older structures.

The other exit must be out there. How far, though? Nothing about the White Mountain suggested a magnificent or any kind of tomb lay inside. *If the pits were looted graves, that might show burials made close to a royal or sacred site, but Fathi's right—there's too much symmetry for them to be graves.* He walked away as Tessa and Fathi arrived, not wanting to discuss what they knew about the tomb's back door.

Tessa stopped at the back of the White Mountain and watched Darwin wander away. *There's nowhere for him to go up here,* she thought, and studied the ground far below. She scrolled to the section of Hypatia's diary about her final exit from the tomb:

> *We found the rear exit built by Alexander, but it was blocked. Over four years we dug downward and under the plain. Masnsen's men built a well in a palm grove. The new corridor to the tomb enters from the well just above water level. We collapsed the front tomb entrance to block looters and Masnsen promised to protect the secret of both entrances until they were forgotten.*

"What about that well? Could we get in from there?" she asked, pointing to a dark circle of water in the palm grove.

"It could be any of a dozen wells down there, and the water level has risen in the last thousand years," he said. "And look at the distance, it's two or three hundred meters, at least. We should begin work on the front," he said.

"Then let's get your men started," she said.

"Tomorrow. It's too hot today."

"It's hot every day. What about this afternoon? The front will be in the shade," she said.

"Tomorrow, Tessa. There's a rhythm to life here. Men do hot work in the early morning and one day won't matter," he said.

"One day— Where's Darwin?" she asked, turning to the empty plateau.

"Shit," said Fathi and began running.

Two minutes later, Tessa scrambled down the chimneys close behind Fathi. They reached ground level and looked around. No sign of Darwin.

"Where is he you idiot? You were supposed to watch him," said Tessa.

"Me?!"

"Find him. He can't have gone far," screamed Tessa.

Fathi ran to the car and raced the shorter distance toward the west side of the mountain while Tessa scanned the mountain and the longer path to the eastern or front face. She kicked at the soil, which did nothing but blow sand back in her face. A couple minutes later, the Land Rover with Fathi returned and they drove to the front side.

"Where the hell is he!" She pounded the dash.

55

The Palms Ecolodge

Eyrún read a book to keep herself occupied and looked again at the door as if staring it down would hold it closed. She had put a chair under the handle, hoping to make up for the lack of a privacy chain. She had also tested the windows. They opened, but not wide enough to allow escape.

Hours ago, a middle-aged woman had brought breakfast, and when Eyrún tried to explain her kidnapping, the woman just smiled. While the woman set down the food, Eyrún ran to the door, but met a man whose crossed arms and wide stance filled the frame. When she yelled for help, the man stepped toward her, and she retreated to the bathroom and bolted the door.

The aroma of baked bread drifted into the bath and her growling stomach had won over fear, and she explored the food. It was not a familiar breakfast meal and, at first, she picked at it until a ravenous hunger kicked in.

They served yogurt with olives and dates with pita bread and coffee. The sweetness of the dates blended with the tart yogurt, and the pita was hot and full of flavor. She tore the pita in small bits and wrapped it around the olives. It was a pleasing, salty and oily combination.

She now closed the book, holding her place with a finger and thought through her situation again. *Darwin's been gone about seven hours. Stevie and Zac are probably close, and they know I'm here. What if there's a fight?* She imagined Zac against the large man by the door. *But he's smarter than to just attack first. What if they figure out where I am by seeing the man at the door, then... Stevie would go outside to the window?*

She stood and opened both the room and bath windows just enough to hear a voice if someone were calling her name. *And then what? Darwin's at some mountain. How would we get him? These assholes dropped him in the desert once. They're clearly capable of killing.* She felt her stomach drop, but then reassured herself, *No, we'll figure this out. We've done it before. Stevie and Zac are coming,* she repeated as if a mantra.

She put an ear to the open window and listened. Nothing but cicadas and the gurgle of a fountain by the pool. A knock at the door startled her, and she turned to see the door handle turn and push inward against the chair.

"What?" she said, rushing to the chair and bracing its legs with her foot. The door opened a little more than a centimeter. A note appeared through the crack. She took it and read the one word:

lunch

An aroma of chicken soup wafted through the opening. Breakfast had been tasty, but she had not eaten a substantial meal since dinner in Cairo two nights ago.

"Come in," she said, moving the chair and retreating to the bathroom where she watched through the door crack ready to close and bolt it if needed. The same woman placed the new tray on the table and removed the breakfast setting. When she had gone, Eyrún ran out and put the chair back under the door handle and explored the food.

Steam rose off a light broth that contained carrots and zucchini. A plate of chicken with pasta and eggplants rested beside the soup and pita with olives completed the meal. She sat and sipped the broth, the fragrant spices reminding her of Darwin's favorite Moroccan restaurant in London.

After eating, she washed her hands and listened at the window again. *Stevie and Zac should be here about now.* She paced the room, thinking of how she should be ready for their arrival. *Patience*, she thought and sat down to read. A few minutes into reading, the warm air drifting in the open windows and a full stomach brought on heavy eyelids. *Stay awake*, she commanded, but her chin dropped, and she reflexively pulled her head up.

Zac and Stevie... are coming. Her eyelids drew together. *I shouldn't feel this tired. Unless they drugged...*

A few minutes later, the door opened, and a flat piece of wood pushed at the chair legs, and it crashed to the floor. Eyrún grunted but stayed asleep.

"Zac?" said Eyrún as the large man cradled her in his arms. The woman closed the door as they left and led them to a back door opposite the lobby.

56

The White Mountain

Darwin laughed to himself at their comical panic. He had stopped to explore a crevice when he heard them run past within a couple meters. He almost called out, but waited to see their reaction. He walked toward the returning Land Rover as it bucked over the rough ground.

"Where were you?" Tessa yelled, jumping out of the vehicle before it stopped.

"I had to piss," he lied.

"You didn't tell us."

"What? I need to ask your permission?" he said, walking around her and climbing into the rear seat. "Let's go."

Tessa said something in Arabic that Darwin guessed it was not praise for a job well done. Fathi waved his hand in a dismissive gesture. *Good. He doesn't like her any more than I do.*

After a late lunch at Adrère Amellal, the luxury ecolodge named for the mountain, they returned to the cliff to determine where to dig. Fathi said he had recruited six men to dig and their sons to haul the baskets.

"We need more," said Tessa.

"We don't want the attention from hiring too many people. I trust these men, and we can help," said Fathi.

"I'm not digging," she said.

"Don't want to get blisters on your pretty hands, or aren't you a real archaeologist?" said Darwin.

Tessa did not take the bait, but while walking back down, informed Darwin that they were moving to this ecolodge for convenience.

"Fine with me. As long as I'm with Eyrún," he said.

"About that..." she said with a smug expression.

Darwin stopped. *What the fuck now?*

"We moved her," she paused watching the color leave his face. "Oh, don't worry, she's somewhere safe, as long as you cooperate."

Darwin erupted, "How much is enough, Tessa? I AM cooperating. Eyrún has nothing to do with this. Bring her here or I quit."

"It's not that simple Darwin," she said.

"The hell not. Where is she? Send him to get her," he said, pointing at Fathi.

"She's in a safe place. We find the tomb and you get her back," she said.

"Where... is... she?"

"In Siwa," she said.

"Ugh," he grunted and turned away to look first at the mountain and then toward the lake. He sighed and scuffed at the dirt. "Look, you already know where the tomb is. Let us go. Eyrún and I leave, *together,* and you never hear from us again. Keep your library," he said in a defeated tone.

"We can't trust you," said Fathi.

"Stay out of this asshole," he growled and turned back to Tessa.

"He's right, Darwin. We don't trust you. Maybe the tomb is there and maybe it's not. You've lied continuously to us," she said.

"You used me to get at the diary and decipher it," he said.

"We used each other Darwin. Did you also lie to the Vatican? Or did you give them the exact translation?" she said, smiling.

He folded his arms and stared at her, concentrating on keeping a flat expression, then he looked at Fathi. *How dangerous is he, really? That big man outside our room didn't look that threatening.* His vision drifted across the lake to the town of Siwa and the mountains beyond. *I need to see how they're keeping her. Let her know I'm safe and that she's safe. Buy some time for Zac and Stevie. Maybe they can get her. Siwa's not that big.* But he realized the town looked deceptively small. At its current population, there were several thousand dwellings, maybe more.

He turned to Tessa and said, "Take me to see that she's safe. Blindfold me, drug me, I don't care. When I know she's safe, I'll help."

"You're not in a good bargaining position Darwin, but I'll consider it," she said.

As Fathi led him to his new room in the Adrère Amellal, ecolodge. Darwin felt a weight descend on him. *This is my fault. I didn't listen to Richard or Zac and now Eyrún...* He tried to picture her, but his brain would only conjure images of dark basements with Eyrún tied to a chair as her captors... he shook away the vision.

"You better not harm her," said Darwin with as much venom as he could muster.

"She's safe as long as you cooperate," said Fathi, stopping at Darwin's room.

Once inside, he waited a few minutes, then tested the door. It opened. *No locks. Good to know*, he thought and re-closed the door.

57

Siwa Oasis

Eyrún awoke hours later in a dark room. Her nose registered a combination of rich spices and strong human odors, as if the fabrics and furniture had not been changed in many years. A donkey brayed somewhere outside as the room resolved into a five-meter square where the only light came from small windows in adjacent walls.

Voices in an unknown language carried on a conversation beyond a doorway that was veiled by a drape. Her head slowly cleared as she remembered the hotel room and lunch. She pushed up to a sitting position to find herself in a corner surrounded by pillows.

"Where—" She stopped and looked at a dark figure sitting on the other side of the room.

"You are safe," said a girl's voice.

"Who are you? Where am I?" said Eyrún, standing and looking out the window. A man smoked a cigarette and stood by a gate. She crossed the other window and saw another man working on a cart, the donkey used to pull it wandered near a wall.

"You are safe," repeated the girl as Eyrún poked her head around the drape that separated the rooms. A group of women and girls in what looked like a kitchen area stopped their conversation. The middle-aged woman from the hotel walked toward her waving a hand and saying, "No, no." Eyrún let the drape fall closed and retreated to the cushions. Her head felt thick, like a hangover, and she was thirsty.

"Where am I?" she asked the girl slowly.

"You are in my house. You are safe," said the girl. "Safe from the bad men."

"Bad men?"

"Yes. Bad men at the ecolodge."

What? This makes no sense. She looked at her wrist to check the time, but her watch was gone. *Shit.* She went to the window again and judged the time to be late afternoon.

"How did I get here? Why did they bring me here? Who are you?" Eyrún asked the girl.

"Many questions. Speak slower," said the girl. "My name is Illi. What is your name?"

"My name is Eyrún."

"Ay-roon," said Illi.

"That's right," said Eyrún. "What is this place?"

Illi said this was her home and that her father, the big man by the ecolodge door, brought Eyrún here to protect her from some bad men, but she did not know more. Illi said she had learned English in school and from watching YouTube.

"I do not want to be here. My fiancé, the man I am to marry," said Eyrún, explaining after seeing Illi's perplexed look. "He will look for me."

"He too is safe. At the mountain. But I do not know which one," said Illi. "I have a fee-ahn-say, but I do not want to marry. I am only fourteen and want to be an astronaut scientist. Where are you from?"

"Iceland," said Eyrún.

"I know Iceland. There is Björk?" said Illi excitedly.

Eyrún talked about Iceland and the music star Björk. As her head cleared, she realized she might use the girl to her advantage. "Do other people here speak English?" asked Eyrún.

"No. Only me," said Illi.

"What did they tell you about me?" asked Eyrún.

Illi repeated the story about protection from the bad men, which confirmed she knew little more. Eyrún stood and looked at the window again. The man by the gate now sat on a chair, arms crossed, and had nodded off in the lingering heat.

I could run, but where? She realized her arrival from Cairo by helicopter gave her no sense of location, just that it was far. *Far from anything.* After two hours of flying over a rough desolate landscape, she remembered the town was a tight cluster of buildings set amidst palms between two large lakes, *surrounded by a vast desert. No. There's no place to run.*

She scanned along the fence top and saw palms, a streetlamp, and a metal tower bristling with rectangular boxes and black cables about a hundred meters distant. *A cell tower! The Internet!* Eyrún turned and saw Illi tapping on her mobile. *She's got access, is friendly and wants to learn. What's Stevie's number? Wait! I know her email. I just need to get at her mobile.* She remembered Darwin once saying, if you want to win people to your cause start by asking them for help with something small.

"Illi. I am thirsty. May I have water?"

"Yes. I bring it," said Illi, disappearing through the drape.

Eyrún walked over to a small table for a closer look at Illi's mobile. The brand was unknown to her, but it looked like a recent version and would have full Google functionality. Eyrún dropped into a yoga pose to disguise her investigation as Illi returned with the water.

"What are you doing?" asked Illi.

"Yoga," said Eyrún. "I like to keep fit."

"Can you show me?"

"Yes, and I can show you pictures of Iceland where I live. I am a scientist of volcanos," said Eyrún, gulping the water and putting the glass on the table next to the mobile device. Illi's eyes brightened as if she was granted a wish. *This is working out nicely,* thought Eyrún, and showed Illi a few basic yoga positions and explained how it worked muscles and balance.

58

Adrère Amellal Ecolodge

A little before five the next morning, Tessa closed her room door and walked quietly through the ecolodge, its hallways lit with the barest of light. She entered the empty lobby area and exited on the side that faced the lake, feeling the cooler air wash around her as she cleared the mud brick structure. She stopped and breathed deeply.

This is it. Today we find the tomb, said the Hypatia voice.

Maybe, thought Tessa. *But we've a lot of digging.*

Yes, but we know it's here. Soon, very soon, you will find the wonders I left for you.

Tessa smiled and gazed across the mirror-glass lake at the dark line of Siwa still asleep beneath the pale-yellow bulge on the horizon. Venus hovered a few degrees skyward and would soon hide behind the brilliant sun god Ra. The sky dimmed as she followed it overhead, first to a steel-blue, then deep navy-blue before it lightened again. At this time of morning, the mountain was a black outline against the horizon. She walked towards the Land Rover that Fathi had parked near the mountain's base, and a few small critters scurried from her path.

Shit! Vipers! She froze in her tracks and tapped the flashlight app on her mobile to scan the ground. The Saharan horned viper was a legendary danger around archaeologic sites, and one never entered a tent before first checking for snakes. A single bite was not fatal, but without immediate treatment, the toxicity led to swelling, hemorrhage, and necrosis. She shuddered at the thought as she passed the Land Rover and heard the scraping sounds of shovels up-slope. Fathi yelled some instructions, probably in Siwa, and she felt a passing sadness knowing the Berber dialect would end up in the great pile of lost languages as the world modernized.

So much is lost, said the Hypatia voice. *Remember how you loved the languages and the cultures you studied. The Coptics destroyed mine. Centuries of our knowledge, burned.*

Men burned it. Look what they have done. Even Alexander was just another superpower making the world in his image, replied Tessa.

But Alexander created the library, said the Hypatia voice. *And Darwin, he seems different. He helped us get my diary. He wants to return the knowledge to the world.*

No. He lied to me. He tried to take it for himself and give it to the Vatican, more men who will bury it some place else. No. This is mine, our library, thought Tessa overruling the Hypatia voice. She reached the cliff-base, where Fathi absently tossed a blade of dirt on her feet.

"Sorry Tessa. When did you get here?" he asked.

"Just now. What have you found?"

Men heaved dirt into buckets that boys dumped farther downslope. Another man swung a pick-axe, breaking up larger rocks wedged against the cliff. A single light perched on a nearby boulder provided enough light for Tessa to see that, judging by the exposed rock, they had moved half a meter of soil.

"Nothing yet. We're removing dirt beneath these larger rocks and the plan is to topple one of them later this morning. If we guessed right, this section fell away from the cliff and covered the tomb," said Fathi.

Tessa looked up to where the cliff had collapsed to form a meter-long overhang a dozen meters above them, which meant a considerable amount of rock needed moving. She stepped back to avoid a boy swinging a heavy bucket and asked, "How much can you move today?"

"At least two meters before it gets too hot. I figure we can work no later than ten this morning. I have a different crew who can dig after four when the mountain shadow cools this spot again," said Fathi.

"Maybe tomorrow, we'll know we're in the right spot?" she asked and walked to the largest boulder.

"That's the plan," he said.

"What about this?" she asked, patting the rock.

"A friend visited a construction site last night and borrowed some explosives."

"Good. I'm going to find breakfast," she said and left.

A short while later, Darwin entered the dining room, ignoring Tessa who sat alone drinking tea, and went to a table on the opposite site of the room where he asked the waiter for coffee. He had slept reasonably well in the air-conditioned room, but had awoken several times worrying about Eyrún. He ordered breakfast when his coffee was set down.

There has to be a way to find her. He looked at his watch to estimate the time of Zac and Stevie's arrival, his bare wrist reminding him they took all his devices. *Shit!* He closed his eyes, breathed in deeply and slowly exhaled, trying to release the tension. It was not working. *At least eat to keep your strength.*

He ate eggs and yogurt with dates but took no pleasure in the meal. Even the coffee that normally got his day started remained half-drunk. He finished his plate, figuring it could be a long time before eating again, and walked over to Tessa's table.

"What's your plan for today?" he asked.

"Good morning to you too," she replied.

Darwin did not respond.

"Fathi is already on the mountain with the men hired to dig out the cliff. The plan is for them to move enough dirt for us to find the entrance," she said.

"When can I see Eyrún? I won't work unless I know she's safe," he said, feeling his face grow hot.

"Maybe later today. It depends on our progress," she said.

Darwin crossed his arms as if trying to contain his rage.

"Eyrún is safe, with a local family, women only. I may be many things, Darwin, but I abhor men who abuse," she said.

59

Illi's House

Eyrún awoke too hot and pushed off a covering someone had laid across her. All the women of the household slept in the same room, and the combination of noises and heat made for difficulty sleeping. She got up to peer out the window facing the front gate and watched the man sleeping there. He lay stretched out to one side of the opening.

I could get by, but where would I go in the dark? And what if I ran into... She shuddered and pushed away thoughts of the atrocities. She had heard too many horror stories from her uncle who had served with NATO in the Bosnian War. She lay down again and looked at the women around the room. *No, this place can't be like that*, she reasoned, watching Illi asleep next to her. *She seems good natured and unafraid.*

Eyrún smiled at Illi's dream of being an astronaut scientist and tried to fathom her frustration at not being able to pursue it and, in addition, having to marry someone she did not love. *It wasn't so long ago for women in Iceland;* she recalled her grandmother's stories of women's suffrage. *What would I have done?*

A metallic *clank* from the yard startled her awake again. It was light. *Thank God*, she thought and sat up. She had had to pee since before sunrise, but did not want to wander the house by herself. Fortunately, yesterday she had discovered the single tiny bathroom contained a western-style toilet.

"Good morning," said Illi as Eyrún walked through the kitchen toward the toilet. The women sat at a table eating a kind of porridge with dates. A chair was ready for her when she returned.

"Are you hungry?" asked Illi.

"Yes, thank you," said Eyrún and was served a small bowl with the porridge.

Besides Illi and her two younger sisters, were her mother and the older woman who delivered meals at the ecolodge who, Eyrún learned, was Illi's grandmother. Eyrún sensed an awkwardness as each of them looked away when she made eye contact. In addition, they spoke little between themselves, unlike the non-stop conversation the day before.

"Illi, I don't think they like me. Please tell them I am sorry to interrupt their home," said Eyrún.

Illi said something to her mother and translated the reply.

"My mother says you are welcome here and asks if you are comfortable," said Illi.

Eyrún asked Illi how to say, "Yes, thank you," in Siwi and repeated it to Illi's mother, who laughed.

"She said your pronunciation is good," said Illi.

With the ice broken, their conversation opened up only hampered by the need for Illi to act as translator. Her sisters engaged more quickly and one asked Eyrún why she did not wear a head covering like other women. Eyrún explained she wore scarves when it was cold.

She learned that this was the first time any of the women in Illi's family had talked to a European woman. They had seen many tourists but had never engaged in conversation. Illi explained that Eyrún was an important scientist who led a big project in Iceland, showing them pictures of the Northern Atlantic Tube on her mobile.

"Why are you in Siwa?" asked the grandmother.

Perfect opening, thought Eyrún, and considered her words before speaking.

"I am here on holiday with my fiancé. He is a famous explorer who discovered the lava tube in Iceland. He thinks there is a discovery here in Siwa, but he is troubled by the people he is working with," she said, letting Illi translate and watching for reactions.

"What discovery?" asked the grandmother, head cocked in skepticism.

"An ancient tomb made by Alexander the Great."

The grandmother laughed, waving a hand in disbelief.

"My father said people have looked for treasures for many years and found nothing but water. What makes you think there is a treasure?" the grandmother asked.

"He found a diary written by a famous woman named Hypatia of Alexandria. The treasure is not gold, but a great library. My fiancé wants to find it and help Siwa," said Eyrún.

"How?" asked Illi after she translated.

"The people with my fiancé want to take the treasure and leave nothing to Siwa," said Eyrún and watched the mother and grandmother talk.

They're interested, good, thought Eyrún. *Maybe this will change their opinion of me. I just need a distraction to get away.* She looked at a blue garment hanging on a hook by the door and guessed it was the covering worn by the women of Siwa when outdoors. *No one would know who I am.*

Illi looked like she was bursting with more questions, and Eyrún figured she might be a good ally. The mother stood and said it was time to begin chores and hurried the younger girls out of the room. The grandmother followed, but Illi remained listening until she was alone with Eyrún.

"What is this library?" she asked.

"The lost Library of Alexandria," said Eyrún.

"I have read of it. Are you sure it is here?"

"We have good evidence that it is here, but the people with my fiancé want to steal it," said Eyrún, then leaned in and whispered, "will you help me?"

60

Siwa Oasis

"Whoa, this is amazing," said Zac later that morning while looking out the window as Stevie drove them into the Siwa Oasis. He had been deployed in the Afghan and Iraq deserts during his military service with the US Army 3rd Ranger Battalion, but had never seen an oasis like this. Siwa Lake, a five-kilometer long body of water, shimmered in the mid-afternoon sun, and had they not driven across eight-hours of nonstop desert, he would not have believed where they were deep in the Sahara.

"Holy shit. It's one thing to look at satellite maps, but this is fantastic. Well, I mean it would be in other circumstances," said Zac, using a GPS app to locate the sat-phone in Darwin's car.

"It's moved since this morning," he added.

"What moved?" said Stevie.

"Sorry, Darwin's car," he said.

"It's now..." He looked several times between his iPhone and the windscreen. "It's over there, by that big mountain." He pointed across the lake.

"Why would they move it?" asked Stevie, slowing to avoid a donkey cart crossing their path.

"I don't know. Maybe they moved to that other ecolodge like he said yesterday, or was it the day before? Man, I'm so jumbled up. Keep going straight on this road. It goes through the town and joins a road along the south side of the lake."

"What about Eyrún?" asked Stevie.

They supposed Eyrún was moved as it made little sense to leave her separate. They stopped a couple minutes later at the main market in Siwa to get a sense of the oasis. Stevie wrapped a hijab around her hair and Zac pulled on a New York Yankees ball cap and designer sunglasses, playing the part of a rich American tourist.

Walking through the stalls, Zac took stock of the people, their movements, and any police. It was a market like the many he had been through in Arab countries; however, listening to a few men talking, he picked up a different language. *Must be Siwi*, he recalled, reading about the local language in Wikipedia.

Stevie asked a vendor if he spoke English. "No, no," he said, and Zac listened to him continue in Arabic while Stevie shook her head that she did not understand. *Good, they use both languages.*

He and Stevie had agreed to speak only English as part of their disguise. If they appeared ignorant of the local language, then it might be possible to learn something of Darwin's and Eyrún's whereabouts. Stevie purchased two oranges at full price to further the illusion of rich tourists who had no clue about bargaining.

Zac spoke passable Arabic, having learned during his tours of duty. He knew the better part of gathering intelligence was to act intelligent and take an interest in people. His amiable style also helped put people at ease. And he truly enjoyed many of the foods in Afghanistan and Iraq and conversing with the local people on market day.

Stevie had a facility for languages and accents and spoke Arabic fluently. *She'll probably pick up some Siwi while we're here. Or maybe not*, Zac thought, hoping this was a quick in and out job. Back in the car they exchanged what they learned, which was not much.

"Let's check in to the ecolodge. I'm famished," said Stevie.

"Works for me," said Zac. While he had napped in the car, the early morning start did nothing for his jet lag.

They reached the Adrère Amellal ecolodge about twenty minutes later, and Zac thought it resembled the adobe lodges in the old American southwest. Stevie made a face and asked, "Are you sure this is the place?"

Her question was answered when they wheeled their cases into the lobby. Exquisite marble covered the floor and colorful desert tapestries adorned the walls. A large round glass table supported an enormous bouquet featuring of Birds of Paradise and a few real birds flitted about the open airspace. Everything about them moved at a relaxed holiday pace.

"American?" said the clerk when he looked at Zac's passport. "We don't get many Americans of late," he continued in English that suggested a London education.

"Well, my girlfriend says it's safe now. Let's hope she's right," said Zac.

"Yes. It's safe. Especially here, as we are apart from the main oasis. If you go into the desert, we can recommend a very safe tour company. We have drivers who speak English," said the man. "I am Hassan. If I may be of any service during your stay, please call on me or any member of the staff."

"We're hungry. Is it too late for lunch?" asked Stevie.

"Certainly not. You can have tea in the garden. I will send your cases to the room. Please, follow me," said Hassan.

They followed him through a hallway off the lobby that exited onto a walkway covered in palm fronds and ended in a grove. Cicadas quieted as they approached and resumed their racket as they reached a table beside a large fountain. Four streams poured off its top bowl into a larger pool where koi swam beneath lilies. The fish gathered as Stevie looked in.

A woman entered from a side gate carrying a platter with a tea service and various treats ranging from savory to sweet. Zac popped an olive into his mouth, bit down, and extracted the pit placing it in a small dish. “Mmmm. I miss little from my Middle East tours, but I do miss a good olive,” he said, tearing a pita and swiping it through a puddle of olive oil floating in a bowl of hummus.

“OMG,” said Stevie. “Try the dates. I read about them in Cairo. It’s true. I’ve never had one that tasted this good.” She sipped the tea and sucked in through her teeth. “Try the mint tea and date together. I could like this place.”

Zac looked about to see that the staff had retreated out of hearing and said, “Well, yeah, if we're here on holiday. Darwin’s car is here somewhere. I checked in the lobby, and its dot location is on top of us.”

“Where?” she asked.

“Probably parked in the palms,” said Zac.

“Well, we’re tourists on holiday. Let’s finish and go exploring,” said Stevie, taking a piece of date cake that was described as a local delicacy.

Stevie led Zac to the lake where stone benches and woven chairs dotted the shoreline. She probed the water and rolled the mud between her fingers. It smelled of organic decay, like flowers left too long in a vase. *There must be unique species in here.*

Stevie Leroy was French, named after the musician Stevie Nicks by her free-spirited parents who had had an off and on relationship. Her father, a motorcycle loving Australian, and her mother, a flower-child rebel from a wealthy French family had met at a music festival in Provençe where Stevie’s namesake was headlining. She had grown up in the best of both worlds, sometimes in luxury with her grand-parents and other times roaming far-off South America or Asia with her parents.

The wealth had come in handy when she settled into university to pursue a PhD in the microflora that inhabited underground structures. Her love of deep caves had come about when she saw cave paintings as a young teenager. To her, the animals were alive with movement, and she was moved to tears when she discovered a hand stencil. Her small hand fit perfectly atop that of another young person, perhaps her age, but thirty thousand years earlier.

But to her distress, human exploration and discovery also caused the cave paintings to deteriorate and, while she traveled the world solving mysterious organic growth problems in places like Egyptian tombs, her passion was saving the prehistorical art in her native France. A few years ago, she had landed a role as the assistant curator of the Chauvet-Pont d'Arc cave, a beautiful albeit less famous cousin of the Lascaux cave.

She looked up from the handful of mud at half a dozen tall-legged birds standing in the shallows a few meters away. One of them lanced at the water and tipped up its beak with a fish, gulping the wriggling meal. Something startled them, and they ran across the water until their beating wings lifted them in flight. She followed the splash back to Zac, who skipped stones across the flat surface. One long toss had passed close to the birds, and he shrugged when she frowned at him.

"It's beautiful here," she said, rinsing off the mud and shaking her hands dry.

"Indeed," he replied and took her hand as they walked along the shore.

When they had cleared the palm grove surrounding the ecolodge, they looked up at the mountain. The setting sun blinded them from seeing much detail on the cliff face and, after a moment, Zac turned to face Stevie.

"I missed you," he said.

"Me too."

They kissed, tenderly at first, then with more vigor. Zac's hand slid down the back of her jeans and squeezed. Stevie pressed into him, but pulled away when loud voices erupted from the direction of the ecolodge. One voice carried a fury they recognized.

"Enough of this shit. Take me to her or I'm not working."

"It's Darwin," said Stevie. "Is he talking about Eyrún?"

"Sounds like it," said Zac as both he and Stevie looked at Darwin and two other people standing at the edge of the grove. Zac took a step toward them.

"Wait," said Stevie, holding onto his wrist. "We're not supposed to know him."

Zac and Stevie watched them a few moments until the woman with Darwin led him and another man out of view.

"What do you suppose is going on?" asked Stevie as she took Zac's hand and led him away in the opposite direction.

"Hard to tell, but it sounded like Eyrún isn't here, and he's clearly not happy," said Zac.

"Who are these people?"

"I don't know, but I'm more worried about how they're connected to the people in Siwa. This place isn't big, but if the locals are helping, we're screwed," said Zac.

61

Adrère Amellal Ecolodge

Following the argument with Tessa, Darwin stomped off to his room where he yanked off his shirt and threw it at the wall. The heat and frustration were taking a toll, but at least he saw that Zac and Stevie had arrived. He gulped a glass of water and stood under the cool shower. *I need to write a note. Tell them about Eyrún.*

A half-hour later, he walked out of the bath toweling his head and scanning the room for paper. The air from the fan felt cooling and as he walked around the bed to a table that contained a notepad, he saw an envelope on the floor half a meter in from the door. *Ami*, friend, was printed on its front. He picked it up and removed a folded note written in French.

> *I am here. Reply and put the note inside the vase set in the alcove near your room. Do not look for me. I will contact you.*

Must be Stevie. She's the only French friend I can think of. He sat at the table to write a response. *But what if it's one of Tessa's tricks?* His hand paused over the paper. *Screw it. I don't have many options.*

They took Eyrún to a house, some friend of Fathi, the man here with Tessa. They say she is safe as long as I cooperate, but I'm worried. These people are crazy.

We are digging out the tomb entrance behind where you saw us standing today. The back of the mountain looks deserted. Find the exit well. They know it exists, but think it is farther into the grove behind the mountain. I think it's closer. If you can get in, we can surprise them, but we cannot endanger Eyrún. What do you think?

Darwin opened the door, and seeing no one in the corridor, located the vase, and dropped in the envelope.

The next morning, he got up at first light and performed body-weight exercises. During pushups, he saw a larger, fatter envelope on the floor and willed himself to finish the set before opening it. Inside was a handwritten note and the sat-phone that he had stashed in the SUV. *Zac, you thief, but nice work.* He read the note.

Agreed on plan. Focus on task. Eyrún will be okay. Will contact you later today. Power off the phone when not in use.

He put the sat-phone and the note under the mattress, dressed and went for breakfast. The ecolodge was quiet and he took the same table as the day before. Across the dining room, Stevie sat with Zac, who was fiddling with a drone. They looked at each other once as Darwin filled his plate at the buffet but did not acknowledge each other. A quarter hour later, as he mopped up the remains on his plate, Tessa walked over and said, "I've arranged for you to see your fiancèe this afternoon," she said.

"Great. What time?" he asked, trying to sound grateful.

"Early afternoon, when we're done digging," she said and, looking over at Stevie and Zac, added, "I wonder who they are?"

"Tourists, I guess. Let's get going," he said and walked outside beneath the palms toward the mountain where the sun was halfway down its face and would soon reach the diggers. A few minutes later, he reached them, grabbed a shovel, and got lost in moving dirt. The work did not stop him thinking, but at least created a place to put negative energy.

62

The White Mountain

After their breakfast, Stevie drove the Land Cruiser to the back of the mountain and parked at the base of the slope. The air was cooler in the deep shadow cast by the mountain, and they could see a couple buildings on the edge of a palm grove, but no cars or signs of people.

"I heard Tessa say something about seeing Eyrún today," said Stevie.

"Me too, but I purposefully didn't look. How did he take the news?" said Zac.

"He smiled, but I know him. It seemed forced."

"No doubt he's pissed. Pull over there," he directed her to a spot based on GPS coordinates he collected from satellite scans made before leaving California. During that frantic morning after making the flight reservation to Cairo, he used Google Earth to zoom into the White Mountain and study the basic area. The public domain images limited Google's zoom to about a thousand meters, but he recorded the GPS and phoned a friend at a global imaging company.

His startup, Quake Predict, worked closely with a nano-satellite company to develop its plate-tectonic algorithms. While the software was still in the learning phase, they had successfully forecasted a small earthquake in central California. They benefitted from the rapid deployment of the satellites, less than half a meter cubed, which produced three-dimensional models of the Earth's surface in both visible and invisible ranges.

The images now on his iPad showed the palm grove to the western edge of the mountain. His challenge was zooming into the enormous image files over the cellular or sat-phone network as each screen refresh took more than thirty seconds. He climbed onto the roof of the Land Cruiser and braced his feet against the rack.

Stevie followed him and scanned their surroundings. The mountain stood about thirty meters to their right and had the same forty-five-degree slope as its eastern side where Darwin was digging. The surrounding plane was level, but uneven and dotted with pits. The closest dwelling was to their left a couple hundred meters.

"What are we looking for?" she asked, peering at the tablet, and holding on to Zac's waist for balance.

"The remains of the well that Hypatia wrote about, but I'm not sure what it looks like from here," said Zac and asked her to hold the iPad while he made a call on his sat-phone.

"Hey, Malika. Are you ready?" asked Zac, switching on the speaker mode.

"Got everything on screen now," said Malika.

"Great. I've got Stevie with me. You sure it's not too late?" asked Zac.

"No. It's only nine o'clock. Hey Stevie, long time no see," said Malika.

"Hi, Malika. It's so nice to hear your voice again. I hope Zac isn't too much of a pain in the ass," said Stevie.

"Well... you know Zac," said Malika in a tone that sounded like she was rolling her eyes.

"Hey, I'm seriously outnumbered here. Can we get on with this?" said Zac.

Malika had been one of Darwin's teaching assistants at the

University of California Berkeley and had completed her PhD in the field of space archaeology and now worked for a nano satellite company as its chief imaging technologist. "Okay. I see you in the live feed. You're standing on a car," she said.

"You can see us?" said Stevie.

"Yes. Let's get to it. I can't hold the satellites for long," said Malika.

"We're ready," said Stevie.

"The area you're parked on looks empty, but there's an old settlement with maybe three or four dwellings about two hundred meters to your left near the base of the plateau. The images you got before flying to Egypt were rough. I've got higher resolution scans that also penetrate the soil about a dozen meters," said Malika.

"Looks like just a sandy pock-marked plain from here," said Zac.

"Probably looting, but those holes could have been dug anytime in the last millennium," said Malika.

"Shit," said Stevie.

"No, no, we're good. Here's what I need you to do," said Malika.

Stevie and Zac climbed down from the SUV's roof and walked in a diagonal toward the mountain until Malika called for them to stop.

"You're standing atop a stone circle, probably a well. It's surrounded by a wall and has a two-room structure to your left," said Malika.

Zac stayed on the spot while Stevie got a shovel from the Land Cruiser and traced a line in the sand to mark the wall. Malika directed her movements and then had her mark the dwelling.

"There's something else in this," said Malika.

"Really?" asked Stevie.

"It's faint, which means it's at the maximum depth the satellites can penetrate, but there's a wide line running from the well to the mountain," said Malika.

Stevie grabbed a shovel and scraped a trench from the well to the mountain until Malika confirmed it was straight. The last couple meters were difficult as the slope turned up sharply, and she jumped to the side to avoid messing up the line.

"Look, I gotta go. The satellites are committed elsewhere in a couple minutes," said Malika, but before ending the call, promised to upload high-resolution images and a video of their work mapping the structures.

Stevie pocketed the phone and made more detailed markings of the structure's outline while Zac dug a trench from the middle of the well towards one of the walls. She joined him, digging from the opposite direction, and was soon drenched in sweat.

"Ouch!" said Stevie as her shovel rang from striking rock about a meter and a half down.

"Cool," said Zac and waddled across the trench to help her expose the wall.

A few minutes later, the top few bricks of a wall were uncovered, and they made more precise measurements to where the well should be. Within a half hour, they hit the well and exposed both sides of its circular shape.

They climbed out of the trench as the mountain's shadow retreated and the sun baked the oasis. Another typical day in the Sahara. *We're starting earlier tomorrow, for sure*, thought Zac. He remembered Darwin talking about Egyptian archaeologists beginning their days long before sunrise.

"Shouldn't we be doing a proper archaeology site survey? You know, marking this with a grid. Photographing and all that," said Stevie.

"Probably, but we don't have time," said Zac.

Before they finished for the day, they used the drone to photograph the site from the height of the mountain. Later, they would look at the video and compare it to the satellite images from Malika. They packed the drone back in the Land Cruiser and were brushing the sand off their clothes when they noticed a man walking towards them from the buildings on the far side of the plane.

"Uh-oh," said Stevie.

"What are you doing?" asked the man in Arabic.

"You handle this, Zac," said Stevie as the man approached.

"Who gave you permission to dig on my land?" the man

continued in Arabic. Zac shrugged in the universal language of *I don't understand* and tried to defuse the confrontation.

"*As-salāmu 'alayka*, Peace be upon you. Do you speak English?" asked Zac.

"*Wa 'alaykumu s-salām*, and peace be upon you, too. I speak little English," said the man.

"I am Zac from America. This is my friend Stevie," said Zac, gesturing with his palm toward Stevie.

"Moammar," he said, extending a hand and Zac shook it in greeting.

Stevie placed her right hand over her heart and nodded. Moammar did the same and Zac explained they were amateur explorers and showed one of the satellite photos to Moammar, who was curious, but more interested in the drone. He seemed to be asking if the drone could take photos, and Zac nodded to Stevie.

"*Ana 'atahadath alearabia*, I speak Arabic," she said.

After a couple minutes of back and forth, Stevie explained to Zac that Moammar's clan was having a clean water issue with a neighboring family in the westerly part of the oasis. He claimed his neighbors blocked off an ancient canal, and his family's date palms were suffering from not enough clean water flow.

"Can this drone prove the existence of the dried-up canal?" asked Moammar.

"I think so. If it does, can we dig?" asked Zac.

"Maybe," said Moammar, and they followed him to the palm grove.

63

The White Mountain

The sun felt like it had moved closer to the Earth as its energy amplified in the space between the cliff and rocks. Sweat stung Darwin's eyes as it poured off his head and down his face and he finished a second bottle of water. He had heard colleagues complain about Egyptian digs, having to begin work before first light to beat the oppressive heat. *How the hell did the ancients live here? How do people stand it now?*

Fathi stopped the workers, and Darwin trudged back to the ecolodge, where he stripped off his clothes and stood under the shower. A quarter hour and two glasses of water later, he felt somewhat revived. A knock at the door interrupted his shaving, and he wrapped a towel around his middle.

"Who is it?" he asked.

"Tessa. We can go to Eyrún now," she said.

Darwin eased open the door a crack and saw her alone and wearing a hijab.

"I need to get dressed. Give me couple minutes," he said.

Not long afterwards, he sat blindfolded in the back of the Land Rover with Tessa beside him to enforce their no peeking rule.

"If I see your hands even touch your face, we turn around," she said after tying a scarf around his eyes.

He imagined their progress as they drove toward the back of the mountain and the U-turn toward Siwa. The road was smooth for several minutes, then they made a series of turns mainly, he thought, to disorient him. He guessed they moved off the paved surface on one turn as he had to tighten his core to keep from being whipped around like a rag doll. At one point, his head banged the window as the vehicle bucked.

"Shit. Can I at least grab the hand-hold?" he asked. *Where the hell are we? I hope they're not keeping Eyrún in some shit-hole shack.*

"Fine," said Tessa.

The rest of the journey was on the same uneven road, but it was easier to sit while pulling up hard with his right arm and, fortunately, the car stopped a couple minutes later.

"Wait. Fathi will open the door," said Tessa.

Darwin said nothing but strained to discern any recognizable sounds. Children played nearby. A donkey brayed and was answered by a rooster, but there were no sounds of cars or other machinery. The door opened and he sneezed from dust that swirled about on the hot afternoon wind.

"Grab my arm," said Fathi.

He felt with his right hand, seized the offered arm, and stepped to the ground.

"Go slow. Do not speak until I say so," said Fathi.

A minute later, the light dimmed and the air stilled, growing stale as he walked inside a dwelling. A couple voices murmured in a language he did not understand and he felt hands untie the blindfold that dropped away, revealing a narrow drape hung over a doorway.

"Keep your eyes forward," said Fathi, pulling back the drape and pushing him through the opening. "Five minutes," he added, and the drape closed.

"Darwin," said Eyrún, crossing the small room to hug him. He sighed into her, and she tightened her grip like a python.

"Are you al—" he was about to say more when she drew back and kissed him.

"Yes. I'm okay. They're treating me well enough," she said after the kiss and pulled him close to whisper, "There is a girl who speaks English. I think she might help me."

"Are you sure?" he asked.

"Yes. She asked a lot about Iceland. I showed her pictures on her mobile. I think I can convince her to let me email Stevie. Zac can find the location from the email, right?"

"I dunno. Maybe. I saw them at the ecolodge this morning. They also passed me a note," he said.

"What are you doing?" she asked as his hand moved to the front of her jeans. She felt something being pushed into her pocket.

"Shhh," he whispered. "It's my sat-phone. Zac got it back to me. Keep it in your pocket or hide it somewhere. They can use it to find you."

"What about charging?" she asked.

"It should run for at least a day. I shut down all the apps," he said.

"Okay," she said and resumed their conversation at a normal level. "Did you find the tomb?"

"Not yet, but I think we have the right spot. Fathi hired men, and they dig from first light until late morning. I'm guessing we'll find it tomorrow or the day after."

He moved apart to look at her face, searching her eyes.

"Are you sure you feel safe?" he said and leaned to whisper, "I'm sure Zac can get you out of here."

"I'm safe for now. It's only women in the house. There are men outside, but they don't look dangerous. One sleeps most of the time."

"Where?" he asked, as if gathering intelligence on a raid.

"That side," she said, pointing to a window that looked out the opposite side of the yard from where Darwin entered.

Darwin walked to it and squinted against the sunlit yard. A middle-aged man with a pot-belly sat leaning against the wall, head on his chest. The space beyond the gate looked just wide enough for a cart, and another dwelling stood behind a mud finished wall.

"Two minutes," said Tessa through the curtain.

He motioned her to the window away from the curtained door.

"Contact Stevie tomorrow, or whenever you have the chance. We'll work the timing through her. If we don't hear from you by tomorrow night, then we'll know you haven't been successful and we'll work on plan B," he said.

"What's plan B?"

"Dunno. I'm making this up as we go."

Eyrún's eyes widened.

"No, no, don't worry. We'll get you out of here," he said and kissed her as Tessa said time was up and flung open the drape.

"I love you," said Eyrún.

"I love you, too," said Darwin as the blindfold covered his eyes.

Eyrún watched through the small window as they led Darwin across the yard and out the front gate. The large man who had carried her from the first ecolodge stood as Fathi walked past, but said nothing. A car engine started and moved away. She sat against the wall facing the covered doorway and sighed. She did not feel unsafe, but neither did she like being held prisoner.

At that moment, Illi burst in and said, "I saw him, your fiancé. He is cute."

"Yes, he is," said Eyrún thinking, *She's a teenage girl who's seen things on the Internet*, and asked, "Do you like someone? I mean someone besides your fiancé."

Illi glanced at the doorway and scooted closer to Eyrún. She took out her mobile and opened a photo of a boy maybe a couple years older.

"Him?" asked Eyrún.

Illi nodded with a big smile.

"What's his name?"

"Mohammed."

"He's cute, too. Tell me about him," said Eyrún in her best girlfriend voice.

Illi described Mohammed and said he lived on the far side of the oasis. They used WeChat to talk with each other with Mohammed masquerading as a girl, so their parents would not be suspicious. Illi said she hoped she could get permission to marry Mohammed after she went to university, *inshallah*, but her tone suddenly changed.

"It will never happen. My family cannot afford to send me to university, and they arranged my marriage to a cousin," she said, and a tear welled up in one eye.

"Maybe I can help you, with university, anyway," said Eyrún.

"How?" asked Illi, almost levitating.

"Shhh," admonished Eyrún with a finger to her lips. "I have a friend in Iceland who helps girls from countries like Egypt go study at university."

Well, sort of, she thought. A woman she got to know on the last project in the North Atlantic Tube had told her about an organization that worked with young women wanting to break the male-only barrier to higher education. Eyrún explained the organization to Illi and wrapped up by proposing they email.

"I have to think about this," said Illi.

"Okay," said Eyrún

64

Behind the White Mountain

Zac drove the Land Cruiser as Moammar gave directions to his home behind the mountain, and they soon parked beneath palms next to a dwelling where he invited them to sit at a shaded table. "Please, wait here. I will ask my wife to bring us tea."

"What do you think?" asked Stevie.

"He seems like the real deal," said Zac.

A couple minutes later, Moammar returned and, while spreading a map on the table, asked them, "Where did you learn Arabic?"

Zac gave a short account of his military postings and Stevie mentioned living a year in Algeria in addition to traveling throughout the Middle East. They paused while tea was served, and then Stevie continued her explanation of living many places in the world while she studied the microflora that inhabited caves and other underground structures like tombs. Moammar was particularly interested in her work helping to preserve Egypt's heritage.

Zac relaxed as they talked as he knew it was impolite to rush into a conversation. Moammar's daughters brought plates of olives, pita bread and cheese, and he introduced the visitors as from America and France. Stevie exchanged few words with the girls. Zac smiled in greeting but did not speak, knowing that non-family members of the opposite sex had limited interaction in Arab cultures.

Moammar opened the map after his daughters left. The hand-drawn images showed the mountain, the surrounding lakes, and the palm grove where they sat. He traced several straight lines with a finger, explaining how fresh water moved from the main well, about two hundred meters to the south, through the groves and houses. The irrigation canal that reached Moammar's property ended just outside the wall where they sat.

"I own all the land up to the mountain, but I cannot get water there, and the palms died long ago. My grandfather says a hundred years ago, our palms extended to the base of the mountain. Now, the palms here are dying," said Moammar.

Zac now understood and asked questions about the location of the old canal.

"We have looked but cannot find it. The elder says it does not exist, but I do not believe him. He wants the water for his family," said Moammar.

"May I look at the palms?" asked Stevie. "Perhaps I can learn what is killing them."

"Yes, of course. Please," said Moammar.

She walked out the gate to examine the date palms while Zac showed Moammar the satellite images and how the drone could see through vegetation to reveal ground structures. "We call it LIDAR," said Zac.

"What about this?" asked Moammar, pointing to the dwelling outline on the upslope. "My grandfather mentioned ancient family buildings."

"We think it is connected to the mountain, but Stevie must explain. My Arabic is not good enough," said Zac.

Stevie rejoined them, holding a handful of sandy soil and slimy strands of palm roots. Moammar raised his eyebrows. "I think the roots are weak from a fungus that grows in higher salt concentration. Better water would make the palms stronger and resist the growth," she said, going on to say the drainage was also poor due to the rising water table.

"Yes. There are too many wells and no place for the water to drain," said Moammar.

"If we can find the water canal, you could plant palms on the slope. You said it is your land, right?" said Zac.

Moammar smiled. Stevie nodded to Zac as if to say, *This guy could be our ticket to excavating the well.*

Zac and Stevie spent the remainder of the morning flying the drone in a grid pattern across Moammar's land on the westerly side of the mountain and carefully flew several passes over the land owned by the clan leader and his family. They gathered at Moammar's for a sumptuous lunch of chicken stew and a tomato salad. By the time tea and date cakes arrived for dessert, the software that was crunching the video data had worked its magic, and they leaned in around the iPad.

"You have a canal, here," said Stevie, running a finger along a dark line.

"I see nothing but a line," said Moammar.

"The canal is buried, but it is there. Look here," she said and talked Moammar through what the drone revealed. "You see, the LIDAR makes all the vegetation disappear and shows only the ground. You could walk over this old canal and miss it, but the soil is different, filled in or overgrown."

"This data proves your water rights," said Zac.

"But the old man will argue. It could take years," said Moammar.

"Maybe we have another way. Look at the well we found with the satellite," said Stevie, scrolling and zooming in and out to show a series of lines that fanned out from the well on the slope. "You can see an old canal network all across the plane," she finished.

"Do you think this contains water?" he asked.

"I think there's only one way to find out," said Zac. "Do you know men who can dig?"

65

Adrère Amellal Ecolodge

Darwin stayed in the relative cool of his room that afternoon, running through various scenarios to get Eyrún to safety. The morning's heat had sapped his energy, and having seen that Eyrún was in no immediate danger, he felt the knots in his shoulders unwind. His leg muscles twitched resisting sleep, but they lost the battle and he drifted into a dream where he walked into a massive temple complex lined with columns dozens of meters in height.

People shoved and pushed past him as he walked across the flow, their voices loud and angry sounding. Vendors hawked their wares, food offerings for the gods and animals for sacrifice, but the creatures were human-shaped with Egyptian animal-god heads. A Horus-headed creature screeched a hot foul breath, and he dodged its massive beak as he ascended the temple steps.

The crowd noises receded beyond the entrance, and he walked across a wide, mostly empty space toward a black-draped door. He ducked inside and was blinded by a blaze of electric neon hieroglyphs that emitted a cacophony like a Tokyo arcade. "Tombs" beckoned a sign above a door on the right, and he pulled its handle. Instantly, the building shook and chunks of its ceiling crashed down with a massive *boom*. He dove to the side.

He awoke. *What the hell?* He tried to sort out the dream, but was certain the explosion was real. Jumping off the bed, he pulled on his shoes and ran from the room. Two staff members dashed by and he asked what happened.

"The mountain," yelled one of them, but they kept going. He followed them and was soon in the courtyard behind the ecolodge. He stopped behind them and looked up at a dust cloud roiling up the cliff.

"What happened?" asked Darwin.

"The cliff collapsed. Stay here where it is safe. We will secure the ecolodge," said the staffer.

Darwin walked to the lake shore and shaded his eyes against the lowering sun to assess what had happened. *Shit! This was no random cliff collapse. We only started work yesterday.*

The late afternoon breeze carried the dust to the north and, after a few minutes, the cliff was clear. The large boulder near their excavation spot was gone. He walked closer. All around him lay chunks of sharp-edged rock that had been thrown from the explosion. He lowered his hand once in the cliff's shadow and saw a dark spot where the boulder had been. *Could it be?* He moved closer, but still wary of the danger of falling rock.

"I think we found it, Darwin," said Tessa, who had walked up behind him.

"Someone could've been killed. What if the whole cliff came down?" said Darwin, examining the carnage surrounding the slope.

"It's not likely. We're quite a distance from the town, and this cliff has collapsed before," said Tessa.

"Where is Fathi? And where did he get the explosives?" he asked, looking around.

"Fathi got the dynamite from a construction site north of Siwa, and he doesn't want to be seen if any authorities do come," she said.

The manager walked over and cautioned them to stay away from the cliff. He was calm and informed them that the rocks fell from time to time, but was evasive when asked about the last time it happened. The manager left them, and Darwin watched the staff return to their normal duties. No one seemed to care once they determined there was no danger. Tessa started toward the opening when a chunk of the cliff near the opening broke off and shattered on the rocks below. Darwin seized her arm as more dust spilled in their direction.

"I think we need to give this some time to stabilize," he said.

She shrugged off his grip. "I think if anyone comes, they might not let us in there. Are you coming?" she asked, trudging up the slope and holding out a small torch for him.

This is stupid, he thought, but took the torch and picked his way through the debris.

Closer to the opening, they had to choose their footing carefully around the loose rocks. The newly opened cliff formed a tight wedge about twice body width at its bottom that narrowed to less than a hand-width at Darwin's head-height. The air stung his nostrils with the pungent reek of explosives.

Tessa squeezed sideways and ducked into the crack as Darwin looked up at the overhanging cliff now extending two meters beyond the wedge. His body screamed retreat as the images from being trapped in the Iceland lava tube replayed.

Screw it! He squatted and ducked his head to follow her. He shuffled sideways, touching the rock as little as possible. A couple meters in, the walls widened, but there were rough chunks that looked unstable. He jumped at the sound of tumbling rock as Tessa had dislodged a piece that tumbled near his feet.

"Jesus, Tessa. Stop it! This whole place can come down," he yelled.

"Sorry," she said.

"Just move ahead. Don't touch anything."

The floor was strewn with rockfall, and she stepped over the biggest pieces. Darwin moved his torch along the wall, examining it for stability, and turned to see Tessa step through a doorway. Through the opening, he saw colors, red and yellow, animal headed figures, and… *hieroglyphs!*

"*Dio mio, è bellissimo*," came Tessa's voice as she disappeared into a large room.

Darwin followed her through a carved doorway into a space twice his height and double that in width. Tessa stood in the middle of the room shining her light on one wall, mouth hanging open in wonder. Dim light streamed through the opening in the cliff, highlighting the dust stirred by the collapsing rock as he turned his light to the wall. Life-sized figures nearly sprung from the surface, each intricately chiseled into the rock. The shadows cast from the hard lighting added a third-dimension.

Mon Dieu, it's like they're in the room with us, thought Darwin, reaching out to touch the figure of a priest holding a small bowl in one hand and reaching across his body with the other arm. Darwin's finger poised millimeters from an amulet painted around the man's red ochre arm, the colors as fresh as the day the artist applied them over two millennia ago. Slowly, he scanned toward the opening they had just entered, a doorway of cut-blocks a half-meter thick, and breathed a sigh of relief, knowing the room was stronger than the rough-cut opening. But entering and exiting would be precarious.

The opposite wall contained similar carvings with much of the surrounding space covered in hieroglyphs. A light drew his eyes upward as Tessa had illuminated the arched ceiling that depicted the night sky, a midnight blue so intense it looked like velvet. It reminded Darwin of the walls in Sainte Chappelle Paris, where the Louis kings had spared no expense in their private chapel. The artisans here had done no less as the celestial objects in this sky blazed with gold.

A series of lines divided the ceiling into sections, and in the bottom section, a procession of Egyptian deities walked towards the rear of the chamber. The upper sections were filled with stars and symbols. *Zodiac? No, not exactly, but the stars, the symbols, this must be the Egyptian equivalent. But how do we know this is Alexander's tomb?*

He stepped backward to secure his balance from craning his neck upward, and gravel crunched under his shoe. He turned to the far end of the room. The Egyptian motif transitioned as the hieroglyphs ended at two columns that glowed in the torchlight, each one hugging a wall, part in support and part as a divider of merging worlds.

Marble with Corinthian capitals? thought Darwin. *These came here at fantastic expense.* The curling leafy frond pattern that flowed outward from top of each column confirmed their Greek origins, or at least the origin of the artistic style.

"Oh, my God," said Tessa, and he turned to look at what triggered her comment.

A couple meters past the columns another doorway mirrored the one they had come through from the outside. But whereas the front wall blocks were local stone, the rear wall was marble similar to the columns and double the thickness of the front wall. Its lintel stretched in one solid piece between the side walls and was topped by an elaborate shelf. The space above and beyond the shelf was recessed, and Darwin's light settled on what had taken Tessa's breath away.

Sphinxes.

Two massive marble statues perched atop the wall and grinned downward at a spot directly between the columns. The muscles in their lean feline bodies betrayed a ferocity and hunger, and their claws, as large as a grown lion's, menacingly grasped the lintel.

Wings curled upward from each shoulder as if the creatures could drop from their perch in the blink of an eye. But what captured Darwin's attention were the heads. Human female faces adorned the fantastic beasts. Each creature's lips curled upward beneath broad cheek bones that supported large round eyes. Delicate curls flowed under simple curved crowns and spilled in long braids down each shoulder.

But it was the eyes that added a sinister feel to the inhuman appearance. Devoid of any pupil, the empty expression from the ocular cavity belied their deadly purpose. In Greek mythology, sphinxes were merciless guards of sacred spaces. An incorrect answer to their riddle and the ravenous monster ripped you apart.

Darwin shivered as a line from Percy Shelley's poem about Ramses II popped into his head: *Look on my Works, ye Mighty, and despair!*

The sphinxes were beyond any doubt Greek and their presence shouted:

I AM ALEXANDER THE GREAT!

66

I *found it*, thought Tessa as she walked through the doorway beneath the sphinxes, sweeping her light across a corridor that climbed at a steep angle. She could touch the ceiling, which meant it was just over two meters in height, but not quite a full arms' width across. About fifty meters in, she reached a switchback to the left and continued up the corridor.

We found it, said the Hypatia voice.

Tessa pushed the Hypatia voice away as a series of fantasies played, one where she stood at a press conference while someone spoke accolades of her discovery. She took the microphone as cameras clicked away and reporters shouted their questions.

"How did you find it? What will you do now? Tell us about the library?" And, she envisioned traveling the world as the woman who found Alexander's tomb and the lost Library of Alexandria. *Not lost anymore. I found it, and I don't need anyone. Especially not Nahla and her grave robbers.*

The tingling of self-adulation receded as the passage switched back on itself and kept climbing. Her thoughts turned to her most urgent desire: *Alexander's scroll. This is the true treasure here. Not just the tomb in Egypt, but his buried treasure across the ancient world. I need to get it. Once the antiquities authorities arrive, I'll lose access.*

Her legs burned from the uphill walk as she approached another switchback. Looking back, she saw Darwin about half a passageway behind and turned back to navigate the upcoming turn. It was the third since they left the entry chamber, and she stopped in the corner to catch her breath.

"How many turns are there?" she panted, hands on knees as Darwin reached the bend.

"Dunno. Hypatia only described going up to the tomb level," he said, also breathing heavily. "But it's half-past five now, and we only have these tiny torches."

"Let's keep going. We need to scope out the tomb," she said, taking a breath. "Find out what we need to bring in tomorrow."

"Agreed, but if these run out," he said, waving the light, "it's going to be a difficult walk out."

"There's only one way out. A blind man could do it. Let's go," she said, starting up again.

What the hell is driving her? thought Darwin, but he understood her logic. They likely had a limited time to explore before news of the discovery got around.

But I need the antiquities authorities to stop her. This is too great a discovery to sell off to private collectors. He ran through various scenarios. *I can tell Stevie. She'd know how to alert the right archaeologists. Or Richard. Maybe the Vatican has connections to the Coptic Church leaders.*

No. First priority is Eyrún. While relieved she was safe for now, he knew the situation had changed. *They don't need either of us now. I need to get her to the ecolodge, or at least with Zac and Stevie. Then stop this mad woman before she destroys the find of the millennium.*

Walking became easier as the floor had levelled. The corridor ran straight, although too far to see an end point, and Tessa's body blocked most of the view, anyway. She turned to say something, and he saw a black hole in the floor.

"Tessa, stop!" he yelled, pointing at the floor behind her.

She froze as he ran the short distance between them. He stopped next to her, and they looked at a hole that spanned wall-to-wall. A two-meter gap in the floor plunged into a pit maybe ten meters deep. Palm trunks bridged part of the hole, but several had decayed and collapsed into the pit.

"You need to slow down. There are probably other traps in here," he said.

She pushed his arm away and tested the remaining palm trunks with her foot. "They're solid. Look, it was a section of rock that gave way," she said, pointing to a shelf cut in the floor on each side of the pit. The shelf had broken away in the collapsed portion.

"You're mad," he said as she moved to the other side.

"Are you coming or not?" she said, turning down the corridor.

He tested the palm log. It creaked but was solid. He stepped back and watched her light recede in the passageway. He quick-stepped across the bridge and ran after her as his brain played the opening scene in the first *Indiana Jones* movie where his partner had escaped with the treasure only to be riddled with poison darts. A half minute later, Tessa's light disappeared.

He soon reached a framed doorway where he figured Tessa must have gone and entered it. He gasped!

Darwin had thought about the library for years but had never considered what it would look like if ever found. The sheer size of the chamber sucked away his breath as he cast the tiny light about. It struck furniture, shelving, and pillars in a room whose underground size defied belief. It was like one of the giant caverns whose pictures he had seen on the Internet. The ceiling arced overhead six or seven meters and felt larger by curving downward toward the side walls, themselves more than fifteen meters from where he stood.

Above him, artists had painted a perfect nighttime sky with constellations rendered in gold stars and their astrological figures outlining the star patterns. It was executed in the same rich colors as the entry chamber, but with more precision. The sheer amount of dark blue pigment would have kept an ancient factory in production for years. The sky was interrupted by four stout columns, each a meter and a half in diameter. These resembled the columns in the entry room in style except for the capitals which were carved in a simple ringed Doric style and reminded him of the Karnak temple in Luxor.

Except for Tessa's footfalls across the room, there was no sound. Deep inside the mountain, the chamber was so preternaturally quiet he could almost hear his heartbeat. *And there's something else, the light? Yes, that's it.*

Moving his light across the floor, he noticed a radiance. Travertine tiles, like the marble columns, were polished to an eggshell gloss and the reflected light activated the ceiling depending on the concentration from the beam. He looked upward while sweeping the torch and saw his eyes did not deceive him. The gold in the constellations winked and gave life to the night sky. He felt an ache in his jawline and realized he was grinning.

"I see it, too. Isn't this fantastic? Come look at this," said Tessa, moving to the far wall.

He walked across the tiles to wooden racks built into the space and fitted tightly against the sloped ceiling. A quick glance showed the shelves ran the circumference of the chamber broken only by the doorway. He touched the wood. It was smooth, and he peeled off a small piece and sniffed it.

"Cedar," he said. "The Egyptians used cedar, right?"

"Yes, the wood for shipbuilding and resin for mummification, and also." She paused and gently rocked a wooden box from its place on the shelf. Cracking sounds from the ancient joints reverberated in the chamber. "To hold papyrus rolls intact," she finished, now supporting the box with both hands.

Darwin shined his light on the contents.

"Oh my..." Tessa's voice faded as if in reverence.

Perhaps ten tightly rolled scrolls stood on end, each spooled on dark wooden dowels. Darwin's nostrils registered a mixture of wood resin, dust, and ancient straw. Tessa shifted one hand beneath the box and reached into it with the other. Darwin put a hand on hers, holding it back.

"Wait," he said. "I want to see them, too, but we need the right equipment."

"We need to confirm..." she said, resisting his grip, but he held firm.

"I'm serious, Tessa. This is fantastic, but you're an archaeologist, a scientist. This chamber is confirmation enough. What the hell else would be in here. C'mon," he withdrew his hand. "Let's come back tomorrow and do this right."

"You're right," she said and slid the box back. She stood for a moment like she would pull the box out again, and then said, "We need to look at the rest of the space. These lights won't last."

"Agreed," said Darwin. As Tessa turned to go, he looked around the chamber, estimating the number of scrolls. *Must be thousands.*

He exited the chamber and walked farther down the corridor from the entrance until they reached another door a couple dozen meters on the left. This time, Darwin entered first into a smaller chamber, perhaps ten meters square with a flat ceiling.

On first glance, he felt let down after the magnificence of the columned chamber. The ceiling was the same deep night blue as the other chamber, but it had just a few constellations, and its walls depicted a funerary procession of Egyptian gods. He flinched as Tessa's voice broke the silence.

"This must be Alexander's tomb, but where is the sarcophagus?"

"Dunno," he said and looked down at the mosaic tiling laid in the floor. The centimeter square tiles depicted battles alive with men in fighting regalia and horses drawing chariots. Browns, reds, yellows, the ardent hues reminded him of a Delacroix painting, whose use of color and brush strokes portrayed violence and lust. A portrait filled the center of the mosaic.

"That's Alexander," said Tessa.

"How do you know?

She tapped her mobile and brought up pictures of Alexander. "Definitely him," she said, comparing the picture to the mosaic.

"Shit!" said Darwin as his light winked out.

Tessa's light dimmed. She tapped it against her thigh and it, too, went out.

Darwin's head spun in the complete and sudden darkness, causing him to sidestep for balance. One hand bumped into Tessa, followed by a clattering sound that skipped across the chamber. She clutched at his arm, and he grabbed her hand.

"*Cazzo!* My torch!" she yelled and pulled at his grasp.

"Wait," he said, tightening his grip.

"We need the light. It's over there," she said, tugging Darwin's hand toward his left.

"Stop," he said and held firm. "Didn't you say you had a spare battery?"

She relaxed, and a moment later, laughed. "I'm an idiot. It's in my pocket. Help me find the torch. It can't be far," she said.

"Won't the battery fit mine?" said Darwin. He found her hand. She took his torch and he moved the hand to her shoulder to keep them both steady in the disorienting blackness. A small object hit the floor followed by clicking sounds, then her light switched on. He retrieved her torch and pocketed it once it was clear she would keep his. *Control freak,* he thought, but it was followed a second later by *not unlike yourself.*

Tessa stopped in the corridor outside the chamber and shone the light in the direction they had not gone. The beam penetrated a few dozen meters before the darkness swallowed it. "We'll explore that tomorrow," she said and turned right toward the tomb entrance.

"How do you want to do this?" asked Darwin after they had passed the library chamber and the corridor sloped downward.

"What?"

"The exploration. We need more light than small torches, and we need to catalog the space properly beginning with photographs," he said.

"Fathi has a generator and cabling for lights," she said.

He began a mental project plan, beginning with the distance. He started counting paces and made a quick estimate of their steps since passing the library. *Maybe a hundred meters to the switchback...* he glanced down at his stride and calculated each was just under a meter.

They reached the next switchback as his count reached eighty-five, and the corridor leveled out at a count of ninety. When they reached the entry chamber with the sphinxes, Tessa took photos while Darwin calculated the distances. Estimating the eight-five steps to fifty meters, he figured the distance to the library chamber was around two-and-a-half football field lengths.

"Let's go," she said and wedged herself into the crevice to the outside.

Darwin paused, watching her sidestep, leaning backward to avoid the rock like a limbo dancer. *This will be a major challenge. Everything has to come through here.*

67

Adrère Amellal Ecolodge

Darwin and Tessa got back to the ecolodge just before eight PM. During the hike down the slope, his mind raced on what to do next, and he had no doubt Tessa was working on her own plan. They split up when entering the lobby, and Darwin headed for the dining area, hoping to see Stevie and Zac.

"Hey, are you an American?" asked Zac as Darwin lingered with a glass of water.

Perfect, thought Darwin and answered aloud, "No, Corsican, that's French." He walked over to their table and introduced himself, feeling awkward in his pretend role.

"I'm Zac Johnson, and this is my girlfriend Stevie. She's French," said Zac, shaking Darwin's hand. Stevie also shook his hand and introduced herself, "Stevie Leroy. Nice to meet you."

They talked a couple minutes and, noticing they were nearly finished with their dinner, Darwin excused himself, saying in French to Stevie, "Meet me by the lake in thirty minutes."

Tessa left Darwin at the lobby and went to Fathi's room, where she knocked and pushed through when he opened the door.

"We found the tomb! Oh, my God, it's spectacular! All the scrolls are there," she said, and described how they had entered the cliff-face and chambers. After a minute, she stopped and asked, "What's been going on here? Has anyone come about the explosion?"

"I came back an hour ago. No one in the town mentioned hearing anything, and the lodge staff doesn't care. The manager said part of the cliff collapsed and that was it," said Fathi.

"Good," she said.

"Where's Darwin?"

"In his room, but we no longer need him," she said.

"Don't be so sure. We need time, and he could disrupt things if he contacts anyone," he said.

"Who would he call? And, we still have his fiancée."

They argued about what Darwin could do and how to control him, agreeing to use Eyrún's kidnapping to keep him in check.

"What about the tomb? What do we need?" asked Fathi.

Tessa talked him through the distance from the opening to the chambers with the scrolls. Fathi confirmed he had acquired a generator and enough wire to support low-voltage lighting.

"The power goes out here frequently, and my friends keep a large stock of batteries. I have enough to support us for a few days," he said.

"Good. Prepare everything tonight and have men bring it up to the opening tomorrow morning. Do NOT let any of them inside, for any reason," she said.

"Got it. We are you going to do?"

"Get something to eat and get some sleep," she said and left his room.

Get some sleep, right. Like I can sleep after what we just saw, she thought. *I need to get back in there, tonight.*

Darwin waited in the palm's darkness until he saw Zac and Stevie walking hand-in-hand along the lakeshore. He whistled when they got close and stepped momentarily into the moonlight until Stevie recognized him and turned toward the palms.

"Darwin we've got to stop meeting like this," said Stevie.

"Normally, I'd think that was funny," said Darwin.

"Sorry," she said.

"No, no, it's okay. Have you heard from Eyrún? I gave her the sat-phone this afternoon."

"No," said Stevie and checked her iPhone in case she had missed a message.

"What's the tomb like?" asked Zac.

"Amazing. We've heard about the library of Alexandria our whole lives. To be looking at the scrolls, it was... I dunno..." his voice trailed off.

"I hope we get to see it. Give us the layout and what about this Tessa woman? What's she going to do?" asked Zac.

Darwin described the entrance and the walk to the main chambers, including the distances and chamber locations. Zac closed his eyes while listening, and Darwin knew he was mentally mapping the space.

"How dangerous is the opening?" asked Stevie.

"It seems strong enough, but we won't be able to move anything bigger than a person through it. What have you found?"

Zac filled him in on the well location. "It's much closer than we thought. Based on what you told me, if we've found the right well, it's a straight shot into the mountain. Probably a handful of switchbacks to get to the right level, then a few hundred meters down that corridor to the tomb," said Zac.

"If we found the right well? I don't like the sound of that," said Darwin.

"It's the right well, Darwin. The satellite images show a tunnel running straight at the mountain. If only we could get the technology to work deeper underground," said Stevie.

"I got a buddy who's working on that tech. Has to do with correlating the magnetic waves propagating from the Earth's core and the inbound solar—"

"We need to get Eyrún," said Darwin, bringing the conversation back to urgent matters. Zac was brilliant and loved geeking out on new technologies.

"Right... sorry," said Zac.

"I see a dot," said Stevie, looking at the GPS app, "but the map is poor. I can't see exact streets."

"That's okay. Wait for Eyrún to contact you. Don't go looking for her until we know precisely where she is," said Darwin. "And there's something else. Hypatia wrote that she hid a scroll written by Alexander. I'm not sure what he wrote, but its historical value is incalculable. I redacted it from the translation I gave Tessa, and I need to find it before she does. Stevie, do you have any contacts with the Egyptian antiquities authorities?" said Darwin.

"*Oui*, through Philippe. I'll call him tonight," she said.

"Good, we've got to shut these two down, but not before we get Eyrún. Understood?"

"You got it, bro," said Zac.

"We understand, Darwin," said Stevie, reaching up and hugging him. "She's my best friend, and we love you both. Stay strong."

"I'm trying," he said as Zac embraced them both. They held each other a few moments, then agreed to make contact by mid-morning. Darwin stayed in the shadows as Zac and Stevie walked along the grove then back to the water, then he turned back to the ecolodge.

68

Illi's House

Eyrún closed the door on the toilet and turned to lean against the door. She removed the sat-phone from her jeans pocket and swiped down and to search for Stevie's contact info and tapped the message app.

> Stevie, it's Eyrún. I'm using Darwin's sat-phone. Tomorrow, I will escape from here using a tarfottet, the blue burka-like cover the women here wear. Mid-morning, I think. I'll text when I'm outside on my way.
>
> No one will bother a woman in a tarfottet. I'll use Google maps to head to the ecolodge, but it's a long way. Use GPS to locate me.
> I'll try to stay on main roads.
> See you tomorrow. Fingers crossed. Love, Eyrún.

Her heart pounded like she was about to jump off a high-dive. She read the message again, checking that it was clear and, when satisfied, tapped the arrow to send. Now, she really had to pee and sat on the toilet while confirming the message sent.

Pocketing it, she splashed water on her face and fanned it dry. *Please, please, please, let this work out*, she thought, closing her eyes, and breathing deeply in order to look relaxed when she rejoined the women. She walked back to the main room and sat next to Illi, who leaned in against her. Illi had not answered about emailing Stevie, but Eyrún decided earlier that she could not wait. The other women in the room laughed at a TV show.

She glanced at Illi, who was also looking at the TV, and felt her stomach drop. *I'm breaking her confidence. What if her mother finds out she was helping me?* Eyrún had been serious about helping Illi with schooling. *I still will, but how will she feel about my leaving?* Eyrún debated telling Illi she was escaping, but decided against it. *I can't leave my safety in her hands.*

Illi laughed loudly at something, and Eyrún put her head against the wall and closed her eyes. *She's lovely, but I don't trust the adults.* She envisioned the aunt and the men in the yard. *I'll come back and will help, if I can. It's best if she doesn't know anything.* Sometime later, she awoke in darkness and found a blanket pulled over her. Rolling her shoulders to work out a kink, she lay down on her pillow and fell into a deep sleep.

69

The Tomb inside the White Mountain

Late that night, Tessa paused to catch her breath at the tomb entrance. She had spent a fitful few hours in bed, her mind racing through the locations for Alexander's scroll. She knew the librarians in Alexandria had devised a system to catalog the scrolls that included alphabetical ordering but, *Did Hypatia keep them organized? There're thousands of them, and they're fragile.*

This needs a proper excavation, said the Hypatia voice.

I don't have time. She had planned on starting at four, but when sleep would not come, she got up a little before two and, twenty minutes later, stood at the tomb looking over the oasis as the lake rippled in the moon glow and palms fronds flickered the light breeze.

Turning to enter the mountain, her pack caught on the opening, and she slipped it off and held in her left hand as she sidestepped into the crevasse. It got stuck again halfway through the crease, and she tugged. Several rocks broke free, and several small pieces struck her arm. *Shit, shit, shit,* she moved quickly, hoping the rest would not come down. The rocks held and, a few moments later, she emerged into the entry chamber where the sphinxes round eyes seemed to follow her across the room.

"This is mine, bitches," she said, passing beneath their perch and adjusting her headlamp to highlight the ground a couple steps ahead. She planned to find Alexander's scroll, hide it, then catalog and remove the most valuable scrolls for Nahla. *Then I'll part company with her and a wait a year to work on Alexander's scroll.* It was risky, and Tessa hoped there would be other treasure to placate Nahla's greed. *I'll figure it out. I always do.*

The corridor leveled, and she thought about the empty chamber as she approached the library chamber. *Did looters empty it? No, they would have taken the scrolls or, at least, torn them up looking for gold.* She put those thoughts aside as she entered the doorway and moved to the left side shelves. Her first action would be to determine if Hypatia left the scrolls in any order.

She reached for the first box and froze. *What's that?* She heard something and looked behind. The marble floor and columns glowed faintly from the small light she had placed the floor. Shaking it off as nerves, she turned back to the box.

There it is again. Every muscle caught in momentary fright. Her heart pounded. A part of her brain yelled, *run!* But the logical side reasoned her to be still. *Listen. There's nothing here. It's an empty tomb.*

She resumed movement and slid the box from the shelf. The scrolls inside stood vertically in their leather wrappers, and she gingerly lowered it to the ground. A clear scraping noise came from behind like something dragged a foot, and she whipped around.

"Who's there?" she shouted.

She stood and waved the light about the chamber while pushing down a rising fear. Her brothers had teased her for years after she had screamed and clung to her grandfather while watching *The Mummy*, a movie about a legendary female Egyptologist who had remained strong while facing the reanimated corpse of Imhotep, high-priest of Seti the First.

Tessa smiled at the memory, knowing how she had turned that fear into strength as she styled herself after the actress Rachel Weisz who played the fearless archaeologist. She exhaled and refocused on the scrolls, reaching inside the box to slide out the first one.

"Stop," said a voice from behind her.

"Jesus, Darwin," she yelled after recognizing him but still panting from the fright.

Darwin said nothing. He too had not slept, partly because of excitement, and part knowing Tessa would not wait until morning. After talking with Zac and Stevie by the lake, he ate a large meal and gathered supplies to spend the night in the tomb.

"You could have told me you were coming here," she said.

"As well, you could have told me," he said.

"I couldn't sleep," she said flatly, as if an argument was not worth the time.

"Me neither. What are you looking for, Tessa? There's a whole tomb to explore and you want to read scrolls?" he said. *Could she somehow know about Alexander's scroll? Who would tell her? Lupita?*

"We have to know if this is the Library of Alexandria," she said.

"How exactly will you determine that? It's not like anyone has a list. Besides, these are ancient works and should be examined in a controlled environment," he said.

"You do it your way. Someone's bound to notice we're in here, and I plan to know what we've found," she said, turning back to the box.

"Fine," he said. *This is useless. She's a thief, probably just looking for the most valuable scrolls.*

"But I propose we probe as few boxes as possible. These things will crumble if not handled properly, and we still have to get them out. Have you noticed they won't fit through the front entrance?" he said.

"What about the back entry Hypatia described?" she asked.

"We don't even know if it's still there. Let's survey a few boxes to accomplish what you want, then go look at the rest of this place," he said.

"Agreed." she said and turned back to the box on the floor. "Let's see what we have." She removed a couple pairs of cotton acid-free gloves from her pack, slipped them on, and handed a pair to Darwin. She then pulled the first scroll out, placing a hand underneath its bottom for support. Its leather ties crumbled and fell back into the box.

Darwin swept an area of the floor before donning his gloves, and Tessa laid the scroll on the spot. They looked at each other. Tessa put her left fingers on the cover's edge and used her right hand to gently roll it open a few centimeters. The leather made crackling sounds at its first movement in at least seventeen hundred years. Darwin helped hold down the upper left edge that had started to curl, and Tessa shifted her hand to the bottom. Letters emerged, and she paused.

"It's Greek, but not enough to read. Keep going," he said, and she continued unrolling about an arm's length. The papyrus, while fragile, unfurled surprisingly well for its age.

"Looks like the manufacturer used natron in the process to strengthen and preserve the cellulose," she said.

Darwin read the text while Tessa examined the papyrus. "It's Aesop's fairy tales," he said moving a finger over the text while reading aloud. "The works of Aesop as recorded from oral tradition. Androcles and the Lion. The Ant and the Grasshopper. The Boy Who Cried Wolf. And so on. Nothing new, but it could be an early source." he concluded.

"Maybe this means the scrolls with authors beginning with A start here," she said.

"Can't tell from one example."

They re-rolled Aesop's scroll and placed it beside the box. She removed a second scroll, and they repeated the unrolling process.

"Aeschylus. Also, Greek. The scribe conveniently listed the title and the author on this section," said Darwin, describing that some libraries added the equivalent of title pages to both ends of a scroll to ease the job of re-shelving works when the patrons did not rewind the scrolls.

"I'll keep working on this box. You move down a few sections and confirm if it's alphabetical," she said.

He did as she suggested and the first scroll had an author whose name began with C. He watched her a few moments. After confirming another three scrolls authors begin with C, he skipped another few sections where he found Hesiod and Homer. *My God, this is unbelievable...* and he became absorbed in reading their ancient works.

A couple minutes later, the noise of Tessa replacing a box and removing a new one brought him back to the present. He walked back to Tessa and read the latest scroll over her shoulder.

"You're right, this will take days," she said, putting the scroll away and looking at her watch. "I told Fathi to be here early. Let's explore the rest of the tomb before he gets here."

70

After peeking in the empty tomb chamber, Darwin explored the long corridor through the mountain. His powerful LED light penetrated the dark, but the lengthy corridor still swallowed the beam.

"What time is it?" he asked.

"Four twenty-one," she said.

They had spent more time in the library chamber than he thought. He felt a jet-lag heaviness from having slept only a few hours on the hard floor before Tessa's arrival awoke him. *This will catch up to us.* But he knew he had considerable reserves having experienced true survival mode in his time underground in Iceland.

A quarter-hour later, they reached another pit bridged by palm trunks. Five wide trunks about two meters spanned the invisible gap over the hole. Tessa gathered a handful of grit from the floor and tossed it on the trunks. The granules disappeared in the spaces between.

"Doesn't tell us much, but we have to assume it's the same as the trap in front," said Darwin, removing a coil of rope from his back.

"I'll go," said Tessa. "I'm lightest."

Darwin had a momentary vision of letting go of the rope and

letting her fall in the pit. *It would be so easy. Walk away and come back in the morning surprised as everyone else,* he smiled. Unfortunately, Tessa walked easily across. He followed, and despite the ancient palms creaking under his mass, he reached the other side. They continued with Tessa now in the lead and, in a distance that felt like half a football field, the floor sloped downward and reached a series of switchbacks.

"I guess this is the way out," said Tessa, who stopped after the fifth switchback and rubbed the side of one knee.

Darwin moved around her.

"Wait," she said and started up again.

Keep up, bitch, he thought, thankful for his running in addition to the high-intensity training. He picked up the pace and moved through three more switchbacks before the corridor made a right-angle turn in the direction he figured led away from the mountain. The slope eased and, after a minute, the walls widened into what seemed like a small room a few meters square. The path was blocked straight ahead by large rocks that sloped upward to the ceiling, but the floor just before the blockage opened in a pit.

This must be the cave-in Hypatia wrote about... Tessa's footfalls sounded her arrival, and he walked across the chamber, but stopped as the floor dropped precipitously down a steep stairway. He shined his light down and moved sideways so Tessa could see.

"Is that—" she said.

"Yeah. Water," he said, moving the light across a reflective surface nine steps down, then lifted it to illuminate the rubble directly across from them. "And that must be the blockage Hypatia described."

"They dug this?" asked Tessa. "Where did they put the rocks?"

"Dunno. Could be outside. Maybe they dug from the outside inward," he said.

Darwin turned and braced against the walls as he stepped down to the water level. Each step was a full shoe-length in height, but only two-thirds as wide, so a sideways descent gave him better stability. Tessa followed, but he suggested it would be best to go one at a time.

Halfway down, he had a vision of her dropping a rock on his

head. *Shit!* He looked up where she stood in the same position, and his downward foot slipped, causing him to fall back on the steps. His arm shot out against the forward wall, catching his body from tumbling below. *Idiot! Stop thinking about what she might do. Focus.*

"That was graceful," she said.

He made no reply and continued to the step just above the bathtub clear water. He counted seven steps to the bottom and squeezed into a sitting position to shine his light in the corridor's direction under the water, but could only see a couple meters before the ceiling interrupted the view. Looking up and down the staircase, he estimated the water's depth at less two meters. He put a hand in it and touched the underwater step and felt a slight slipperiness, and the water clouded from the disturbance.

"Do you see anything?" she asked.

"No. It angles away. We could look if we had proper diving kit," he said.

"How far to the outside?"

"No way of knowing unless we swim it, and we have no idea if it reaches the outside. You saw how far the wells were from the mountain," he said.

Why would Hypatia dig this? He thought about the space and distances. *If the blockage above is like the front entrance, then we must be near the mountain's backside. Hypatia's people dug below a cliff entrance into the side of a well. But why would the well she described go so far out in the plain? I need to work this out with Zac*; he concluded and climbed out.

Tessa went down to the water as Darwin stood in the chamber and made mental notes about the structure. When Tessa returned, he again led the way in order to keep a consistent stride length to calculate the distance. He started up the corridor from the top step. A few minutes later, Darwin curled a second finger into a fist as he counted two-hundred strides, and another couple of minutes brought him to the first switchback.

He paused to catch his breath and mentally log the distance. *How am I going to do this?* He normally took notes on his iPhone. *Should have brought my notebook.* But, fortunately, the first few section lengths were each within a few paces of each other, but then he realized the distance between the switchbacks did not matter as much as the height gain.

Oh, hell. This is geometry. I sucked at geometry. He looked up and down the slope as he walked. *Wait!* Something caught his eye. He stopped and ran the light along the floor wall. *That's it. The brown layer we saw from the outside.*

A darker brown layer of rock, about a meter thick, cut a near perfect line across the corridor and continued on the wall. He turned and followed the line dividing the different colored rock as the floor angled down. The line on the wall met and continued across the ceiling about ten meters distance. It was as if he had bored through a layered cake.

It's a reference point that runs through the mountain. It's got to happen on the front side, but...there are not as many switchbacks because the entrance is higher on the mountain. We can use it to figure out how deep underground the exit tunnel is in the back, remembering Zac's ability to visualize underground spaces. Tessa rounded the corner below, panting heavily, and he started walking again.

Fathi was in the library chamber when Darwin reached it about a quarter hour later. He had set up a few battery-powered lights, and two men ran a black wire along the corridor. Darwin's stomach growled at the sight of cheese and pita bread laid on a small cloth inside the chamber.

"Where's Tessa?" asked Fathi.

"Back there," said Darwin, moving his head the direction he came. Fathi headed that way, and Darwin cut off a chunk of cheese, and went to his small bag to empty his memory into the notebook.

I need to get this to Zac, he thought, finishing a line drawing of the route through the mountain from the front slope to the water. He wrapped more cheese in a pita and headed toward the front. Along the way, he noticed low voltage lights attached to the wire at ten-meter intervals.

The corridor continued flat until the first switchback where it sloped downward. At forty-three strides, he reached the brown layer and measured its height from his shoe to hip-level. He looked up and down the corridor. *It looks like the same slope as the back.*

He resumed walking and counted the steps to the switchback and found their lengths nearly the same as those on the backside of the tomb. He stopped behind the sphinxes to record everything in his notebook, then continued into the entry chamber. They stacked supplies, including a generator to one side, and he squinted against the daylight pouring through the opening.

"What time is it?" he asked one man.

"Almost seven."

Darwin moved to the entrance, figuring he had about thirty minutes to get his notes to Zac.

71

Illi's House

Eyrún fidgeted with a strand of hair, her fingers looping the ends and letting it unravel. The women of the household were about their chores, and Illi had just left for school. Eyrún tried not to stare at the robe hanging on the wall. *Don't take it. Don't take it,* she repeated, hoping Illi's mother would not be going out today.

All married women in Siwa wore a tarfottet, the traditional head-to-foot body covering, when outside their homes. Its sky-blue outer shell had intricate red embroidering that made it look more like a hooded robe. The inner layer exposed at the front was a royal blue, interspersed with white and red vertical stripes. The voices receded, and Eyrún went to the drape covering the kitchen door and peered into the other room. *Empty!*

She heard chatter from the side window and quick-stepped over to see the women outside, working in the vegetable garden. She went to the opposite window and saw the man at the gate was looking at his mobile, laughing about something. *Now!*

She took the tarfottet off its hook and wrapped it around her shoulders. *No scarf! Never mind, the man won't look.* She pulled the hood around her face and went into the kitchen, pausing to confirm the women were still in the garden. A strong, earthy perfume wrapped around her as tightly as the garment.

She turned and left through the front door and across the small yard, not looking at the man. He said nothing, and Eyrún exited the gate to the left. *Now where? Shit, shit, shit. Just keep going. Get away from the house.*

The road was empty and after passing a couple homes. She turned left on a larger road. She now thought she headed west and, feeling more comfortable, slowed, and looked about. Mud-brick walls lined the dirt road on both sides, punctuated by gates or wider car ports. Palms towered overhead, making it difficult to figure out her direction, but judging by her shadow, she figured it was westerly.

She reached under the tarfottet for the sat-phone in her jeans pocket and texted Stevie.

> Stevie, I escaped and am on a road heading west. I think. No signs, so I don't know its name. I'll keep walking this direction. Text or call me.

She clutched the device in her right hand and regathered the tarfottet around her chin with her left. The dust roiled around her ankles, and the heat built under the garment. *I should have brought water.* She thought of the glass bottles Illi's family used for drinking. The sat-phone rang.

"Stevie!" she answered seeing the caller ID.

"Eyrún, Hi!"

"Oh, my God, Stevie. You can't know how happy I am to hear your voice," she said, and then added, "I don't know where to go."

"Just keep walking. I'm driving toward you in a white Toyota Land Cruiser, not like that'll help as there are dozens of them here. Does the sat-phone have anything like Google Maps?"

"Not that I can tell. Which way should I go?" asked Eyrún.

"I can see your dot on my GPS app, turn right when you can. That will take you towards town. I should be there in less than five minutes. Keep the call open," said Stevie.

"Okay. I'm turning now. See you in a few," said Eyrún and continued walking.

The number of men increased as she moved toward the town center, and she could see the main market ahead and slowed to give Stevie time to reach her. A young woman emerged from a side street near the market. Eyrún kept the same pace when, suddenly, the woman crossed the street and intercepted her path.

"Eyrún, what are you doing?" asked Illi.

Shit! This can't be happening. How does she know it's me?

"You wear my mother's tarfottet. Each one is special. Made only for one woman," said Illi.

"Stevie, Illi found me," she yelled in the sat-phone.

"I'm almost there. I'm turning on that main street now," Stevie's voice came out of the sat-phone.

"Eyrún, why are you doing this? I was going to help you. My mother called me at school. Everyone is out looking for you. Come in here," she said, pulling her into a narrow street.

"Stevie, I'm in a side alley with Illi Do you see a small blue car parked against the wall? I don't know if it's on your right or left," said Eyrún.

Illi tugged on the tarfottet, pleading for Eyrún's attention, who had Stevie talking in one ear and Illi in the other. Her heart raced as she moved to the alley corner to better see the street. She turned to the girl and said, "I'm sorry, Illi. My fiancé is in trouble. I couldn't wait."

"I see the blue car," came Stevie's voice from the speaker. "It's on my right."

"How long before you get to it?"

"Thirty seconds, and there's a large group of women up ahead. I can't tell what they're doing," said Stevie.

"Stop at the back of the blue car. I'll run across as soon as I see you."

"Okay, nearly there."

Illi took her robe off to reveal jeans and a colorful blouse and motioned for Eyrún to do the same. "Take off the tarfottet, Eyrún. They won't bother a western woman. Hurry," she said.

Eyrún unfastened the gown and rolled it up, and Illi stuffed it in her pack just as a white SUV stopped behind the blue car.

"Wait," said Illi, pulling Eyrún back and stepping out herself. "Okay, it's safe. Let's go."

"Illi, you can't go with me," yelled Eyrún as they sprinted across.

"I go with you," she said.

Eyrún glanced left and saw the women pointing at them, and one waved her arms and looked like she was yelling to someone. Stevie's auburn hair shone in the light slanting in the Land Cruiser's windscreen, and she motioned them to hurry. Eyrún pulled open the passenger door behind Stevie. *No time to argue*, she thought and swept Illi into the rear seat as she jumped in behind her.

"Go," shouted Eyrún, pulling the door closed as the vehicle lurched forward, and it threw her against Illi as they U-turned while accelerating. The Land Cruiser shot down the street opposite the women who Eyrún saw receding through the rear window.

"Turn right. Turn right," yelled Illi, and Stevie did so.

A wall loomed before them.

"Illi!" shouted Eyrún.

"It's okay. Go left at the wall. I promise. It's safe," said Illi. Stevie followed a series of rapid turns as Illi shouted instructions. "Slow down now," she said, and the vehicle slowed to normal speed.

"Stevie, this is Illi. Illi, this is my best friend Stevie," said Eyrún when the initial panic had subsided.

"Hi, Illi. *As-salāmu 'alayki.*"

"*Wa 'alaykumu s-salām,* Stevie. You speak Arabic?"

The two of them chatted while Eyrún watched the road out the rear window. *Shit, what are we going to do with her?* In half a kilometer, they reached the main road along the southern side of the oasis and turned toward the White Mountain.

"Won't they know where we are going?" asked Eyrún, worried that someone was watching.

"Zac and I are on the western side of the plateau and have met some locals who can protect us," said Stevie.

Eyrún heard a sniff as if from crying and turned to Illi, who stared at Siwa Lake on their right.

"Illi?" asked Eyrún.

Illi turned, tears streaming down her cheeks. "I'm sorry, Eyrún. I'm sorry," she sobbed, leaning into Eyrún, who embraced the girl and met Stevie's eyes in the rear-view mirror. They exchanged a wide-eyed, perplexed look, before Stevie turned her attention back to a donkey cart on the road.

"I didn't want them to capture you, but now I'm in trouble. My mother..." she burst into tears again.

"It's all right, Illi. Thank you for helping me. I will talk to your mother when this is over," said Eyrún, rubbing Illi's shoulder and looking again behind the Land Cruiser. *But what if the mother is involved?*

They drove in silence until a few minutes later when Stevie turned onto the peninsula with the mountain and pulled over.

"Eyrún?"

"I know," she said, turning to Illi. "We can't take you with us."

72

The Tomb

Darwin reached the top of the slope and grasped a coil of low-voltage wire and a box of lights and fell in behind another man entering the crease. He paused, letting the man get a few steps ahead, and sidestepped his way into the tomb.

Once inside, he found a box containing food, and he shoveled in some olives while wrapping dried meat in a pita. He bit into the makeshift sandwich. *Water!* He looked about and grabbed two bottles before heading deeper into the tomb. He tried to imagine what Tessa had been doing in the time he was out of the tomb as Fathi came toward him in the corridor, just below the first switchback.

"Where did you go?" asked Fathi.

"Toilet. What's Tessa doing?" he asked.

"She's in the library chamber looking for…" said Fathi, abruptly stopping.

"Looking for what?"

"Scrolls. She said she wants to catalog the scrolls," said Fathi.

I knew it. Somehow, she knew. He frowned at Fathi, who had looked away.

"I'm going up there. What're you doing?" asked Darwin.

"Setting up lights," said Fathi.

"Good. We need to work fast. It was quiet at the ecolodge. But this news will spread no matter how much you trust your men," said Darwin, trying to sound like he was on their side of keeping the discovery private.

They parted, and Darwin rounded the two switchbacks, but paused at the pit to study it closer. Three palm trunks still bridged the gap, but their desiccated condition had reduced their holding strength. He stomped lightly on one and it crackled like a dried corn husk. The pit bottom had the remains of two trunks that had fallen in. *By themselves, or had someone else been in here*? he thought but decided it was a rhetorical question as anything removed from the tomb had occurred long ago.

He reached the library, where Tessa meticulously worked her way along the wall of scrolls. He stood in the doorway a few minutes, watching her remove a box, open each scroll to identify its contents and make notes. *Is she estimating the value of each scroll? Like how much it would sell on the black-market.*

Tessa placed a box of scrolls back on the shelf and made notes before she removed the next crate from the shelving.

Where is it? You could not have moved every scroll in the Serapeum, even in six years. You must have chosen the most significant and valuable writings.

Of course, I did, said the Hypatia voice. *It's here. I assure you.*

Where?

Tessa froze when she heard Darwin's voice asking if he could help. She closed her eyes and sighed. *How can we make him go away?* Fathi had suggested the pit with the broken trunks, but she had argued that his body could be examined and forensics would discover any foul play.

"It needs to happen somewhere deeper in the tomb," she had said.

"A cave in," Fathi had replied. "It would be months or years before anyone dug it out. We could say nothing is back there, and they would believe it. The tombs are in the front."

"Yes," she said. "We need to catalog the scrolls. Once the antiquities authorities learn of this discovery, I doubt we'll have any access to them."

"Okay. Where do I start?"

"Over there," she said, explaining how to log each scroll by box number. *God, I'm tired of this fake cooperation.*

They continued working on the scrolls, each occasionally walking around to loosen stiff knees. At one point, about two hours into their work, a light came through the doorway, and they turned to see one man unrolling the black wire into the chamber. He stretched the wire along the floor between the columns while a second man attached low voltage light fixtures. The chamber brightened, and both men studied the ceiling when their work was finished. Tessa barked a command at them, and they left.

"Well, that makes it easier," said Darwin, switching off his headlamp and stretching.

"My God, that's stunning," said Tessa, studying the ceiling.

While the four lights on the wire were only twenty watts each, the reflection off the marble tiles amplified their effect and caused the gold lines and objects in the ceiling to glow evenly. The peaceful moment burst by Fathi who shouted. "Where is he? Eyrún's escaped."

"Stop him," yelled Tessa.

Darwin raced around the column toward the door, but abruptly halted. Fathi had blocked the doorway and levelled a pistol at Darwin's chest.

73

Adrère Amellal Ecolodge

Stevie and Zac discussed the situation and decided that since neither of them knew what Darwin was doing, it made the most sense to take Eyrún and Illi to their room at the ecolodge, especially after Illi related overhearing the men in her yard, who guarded Eyrún. She said the men worried that the digging at the tomb was illegal and Fathi would bring trouble to their families.

Once in the room, Eyrún let Illi text her mother she was safe and, when Illi sent the text, she handed her mobile to Stevie who pocketed the device after switching it off.

"Illi, I need to talk with Stevie in private. I'll be just outside the door," said Eyrún and closed the door after seeing the girl nod. She turned to Stevie and whispered, "What about Darwin? We need to find him, then get out of here."

"As best we can tell, he's in the tomb. Went in last night," said Stevie.

"But they have to come out right? He can't know I've escaped," said Eyrún.

"I'll put a note in his room, telling him you're in here. I'm going to Zac now. Call me if Darwin comes back. We'll drop everything and leave the oasis," said Stevie.

"Okay," said Eyrún and hugged Stevie before going back into the room.

74

The Tomb

"How did she escape?" Tessa asked Fathi, who described what he knew about it.

"The daughter helped Eyrún contact someone who picked them up in town. We don't know where they went. The girl's mobile is turned off," said Fathi.

"She didn't escape on her own. Who's helping her, Darwin?" said Tessa.

"I dunno."

"I don't believe you. What the hell were you doing outside the last hour?" she asked."

"Went to use the toilet in my room, like I said. If I helped her, why would I come back here?"

Fathi raised the gun again and took a step towards Darwin.

"What are you going to do? Shoot me?" he said, heart racing.

"Fathi, leave him be. Darwin, sit there," she said, pointing. "I need to think."

Darwin sat at the wall by the entry and watched Fathi lean against one of the Doric columns, fish a pack of cigarettes from his pocket and light one.

"Don't smoke in here, you idiot," said Tessa, turning toward the pungent smell. "This whole place could go up and its contents are worth more than your sorry life."

Fathi ground out the smoke on the marble.

"Do you people even care about what this place represents?" asked Darwin. "My God, think about it. This is the discovery of a career, no, a lifetime. You want fame? Look around you. Tessa Santarossa found The Library of Alexandria. But no, you want to gut it piece by piece. I got news. You won't get away with it."

"Shut up, Darwin. What do you know about what I want?" she said. "Guess what? You're now the hostage, and you better hope Eyrún wants you back. Tie him up."

Fathi bound Darwin's ankles and wrists with Zip Ties and left him sitting against the wall. He then went back outside to organize the search for Eyrún while Tessa went back to cataloging scrolls. Darwin was left to his own thoughts and a soreness building in his ass from the hard marble. He felt sleep creep up on him and leaned sideways, using his pack as a pillow.

75

Adrère Amellal Ecolodge

Stevie walked the short hallway and turned into the lobby where two people stood with their luggage at the check-in desk. She aimed for the front door, hoping to make it outside unnoticed.

"Mademoiselle Leroy," called the desk manager.

"Yes," said Stevie, wincing and turning toward the desk.

"I have a note for you. The man who left it said it was urgent and to hand it to you personally," said the manager, removing an envelope from his pocket.

"Thanks," she said, taking it from him. "What time did he leave it?

"A few hours ago. He was very insistent that I give it to no one besides you or...the man with you. Then he said he had to get back to the mountain," said the manager, returning his attention to the couple at the desk.

"Thanks again," said Stevie, walking across the lobby and slitting open the envelope with a finger.

We found the tomb. The library's intact! OMG, it's the most fabulous thing I've ever seen. Stevie, as soon as Eyrún contacts you, get her someplace safe. Zac, when Eyrún's safe, come in the tomb to get me. They don't appear to have any weapons but be careful at the opening. It's unstable and could collapse.

Eyrún's our first priority, but we need to shut Tessa & Fathi down somehow. I'll stall them as much as I can, but we need the antiquities authorities to stop the looting. Tell Pierre to hurry.

I've been to the back exit, it's full of water, but it must link to the well on the plain. The diary makes the tunnel section sound short, but I dunno. I listed the distances below using my steps as a guide. Zac, you're good at figuring this out.
We can't let Tessa keep this. It belongs to Egypt, to the World. I'll try to get out again around noon. Hopefully, you got Eyrún by then.

The rest of the note listed distances on a crude side-view sketch of the mountain. She pocketed the note as she heard an angry voice and turned to see Fathi run into the lobby yelling into his mobile.

"Find her. I don't care how. Use the find people app to locate the girl's mobile. They can't have left Siwa," he raged.

Stevie guessed what was coming next and quickly walked out the entrance. Nearing the SUV, she heard Fathi yell, "What woman picked her up? What was she driving?"

She didn't wait to hear more as she hopped in and sped away from the ecolodge toward the back of the mountain. The steering wheel rattled as the Land Cruiser bounced hard on the dirt road, and she glanced between the roadway and the rear-view mirror. *Shit! Don't follow. Don't follow. Eyrún, stay in your room, but what about Darwin? Shit!*

Within two minutes, she reached the other end of the mountain and slowed just enough to steer over the rutted embankment. The vehicle bucked on the uneven surface of the plain, and another glance in the mirror showed a plume of dust.

"Fuck!" she yelled and rounded the mountain's backside and

wheeled up to the men digging out the well. She jumped out as soon as the car stopped.

"Zac! Where's Zac?" she yelled at Moammar. Zac popped his head up from below a rock wall.

"What's up, babe? Where's Eyrún?" he asked, leaping over the rocks.

"She's safe at the ecolodge, but they know she escaped. Darwin's in danger. We've got to get him now!"

76

The Tomb

Darwin awoke to footsteps and a man's shouting, "They located the girl's mobile. It's on the other side of the oasis."

"Show me," said Tessa, and she was reminded there was no signal inside the tomb. "Right. Help me move him to the other chamber. There's nothing for him to disturb in there."

She and the man lifted Darwin under each arm and dragged him to the other chamber where they laid him on top of the mosaic in its center.

"Let me at least have my pack to put my head on," said Darwin.

Tessa nodded, and a minute later, the man returned with the pack. Darwin lifted his head and the man slid it under Darwin's cheek.

"Let's go," yelled Tessa from the corridor.

Darwin struggled to sit up as the footsteps retreated. Fortunately, the low-voltage lighting extended to just outside the chamber. *Eyrún, what are you doing? Where are Zac and Stevie?*

77

Adrère Amellal Ecolodge

Eyrún sat on the edge of the bed nervously tapping her feet on the floor when the mobile finally vibrated.

Stevie: they leave now

Eyrún: text again when you see them pass by the road on the other side of the lake

Stevie: yes

Stevie's iPhone was in Illi's hands, somewhere outside the ecolodge where she could watch the road. *Please keep going.* Eyrún bounced on the mattress and willed Fathi and Tessa to keep driving into the heart of the oasis. Stevie paced the floor across from her when a coded knock at the door meant Zac had returned. Stevie moved the chair and let him in.

"I got to hand to that girl. She'd make a good agent for somebody," he said.

"How'd it go?" asked Stevie.

"Fine. Just like we planned. I left Illi's mobile behind some canned goods in the market stall she described," he said, holding out some snacks he had bought.

Eyrún tore open a bag of crisps. She was always hungry when nervous. "How long do you think?" she said through a mouthful.

"There's your answer," said Stevie as the sat-phone chimed.

Stevie: they passed. I come back now

Zac went to his case and took out a small sack. He withdrew a compact Sig Sauer P320 nine-millimeter pistol from the bag, inspected it, and inserted a loaded magazine.

"Do we have to do this, Zac?" said Eyrún.

"If everything goes to plan, then we won't need it. But it's best if we don't take chances," he said, snapping the magazine in place and checking the safety before sliding it in the back of his waistband.

"I don't like it," she continued to protest as another knock on the door announced Illi's return.

Stevie let her in and helped Eyrún put on the tarfottet while Illi put on her own cover-up.

"Let's go, ladies. We've only got an hour at the most," said Zac.

They left the room with Eyrún and Illi carrying a food basket and the tea canteen. Earlier, Stevie had asked about a desert picnic and had ordered food for six people.

"This is exciting," said Illi.

"Yes, it is, but these are dangerous people. Remember what Zac said. If there is any fighting, you run. If you can't run, then lie down someplace out of the way," said Eyrún as they began walking up the slope.

"Is it true he was in the American Army?" asked Illi.

"Yes. But let's stop talking now. We can't let them hear us speak English," said Eyrún, and Illi nodded.

The slope grew steeper, and Eyrún had to concentrate on her steps. The men by the entrance stood and walked toward them. *Stay calm, stay calm,* thought Eyrún, grateful they could not see her face and kept her head lowered as Illi spoke to the men. Eyrún did not understand, but they had agreed Illi would say someone had ordered food from the ecolodge. If the men asked who, she was to say she did not know; she was only delivering it.

Eyrún's pulse thrummed as she opened the basket and handed some food to the men and glanced up to see Zac and Stevie move across the top of the slope behind the men. *C'mon, c'mon. It's hot as hell under here.* The day's heat radiated from the rock like baker's kitchen.

Suddenly, the men stood, and she heard vehicles. She turned to see three SUVs, two of them with police badging and lighting, race partway up the slope and stop. A man in pressed khaki pants and white shirt got out of the passenger side of the unmarked vehicle and began shouting as the police officers surged out of their cars.

"Illi, I've got to go. Stay with Stevie," said Eyrún as she pulled off the tarfottet and handed it to the girl. She pressed Illi away with the garment as another vehicle's approach attracted her attention. Fathi's white Land Cruiser plowed up the slope behind the police cars. *Oh, fuck!* She turned and ran the short distance to the tomb opening and slipped sideways into the gap.

She pushed in deeper as she heard Zac's voice yelling, "Eyrún, keep going."

"Ouch," she said aloud after whacking her head on one of the rocks hanging down. She rubbed the spot and looked at her hand. *No blood, good.* She rubbed again as she squeezed through to the entry chamber. The crease cast a dim light, and she paused to catch her breath and dig her headlamp out of the small bag Stevie had given her.

The yelling from outside, Zac's voice in particular, told her she was alone for now. *But that can change. Focus. Get to Darwin. Zac and Stevie will sort out whatever's going on out there.*

Switching the light on brought a riot of colors as the hieroglyphs came into view. *Oh, my God,* she paused and looked about the room and took a reflexive step back when the beam hit the sphinxes. *This is beautiful*, she thought, taking a moment to get her bearings, and started on the only inward direction possible.

"Zac," yelled Stevie as Tessa and Fathi had returned from town and ran up the slope.

Zac chose the only option that made sense and wedged himself in the crack. When the police tried to pull him out, Zac grabbed the pistol from his pants and held it out, barrel pointing up. The policemen backed out of the cliff, palms forward in a universal gesture of surrender. *Shit, everything was going to plan. I hate these people. Where's Stevie?*

"Who are they, Stevie?" yelled Zac, after seeing her walk into view.

"Police, but the man is saying he's an Egyptian official from the antiquities authority," she yelled back.

"Get him out of there. This is our find," Tessa raged at the police.

"Where are your permits for this operation?" said the man in the khaki pants.

"He has it," said Tessa, pointing at Fathi.

"This is an illegal dig and a crime against the state of Egypt. Arrest them," the khaki pants man said to the police and walked toward the opening.

Stevie followed him, with Illi close by her side. "Zac, I think he just wants to talk. Don't do anything," she said.

"I'm cool. I just want to make sure Darwin and Eyrún will be safe," said Zac.

"I am Abbas Kamal of the Egyptian Ministry of State for Antiquities. Come out of there," said the man in heavily accented English.

"No, sir. Not until I know my friends inside are safe. Those two behind you kidnapped them," said Zac.

"He's lying. How could we kidnap someone if we are out here?" said Tessa.

"She's lying. The woman who went inside was kept prisoner at my house. I helped her escape to save her fiancé in the mountain," said Illi.

"That's another lie," shouted Tessa as an argument broke out among the five of them. Zac was the only person whose position was clear and backed up by the argument in his right hand.

"Stop it, all of you," shouted Abbas, waving his arms. "You," he pointed to Tessa, "what is in there? I got a phone call from a French archaeologist saying you found Alexander the Great's tomb."

"We don't know what it is," said Tessa.

"She's lying," said Stevie. "She—"

Abbas held up a hand and said to Tessa, "Her friend, Philippe, is a trusted partner of our department. He does not exaggerate. Now, what's so special about this cliff you had to blow it up to get inside?"

Tessa folded her arms and said nothing. Abbas turned to Stevie and nodded for her to speak.

"They found the Library of Alexandria in there," said Stevie, pointing.

Abbas's eyebrows shot upward.

"It's true. I called Pierre, who called you," said Stevie, and she pointed at the crease. "The man being held captive inside was working with her." She nodded at Tessa. "I can't comment on their permits, but I know they found a vast tomb and numerous scrolls."

"Have you seen it?" asked Abbas.

"No," said Stevie.

"I need to see it. Sayed," said Abbas to one policeman, "keep them out here while I go inside." He turned to Stevie and smiled as he asked, "Can you persuade this man to let me pass?"

Stevie talked with Zac a few minutes before he agreed to come out of the opening and let Abbas inside. Zac immediately took up a position blocking the entrance, the gun visible in his crossed arms.

78

The Tomb

Darwin worked himself into a more comfortable sitting position, careful to keep the pack close. He sat almost dead-center on the mosaic. *There's something familiar about this. What is it?* he thought, considering the circular pattern more closely. The first time he and Tessa were in the room, they considered it empty and moved quickly elsewhere.

His hands worked on his primary task of opening his pack to retrieve a pocket-knife. He sorted out the top from bottom of the pack and unzipped it. *Careful*, he chided himself as the zipper pulled a few centimeters. *It won't do to spill the contents over the floor.*

Once open, his fingers worked along the inside of the nylon fabric as he visualized the internal zippered pocket. *Ugh*. His shoulders ached from the backwards pressure, and he let them go slack a moment. His eyes focused on the edge of the mosaic tiles as his muscles eased. *There's a gap!* Instead of grout filling the space between the tiles at the edge of the circle with Alexander's face, there was a distinct gap. *Could this be a cover?* he thought; referring to the mosaic circle.

He knew the evidence was beneath his butt and after a minute, when tingling fingers indicated the return of feeling, and he completed opening the zipper. Reaching into the small pocket, he removed the knife. Running his fingers over its surface, he found the blade, stuck a thumbnail in the notch, and slowly worked it open.

He rested again after testing the sharpness. *Best to not cut myself.* He felt the Zip Tie around his left wrist: tight, but manageable and, ignoring the cramps in his arms, worked the blade under the plastic tie and began to cut.

"Ow! Shit!" he yelled as a sharp pain caused a reflexive jump, and the blade dropped. He checked his wrist. *No blood. Where's the knife?* He did not hear a clattering of metal on stone and figured it must have fallen in the pack. He sorted through a few items and found it a minute later, resting on the nylon.

Easy this time. He started to cut again. At first, it felt like nothing was happening, and after a dozen or so cuts, the stiff material yielded. As the knife edge bit into the plastic, he had to twist his wrists to keep the Zip Tie from binding against the blade. He rested again, but the blade stuck. He wiggled. *Shit, it's almost through.* His shoulder joints blazed.

"Ahh," he yelled, turning his wrists to part the cut in the Zip Tie, then bore down on the knife. The tie broke, springing his hands apart. He collapsed and banged his head on the floor. He winced from the pain and brought his hands around the front of his body, alternately rubbing his shoulder and wrists. After a couple minutes, he bolted upright. *The sarcophagus is below me!*

Eyrún stopped at the pit with the three palm trunks. Nothing was visible farther down the corridor in the dim lights interspersed at ten-meter intervals.

"Darwin!" she yelled. "Dar-win!

Nothing. *Where the hell is he?* She tested the trunks with one foot.

They seem strong enough. She put more weight forward. It *crunched.* She backed off.

"Darwin!"

She backed up and ran at the trunks hitting the edge like a long-jumper and landed on the opposite edge, her momentum carrying her a few strides down the corridor before resuming a normal cadence. In a few more meters she noticed crude sketches emerge on the walls.

This is spectacular. She traced her fingers along a figure before recoiling at the thought of harming an ancient work of art. A few steps more, and she reached the doorway open on the right.

"Oh, my..." she gaped at the library chamber. *It's like... it's...* Her eyes scanned the heavens above, and she felt the same wonder as when she stood in the glow of the Rose Window beneath the vaulted ceiling of Notre Dame. She closed her eyes and sighed.

Opening them again, she saw a box on the floor and some bedding scrunched up against one column. "Darwin?" she called and made a quick loop around the columns. *Where is he?*

"Darwin!" she yelled again in the corridor.

"Eyrún?" came his voice from farther along the corridor.

She ran toward a second opening on the left and nearly collided with Darwin coming out.

"Darwin!" she said, throwing her arms around him.

"Oh, my God, Eyrún... Eyrún," he said as she squeezed him.

After a moment, he pushed her an arm's length away and asked, "How did you... Where did—"

She crushed him in a hug and a moment later; she pulled back, sighed and launched into an explanation of what had happened. She stopped and noticed a large hole in the floor that was lit from below.

He saw her looking and said, "It's Alexander's tomb, well his sarcophagus. I—"

Eyrún put a finger to his lips, then to her ear.

"I said is anybody else in here?" boomed a deep voice.

79

The White Mountain

Abbas had been inside the tomb about a quarter-hour when Fathi made his move. Stevie talked with Illi, telling her everything would be okay, when an arm pulled across her chest and something hard pressed against her neck.

"Get back," yelled Fathi, who stood behind Stevie and pressed a gun into her throat.

Illi screamed and Stevie's hands waved in fright as she watched everyone step away. *Oh, God, oh, God.*

Zac stepped out of the cave.

"Don't," said Fathi, pushing the barrel hard into Stevie.

"Zac, nooo," she screamed.

"Give me the gun, Zac," said Tessa, carefully stepping towards him.

Zac slowly lowered the gun, but just before handing it to Tessa, he ejected the magazine into the dirt and stepped on it. She snatched the empty pistol from Zac and tried to shove him back to retrieve the bullets.

"Stop," yelled Fathi. "We don't need it. Just pocket the gun and get inside."

Tessa went inside the mountain as Fathi backed his way toward the opening, pulling Stevie along. When he got to the crease, he whispered in her ear, "I'm moving the gun, but it's still pointing at you. Any sudden movement would cause me to pull the trigger which would be fatal at this distance."

"I'm not moving," said Stevie, trying to control her shaking hands.

"Zac," said Fathi.

"What?"

"Stay out here. If I see you, then I shoot Eyrún. Understand?"

"Let us go. We mean you no harm," said Zac.

"Do you understand?" said Fathi.

"Yes. You can't get away. This is the only way out and the police will still be here," said Zac.

"Don't be so sure," said Fathi and disappeared inside.

Zac started for the entrance when the head policeman, Sayed, blocked his way and the other policemen motioned for Stevie and Illi to join Zac at the cliff face.

"Oh, fuck," said Zac.

80

The Tomb

"I thought you controlled the police?" Tessa asked Fathi as she jogged up corridor past the sphinxes.

"I do. Why do you think Zac's not right behind us?" said Fathi.

Clever, she thought, but a moment later realized their predicament. *But how're we going to get out of this? The antiquities man will have backup.*

We? I don't think he'll help you, said the Hypatia voice.

Shit, you're right, she thought, watching Fathi stride up the slope, and they reached the second switchback. *He's got people in Siwa who will help him. What can I do? Think.*

Her brain cycled through multiple possibilities, each one dead-ending in the same arrest scenario. She crossed over the pit without thinking and within a minute passed the library chamber to join Fathi at the door to the sarcophagus chamber. He pressed a finger against his lips, and she raised up on tip-toes to quiet her approach and heard Darwin's voice explaining to Abbas what they had found.

"... and I remembered that some tombs built a chamber beneath a false floor," said Darwin.

"Where's Eyrún?" Tessa whispered to Fathi.

"In there. She talked a moment ago," said Fathi, who turned into the chamber, pistol leading his charge. "Stop. Stand against the back wall."

"What?" said Darwin, turning to face them and sidestepping next to Eyrún.

"Where's Zac?" asked Eyrún.

"Arrested. As you will be as soon as we get you out of here," said Tessa.

"You cannot do this!" protested Abbas.

"Already done, old man. Your kind may be back in power in Cairo, but not in the provinces," said Fathi.

Tessa walked to the edge of the meter-wide hole in the floor. Darwin had set a small light on top of a marble sarcophagus which reflected around the space below that was only a meter wider in each direction around the man-sized box.

"What's in it?" she asked.

"I didn't open it," said Darwin.

"It needs proper documentation, photographs, and study," said Abbas.

Tessa pulled out her iPhone and snapped pictures of it, then lowered herself in the hole and took more pictures. "Done," she said and ran her hands around the lid. *Hmm, five centimeters thick and a little more than a meter and a half long.* "Alexander was shorter than average height, right?" Before anyone could answer, she swiftly grabbed a corner of marble and spun it open.

"No," yelled Abbas.

"Well, look at that," said Tessa, and she bent into the sarcophagus.

Fathi moved in front of the door as Darwin, Eyrún, and Abbas stepped forward from the back wall to look in the hole.

"No Alexander, but I wonder why someone would bury a scroll?" she said, standing upright and reverently holding a leather tube in her two hands.

A half hour later, Tessa prodded Eyrún to keep walking when she paused at the pit. Darwin took Eyrún's hand from the other side and helped her across, then turned away to let Tessa find her own way over.

"Catch up to Fathi," she waved Zac's pistol at them.

It has a nice feel to it; she thought as she followed Darwin and Eyrún out of the tomb. She remembered it was in her pocket as Fathi got them ready to leave the sarcophagus chamber. One hand cradled the leather-bound scroll, and the other carried the empty Sig Sauer.

She had to keep herself from laughing as Eyrún was mortally afraid of a gun that, without bullets, was as dangerous as a rock. *Maybe I'll carry it with me around Rome.* She started thinking of her escape plan once they got out of the tomb.

She knew more of Abbas's people would arrive and seize the discovery, but Alexander's scroll would more than compensate for losing the tomb and library. Darwin and his group would be arrested by Fathi's corrupt police and held for at least a day before somebody figured out what had happened. *By then, I'll be out of Egypt. It's only late afternoon now. I can make it to Cairo tonight and be on an early flight tomorrow morning,* knowing she had both her Ukrainian and German identities in her case at the ecolodge.

Fathi walked ahead with Abbas, and they stopped just outside the entry chamber with the sphinxes, where Tessa reviewed how they would leave. "Abbas, you're out first. Fathi will be right behind you. Darwin, you follow Fathi, then Eyrún. I'll come out last. Once we're out and away, we let you go," she said.

"You mean to be arrested by Fathi's buddies," growled Darwin.

"A misunderstanding that will be sorted out tomorrow. And, guess what, you and Eyrún get to go home like you want, and Mr. Abbas here gets his library," she said.

Darwin glowered.

"Move," she waved the gun at him.

81

The White Mountain

One of the policeman standing outside the tomb opening said, "Someone's coming."

Stevie looked up from the cliff base, where another officer had made her sit next to Zac.

"Don't shoot. Don't shoot," came the voice of Abbas from the crevice and the policeman backed up to give them space to come out.

Zac moved in a flash, sweeping the legs from the policeman closest to them. Then he pivoted to the officer in front of the cave who went down hard with an elbow to the temple. Zac disarmed him and lunged for the cave, pulling Abbas by the arm and throwing him clear of the opening.

He folded against the rock as Fathi aimed his weapon, but Zac pushed Fathi's arm upward, discharging the gun into the cliff. He raised the police pistol to shoot Fathi but was struck by falling rocks. "Zac, get out of there," yelled Stevie.

He spun away, and Fathi disappeared behind a hail of rocks and dirt. Stevie screamed and covered her face as rocks bounced out of the opening. She turned away as a dust cloud spread across the cliff face. Sand hissed against her clothing with the force of a water spray.

A minute later, breathing through her shirt collar, she carefully opened her eyes. Dusty, but she could see. Illi next to her was covered in dirt except for her face. *Zac!* The last she saw him it looked like half the mountain was falling on his head.

"Zac!" she called, running to his prostrate figure, legs half-buried in gravel and sand. She knelt next to him as he moved his head and pushed up with his hands.

"Hold still. You're hurt," she said, looking at a dark muddy spot on the back of his head.

"I'm okay," he said, pushing up on hands and knees, the dirt pouring off his backside.

Stevie examined the wound which appeared to be clotting. "Look at me," she told Zac as he sat back. She studied his eyes, looking for signs of a concussion. "How do you feel? Can you see me?"

"Like someone hit me in the head, and you look beautiful, babe," said Zac.

She helped Zac to his feet, and they turned to look at the mountain.

"Dammit!" said Zac and made his way to the opening now behind a one-meter pile of sand and gravel. The crease was jammed full of rock. He inspected it closer, but stepping on the pile caused rocks to tumble out with a coarse grinding sound. He jumped back.

82

The Tomb

Darwin coughed violently. Each breath seemed to suck in more dust than it expelled. He pulled the neckband of his shirt over his mouth and was wracked with another spasm. *Eyrún. Where's Eyrún?* He knew she got back in the chamber as he had pushed her on his way in, but something large hit him in the back, and the lights went out. He supposed he was in the middle of the chamber, but it was pitch black. *Coughing. Eyrún's coughing!*

"Eyrún!" he yelled

"Over h—" she sputtered.

He crawled toward her voice, and she switched on a light as Darwin closed the gap. She was covered in pale dust, and the marble floor between them was scattered with small rubble.

"Are you okay?" he asked, looking her over.

"Yes," she said, sitting back on her heels. They checked each other for injuries and found nothing beyond scrapes and sore spots that would later bruise.

"What did you do Darwin?" came Tessa's voice from across the chamber.

Eyrún moved the light, and they saw Tessa sitting against the wall. Darwin ignored her for the moment and turned toward the front of the chamber where the collapse had occurred. Fathi lay face down, his legs covered in rubble. The air danced with particles of dust but was clearing as the heavier bits settled. In his periphery, he saw Eyrún scamper towards something, stand up, and walk toward Tessa.

"Eyrún, don't," said Darwin when he saw her holding the gun that Tessa had lost.

"I'm not. I'm just keeping her away from us," said Eyrún.

Tessa laughed. "It's not loaded. I took it from Zac, but not before he dumped the bullets out. You were afraid of an empty gun," she said, speaking to Eyrún like she was a child.

Eyrún screamed and hurled the pistol. It's metal flickering in the faint light as it arced across the chamber. Tessa twisted, but it struck her temple, and she slumped.

"Oh, my God," said Eyrún as both she and Darwin crossed the room. Blood poured from the cut in Tessa's head, not deep, but deep enough. Eyrún tore a piece of Tessa's blouse and pressed it against the wound. "Get a cloth or something from those boxes."

Darwin found a packet of cotton gloves and tossed them to Eyrún, who pressed it on the wound. Tessa moved and grunted. He then rummaged in the boxes for batteries, water bottles and food. Near the bottom he found a bag with Zip Ties and smiled. *Let's see how you like it.*

He secured Tessa's ankles and wrists and walked over to Fathi, who had not moved. He looked around for Fathi's gun and, when he could not find it, scanned the tomb. A wave of relief passed through him, seeing the tomb was unscathed aside from a debris shower.

Turning back to Fathi, he checked for a pulse, *nothing*. He stood and noticed the leather roll containing Alexander's scroll against the tomb wall. *It survived!* He picked it up and cradled it under one arm.

"Fathi?" asked Eyrún.

"He's dead."

"Let's go," she said, walking to the doorway under the sphinxes.

"Wait. We can't be cruel. That's not who we are," said Darwin, insisting on leaving a water bottle within reach. He tied a makeshift bandage on Tessa's wound, and then they left.

83

The White Mountain

"What are you doing? We have to get Darwin," yelled Zac, backing away from the tomb opening..

"Get away," said Sayed, the policeman who had a pistol drawn and was waving them all to one side.

Stevie said something to him in Arabic, and they engaged in a rapid exchange. "He says we're all under arrest for attempting to kill Fathi," she said.

Abbas now argued with Sayed, and another policeman shoved him backward, driving him to the ground and kicked him.

Suddenly, the sound of vehicles drew their attention. Several pickup trucks and a handful of cars pulled up at the bottom of the slope, and men poured over the sides of the trucks, most of them carrying rifles and shouting angrily.

"Oh, shit," said Stevie, reaching for Illi, but the girl pulled away, yelling, "Baba!" and ran to a big man, who had stepped out of the driver's door of the closest pickup.

"Her father?" said Stevie, grabbing for Zac's hand. They watched Moammar walk around from the passenger side of the same truck.

Sayed lowered his revolver, and the other two police held out their hands as the men with rifles surrounded them.

"These men are not police. They're a local gang Fathi is using," said Moammar.

"How did you find us?" asked Stevie.

"When you drove off, I texted relatives to ask if any knew about a kidnapping. Baseem is a cousin of my wife and suspected something was not right when his daughter left school early without permission. We are a tight community," he said and directed his men to move the corrupt police away.

Zac picked his way back to the crevice and carefully put an eye to a small opening. "Darwin," he yelled. "Darwin!" He loitered another moment and turned away, saying in frustration, "I can't see anything."

"What of this well behind the mountain?" asked Abbas.

Zac summarized what he knew of the diary and its description of an exit. He continued with the satellite confirmation of the ruins behind the mountain and the work at uncovering the ancient property.

"My property," interrupted Moammar.

"Right. It's on Moammar's land and could restore his water," said Zac, glancing at Stevie, who made a small skip-ahead gesture with one hand. "The well also could be the terminus of a rear exit to the tomb structure."

"These are ancient buildings and must be examined carefully," said Abbas.

"With all due respect, sir, those people inside are my friends, and their lives are in danger. We don't have time," said Zac.

Stevie translated for Bassem, who said, "The man, Fathi, inside is a bad man. He deceived my family into kidnapping the woman, Ay..." He paused, looking at Stevie.

"Eyrún," said Stevie.

"What about the other woman?" asked Abbas.

"She's a known antiquities thief. I don't know the details, Darwin does, but she's dangerous," said Stevie and related how Tessa left Darwin in the desert. "There's no predicting what she might do to

Eyrún and Darwin or," she looked directly at Abbas, "the treasure inside."

Abbas turned to look over Siwa Lake and seemed to consider what to do. After a minute, he turned back. "Let's assume they are alive, inshallah, and they will go to the back-exit tunnel. Can we get them out?"

"Yes, sir, I believe we can," said Zac.

"Let's go then. Bassem you can take care of these corrupt police and watch the front of the tomb?" asked Abbas.

Bassem nodded.

"Good. You have a very brave daughter, and you should be proud. She may have saved a priceless Egyptian treasure."

Bassem smiled, and Illi hugged him.

"Move nothing at the front of the tomb. It's too dangerous. I will call in experts from Cairo," said Abbas.

Illi hugged Stevie and apologized for the trouble she caused. "I hope..." she lost her words.

"You are magnificent, Illi. Now stay with your father. Eyrún and I will visit you when this is all over," said Stevie.

Stevie drove the Land Cruiser to the back of the mountain as Zac called Malika to ask for another satellite scan. Now that they had removed two meters of dirt, the satellite ground penetration might reveal more about the underground structure.

"Thanks, Malika. Let me know as soon as you can," he said.

"What did she say?" asked Stevie.

"She thinks they can do it, but it might not be until our nighttime," he said.

"Zac..." she started but choked up. The SUV slowed. He leaned over and put a hand on her arm. He had been thinking the same thing. *Did they get back inside the tomb?* One good-sized rock had pelted Fathi's arm as Zac saw him push backward in the crevice, but it was too dark to see Darwin.

"I know Babe. I'm worried, too, but we have to assume they got back in the tomb. As best I could tell, it collapsed from the front. So that would give them time to get to safety," he said.

"But what if they're hurt?"

"We hope it's minor. The best we can do is get in that back door and get them out," he said, and they drove in silence the remaining few minutes following the vehicles with Abbas and Moammar to the ruin.

In the days that Zac, Stevie, and Moammar had been excavating, they mapped out a site about the size of two basketball courts. A rock wall formed a rectangle around a two-room dwelling. They had dug deeper in the enclosed yard and exposed the well which was full of sand.

Abbas followed Zac inside the gate Stevie had marked off to preserve as much of the site as possible. She explained the layout to Abbas as they approached the well.

"Who knows what you have destroyed," said Abbas, shaking his head. "Now, what about the well?"

"We planned to dig out the inside of it today, when we got distracted with the kidnapping," said Stevie.

Show me this underground structure you saw on satellite," said Abbas.

Zac scrolled through photos on his tablet and described how the satellites detected a slight settling of the soil in a straight line between the well and the mountain. "Using multiple nano-satellites gives us a three-dimensional scan for more sensitive views."

"How deep is this?" asked Abbas.

"Five point four-nine meters," said Zac.

Abbas tilted his head in disbelief, and Zac pointed to two drones on a makeshift table under a sunshade.

"LIDAR. These babies are accurate to at least fifteen meters, but my start-up is tweaking the algorithms..." He paused as Stevie put a hand on his arm and continued, "Right. We can talk about that another time.

"This means there's an underground passage from the mountain to the well?" Abbas.

"Yes. Given the description in Hypatia's diary and the physical evidence," said Stevie.

Abbas's mobile rang, and he took the call to coordinate resources coming in from Cairo. A minute later, he looked at them, put a hand over the phone, and said, "Start digging."

Moammar's men began shoveling out the sand, but he pulled Zac and Stevie aside and said, "We have a problem with the water table. It has risen since ancient times. The tunnel will be flooded."

84

The Tomb

At the top of the second switchback, Darwin sat down, saying he needed a brief rest. Eyrún opened a water bottle, and each drank. His leg muscles cramped slightly, and he felt a heaviness spread through his head and chest. He nodded and bumped the wall with his head.

"Darwin?"

He sat forward, pulling his knees up and massaging his temples. "Tired. I'm just tired," he said.

"When did you last sleep?

"Last night... well, a couple hours maybe, and it was on the floor in the library chamber," he said.

"What about your last proper meal?"

"Yesterday?"

She made him eat some cheese and dried meat from the small bag of food. A few minutes later, he felt the caloric energy boost.

"What should we do? Can Zac and Stevie get in here? Do you think they're okay?" she asked.

"One thing at a time," he said. He drank some water and continued, "I'm sure they're okay. I saw Zac dive to the side before the rocks hit Fathi. But I don't think anyone can get in the front entrance, at least not for days, weeks maybe. They'll go to the back exit and start digging. That means we need to figure out what to do from this side."

"What about Tessa?" asked Eyrún, putting the food back in the bag and helping each other up.

"We'll get her out after we get out. It's a long way back and forth across the mountain, and we need to conserve energy, if she suffers, I'm not worrying about it."

They reached the first chamber and collected the cheese and pita bread that had been left there. "I have three waters. How about you?" asked Darwin.

"Four."

"Just under two liters. A day's worth. Another reason to conserve energy," he said as they turned into the corridor towards the back of the mountain.

Eyrún led the way this time and kept a slow, steady pace. Darwin paused at the sarcophagus chamber and thought a moment of putting the scroll back under the marble lid, but decided against it. *The library belongs in Egypt, but the scroll's treasures are buried outside of Egypt where Alexander found them. Best to keep it close until we assess its value.*

They stopped to rest a few times on the switchbacks and, in less than an hour, reached the small chamber at the top of the steps. "What now?" asked Eyrún as they looked down the stairs.

"I'm not sure. Hypatia didn't write about water, but it sounded like that tunnel wasn't long. She wrote she could see light."

"Swim?"

"Perhaps. The drawing I gave Zac and Stevie should give them an idea of how close it is to the mountain. They told me they found a dwelling near to the mountain and would excavate starting today. But it's full of sand. They have to dig it out to get to the tunnel level and hope it goes through. We have to wait."

"How long do you think?"

"Dunno, but they'll be moving fast. I hope," said Darwin.

“Let’s wait here then,” she said and directed them to a spot away from the steps. They ate the rest of the food and drank more water. Darwin leaned his head on her shoulder.

“I’m sorry, Love, for dragging you into this. I had no idea she was so twisted,” he said.

“How could you know?”

“We’ll get out. Zac and Stevie will get through,” he said with a weakening voice. “And then, we’ll go to Mykonos.” A minute later, he drifted off to sleep.

85

The Well behind The White Mountain

The indigo sky faded to black and the stars brightened as darkness settled in the oasis. A small generator growled on the opposite side of the low rock wall and power cords snaked their way to a series of lights around the ruin. Zac descended the ladder after two of Moammar's relatives climbed out of the well and headed to dinner with their families. Stevie stayed up top to pull up the buckets and empty them.

"Less sand Zac," Stevie yelled into the well. "The last bucket was too heavy for me to move. Send them up half-full."

"Got it," he said attaching a bucket to the line. Earlier, Moammar's men had rigged a frame and pulley system over the well. "Ready," he yelled, and the slack tightened as the bucket lifted overhead.

He estimated the well at two meters in diameter as his outstretched arms left a hand-width gap on one side. He studied the amount of exposed rock and estimated they were halfway to the top of the tunnel. *Like I ever wanted to do this again*, he thought, remembering his last assignment with the Army Corps of Engineers in Iraq, and pressed the shovel into loose sand. Most of it ran off the blade as he poured it into the bucket.

An hour later, he and Stevie swapped places and, between dumping buckets, he watched a quarter moon rise and highlight the northern ridge of plateaus. He checked the petrol tank in the generator and topped it up.

"Zac! Zac! Where are you?" he heard Stevie yell as he jumped back over the surrounding wall.

"What, babe?" he said, running to the well.

"The sand is getting wet."

"Really?" He climbed down and found the sand clumping like digging below the sun-baked surface at an ocean beach.

86

The Tomb

Tessa jerked awake. A grunt and the sound of sliding rocks came from her right. "What's that?" she asked the darkness and cocked her head to listen. *Ow.* She winced at a crushing pain in her temple and tried to move her hands.

"What the..." she shouted, realizing her legs were also bound. The last thing she remembered was Eyrún throwing the pistol. "Goddammit!" she yelled, and a moment later, "Fathi, where are you?"

A coughing fit followed another grunt.

"Fathi!"

"What?" came his hoarse reply.

"Get over here and untie me."

A few minutes later, he switched on the light, which she directed him to take from her pocket. "What happened?" he asked, cutting her binds.

"That bitch hit me with something, and they...", she said, jumping to her feet. "Ooo." She squeezed her temples, sucked in a breath, and steadied herself. A minute later, the hieroglyphs stopped spinning, and she circled the chamber.

"What are you doing?" asked Fathi.

"Where is it? Dammit, it's mine," she spat and winced again from the pain. "He took it. Come on."

Fathi did not immediately follow, and she returned to find him surveying the remaining supplies. When they had gathered all they deemed useful, Tessa set out again, with Fathi on her heels. At the first switchback, she finished the bottle Eyrún left. He watched the last of their water with the eyes of a dog whose master ate first. She tossed him the half-empty bottle and continued walking. A few minutes later, she paused after crossing the palm trunk bridge and shined the small light down the corridor.

"You lead," she said, waving Fathi forward. He crept forward leading with his light, but held a knife at the ready in his opposite hand as he had lost the gun.

When they reached the library chamber, Tessa took up a position just inside the door as Fathi moved along the shelving. In less than a minute, he had circumnavigated the room. "Not here," he said, and they moved on to the sarcophagus chamber. It was also empty.

"They must be at the back exit. It's where I'd go," said Tessa as she started down the corridor. *Where did you think you were going, Darwin?* She grinned, fingering Darwin's pocket knife.

"Darwin," said Eyrún, rocking his shoulder. "Darwin."

"Wh—"

She put a hand over his mouth and whispered, "I hear footsteps. Someone's coming."

A moment later, a dim light grew in the corridor, bouncing as it moved closer.

"It's got to be Tessa," he said.

"Maybe someone got through," she said.

"I don't think so. Too much rock."

"How did she get untied?"

"Maybe she had a knife. Did you check her pockets?" she asked.

"No," he said as he stood up and, grasping Eyrún's hand, helped her stand. "Wait until they get close, then shine your beam in her face." He rubbed his arms to ward off the coolness of sleep.

"Shit," Eyrún whispered. "There's two of them. I thought Fathi was dead."

"He had no pulse."

"Pulse can be very weak when someone's in shock. Siggy told me once," she said, referring to her sister who was a medical doctor.

"I should have tied him up, too."

"Nothing we can do about it now," she said.

"We see you, Darwin," yelled Tessa. "There's nowhere to go."

Eyrún turned on the light. Tessa's and Fathi's forms pressed against the wall as if Eyrún had pointed a lethal weapon.

"If you're still here, it means the exit's still blocked," said Tessa and shaded her eyes as she closed the gap between them. A few meters out, she stepped sideways and let Fathi pass, the light glinted off the steel blade he waved about like a divining rod. Darwin and Eyrún pressed against one wall of the small chamber as Tessa and Fathi entered.

"I'll take that," said Tessa, picking up the leather-wrapped scroll on the floor next to Darwin. "Did you read it?"

"No," said Darwin.

"Are your friends outside?"

Eyrún and Darwin said nothing.

"Oh, come now. I've figured it out. They came to the ecolodge posing as lovers to rescue you. And if that didn't work, it was a smart move to call the antiquities authority as a backup, but their mistake was sending only one man. They didn't figure on the local police being on our side. Siwa's a long way from Cairo," said Tessa.

"Zac had another gun," said Eyrún. "I saw him try to shoot Fathi."

Tessa lunged, her forearm pinning Eyrún against the wall and the pocket knife pressing against her neck.

"It was Zac's gun that nearly killed us," Tessa breathed into Eyrún's face.

Darwin moved, but Fathi jumped between them, knife at the ready.

"How does your head feel?" Eyrún said through clenched teeth.

"Tessa!" yelled Fathi, backing up and pushing her off Eyrún. "We need them. She's right, Zac had another gun. And unless the rocks killed him, we can't assume the police are in control."

"Arrgh!" Tessa growled and walked away to look at steps leading down to the water. Fathi moved toward her, looking over his shoulder. Eyrún ran to embrace Darwin.

"Control yourself. We might need them as hostages," said Fathi to Tessa.

"What about the well?"

"My men know about it, and more will come from the oasis to help us get out," he said.

She turned. *He's not as stupid as he seems.* She looked back at the water below. "What if your men are not in control and someone gets in?" she asked.

"That's why we need hostages," he said, nodding towards Darwin and Eyrún.

"Darwin, what do you know about the tunnel exit into the well?" asked Tessa. When he did not answer, she added, "Look, it's not like the four of us can hide from each other in here. If we don't get out in a day or so, we'll all die."

"The well is in a ruined settlement much closer to the mountain but buried under sand. That's why we didn't see anything."

"How long before they dig it out?"

"Dunno. If it was filled to the level of the plane, it could be five to ten meters. How deep do wells go?" he asked rhetorically.

"And then there's the water in the tunnel," said Fathi.

87

The Well

"Zac. They're calling you," said Stevie from the well.

He walked from his resting spot against the rock wall and looked in the well. Moammar and one man had come back after their dinner, but he was saying there was too much water.

"Hang on," said Zac and lowered himself into the well. It was nearing midnight and the buckets had come up with more and more water as the night wore on. Ten centimeters of water now sloshed around the well-bottom. Zac's feet sunk in the water-logged sand, bringing the water to his knees.

"This does not work," said Moammar, showing how a bucket filled mostly with water.

"What about the opening?" asked Zac.

Moammar probed the sand on the mountain side of the well. The staff pushed down with relative ease compared to the side away from the mountain.

"That must be the tunnel which means only the well is full of sand. It must slope into the tunnel, but it should be open past that," said Zac.

"True, but it will still be full of water," Moammar had replied.

"How the hell are we going to get the water out?" Zac asked.

"I know a man with a large pump," said Moammar.

"My friend you are a man of many resources," said Zac slapping him on the shoulder.

Moammar smiled and said, ""But we cannot get the pump until morning."

88

The Tomb

Eyrún and Darwin sat against the front wall where Tessa told them to sit after leading them all back to the library chamber.

"What's she doing?" asked Eyrún, adjusting her ankle that was Zip Tied to Darwin's.

"Reading the scroll, I guess," he said, looking at a glow spilling around the column where Tessa had gone with Alexander's scroll. He then scanned the ceiling, its gold stairs faint in the small light Tessa used. Aside from the occasional insect, he had seen nothing living inside the mountain.

A good thing, he thought, knowing that cellulose in papyrus was food for some life forms. He sipped from one of their two water bottles and handed it to Eyrún. Tessa had divided the water, which left each person a little over one bottle.

"What time do you think it is?" asked Eyrún.

"It was about six when the cave-in happened. I asked Abbas the time when I saw him look at his watch just before we got to the entry. How long was I asleep?"

"I don't know. I cat-napped a little. At least, I remember having a dream."

Darwin factored a couple hours sleep time and approximated how long it would take Tessa and Fathi to traverse the mountain and their long trek back to the chamber.

"Could be anywhere from four to eight, but that seems long, so let's say five or six hours. That would make it before midnight," he said.

"Will they dig in the dark?" she asked.

"I would, and knowing Zac, he will."

Eyrún looked at the ceiling and said, "I've had to dig in Iceland, but the soil was volcanic mud and rock. If it's just sand, they could probably move a meter an hour. You think?"

"It's plausible," he said.

"What do you suppose they know," she said, nodding toward Fathi, who sat against a pillar, head bobbing against sleep.

"Dunno."

"We could fight them," she said.

"They've got knives! We can't risk it. What you did with Tessa was stupid. What if she cut you? Any injury here could be fatal," he said, focusing on her face.

"Shh, they can hear you," she said, pointing toward Tessa. "I don't know why I did it. Maybe because she left you in the desert."

"I know," he said and put a hand to her cheek, "but there's no treasure in the world more important to me than you."

Her eyes welled up and a tear spilled down one cheek. Darwin wiped it away with the back of his hand and leaned in to kiss her. After a moment, he said, "Let's get some rest. We'll need it later."

On the other side of the chamber, Tessa concentrated on the scroll. *My god, this is everything I dreamed of*, she thought.

It's why I hid it for us, said the Hypatia voice.

I don't need you anymore.

You're not out of here yet, said the Hypatia voice.

Tessa ignored the voice away as she became mesmerized by Alexander's descriptions of conquests and the treasures he described. She inhaled sharply at one passage.

> *We move to Egypt soon and cannot carry gold. While the army took its revenge on the insolent city of Tyre, I used the distraction to bury the 20,000 Talent bribe sent by Darius in an unmarked tomb beneath the temple of Heracles. My personal guards killed the slaves who transported it.*

She squinted at Alexander's hand-drawn map, but Darwin's rising voice on the other side of the chamber distracted her. She stood and looked around the pillar and saw the pair still against the wall.

Where's Fathi? She stepped out and saw his legs stretch outward from the base of the pillar nearer the door. Their voices lowered, and she stretched before returning to the scroll.

Hours later, Tessa's light dimmed, its batteries running out. She retrieved more batteries from a box near Fathi and noticing Eyrún and Darwin were asleep, motioned him to follow her into the corridor.

"It's been three hours," she said, looking at her watch. "We should check the exit again."

"I'll go. I need to stay awake," he said.

"Come back in no more than an hour. Take extra batteries," she said, remembering her light and rubbing her sore knees while Fathi disappeared down the corridor. She stretched, and a thought burst in her head.

How will you get the scroll through the water? asked the Hypatia voice.

Shit! She flinched at the shock of the realization. She had no answer and ran on tiptoes back to the scroll. *What can I do? Write it all down?* She felt for the notepad and, feeling another object, tipped her head back. "Stupid," she said aloud and withdrew her mobile from behind the notepad.

For the next half hour, she snapped photos with and without the flash, then zoomed into each one to ensure readability. Once satisfied, she re-rolled the scroll. *I need to hide it.* She looked at the shelving. *I'll swap it with one of those.*

They won't let you back in, said the Hypatia voice. *Hide it, yes, but put it someplace where no one else will look.*

But I need a decoy or Darwin will suspect something. She thought a moment, and then grinned. *The boy who cried wolf. Perfect.* He walked to the box that contained the Aesop fairy tale scroll, removed it, and rolled it in the leather that had bound the Alexander scroll. *Now, where to hide this*, she thought, palming the re-wrapped treasure scroll.

89

Adrère Amellal Ecolodge

The sound of running water brought Stevie out of a deep slumber and disoriented her as the shapes of their room at the ecolodge resolved. A sharp line of yellow light sliced from beneath the bathroom door where Zac was showering. They had gone back to the ecolodge about midnight to get some sleep.

She stretched her arms overhead as her shoulders and lower back protested. Her neck down through her shoulder blades nearly refused to move. She rolled over onto her knees and slid her arms forward in a prayer stretch. The water in the bath shut off and, a minute later, the ache in her neck eased. She was about to get up when the bath door opened.

"Now, there's a view," said Zac, sliding on the bed next to her and massaging her neck and shoulders.

"What time is it?" she asked.

"Four thirty."

"Right there. No, down a little. Ah, yes, under there," she sighed as Zac dug his thumbs under the wings of her scapulas.

A few minutes later, she was in the shower, letting the water scald her back muscles as she scrubbed sand from her hair. *Ugh, it's everywhere.* She swished out her mouth again, remembering a face-full she got from a random hot gust off the desert.

When she stepped out of the bath, Zac's face glowed in the blue light of his mobile. Shaking out her jeans before putting them back on, she asked him, "Anything from Malika?"

"Nothing new from the satellite pass, although she mentioned the new debris field at the front of the mountain is visible. She also confirmed the water table is higher, maybe two to three meters, but data going back to more than a hundred years are just estimates," he said.

"What about Eyrún and Darwin?" she said, head slumping as she laced her boots.

Zac crossed the room and put an arm around her. "I'm worried, too, but they're tough. We're getting in the tunnel today. C'mon, let's get some food. Moammar said he could get the pump early," he said.

90

The Tomb

Thirty minutes after deciding where to hide the Alexander scroll, Tessa met Fathi in the corridor outside the sarcophagus chamber.

"The water's moving," he said, explaining how its surface undulated like the passing of a swell. "The surface stilled after a couple minutes, but left wet marks around the bottom step."

"Did you see anything? Lights?"

"Nothing. No light. I flashed my light as a signal, but nothing came back," said Fathi.

"It's almost five, and sunrise is half-past. We need to make the first move. Keep them on their back foot," she said.

"I can swim out."

"No. We need hostages to get away. We send Darwin out and hold Eyrún hostage. He tells them we get safe passage or something happens to Eyrún. He comes back. We go out," she said.

"That's not exactly solid. What if they capture us and go in to rescue them?"

"We'll work on it, but let's get them down to the exit first," she said, and they entered the chamber to wake up, Darwin and Eyrún. She tapped on their feet with her boot. "Let's go."

"What time is it?" asked Eyrún, snapping awake.

"Five oh three," answered Tessa.

Darwin stood and rubbed the small of his back. He took a large gulp of water from the bottle and handed it to Eyrún. She drank and handed it back.

"I've had enough. You drink it," he lied, and she finished the bottle.

"Let's go," said Tessa as she led the way out. Darwin followed Eyrún, with Fathi bringing up the rear.

A few minutes into the walk, Darwin's stomach growled, and he rubbed his midsection. They had eaten the last of the food hours ago. He motioned for Eyrún to slow down and, when Tessa was out of hearing, he looked back to confirm Fathi could not hear them.

"We need some kind of plan," he said, not having any in mind, but felt the urge to at least talk about it.

"I think it depends on getting the well open and how long that tunnel is. Could we swim it?" she asked.

"Dunno," said Darwin thinking about the last time he had to hold his breath for a lengthy swim. He was nineteen and trapped in a sea cave with a buddy on Corsica. The tide had shifted faster than they had planned for and closed the narrow air gap in the entrance.

He recalled it was something like twenty meters, but they also had to deal with the forces from the waves. It took a few tries to figure out how to swim with the outgoing flow and, even then, he had felt on the edge of blackout when he emerged in the open ocean. He shuddered at the memory.

"What?"

He told her about the incident in Corsica.

"I never swam much outside of a few resorts where the water was warm," she said.

Good to know, he thought, remembering the fear factor. *It's one thing to hold your breath across a swimming pool, but totally different when you can't pop up to breathe if you panic.*

"What did you think of Tessa as a fighter?" he asked. "I mean, was she strong? Did she seem to know what she was doing?"

"She's strong, but I couldn't tell much from that moment," she said.

"I can take Fathi. We fought once before getting in the tomb."

"But the knife?"

"I can get it from him. Be ready," he said.

She took his hand and squeezed it before separating. They had reached the palm trunks over the pit and crossed separately. Darwin felt one trunk sag and crack as he reached its opposite edge. He walked a few steps farther and stopped to wait for Fathi.

One trunk split and went down as Fathi stepped on it. He fell with it but rolled onto the remaining trunks as the broken pieces dropped. Darwin rushed in, but Fathi sprung to his knees, knife up. Darwin froze, and Fathi grinned as if to say, "Nice try."

"What happened," yelled Tessa.

"One of the trunks fell. Too bad Fathi survived," yelled Darwin as he turned to catch up with Eyrún.

"Fathi?" called Tessa.

"I'm fine. Keep going," he said.

"Damn, that was so close," said Eyrún.

"Yeah, unfortunately, he'll be more alert now, but I could see he's weak. His body was shaking. He got hit hard in the cave-in."

They rounded the first switchback and saw Tessa was almost at the next turn ahead of them.

"I could distract him," said Eyrún, "then you disarm him."

"When we're in the lower chamber, and Tessa's apart from him. I'll watch for your move," he said.

91

The Well

The night sky had given way to a pale blue horizon when they arrived at the ruin. Two cars were already parked nearby, and a small group of men listened to another man, who pointed around the site.

"*As-salāmu 'alaikumā,*" said Zac, greeting the men.

"*Wa 'alaykumu s-salām,*" said Moammar's brother, Tariq, whom they had met yesterday.

Stevie who had pulled a scarf around her neck against the cool morning air translated the conversation. Moammar had spread the news about a well and the men knew there was an urgency to excavate because of people trapped in the underground.

Tariq directed them into the well, and Zac watched from the edge as one man sunk up to his knees before the wet sand supported his weight. They fumbled awkwardly with the buckets, pushing them down to the sand with their feet, but hardly getting half a bucket-full.

"What about the pump? Moammar?" Zac asked Tariq.

"He is coming," said Tariq, but he admitted he did not know when as the pump was at a job on the far side of the oasis.

Zac asked one guy to come out so he could climb in for a closer look. *Looks close to five meters*, he guessed while sliding down the rope. He knelt and dug down about half an arm's length, then walked his fingers down the rock wall. Just as his face neared the water, he felt a gap in the rocks. *Yes!*

"I found the opening!" he yelled.

92

The Tomb

"The water's moving more than it was before," said Fathi.

"Let me see," said Tessa sliding in next to him at the top step and peered down as Fathi moved back. The water rose and fell as a pressure wave moved in the tunnel, leaving a mark now several centimeters high.

"What time is sunrise," she asked Fathi.

"About now, but it won't be fully bright for an hour on this side of the mountain," he said.

"But they'll be using lights to work? Shining them down the well?" she said, switching off her light and climbing down to the water.

She braced against the walls as she felt for each step. When she reached the eighth step, she sat back. A faint light from the chamber above barely illuminated the stairwell, and no light came from the underwater tunnel.

Someone needs to look in the tunnel, said the Hypatia voice. *You need the element of surprise. Strike them at daybreak.*

Tessa climbed back up to the chamber and found them sitting

against the walls opposite each other. "This is what we'll do," she said, looking at Eyrún, "Darwin swims out and tells them you're a hostage until Fathi and I get away. When he swims back, we swim out and leave. After we're gone, they can come in here and get you."

"You can't be serious," said Eyrún. "How do you know it's even open."

"That's why we're waiting until it's fully light outside. Lover boy here will see the proverbial light at the end of the tunnel."

Eyrún threw her hands up in frustration and took a step toward Tessa. When Tessa leaned back, Eyrún pivoted and shoved Fathi against the wall. Darwin lunged at Fathi's knife hand, slamming it against the wall. Fathi yelped, and the knife clattered to the floor. Both men dove for it, but Darwin was faster and rolled away with the knife.

Eyrún screamed. Darwin turned to see Tessa's arm around Eyrún's neck and the pocket knife held against her cheek.

"Drop it," said Tessa. Darwin hesitated.

"Ahhhh," yelled Eyrún as the blade punctured her skin. He dropped the knife and backed up. Fathi retrieved it, and Tessa shoved Eyrún toward Darwin.

"Let me see," said Darwin, pulling away Eyrún's bloodied hand. He shined a light close as a trickle of blood flowed from a centimeter-long cut on her cheek.

"Is it bad? It hurts," said Eyrún.

"It doesn't look deep. Hold still a moment," he said and used his sleeve to dab away the blood. He spread the cut gently, but it stayed together. "It's just the outer layers of skin, but press this against it." He tore a piece from his shirttail and folded it into a small square and held it to the wound. Eyrún put her fingers on it, and Darwin let go and whispered, "It's all right. I can swim the distance."

"I'm going to kill that bitch," she whispered back.

93

The Well

Zac had scooped a couple dozen buckets of sandy water and created a small opening at the tunnel's top by the time Moammar arrived with the pump. He climbed out and took a cup of tea that was offered.

"Damn, this thing's huge," he said, admiring the pump on the trailer behind Moammar's pickup. He could barely connect his thumbs and middle fingers around intake and output hoses.

"We can use it today, before the man's boss finds out," said Moammar. Earlier, Zac had given him five hundred US dollars to use as a bribe. "My friend said they move three-hundred cubic meters an hour."

Zac read the specifications plate on the trailer's frame and said, "Moammar, your friend doesn't mess around. This puppy can move over eight-hundred meters an hour. Let's get it on."

"I don't think that will translate," said Stevie, and she related a version of Zac's statement to Moammar.

They dropped a flexible intake hose into the well and connected fat aluminum pipes to the output and ran them some distance away from the ruin. One of Moammar's men said something that ignited a debate.

"Something about sand in the pump," said Stevie.

"I get it," said Zac, tapping Moammar on the shoulder.

Stevie translated that Zac had used similar pumps before to clear sand and relayed the technique. A few minutes later, Zac was back in the well. Moammar started the pump, and they ran it at a low speed while Zac used a trowel to stir up the sand. A minute later, Zac let out a whooping sound as he watched the slurry disappear up the heavy rubber hose.

"We're coming, Darwin," he said to the water. *I hope you're still there, buddy.*

94

The Tomb

Darwin and Eyrún huddled against the wall near the upper side of the corridor as they waited for daylight. Tessa paced like a junkyard dog while Fathi sat resting and playing a game, balancing the knife on his fingers. A minute later, he stood and asked Tessa, "How do we prevent them from holding us when we get out and then coming in here to rescue them?"

"Hopefully, your police friends are out there, and it won't be an issue, but if not, Darwin tells them we've rigged a trap. That will get them to hurry in here, and we get away in the chaos," she said.

"What kind of trap?"

"It doesn't matter. Darwin won't know, and they won't risk their friends.

"I don't like it," he said.

"You got any better ideas?

"I'm scared," said Eyrún, leaning her head into Darwin's. "Do you think Zac is out there?"

"I wouldn't be going if I didn't think Zac was on the other side but, yes, I'm scared, too," he said and turned toward her. "How's your face?"

"It's not throbbing anymore."

"Good, it'll heal, and you won't notice it," he said.

"Let's go, Darwin," said Tessa.

He got up and hugged Eyrún. "I love you. If it's blocked, I come right back."

"You got the message, right?" said Tessa.

Fuck off, I'm not stupid, he thought, but said, "Yeah, I got it. We're hostages until you two get away."

He tested the light, took off his shoes and pants, but left his shirt on against the chill and socks to protect his feet. Eyrún sat down, pulled her knees up, and lowered her head on crossed arms. She told him earlier she could not watch.

Darwin stopped at the lowest step above the water and mentally prepared. *The water will feel cold, but it's not that bad.* The ambient temperature inside the mountain was surprisingly comfortable. He studied the steps and space below the water's surface. *I'll go in easy to not stir up the silt, then look up the tunnel. Then come up, hyperventilate four breaths, drop under, and push off. Relax. The key is to relax.*

He sucked in a breath as the chilled water rose above his socks. *Keep moving.* He went down two more, then sunk his body in the water, gritted his teeth and stood again. He let his body warm a few moments from the shock, then lowered himself back, and sucked in a breath before sinking under the tunnel ceiling. He opened his eyes. A pale band of light ran across the top of the tunnel. "Yes," he said. The bubbles from the inaudible word flowed up his cheeks, and he slowly stood.

"See anything?" asked Tessa from above.

"I think I see a light," he said.

"Thank God," said Tessa.

Eyrún looked up, sighed, and put her head back down.

Darwin breathed deeply. *One, two, three, four*. He lowered himself, feet against the lowest step, and pushed off.

Kick, kick, kick. He dolphin-kicked about ten meters until he reached a pile of rocks in the tunnel's bottom, where he stopped. *What the...* He looked up and saw the mirrorlike surface of the water. *An air pocket?* His breath was still good, and he put a hand up. The temperature told him it was out of the water. He pushed upward until his head broke the surface. *Air!*

He brought the light upward and breathed in a little. *Stale, but breathable.* His feet gained a purchase on top of the rocks that had fallen out of the ceiling. He peered down and saw a brighter light on the outward side of the rock pile. He sucked in a breath and made for the light. *What the fuck!*

He braced against the walls, feeling a sudden suction and a roaring sound. A black shape hung in the tunnel, and the floating grit streamed into it. There was no way he could get around its powerful suction without part of him being drawn in.

How the hell? And he watched a larger piece of debris swirl off the floor and get sucked into the giant hose. His brain called for air, and his lungs pressed against his ribs. On impulse, he pulled off his shirt and let it stream toward the hose. The beast sucked it in, and he retreated to the air pocket. Less than fifteen seconds later, the noise stopped.

He filled his lungs and breast-stroked his way to the hose. Swooping under it, he turned upward and burst above the surface. A powerful light shined downward in his face. "Hey," he yelled as loud as he could.

95

The Well

Tariq climbed from the well and explained he had cleared all the sand he could without going underwater. So far, the pump had run at a slow speed while vacuuming the sand and water from the aquifer had flowed in at an equal rate.

Now, they manipulated the front end of the hose with a rope that attached to a cross-hatched metal frame that protected against large objects being sucked in. Moammar watched the water in the output pipe run clear, then gave the order to turn up the volume.

The engine roared like a large truck pulling away from a traffic light and, a moment later, the water from the output pipe shot outward a couple meters. Zac watched it gouge a hole in the plain before fanning into a mini-river delta. He turned back to the well and saw the water's surface eddy from the suction.

At max power, it should empty in an hour, he thought. Suddenly, the pump made a straining sound, and Moammar turned from the well, yelling at the man at the controls. The engine died as the man hit the emergency stop.

"What is it?" yelled Stevie, her voice reverberated off the cliff in the sudden silence.

"Something went in the pump," said Moammar.

"Didn't see it. I was looking up," said Zac.

Water gushed back into the well from the pipe as the men at the pump disconnected the intake hose. They turned as one man pulled a cloth from the impeller housing.

"Oh, my God! It's Darwin's shirt," said Stevie.

"Yeah, looks like Darwin's," said Zac, holding out a chewed-up piece of light blue fabric. "How the hell—"

"Zac," said Stevie, tugging his arm and running toward the well where Moammar was yelling and pointing. They reached the well together and peered over the edge at Darwin floating in the water.

96

The Tomb

"It's been five minutes. What's he doing?" said Tessa, storming back and forth across the narrow chamber, stopping between passes to look down the steps. "He's with them, planning something. I know it."

She walked over to Eyrún. "He better not be for your sake. What's he doing?"

"I have no idea," said Eyrún. *He's okay. He's okay,* she told herself. *Five minutes isn't long. He's telling them, and he'll be back. Oh, God, please be right.*

"Fathi! Get down there. I need you to find out what's going on. Darwin said he saw light. It can't be that far."

"Why not you?"

"Because I can't swim," she said. "Really, I never learned," she added after seeing his look of disbelief.

He muttered something unintelligible, removed his shoes and pants, and climbed down the steps. "I can see light," he called out after seeing a pale glow on the lowest underwater step. Fathi took a deep breath, then submerged and pushed off.

Tessa turned to Eyrún, who had walked up behind her to watch, "He better not be trying to cross us," she said.

"Shut up, Tessa," said Eyrún, turning away.

97

The Well

Five minutes later, after explaining the hostage demands and their situation inside the mountain, Darwin was readying to go back.

“I can follow you in,” said Zac, who had slid down the rope and stood in the water next to Darwin. “What’s the trap?”

“No, Zac, I won’t risk Eyrún,” said Darwin. “I don’t think there is a trap. Just let them go. Eyrún and I can get out later.”

“We can run the pump full-blast now. Should be empty within the hour. They could walk out.”

"No. They expect me back. Anything else--"

“Understood. Let’s get you in there. As soon as they come out, we crank the pump on full, and you and Eyrún can walk out. But if they’re not out here within five minutes of you going back, I’m coming in,” said Zac.

“Thanks,” he said and began hyperventilating for the return journey.

Darwin used Zac’s thighs as a push-off and was more confident this time as he knew the distance and the air pocket in-between. It was an exercise akin to holding one's breath the length of a standard backyard swimming pool; easy for an in-shape runner like Darwin.

He kicked a few times and used his hands to pull up the rock pile into the air space. Pausing a moment to exhale and suck in another breath, he dove down the other side of the pile.

A dark shape drove him into the floor. His shoulder banged the bottom as Fathi passed over top. Darwin spun like a seal, changing direction to face Fathi, who held the knife and faced him from the outward side of the tunnel.

Fathi came at him like a torpedo. Darwin focused on the knife and shoved sideways from the wall. He grabbed for the arm behind the blade to force it into the ceiling but missed, and a searing pain shot down his arm when the knife struck his shoulder. He drove a fist upward into Fathi's belly, but the water weakened the blow.

Fathi lost air, spun, and scrambled toward the well exit. Darwin pulled the knife from his shoulder, blood clouding the water. In a blind swing at Fathi, he felt the knife grab and tear. The feeling sickened him, and his stomach surged. He bit down to hold his breath. Fathi kicked wildly as the water turned red-orange.

Blackness pressed on Darwin's vision as his oxygen depleted. No way he could make it to the steps. With the air pocket his only option, he seized one of Fathi's flailing legs and yanked backward. Fathi's head hit the rock pile, and air exploded from his lungs. Darwin shoved Fathi down as he climbed into the air pocket and sucked in a massive breath along with some water running off his head.

Pain! He coughed, nearly passing out until his breathing stabilized. The light was gone, lying somewhere on the tunnel floor, its dim glow shone up through orange water. Darwin brought his right hand to the opposite shoulder and felt warm liquid spilling out a finger-sized hole. He pressed it shut and fought against nausea.

Oh, fuck! Oh, fuck! Calm down. Get your heart rate down. He took in a few deep breaths while imaging sitting in a peaceful spot. *Shit, where's Fathi?* He gulped a breath and sunk under to find Fathi. He swam down toward the light, his shoulder seared as the water hit the raw nerves. He pulled the arm to his chest and grasped the light with his right hand. *Nothing. Where is he?*

Darwin shined the light about. The water was thick with silt, stirred up from their fight and tinged with blood. He finally saw a dark shape motionless at the top of the ceiling. It was drifting toward the steps. He was out of air and pushed back into the air pocket where he struggled to maintain consciousness. The air tasted sour. *Breathe!* He forced his diaphragm to pull in air, but the oxygen was depleting, and his legs shook from carbon dioxide buildup.

I have to save Eyrún. One more breath.

He tried to suck in one more lungful of air and willed himself to keep going as he was suddenly caressed by bubbles and a pair of hands. *Eyrún!* He slid downward as his vision faded to black.

98

Stevie lowered herself down the rope, adjusting for the awkward weight of the air tank on her back. She had been adjusting the mask up top when Zac yelled that there was blood in the water. "What happened," she yelled while concentrating on the rope.

"I don't know. The water moved, and then I saw blood. I went under to look. But it's too cloudy," said Zac, grabbing her waist as she dropped the last two meters. She pulled on the mask and switched on the light she had attached to it while Zac opened the valve to check the air flow. She put in the mouthpiece and nodded that it worked.

"Take this," said Zac and slid a knife in the hip band of her shorts.

Stevie patted it and squatted down under the water. Adjusting her mask once more, she pushed off into the tunnel. *What a mess!* She had seen this once before, diving in a cave where a colleague had panicked and stirred up centuries of silt. They had to use guide wires to pull themselves out while fighting off panic in zero visibility.

The tank's weight pressed her to the floor, and she pulled along. After a couple body lengths' distance, she reached to her hip and withdrew the knife. She had experience with a blade from her time dating a French special forces guy, who was aroused by knife play. It was near the end of what she considered her wild youth, and the relationship ended badly, but she had learned valuable defensive skills.

Rocks! She reached the pile and moved her way up. A pair of feet stood on top the rockpile. She readied the knife. The legs were bare except for a pair of yellow-striped socks. *Darwin!* She moved upward as he slumped. She grabbed his waist and shoved upward with all her strength.

Holding Darwin up with one arm, she steadied her footing on the pile. His head rolled back, and she saw blood pulsing out of the narrow knife wound. *Shit!* She shrugged her grip from his arm up to his shoulder. The pressure stopped the bleeding. She shoved the regulator into his mouth and squeezed his side to force a breath. Nothing.

She kneed him in the balls. He spat out the mouthpiece. She pressed it back in as he sucked in. The air in the space was foul, and after Darwin took three breaths, she exhaled and switched the regulator in her mouth for a long breath, then shoved it back in Darwin's.

"Darwin, can you hear me? It's Stevie." She took another breath from the regulator and asked again, "Darwin?"

His eyes opened, and he pulled the regulator out. "Oh, my God, Stevie. Where's Eyrún?" he gasped and breathed again.

"She's fine. We need to get you out of here. Can you swim out with me?"

"Yes. Give me a couple more breaths. Where is she?" he asked again, and Stevie shoved the regulator back in his mouth.

Two breaths later, he said he was ready. Stevie explained she would take a deep breath and that he would keep the regulator. "I'll hug you with one arm. We drop, and both of us push off the rock pile. When you feel my pinch, push like hell. Got it?"

He nodded. Stevie took in three fast breaths, put it back in Darwin's mouth, and then submerged. She brought them sideways and pinched him. They shot toward the exit, and Stevie kicked furiously. Ten seconds later, they burst into the well. Zac hauled them upright.

"Where's Eyrún?" asked Darwin just before he passed out.

99

The Tomb

Eyrún returned to her spot against the wall and continued her mantra: *He's okay. He's okay.* She tried to relax, breathing like Darwin had told her, but it was not working. *Fuck it!* She stood and walked to the steps.

"There's blood in the water," said Tessa and climbed down the steps.

"What!" said Eyrún and shined her light to see.

Tessa reached the lowest step, hands flailing at the water. "It's Fathi," she said, pulling an arm and collapsing backward on the steps. Eyrún's hand went reflexively to her mouth. Blood was everywhere, and Fathi's open eyes had rolled up in their sockets.

"He's dead," screamed Tessa.

"Where's Darwin," yelled Eyrún, who started down the steps but quickly retreated as Tessa bolted upward.

"Darwin killed him," Tessa screamed again and advanced with the knife.

Eyrún looked around and grabbed the scroll leaning on the wall.

She held it like a bat and moved to the middle of the small chamber as Tessa reached the top step.

"Rrrrrr-ahhhh." Tessa charged, and Eyrún swatted at her, forcing the knife wide. She charged again. Eyrún thrust the scroll one-handed like a sword and poked Tessa in the face.

Tessa swung her knife-arm and caught the leather, yanking it out of Eyrún's hand. It hit the wall and cart-wheeled down the steps. While Tessa watched the scroll, Eyrún kicked her in the gut. Tessa flew backward, landing on her back. Eyrún kicked her knife hand, and it released the blade. Eyrún bent for it, but Tessa punched her in the crotch. Pain surged as Eyrún grabbed the knife and landed on her back.

Tessa was on her in an instant, hands around her throat. Eyrún gagged and forced herself to focus on turning the knife in her hand. Tessa lifted Eyrún's head and banged it down. Eyrún fought to remain conscious and, as Tessa lifted her head again, she plunged the blade into Tessa's hip.

"Ahhhh, you bitch," screamed Tessa, arching from the pain.

Eyrún rolled away and got to her feet, but Tessa charged, knocking her into the wall. They fell at the top step, Tessa grasping for the knife, but Eyrún tossed it down the steps where it clattered in the water. Tessa punched Eyrún in the temple and jumped off her.

"My scroll. It's ruined. God damn you," yelled Tessa and kicked Eyrún in the ribs. Blinding pain expelled the air in her lungs. "The lighter. Fathi's lighter. If we can't have the scrolls, nobody can," said Tessa, rooting in Fathi's pants pocket for his lighter. She grabbed it and pressed a hand to her injured hip as she hobbled from the chamber.

Eyrún squeezed a hand against her pained ribs, rolled on her side, and drew her knees up. *Oh, God, where's Darwin?* She tried not to imagine the worst, but she screamed at the vision of Fathi's dead eyes, "Nooo!"

Her side burned and she broke into sobs when the same numbness blanketed her as the day her father died and she shut herself in a closet.

100

The Tunnel

Stevie immediately went back in and moved cautiously after clearing the rock pile. She could barely see a meter ahead and paused. *A body? Not moving.* She poked one heel with the knife and withdrew at the shock realization that it was dead, then jumped at a roaring sound that filled the tunnel. *The pump. Zac said he would turn it on.*

Dipping low under the corpse, she moved forward to the steps and halted, realizing the tank would slow her down. *I need to be ready.* She unfastened the straps, lowered the tank, a took a couple deep breaths. She moved to the steps and burst above the water. She wiped water from her eyes and shined the light up the steps. She heard crying. *Eyrún?*

"Eyrún?" called Stevie as she mounted the steps. "Eyrún?" Stevie's head reached the top step, and she saw Eyrún an arm's length away.

"Eyrún, it's me, Stevie," she said, placing a hand gently on Eyrún's.

"Darwin?" Eyrún sobbed.

"He's alive, Eyrún. He's alive."

"What?" said Eyrún, opening her eyes.

"He's alive. I got him out. He's with Zac now," said Stevie, climbing next to Eyrún and helping her sit up. She briefly described bringing Darwin out.

"Is he okay?"

"Yes. Well, he has a cut on his shoulder, but yes, he's okay. They're draining the water now with a big pump. We'll get out of here soon," said Stevie.

Eyrún was alert now and looking about the chamber.

"What is it?" asked Stevie.

"I have to stop her. She's going to burn the scrolls," said Eyrún, jumping to her feet. "C'mon."

"I don't have any shoes."

"Give me the knife."

"But, Eyrún—"

"I have to stop her," said Eyrún, taking the knife and running up the corridor. "Catch up when you can."

101

The Tomb

Eyrún reached the second bend, stopped, and gasped for breath while bracing herself with a hand on the wall. Her left ribs burned on each inhalation. *I need to get going*. She pushed off the wall and walked at a measured pace. *Six more keep going.*

She counted the switchbacks, and at the seventh, smelled something burning. *No!* She pushed her legs and squeezed her right hand against the pain in her side. Going up the slope before the corridor leveled, she saw an orange glow on the ceiling. A few meters farther and the glow brightened. *It's too close for the library. What happened?*

The answer revealed itself a few steps later as she reached the top of the slope. The glow was coming from the floor. *The pit!* Eyrún paused and shined the light down the corridor, but could see nothing beyond the glow from the pit.

"Ahhhh," came Tessa's pained voice.

"Tessa?" said Eyrún, reaching the pit. The palm trunks had fallen in, except for one against the sidewall. She dropped on hands and knees and crawled up to the edge nearest the intact trunk. The glow came from the opposite side. She looked in.

Tessa lay in a heap propped in the opposite corner holding a piece of burning paper. Her right lower leg bent at a gruesome angle. Eyrún swallowed hard against an urge to vomit.

"Get them away," Tessa screamed and shook the flaming paper at something. Eyrún leaned forward and saw a tangle of vipers across from Tessa. Several smaller snakes writhed around a larger one that was swaying to the moving flame. "Do something!" she yelled and used the shrinking flame in one hand to ignite another piece of paper.

Eyrún looked around the empty corridor. *It's too far to climb down, and the snakes.* She turned, and the pain from her ribs shot down her side. Anger exploded, and she turned back to Tessa. "Why should I help you? You tried to kill my fiancé—twice. You fucking bitch. Tell me why I shouldn't just sit here and watch you die."

"We went back for Darwin. He was never in danger. I swear. I—" Tessa swung the flaming paper at a viper that crawled over her broken leg. "The vipers. Help me. Pleeeease."

Eyrún sat back against the wall again. *What do I do? What do I do?* Sounds of thrashing came from the pit.

"Get away. Get away," Tessa shrieked.

Her fury at wanting to kill Tessa rebounded. *But Darwin's alive,* and his words from yesterday came to her. "It's not who we are."

Tessa screamed. "It bit me. Oh, God, it bit me!" Eyrún looked in as another viper moved. Tessa took her mobile from a shirt pocket and threw it. The big snake recoiled and hissed as the device struck it and bounced into the pile of palm trunks.

"There's a rope in the small chamber," said Eyrún. "I'll get it."

She backed up and ran at the remaining log, springing off its near side, and hitting the opposite at full stride. She reached the chamber in less than two minutes and yanked the rope out of the sarcophagus hole and turned back. A coughing fit from the rib pain held her up just outside the door, but she stumbled along until it subsided. A few minutes later, she approached the pit. *Oh, my God, it's brighter.*

"Tessa. I've got a rope," said Eyrún, kneeling down and lowering the end with the loop they had tied as an anchor the other day. Tessa had lit a frayed part of the palm trunk, and the ancient dried fibers burned fast as she waved it wildly. Sweat beaded on her forehead, and her head lolled like a drunk. *The venom. She's losing consciousness.* "Tessa. Tessa!" shouted Eyrún.

"They took it from us. They can't have it," said Tessa.

"Tessa, the rope," said Eyrún as she settled the loop over Tessa's head. "Put your arms through it. I'll pull you up."

Tessa continued talking deliriously. "We gave it to the sphinxes for protection. They will protect it," she said as her head slumped and the burning fragment fell onto the trunk pile.

"No," shouted Eyrún and pulled at the rope.

Tessa had put one arm through the loop. Her arm and head squeezed together as Eyrún leaned back, keeping one eye on the trunks. At first, smoked billowed nearly smothering the fire but, just as it looked to go out, flames erupted.

A wall of heat drove Eyrún back, and the snakes scattered. She realized the fire would burn the rope from this side and, in a desperate move, crossed the remaining log back to the exit side of the corridor. She gathered the rope and readied to pull again when Stevie's voice came from behind.

"Eyrún. Oh, my God. What's happened?"

"Tessa's in—" the rope pulled free, sending Eyrún into Stevie, and they both tumbled backwards.

They jumped up and moved to the edge. Flames curled up the side of the corridor, consuming the remaining trunk bridging the pit. Tessa lay against the opposite wall, smoke rising from her clothing.

"We have to help her," pleaded Eyrún, but she stepped back from the heat.

"It's too late, Eyrún. She's gone," said Stevie, shielding Eyrún's view.

A couple minutes later, the last trunk crashed into the pit, sending a shower of sparks up to the ceiling. Eyrún and Stevie scrambled away, coughing from the smoke. They stopped at the top of the downward slope and watched until the glow receded.

"Oh, God. It's horrible. I could have saved her. I told her..." Eyrún broke down in tears.

"You did all you could, Eyrún. All this was her own doing. Come on. The tunnel's drained by now. Let's go see Darwin," said Stevie. She put an arm around Eyrún's waist and guided her out of the mountain.

102

Ten Days Later
Adrère Amellal Ecolodge

Eyrún found Darwin at the lake shore outside their room, cooling down from an early morning run.

"Your stitches come out today," she said as he stretched.

"Yeah, it feels pretty good," he said, rolling the shoulder.

The noise from a hammer-drill turned their attention to the White Mountain, where a large team from the Ministry of State for Antiquities was erecting scaffolding to fortify the tomb opening.

"Abbas wants me to stay. Be his second in command here in Siwa," said Darwin.

"Really? You're not Egyptian."

"That's what I said, but Richard called me yesterday from Vatican City. It seems there's some joint cooperation at the highest levels and said Abbas would talk to me about it."

"That's great!"

"But it means I'd have to stay here full time. At least six months, anyway," he said.

"Do it. I've been thinking about my job and decided I need a break. I'll stay here with you," she said.

"Are you sure?"

She kissed him. "Absolutely."

A short while later at breakfast, Darwin was lost in thought, staring at the water flowing from the fountain.

"What is it?" asked Eyrún. "I know that look. Something's bothering you."

"The Alexander scroll. We were so close."

Zac had found a coiled scrap of wet leather on the tunnel floor, but the papyrus inside had turned into goo. They handed it over to Abbas, but they did not say what it was. Zac also recovered Tessa's mobile and sent it to forensics experts in the US, but they said it was too badly damaged to recover any data.

"I know, but you've made the discovery of a lifetime," she said, shuddering at the memory.

"Are you okay?" he turned and put a hand on hers. She had woken up with nightmares several times in the last week.

"It will pass. Stevie was there and helped me. I know we couldn't save her."

"I called her cousin, Joseph. Told him it was an accident but left out all the bad things she did."

"You're kind," she said, turning her palm upward and squeezing his hand.

He smiled. "Still, I wonder what was in that scroll."

"C'mon. Let's get you cleaned up, Mr. Second-in-Command. We have an appointment at the clinic. Later, we can look for a place to live. If we're going to be here a while, I want a house with a view over the whole oasis."

EPILOGUE

Autumn
Siwa Oasis

Darwin flew arms outstretched, overtop ocean waves, sea foam rushing beneath him. He swerved like an aerial surfer into the curl of one massive breaker as the sound of...

... a braying donkey burst his dream.

Merde, he thought as the accursed animal next door once again played the role of a rooster. He squinted against the daylight and willed the peaceful vision to return. But now, a dog barked, and a flock of birds flapped noisily from a palm somewhere in the yard. *Oasis, my ass!*

His front door burst open. "Darwin. Come on. We're going for a swim," said Moammar, who stood with a group of men in the growing light beyond the door. A celebration that had begun two days ago would culminate today. Darwin had seen weddings in the oasis, but this was the first one he had attended.

Today was the actual ceremony of the traditional Siwan wedding. Yesterday, he had taken part with the men in constructing the tents and slaughtering the cow that would become the wedding feast. The younger men and boys competed for the tail of the animal in a tradition that made a rugby scrum look like a committee meeting on peaceful protest. The winner of the tail would possess good fortune for years to come.

Darwin had enjoyed the past months in Siwa after the frantic search to find Alexander's tomb and the harrowing escape. He had settled into his role as second in command behind Abbas, who spent most of his time in Cairo. The first month after the discovery had brought the global media eager to show the world the famed lost Library of Alexandria. But by far his most tense and exciting day was a visit by the Pope, the president of Egypt, and the Grand Imam of Al-azhar.

They made public gestures of reconciling centuries-long angst by proposing a joint study of the newfound Library of Alexandria. The Pope offered the vast capabilities of the Vatican Apostolic Archive. The president of Egypt committed to install a new wing in the rebuilt Library of Alexandria where all scholars, regardless of faith, could study the knowledge of the ancients.

Darwin said a few words at the ceremony and spontaneously moved off-script by saying, "Let us remember, we have this fantastic treasure of knowledge because Hypatia of Alexandria defied the role society expected of her. The time is ripe for all institutions to embrace the full participation of women, especially as spiritual leaders."

The Internet blew up with a gif of the Pope and Grand Imam grinning nervously at each other but shaking hands to seize the moment. Post-ceremony, Darwin had felt like a boxer blocking punches as non-stop microphones and cameras shoved into his face to recount his ballsy moment.

But now after five months, much of the work had become administration, and the urge for new discovery pulled at him. Even Eyrún was restless and had made more trips back to Iceland to check on the NAT.

"Hurry, Darwin," said Moammar as Darwin pulled on jeans and a polar fleece jacket against the morning chill.

About a dozen of them headed to the spring and a warm sensation descended on Darwin as he thought about his acceptance in the Oasis.

"What did he say?" Darwin asked Moammar. One man had said something in Siwi too fast for him to comprehend.

"He said we should go to a cold spring. It's better for the groom's virility," said Moammar, reaching to slap the groom on the back.

Later that day, car horns and gunshots heralded the approaching bridal party. Darwin stood with the groom's families and tribe under the ceremonial tent beneath the shadow of the White Mountain.

The sun cast long shadows and streaked the mountain with orange bands as it sunk beneath the Great Sand Sea. A sudden breeze swirled a dust djinn into the palms on the edge of Lake Siwa and wafted with it the yeasty aroma of Engeel. Served at weddings, the caramelizing dates in the local pita bread made Darwin's stomach growl in anticipation of the coming feast.

Dozens of people from the bride's clan poured from the cars and gathered around the tent. He could see movement as the center of the group parted for the bride, and the crowd hushed. He had read about and seen photos of traditional Siwan bridal dress, but he gasped at the beauty of the real thing as the front row stepped aside, and the bride emerged.

The slanting sun sparkled off silver chains, raining down from large hoops on the sides of her headdress. Her tightly braided hair splayed over her shoulders, and bells at the ends of the chains softly tinkling as she moved. A silver hoop around her neck and shoulders held a head-sized silver disk, adorning the front of the intricately embroidered dress. Cloud-white cotton flowed lightly over her figure as rays of hand-stitched orange, red, and midnight blue patterns mimicked the rising sun.

She turned in Darwin's direction, and the radiance of her glacier blue eyes immediately dulled the silver by comparison. An elbow poked Darwin, and he glanced briefly at the cheek-splitting smile on his friend Zac's face. Darwin smiled and turned back to the bride.

"Hello, Love," said Eyrún, reaching out with henna-covered hands.

He blinked to clear his vision, and their hands entwined. "Hi," he said, swallowing hard to keep his composure.

They turned as one to face their friend, Richard Ndembele, who began their vows.

The morning sun spilled through the kitchen where Darwin sat enjoying a coffee. Eyrún had disappeared into the back of the house. She came back a moment later and laid a rectangular box on the table.

"I was too rushed to get you a wedding present, but I found something in the oasis you might like," she said, sitting next to him.

"I thought we decided to defer gifts," he said, looking up from his coffee.

"It wasn't expensive. It's a local craft to remember our time here."

"Thanks, Love."

He turned and kissed her. They lingered a few moments until she said through their touching lips, "Open it silly."

He sat back, lower lip pushing out.

"Later. C'mon. Open it," she said, her knees swinging excitedly.

He moved the coffee cups, lifted the box, and brushed some crumbs from the table. He grasped the bow and glance at her. She spun her finger—hurry. He pulled the woven grass bow apart, tore off the paper, and lifted the box flaps, exposing one of the custom tubes for storing the scrolls.

They had commissioned thousands of the tubes to transport the scrolls safely. Each plastic cylinder formed a hermetic seal with a medical-grade desiccant built into the end-caps to preserve the ancient cellulose until it was time to examine the papyrus.

"What?" he looked at her with raised eyebrows.

"Be very careful now," she said.

He pried off one end-cap and tipped the tube, gently shaking out a scroll wrapped in acid-free paper. Eyrún moved the box, and Darwin laid the scroll on the table.

"You'll want these," she said, holding a pair of cotton gloves.

He slipped them on and unrolled the paper to reveal an ancient leather scroll. He glanced at Eyrún, who grinned ear to ear. Darwin unrolled the leather and went silent as he read.

"It's..." his fingers followed the Greek text. "Oh, my God... I can't be... How did you? Where did you?"

He pushed back from the table, cautiously moving Alexander's treasure scroll to its center. He hugged her, and after a long minute, stepped back and said, "I thought it went into the water. You have to tell me where you got it."

"Do you remember when I had to go to the NAT about a month ago?" she asked as they sat down.

"Yeah, you were turning over the project."

"Yes. Well, I hadn't been inside for a month, and the second night, something woke me in the middle of the night. I swear there was a breeze, but there's no air movement in the tube. Anyway, I fell back asleep but had a nightmare. I was back in the tunnel with Tessa—"

"Oh no, Love, I'm sorry," he said.

"No, no. It's okay. The dream was mostly about Tessa's last words. She said, 'We gave it to the Sphinxes. They'll protect it.' She was so delirious from the viper toxin that it made no sense and I forgot about it. But this time, I wrote a note on my iPhone. I wasn't sure what it meant, but we know Tessa was devious."

"That's one word for her," he said.

"When I got back to Siwa, I asked Illi to help me check out the Sphinxes. I didn't know what I was looking for, and I couldn't involve you," she said with a mischievous smile.

"How did you get in? I mean past all the guards," he asked.

"I have a little devious in me. I said I needed to find you as some VIP begged for a tour. Illi helped me with a ladder, and I climbed up between the sphinxes and, sure enough, there was a gap at the back of the arch. About an elbow length down, I felt the scroll."

"Wow," he said. "All I can say is, wow. And thank you, Tessa. The only positive thing that came from her psychotic behavior."

Eyrún wanted to know what the scroll said, so Darwin opened it an arm's length. She placed a hand on his back as they stood looking at the ancient text.

"*Merde,*" he said, pausing.

"What?"

"Listen to this," he said, reading as his finger passed over the text.

I, Alexander III of Macedon, King of Upper and Lower Egypt, Son of Ra, beloved of Amun, selected of Horus, and annointed Son of Ammon by the oracle at Siwah, leave the treasures recorded in this scroll to—

At that moment, their front door burst open and Abbas walked in.

"Abbas," said Darwin. "What are you doing?"

"Give me the scroll Darwin," he said holding out one hand palm upward.

"This is our home. You can't just walk in here," said Eyrún.

"Yes, I can. In fact, it's not even my personal doing," he said as two men wearing dark suits walked in behind him. "These are officers from the Ministry of Antiquities recovery department. Step away from the table."

Darwin and Eyrún moved back as Abbas examined the scroll, re-rolled it, and slid it back in the tube, speaking to them as he worked, "There are cameras placed in the tomb Eyrún to prevent just this kind of theft. It took some days to review the video, but the security people at the Ministry take their job of protecting Egyptian antiquities seriously."

"I'm sorry, Love," Eyrún whispered to Darwin.

"Don't worry about it," he said, squeezing her hand.

"Leave us," said Abbas to the men and waited for them to exit before continuing. "Your work here was wrapping up anyway. No?

You've done an exemplary job for Egypt. Let us part as friends and I'll forget this transgression."

They shook hands and Abbas departed, closing the door behind him.

Abbas got in the back seat of the car with the two men. As the vehicle pulled away, he messaged:

Abbas: I have the scroll

Nahla: Good. I'll meet you in Cairo

THE END

AUTHOR'S NOTE

The ancient Library of Alexandria remains an enduring mystery.

About ten thousand words into writing a thriller that takes place in Silicon Valley, I stalled. As usual, I hit the trailhead behind my neighborhood and, two miles later, stopped high on the ridge to gather in a view of the San Francisco Bay. I imagined how the valley looked when diverse tribes of the native Ohlone people made this area one of the most densely populated regions north of Mexico.

In that moment, I realized Darwin did not find what he sought in Roman Ice: proof that the Romans used lava tubes to move about in stealth and store valuable knowledge. Like Darwin, I'm fascinated by the discovery of ancient knowledge, especially when found by accident like the Nag Hammadi and Dead Sea scrolls.

What if lava tubes were used to save the Library of Alexandria?

Researching led me to Alexandria, its library built by the Ptolemaic dynasty, and to Hypatia, a philosopher and mathematician whose fate collided with the power-grab of a rising religious order. Learn more at https://en.wikipedia.org/wiki/Hypatia or watch this film starring Rachel Weisz https://en.wikipedia.org/wiki/Agora_(film).

Alexander the Great founded multiple cities named Alexandria, the most famous on the Nile Delta. After conquering Egypt, he journeyed into the Sahara Desert to consult the oracle of Ammon in the Siwa Oasis. He sought legitimacy as ruler of Egypt and proclaimed the oracle said he was the son of Ammon (Amun Ra) as summarized at https://en.wikipedia.org/wiki/Alexander_the_Great.

Humans have inhabited the Siwa Oasis for 10,000 years, and the Greeks first became aware of the oracle in the 7th century BCE. That Alexander the Great travelled for weeks in a hostile environment to consult the oracle is a testament to its importance in ancient Greece, Macedonia, and Persia. I encourage you to explore: https://en.wikipedia.org/wiki/Siwa_Oasis.

On October 28, 2019, Pope Francis renamed the Vatican Secret Archives to the Vatican Apostolic Archive. He said the new name is a better reflection of the archive's "service to the church and the world of culture." The archive is one of the oldest curated libraries on earth and open to access for all scholars since 1881. Discover for yourself at https://en.wikipedia.org/wiki/Vatican_Apostolic_Archive.

Hypatia's Diary

We all embody Darwin's imagination and spirit of discovery. It's plausible that Alexander the Great commissioned a tomb in Siwa. Hypatia may also have visited the oracle, learned of a tomb and moved scrolls there. With just a bit more stretching of our imaginations, we can see her writing a diary that found its way to the Vatican's archive.

We know at least two people buried scrolls thousands of years ago in Nag Hammadi and the Dead Sea. Why? It leaves us to speculate and to wonder what we would find in the lost Library of Alexandria. Imagine the missing Greek plays, a cipher for the language of cave paintings, or an account of why humans buried and abandoned Göbekli Tepe in ancient Turkey.

Our ancestors squirreled away books in libraries. In the 15th century, Poggio Bracciolini, an obsessive book hunter, found a lone copy of *On the Nature of Things* languishing in a German monastery. Written by the Roman poet Lucretius, the book described atoms as the smallest indivisible particles. Lucretius wrote about atoms and we lost the knowledge!

If you are interested in this real-world discovery, I recommend *The Swerve: How the World Became Modern*. Its author, Stephen Greenblatt, suggests the Renaissance began with the discovery of *On the Nature of Things.*

What else is out there? Darwin, Eyrún, Stevie, and Zac are looking for it.

I invite you to learn about the next Darwin Lacroix Adventure by joining my mailing list at davebartell.com.

ACKNOWLEDGMENTS

My first novel, Roman Ice, was a multi-year journey into the unknown. Hypatia's Diary came to life and published in a year due to help I received from many people.

Thank you Annie Tucker, a development editor of great talent and patience. She is teaching me how to craft stories worth reading. Also, thank you to Simon Firth who helped me think out the Lacroix Adventure Series promise to my readers.

Kudos to the Hypatia's Diary beta-readers: Carol Orr, Tracy DeDore, Karen De Luca, Nick Coleman, and Eric Bartell. They helped smooth the edges and increase the believability of the scenes and character arcs.

A special thanks to my daughters: Sara who read many drafts and Kelly who suggested Stevie's name saying she needed to be unique.

And an ongoing thank you to my wife Diane for her continued support and regular motivating question, "Is there anything new to read?"

ABOUT THE AUTHOR

Imagine the wonder at being the first person to open King Tut's tomb? Dave Bartell loves reviving lost history and his novels breathe "thriller" into archaeology.

As a kid, he was frequently found tinkering in his parent's garage. His insatiable curiosity to understand how things work led him to study biochemistry and, later, fueled a career in high-technology. His what-if mindset and life experiences combine to make his fiction plausible and feel realistic.

Dave lives in Los Gatos California, a small town tucked into the edge of Silicon Valley. He enjoys hiking in the hills behind his home, where beauty is still analog.

He hopes you enjoy his stories and invites you to share your thoughts at dave@davebartell.com. And, visit davebartell.com to get a sneak peek of upcoming projects.

Printed in Great Britain
by Amazon

69527453R00234